THE MASK OF MIDNIGHT

A Gabriel McRay Novel

LAURIE STEVENS

Dear Muriel,
Enjoy!
Laurie Stevens

THE MASK of MIDNIGHT

A Gabriel McRay Novel

By Laurie Stevens

Copyright ©2014 by Laurie Stevens

Published by FYD Media, LLC

www.fydmedia.com

ISBN: 978-0-9970068-0-3

LCCN: 2014921223

In Twilight's Hush excerpt ©2014 by Laurie Stevens

To my parents
Joyce, because you love to read a good scare
and David, the real Dr. B

I am filled with gratitude to the following people: Dr. Sarah Carter for her wonderful input regarding forensics, Dr. Stephen Kibrick, who patiently weathers my questions into all matters medical and psychological, and prosecutor Patricia Campbell, for lending me her legal expertise. David and Petra Vieira, Deborah Templeton, and particularly Scott Templeton gave generously of their creative talents. Thank you to Ronald Jacobs, my sister Debbie, and Jody Hepps who have made wonderful friends and editors, and to Carole and Mickley for test-driving my books. Authors DJ Adamson, Kim Fay, and Connie Archer, I am indebted to your honesty. Alan Nevins and Diane Golden, thank you for believing in my work, and Jennifer Custer, thank you for bringing the Gabriel McRay novels to Blanvalet. Barbara and Bob, your love and support have fed my heart and my creativity. To Steven, Jonathan, and Alanna, knowing we are part of each other makes me joyful each day. Lastly, thanks to the readers, especially the ones who have let me know that Gabriel's journey has touched them in personal ways. I am incredibly grateful for that.

    – **Laurie**

THE DARK BEFORE DAWN
Named to Kirkus Reviews Best of 2011

"Stevens sets the stage for graphic sensory details and a fast-paced, tantalizing mystery that utilizes her passion and research in forensics and psychology... Memorable characters, macabre scenes, and a dazzling portrayal of reality will leave readers anxious for book two in the Gabriel McRay series."
– *Kirkus Reviews* (a *Kirkus* starred review)

"This blood-curdling thriller kept me up at night."
– *Suspense Magazine*

"*The Dark Before Dawn* is a psychologically accurate and profound thriller and has gripped us like *The Hunger Games*."– **Dr. Christina L. Cassel, Psy.D., Mft**

"This is top-notch psychodrama suspense at its best... This story goes beyond other crime novels and actually recreates *Jekyll and Hyde* in a more urban, American setting, with touches of modern forensic science... I cannot get enough of this bright star in the thriller market."
– *A Bibliophile's Reverie*

"This is a very unique, nuanced thriller with multiple layers of intrigue... had me hooked from the first page."
– *Writer's Digest*

"Laurie Stevens may have created a new sub-genre of mystery novel — the *psychiatric* thriller. Stevens' telling of her protagonist's internal and external investigations is taut, suspenseful and surprisingly cinematic."
  – **William Knoedelseder, author of NYT bestsellers** *"Bitter Brew"* **and** *"I'm Dying Up Here"*

"Frighteningly great Indie title... Be sure to leave a light on!" – *The Huffington Post*

DEEP INTO DUSK
Winner of nine awards, IPPY winner
for Best Mystery/Thriller

"Laurie Stevens' *Deep Into Dusk*, has all the ingredients of a hair-raising movie thriller on par with the movie *Fatal Attraction* as it sucks you into wild intrigue with a very unexpected ending... This is one author that I am sure we will be hearing more from in the future."
– **Shelfpleasures.com**

"Stevens deftly intertwines McRay's childhood trauma with the crimes taking place in the present, intensifying the emotional force of the story. The characters have depth and personality, and their internal conflicts are portrayed in a wrenchingly human fashion, both moving and believable." – **IndieReader.com**

"An enticing murder mystery with an unorthodox protagonist. Stevens delights in playing with conventions set forth by past detective novels... Respects the old-school murder mystery while showcasing contemporary characters." – *Kirkus Reviews*

"Stevens has once again brought us to the edge of our seats with her gift for psychological suspense and leaves us scarred forever. Like Ming is drawn to the tortured soul of McRay, we too are drawn into the heat; better to be burned than to have never known the flame."
  – *Suspense Magazine*

THE MASK OF MIDNIGHT
Winner of the Clue Award

"This one is worth the investment. Laurie Steven's Gabriel McRay series is outstanding. Victor Archwood is one of the best villains I've ever seen written. Great writing, pace, characters! Loved it."
  – **Teresa Trent,** *Book Review Blog*

The Mask of Midnight is nothing short of astounding. A psychological thriller of the first caliber, I had to remind myself on more than one occasion to breathe."
  – **Back Porchervations,** *Book Review Blog*

PROLOGUE

Victor Archwood sat in his prison cell and looked around, bored. The room was the size of an average bathroom and offered no visual stimulus other than a postage-stamp sink, a lidless steel toilet, and the bunk on which he sat. He didn't have a cellmate because serial killers were instant celebrities in jail. The chance of them getting killed by their fellow inmates was high.

After his arraignment, they transferred Vic here to await his trial. Terminal Island, a federal correctional facility, had been built in 1938 to house prisoners convicted of crimes such as bank robbery, fraud, tax evasion, treason, forgery, and drug trafficking. John DeLorean had been held there, and Al Capone had spent his last few years at T.I. after being transferred down from Alcatraz. The facility sat on the waters of San Pedro Bay, where the sun and the ocean could wave freely to those held captive inside.

Victor, suspected to be The Malibu Canyon Murderer,

had been a model prisoner and could enjoy certain privileges. Although he was considered too much of a risk to use the gym, he was allowed one hour a day in the north yard. He could mix with some of the other prisoners, but he was supervised carefully.

The long hours of being alone did not bother Vic. It helped him organize his thoughts. He thought about getting out and discussed all possibilities with his defense attorney. As it stood, he faced the death penalty.

Didn't they know he carried the energy flow of multiple souls? Vic could feel that energy pulse through his veins, creating an aura of power around him. The DA wanted to convict him of the deaths of seven people, but Vic knew some divine element would intervene on his behalf.

In his isolation, Vic also thought about Detective Sergeant Gabriel McRay. It was Gabriel who put him in here. He thought about the investigator often, and what he would like to do to Gabriel if he ever had the chance to meet up with him again.

"Here are your magazines."

A guard stood in front of Vic's cell, holding out copies of *Architectural Digest*, *Gourmet Chef*, *American Art Review*, *Wired*, and a copy of *Robb Report*. The guard perused the magazines before he released them to the man behind the bars.

"Think you'll be in the lap of luxury anytime soon?"

Vic gave him a disarming smile as he took the magazines. "One never knows."

The guard frowned. "You got fan mail too."

He stuck a stack of letters through the bars. All the

letters had been opened, of course, and scrutinized for anything suspicious in nature.

Victor thanked the guard and then read through the letters. He had nothing but time on his hands, and he didn't have anything better to do. The prison officials had courteously disposed of the death threats. All of these notes were from women. The Malibu Canyon Murderer was known to be a tall, good-looking blond. No strong dimpled chin, nothing like that, but softly handsome features. That plus his notoriety made him quite popular with the ladies.

"I think what they are accusing you of is ridiculous," one note read. Another asked, "Are you allowed conjugal visits?" Some other lovelorn female had scribbled inside a pink-penned heart, "Marry me!"

He had no real interest in meeting these women, but he wrote back on occasion, asking what they did for a living. Perhaps one of them possessed an interesting personality trait to absorb. That might be worth his while.

ALTHOUGH ACCESS to the Internet was prohibited, Vic's attorney had won him the privilege of being able to read articles from the *Los Angeles Times* archives. His lawyer had pointed out that the bright young graduate student wanted to do legal research to help his case and that Vic was, after all, a model prisoner. The prison board found no harm in allowing Vic to research the archives since they offered only previously published news.

Once a week for fifteen minutes, Vic could scan through the various articles in the prison's email room. A guard always stood by, overseeing his progress.

Today, Vic was back on the computer, searching through the articles. He had only three minutes left before the guard would escort him back to his cell.

Only one item in particular interested Vic. So far, he had been unable to locate it. He had read through many news pieces about Gabriel McRay, how the detective was ordered into psychiatric sessions for having violent behavior and using excessive force. Victor knew all that, of course. He needed another piece of information —a name.

And then he found it. A reckless journalist had let it slip. Gabriel had been under the care of a police-department psychiatrist named Dr. Raymond Berkowitz, better known as Dr. B. Victor yearned to Google Raymond Berkowitz and learn all he could about the doctor, but knew that he couldn't. Not under prying eyes.

Vic offered a big-eyed, innocent look to his jailor and said, "I'm done."

The guard stood his prisoner up and clasped manacles on his wrists. The manacles were attached to a belly chain that wound around Vic's waist.

It didn't matter. The Malibu Canyon Murderer had what he needed.

CHAPTER ONE

D etective Sergeant Gabriel McRay waited at the Seattle-Tacoma International Airport for his sister to pick him up. Years had passed since he had last seen Janet. Her nine-year-old son had been a baby then. Gabriel peered at every woman who drove past him and wondered if he would recognize his sister.

Although it was summertime, the air felt cool and carried with it the promise of rain. Gabriel zipped up his windbreaker jacket. A beachcomber by nature, he lived in Southern California where summertime meant sunshine and heat. This damp climate posed a new twist for him.

A plane took off in the distance, and he viewed its departure with longing. It had taken many discussions with his psychologist for Gabriel to get up the guts to face his family, but now that he'd arrived, he was determined to see the visit through. His father was ill, and Gabriel, burdened by enough regrets, didn't need one more.

An auburn-haired woman pulled up to the curb in a red Ford Explorer. Gabriel didn't make a move at first, unsure if she was his sister. He remembered Janet as a lithe brunette. The auburn-haired lady exited the SUV and approached Gabriel with some trepidation.

"Gabriel?"

Janet. She'd gained some weight. A woman now. A mother. She'd changed her hair color.

"Hi," he said.

"Hi!" she echoed back and came at him with open arms.

Although his arms felt weighted, he forced them to come together around his sister. Janet smelled of perfume... nothing exotic, a commercial fragrance perhaps.

"Let me look at you." Janet pulled away from him although her hands stayed on his shoulders. She smiled sadly. "Yes, it's you."

Gabriel, discomfited, bravely met her smile. "Look at you..." he began and couldn't finish.

She squeezed his shoulders and then let her hands drop. Moving to the car, she opened the hatch. "Just the duffle bag?"

"I travel light." Gabriel placed the bag inside the cargo area.

They took their seats in her car. Tossed DVDs of Disney movies littered the floor along with flattened juice pouches and a discarded fast-food kid's-meal container.

"Sorry about the mess. I didn't have time to get the car washed. I should have."

"Looks like my car, only I don't have kids as an excuse."

Janet seemed to melt a little then. "I'm glad you came, Gabe. Mom and Dad are coming over. We're all having dinner together at the house tonight."

She quickly glanced at her brother to see if he'd stiffen. Gabriel made sure that his features stayed calm and relaxed.

"Nothing fancy," Janet added. "I just..." She left off and concentrated on moving into highway traffic.

"How are your kids?" he asked as he scanned the Seattle scenery from the window.

"You'll meet them. Do you remember Liam at all?"

"As a baby in your arms. That's about it."

Janet smiled. "He's changed."

"I'll bet."

"And I don't think you ever met Amber."

"No, I never did." Gabriel cast a sidelong glance at his sister. "Your hair is a different color."

Janet absently touched her head. "Oh, yeah. I started getting gray, so I figured I'd experiment."

Gabriel looked out the passenger window and commented silently to himself, *my baby sister started going gray.*

~

"THIS IS YOUR UNCLE GABE. Can you say hi?"

Two children surveyed Gabriel dubiously. Liam, the nine-year-old brown-haired boy, appeared to be interested in an exchange. His little sister Amber, all of five years old and adorned with black curls like Gabriel, took a shy step closer to her mother.

Gabriel unzipped the duffle bag and pulled out two wrapped toys. He handed one to his niece and the other to his nephew.

"A truce," he said. "Because you've never met me."

Liam gave him a huge smile. "Can we open 'em?"

Gabriel shrugged. "They're yours."

The two ran off conspiratorially as Janet yelled after them, "Hey, that's rude! You didn't even say thank you!"

"Let them go," Gabriel said, chuckling. "I'm sure they'll let me know how I rate."

He caught Janet staring at him, and the awkwardness fell between them again. Janet lived in a two-story house perched on a hill overlooking the Ballard locks. The view was a grassy downslope that led to the water where the kids had a raft they could swim to. The raft had a sun with a happy face painted on it. Well beyond the raft, one could watch the boats cruise back and forth.

"Your house is big, Janet. It's very nice."

His sister smiled briefly and took his hand. "Come on, I'll show you your room."

She led him down the basement stairs, past a washer and dryer, to a large carpeted rumpus room with wall-length bar, a pool table, and windows that faced the grass and the water beyond.

"The couch pulls out." Janet spoke quickly as if she were in a hurry to leave. "The mattress is really comfortable. Don't worry. I'll make up the bed for you later."

"I can do it. Please don't go to any bother for me."

"It's no bother," Janet told him as she hoisted his

duffle bag onto the bar and then opened a narrow door. "Here is a closet where you can hang your clothes, and behind that other door is a full bathroom. Towels and everything are already in there."

She clasped and unclasped her hands as she turned toward him. "It's more private down here, what with the kids running and yelling through the house. I thought, you know, you can close the door and have some quiet time to yourself if you need it."

"Janet," Gabriel began. "I'm all right."

"Oh, I know! I know." She nodded tensely. "I only want you to be comfortable."

Gabriel looked around the large room. "I'll be fine."

She went to the door, paused and then turned to face him. "See you later then…"

Gabriel nodded. His sister closed the door, and he was alone.

GABRIEL'S CELL PHONE RANG, and he eyed the display. Dr. Ming Li was calling him. Ming held the esteemed position of being the Los Angeles County Medical Examiner. Gabriel had worked with Ming on many homicide cases, but what began as a professional workplace relationship had turned personal. Gabriel had known she'd check up on him.

"Hey," he answered into the phone.

"How is it?"

Ming always drove right to the point. It was one of the things Gabriel liked about her. Some people found her no-nonsense approach obnoxious, especially men who had issues with strong-minded women, but Ming had been a true friend to Gabriel. He supposed she was officially a true girlfriend now.

"Sort of awkward," he replied.

He heard Ming give a gentle "hmm" of agreement.

"Of course it is," she assured him. "Just remember what Dr. B said. This is part of your recovery. Mending the relationship with your family, getting it all out in the open, is important."

"How are you?" Gabriel asked. He didn't want to talk about himself.

"Missing you like crazy. What have I got to look forward to except corpses?"

"Got an examination later?"

"Nothing for you to worry about, Detective. You're on vacation, remember?"

"I'm just curious."

"Mend, Gabriel. That's an order. You'll want to be strong for the trial."

"I'm not the only one."

He heard her sigh. Gabriel knew Ming would be called as a material witness. After all, Victor Archwood, the Malibu Canyon Murderer, had kidnapped her. Archwood had killed seven people that hot summer in a ritualistic manner. He had left notes on the violated bodies of his victims—notes that were addressed to Gabriel, targeting him. Those notes had picked the lock of a mental door to Gabriel's past, a door that Gabriel sometimes wished had stayed closed forever.

It had taken a serial killer to make Gabriel recall a

terrifying childhood trauma. What would it take to bridge the abyss between Gabriel and his family?

"How is your father?" Ming asked, changing the subject.

"I haven't seen him yet."

"I think your mother mentioned he's on Exelon, which can stabilize the Alzheimer's symptoms. Your mother has been very vigilant about his medications."

"He's too young for this, Ming."

"Unfortunately, he's not. Early-onset ALZ can occur in people even in their forties."

Gabriel moved to the windows and looked out at the expanse of green lawn. "I hope I'm not too late."

"It's never too late to mend fences. You say to them what you need to say."

DR. MING LI pulled on her latex gloves, donned her facemask, and joined her deputy coroner in the autopsy room. The body on the table was a young female named April Pennington. April had allegedly overdosed on drugs, which had caused cardiac arrest. That was all well and good, but it was the medical examiner's job to let the body tell its own story. Perhaps there was a suspicious bruise or cut that would indicate foul play. Ming didn't mind being the channel through which the dead spoke.

This girl had been pretty with a pert nose and lustrous chestnut hair. Now her arms lay still at her sides. Her delicate hands were frozen and gray. It was a shame, Ming thought, to die so young. Her family would want answers. Ming would provide them.

Her initial review of the body didn't yield much. There was a needle mark along the vein of her left inner arm that stood out because the other drug tracks were old and healed. As Ming continued the external examination, she paused over another tiny puncture wound on the girl's neck.

Drug users usually avoided injecting their necks because it was too easy to hit the carotid artery. Arteries, when hit, resulted in a painful injection because of the abundance of surrounding nerves. Pullbacks weren't easy either because the syringe filled with fast-flowing blood. The neck could swell and cause breathing difficulties, so the risk of death was high.

Ming regarded the girl. April had been lucky that her neck injection was without incident. Unfortunately, she hadn't been lucky enough to prevent her overdose.

Other than the needle marks, Ming could find no bruises or wounds, nothing that aroused suspicion.

Ming took up her scalpel and cut a line from each shoulder to the sternum, then down the midline of the body. She sliced back the flesh to expose the peritoneal cavity and then examined the abdomen. Her deputy coroner, a wiry redheaded man named Geoffrey, used rib shears to snap the ribs so that Ming could easily lift away the breastplate.

So much loss in this world, Ming thought as she examined the heart and lungs, this poor girl and also Gabriel. He had avoided his family for years, and now he hoped to make peace with them. Ming felt a bit envious of Gabriel being on good terms with his folks. It wasn't that she didn't want them to get along; it's just that when he'd been troubled—a lonely pilot flying through an emotional storm—Ming had been his wingman. Funny, the healthier Gabriel became, the more she worried he'd toss her aside along with his old mental garbage.

Ming removed the girl's organs and handed them one by one to Geoffrey, who weighed and measured them.

Gabriel had shaken the foundation of Ming's controlled world, and that's what she liked about him. When she first started working with Gabriel, she'd been physically attracted to him. His black hair, deep blue eyes, and strong body were enough of a magnet, but it was his instability, the fact that he seemed less man and more smoking volcano, that had really turned her on. Of course, she would only admit that to herself.

Ming dissected the girl's heart, looking for clots, and observed that the valves were intact and normal. Soon, Gabriel would come home, and she'd have him all to herself again. Of course, then the trial would commence.

Ming didn't want to think about the upcoming trial, but it hung like a specter in her head just the same. Victor Archwood had been a master of disguise. He had played various roles to gain access to his victims. When he abducted Ming, he had been dressed as a janitor, mopping the floors. The next thing she knew, Archwood was burying her alive beneath sand and water. She had begged for her life before he rammed a PVC pipe into her mouth, chipping her teeth as he told her to pray for Gabriel to find her. The feel of that hard plastic pipe lodged in her mouth—her only lifeline to air, the frigid wet earth pressed heavily against her body; her shackled hands, her bound ankles, her stampeding heart—they would haunt her forever. How she wished she could forget all that.

Gabriel had rescued Ming from her makeshift grave. Did he realize he was her Knight in Shining Armor? She didn't think so.

Looking back now, Ming was rather embarrassed by the screaming mess she had been, so out of her element, so close to her own death. Now she would have to face Victor Archwood all over again.

Ming sliced representative samples from all the organs and saved them in formaldehyde. She had to smile behind her mask. Examining dead bodies had never made her sick, but seeing her kidnapper again might make Ming vomit all over the courtroom.

Using a Stryker saw, Ming removed the girl's scalp and exposed the brain. She then freed the organ from the optic nerves still attached. She instructed Geoffrey to remove the eyes and glean the vitreous humor from the cavity of the eye socket. Eye jelly, while not the wunderkind postmortem clock it was reputed to be, was still a good marker to determine the body's dehydration levels or to show an electrolyte imbalance.

Ming sighed and thought about all the trials where she had served as an expert witness, a highly regarded forensic examiner. Now she would be called to the stand as a victim, as vulnerable and exposed as the flayed body of the young woman on the table before her.

CHAPTER TWO

G abriel sat at dinner with his mother, father, sister, her husband, and their two kids. He observed his father carefully, looking for signs of Alzheimer's. So far, his father seemed content to be sitting next to his wayward son.

Janet's husband, Michael, a local radio sportscaster, observed Gabriel carefully.

Looking for signs of psychosis, Gabriel imagined. He tried to ignore Michael's nonstop staring. Janet would nudge her husband every so often, and Michael would turn away, but only briefly.

Gabriel's mother sat next to her husband. Mrs. McRay also couldn't keep her eyes off Gabriel, but her look was one of compassion and relief. Gabriel had made the effort. Her son was finally communicative. He was here.

Pete McRay nodded to Gabriel. "How's the police business, Son?"

His dad had aged so much since Gabriel last saw him.

This frail person beside him couldn't possibly be his shoe-salesman father.

"Busy."

"You made investigator yet?"

Many years ago. "Yep."

"I knew you would. I always told your mom, 'Gabriel's the one with his head on straight. Sharp as a tack and smart as a whip.' Didn't I used to say that about Gabriel?"

Mrs. McRay nodded tenderly. "You did."

Janet took an impatient breath, and Gabriel glanced at her. His sister wore a noticeable frown. He wondered briefly what was irking her. Had their parents favored him over Janet? If so Gabriel had been too screwed up to notice. Obviously, some interesting family dynamic existed that he hadn't been privy to.

Liam poked Gabriel's shoulder. "Are you a cop?"

Gabriel nodded.

"I betcha you can't catch me."

"Liam, wait until after dinner," Janet warned. "Let Uncle Gabe eat his food."

Amber eyed Gabriel from across the table. Black Irish like him, her dark curls played around cobalt-blue eyes. She twisted her fork around in her pasta. "I bet you can't catch me!" she baited coyly in her little-girl's voice.

Gabriel, not used to capturing the attention of children, could only shake his head and smile awkwardly.

"Catch us now!" Liam commanded and jumped from his seat.

Michael pointed at his young son. "Sit down and finish your meal."

Liam stuck out his tongue and sat down defiantly, trying to save face in front of the stranger who was his uncle.

"Tell you what," Gabriel assured the boy. "Later we'll go out and you find the best hiding place. I promise to find you." He pointed a comedic finger at Amber. "And you."

The little girl broke into delighted giggles.

At that, Gabriel's awkward smile cleared into one of honest amusement.

Janet cleared her throat. "You don't have to, Gabe. Don't let them pressure you." To her children, she said, "Uncle Gabe wants to spend time with Grandpa. He's on vacation, remember, so just leave him be."

Liam and Amber responded with the expected hurt expressions, and Gabriel regarded his sister curiously. He wondered if Janet already knew the reason he felt uncomfortable around children. If she didn't, she was going to find out tonight.

AFTER DINNER, the kids disappeared into their bedrooms, lured by Janet's promise of video games.

Michael, Janet, Gabriel, and his parents sat in the living room and stared at each other.

Finally, Janet broke the silence. "Did you have enough to eat, Gabe?"

"Yes, thank you. It was very good."

The pasta hadn't been very good, but Gabriel kept that to himself.

More silence.

"Gabriel's a wonderful chef." Mrs. McRay beamed at her son. "What was that dish you made me? You put fish in paper and cooked it."

Salmon en papillote.

Again, Gabriel sensed something negative radiating from his sister. "I can't remember," he answered.

Mrs. McRay nodded to Janet. "You should really let him make something."

"If Gabriel wants to cook, he can cook," Janet replied, but her words sounded disingenuous.

I don't want to cook, thought Gabriel. *I want to get out of here.*

Maybe his years in therapy urged him to clear the air, or maybe he'd had enough of the paralytic pauses that crept into the conversations. Whatever the reason, Gabriel said, "I hope my presence here is not making you all uncomfortable."

He looked plainly at his sister.

Michael cleared his throat and answered for his wife. "Look, Gabriel. We can't help feeling like we have to tread carefully around you. It's pretty much common knowledge that you've had your share of troubles."

A finger of irritation poked at Gabriel, but all he said was, "Okay."

"We're just not sure what will set you off."

Gabriel coolly regarded his brother-in-law. Once upon a time, Gabriel had suffered uncontrollable rages. An asshole comment like that would have very much set him off. It would have sent Gabriel barreling across the room to punch his brother-in-law in the face.

Instead, Gabriel took a controlled breath. "Michael, if

you're worried that my problems are going to cause me to kill your family in the middle of the night…"

"Gabriel!" Mrs. McRay cried. Janet shook her head and chewed her lower lip.

Michael reddened. "I didn't say that."

"Now listen, you…" Mr. McRay stood up from the couch and wagged a finger at Michael. "You just lay off…" Pete McRay looked helplessly toward Gabriel, who was shocked to realize that his father had forgotten his name. "…My son!"

"It's okay, Pops." Michael held up his hands in surrender. "No one's arguing here."

Janet motioned to her father. "Dad, help me put the kids to bed."

Mr. McRay continued to point at Michael. "My son is a good boy. He just acts out sometimes. That's all." He let his arm drop, and his hand went into his pockets to fish for something. "Where's my wallet?" He looked at his wife in consternation. "Did you see my wallet?"

"I have it," Mrs. McRay assured him.

Pete McRay seemed to deflate then. Gabriel gazed at his father and wondered if the comment about him acting out referred to a memory of Gabriel as a boy. How much did his dad remember? Forcing himself to move, he walked over and rubbed Pete McRay's thin shoulders. "Everything's all right, Dad. Michael wants you to say goodnight to the kids with him." Gabriel threw his brother-in-law a stony look. "Don't you, Michael?"

"I'll go," Janet said as she went to her father.

"No." Gabriel stopped her. "We need to talk."

Janet exchanged worried glances with her husband.

Michael took the cue and put his arm through Pete McRay's. "Come on, Pops."

The older man shuffled next to his son-in-law as they headed down the hall toward the kid's bedrooms.

"I need my wallet," Pete complained to him.

Gabriel took a seat on the couch. Janet took refuge in an armchair a safe distance from her brother. Mrs. McRay stood awkwardly between her two children.

"Now let's get it out in the open," Gabriel said bluntly. "Apparently you heard or read about how I was on probation for using excessive force."

Janet eyed him steadily. "I read how you were fired because of police brutality."

Gabriel ignored that. "And you heard or read that I was forced into psychiatric evaluation."

She nodded.

Mrs. McRay sighed loudly and flopped into the nearest armchair.

Gabriel sat back and regarded his sister. "Well, all that is true. I suffered from aggression, headaches, nightmares, and worst of all, memory lapses. They are called fugue states. I would 'wake up' and be in a different place and have no idea how I'd gotten there. All this was happening while I was investigating the Malibu Canyon murders. Are you scared, Janet?"

Janet frowned at her brother but made no reply.

Mrs. McRay shook her head at her son. "Gabriel, stop."

"Enquiring minds want to know." Gabriel couldn't keep the sarcasm out of his voice. He looked at his sister. "Do you want me to continue?"

Janet peered down the empty hallway and then nodded at Gabriel.

"I had symptoms of post-traumatic stress disorder," he continued. "War veterans get it, but everyday people who have experienced a trauma in their lives get it too."

Janet's shoulders squared. This piqued her interest.

Gabriel studied the lines in the wood floor. "Apparently I had blocked out a trauma. I suppressed the memory of it. It was very painful, so I refused to address it. Thus the anger and the generally out-of-control way of life."

Janet glanced at Mrs. McRay and saw that her mother's eyes were wet.

"What happened to you?" Janet asked.

"Victor Archwood—"

"Who?"

"The Malibu Canyon Murderer. He left notes on his victim's bodies, notes that were addressed to me. He seemed to know me, but I couldn't remember him. He was from my past, part of that memory I had blocked. I knew that if I could remember the trauma, then I would remember him and solve the case. It took everything I had, Janet. It took everything out of me. And then I remembered."

"What?" Janet pressed.

The sound of a door closing perforated the silence, and the muffled voices of Pete McRay and Michael became more audible.

"I was molested by our neighbor in San Francisco." Gabriel met his sister's eyes. "His name was Andrew

Pierce, but you wouldn't remember him. You were too young."

Mrs. McRay crossed her arms, looked down, and rocked back and forth in her chair. Janet grimaced as she observed her mother.

"We think the abuse must have occurred several times," Gabriel added.

Janet turned back to him. "We?"

"My therapist and I. And my appointments are no longer mandatory."

Janet stared at the floor, searching for words that escaped her. Finally, and without looking up, she asked, "Is he—is this Andrew Pierce still around?"

"No, he's dead."

Janet looked earnestly at her mother. "Did you know? Have you been hiding this from me?"

Mrs. McRay was a tightly wound ball on the chair. "I only found out last Christmas. It wasn't my place to tell you."

They could hear Michael and Mr. McRay approaching. Janet turned her eyes toward Gabriel. "I never knew. Why didn't you say anything to Mom and Dad?"

"Because Andrew said he would drown you in his pool if I told anyone."

Janet gasped.

"Eventually Andrew told me that Mom and Dad approved of what he was doing because it paid him back for all the movies that he took me to." Gabriel paused and then lowered his voice to a whisper. "I hated you all."

Michael entered the room, took one look at his wife's pained expression, and then stared ruefully at Gabriel.

Mr. McRay entered and, genuinely pleased to see his son, wandered over to him.

"Well!" He wavered a bit, suddenly unsure of whom he was addressing.

Mrs. McRay quietly rose from her chair and tiptoed next to him. "It's Gabriel."

"I know that!" Mr. McRay brushed his wife aside and took a seat on the couch. "How's the police force going?"

Gabriel offered him a sorrowful smile. "It's going well, Dad."

THE NEXT MORNING, Gabriel awoke to whispers and giggling. He opened his eyes to see the faces of his niece and nephew peering over the side of his bed. Upon seeing their uncle awaken, the two children jumped up on the mattress.

"Are you going to play with us now?" Amber asked and then did a somersault across the sheets.

Liam shook Gabriel's shoulder. "C'mon! It's already seven thirty!"

Gabriel, astonished at this noisy show despite being half-asleep, sat up self-consciously. His first reaction to Liam's jostling his shoulder was to push the child's hand away, but he crushed that thought and forced himself to act normally.

"Okay, okay," he said in a cracked voice. "Just let me get dressed."

Amber somersaulted back his way and landed against Gabriel's chest. She unfolded there in giddy laughter.

The three of them heard Janet call from upstairs.

"I think your mom's got breakfast on the table," Gabriel told them.

Amber threw her arms around his neck. She smelled like fresh sheets and soap.

"Carry me upstairs!" she demanded with a smile.

Conscious that he was wearing only boxer shorts and a tank top, Gabriel carefully removed her small hands.

"Okay. You guys go and save me a seat while I get dressed."

Amber pursed her lips together in a pout and jumped off the bed. Liam didn't move.

Gabriel tried again. "I bet if you two ran up the stairs together, Amber would win."

As Liam's mouth dropped open, Amber shrieked gleefully and bolted out of the room to get a head start.

"Uh-*uh!*" Liam yelled and took off after his sister.

Only when Gabriel heard their scrabbling footsteps on the stairs did he get out of bed to get dressed.

AFTER BREAKFAST, Janet drove Gabriel and the kids to Pike Place Market. The sun had broken through, and Janet told her brother he had brought the California sunshine with him. They browsed through the various shops, and when Janet wasn't reining in the kids, she spoke to Gabriel.

"I wish you'd told me before, Gabe."

They stepped inside a used bookstore, which knew wouldn't entertain the children for long.

"I couldn't. I blocked it out."

Janet sighed. "No wonder you never wanted to talk to us. No wonder you pushed us away. But when you realized what had happened to you, why didn't you call me?"

"I had to process everything, Janet. I'm still processing it."

"But how does Victor Archwood figure into all this?"

Gabriel picked up a book with a ripped spine. "Like I said, he was from my past."

"Was he involved somehow with your"—Janet paused —"molestation?"

Gabriel shook his head and set the book down. "I used to babysit him."

"You babysat the Malibu Canyon Murderer?" Janet gaped at her brother.

"When I was a teenager." He perused another old book. "He didn't have a father, and his mother thought a male figure in his life, a big brother of sorts, would help him out. It didn't."

"Why not?"

Gabriel decided the bookstore was too stuffy. He moved to the door and stepped outside into the filtered sunshine. Janet quickly corralled the kids and followed her brother. In the freedom of the street, Liam and Amber began a game of chase. Gabriel watched them, knowing his sister waited for an answer.

"The district attorney wants me to keep my mouth shut because it's all coming out at the trial," Gabriel said. "Archwood's defense is going to make me look bad because I was the lead investigator on the case. They may try to dredge up the past and put a stain on my character. They can discredit me that way."

"But why did Victor Archwood write notes to you?" she pressed. "Why did he target you after all these years?"

"Victor Archwood was abused as well, by his grandfather. When he confided that to me years ago, it brought up my own issues with abuse, and I went off on him. He was just a little boy, but I beat him up. The worst part is, once I was out of his life, his mother told him that it was I, not his grandfather, who had sexually abused him. As far as I know, he still thinks that I'm a child molester."

Janet's eyes went wide. She seemed to be at a loss for words. Gabriel wanted to tell her more, to clue her into Archwood's twisted take on the truth, but Liam and Amber ran up to them. His sister watched in semi-horror as her two children grabbed at their uncle and begged him to chase them down the street.

CHAPTER THREE

Outside the Terminal Island Federal Correctional Institution, the sun bounced merrily over the waters of San Pedro Bay. Inside the prison, Victor Archwood was led into the family visiting room. He wore regulation inmate attire; a khaki shirt buttoned up to the second-from-the-top button that was neatly tucked into khaki pants. His hands were manacled together. The visiting room officer led Vic inside, sat him down at a table, and then stood by holding a sap and a stun gun. A video monitoring system kept a watchful eye over the room.

Victor saw his mother seated across from him. Most of the time, Victor was in a cage, and his mother sat behind a glass window and spoke to him using a phone. This was the first time they didn't have a solid barrier between them, and Victor instantly delved into the possibility of physically attacking her.

His mother smiled sweetly when he took his seat.

"Good morning, Son."

Vic watched his mother give an innocent glance toward the officer. She then turned her face back to Vic.

"I want you to meet someone."

"Another attorney?" he asked dryly.

His mother, Natalie Archwood, was a thin woman. She'd always looked malnourished, but he could clearly see lines in her face—deep gouges that ran parallel across her cheeks as if they'd been carved. Her light blue eyes were rheumy.

A drunkard's eyes, Victor thought. *Well, no surprise there.*

Her hair was gray-blond and frizzy. She had it pulled into a tight bun, but the frizz escaped and popped out all over her head like pubic hair.

An amusing thought occurred to Victor as he surveyed his mother. He could personally give her a facelift. He could do a little carving of his own, stretch back that facial skin, and staple it to her skull. *Voilà! Plastic surgery a la Victor Archwood.*

He must have smiled, for his mother patted his manacled hands, which rested on the table.

"I think this person will really help our case," she said.

Our case?

Natalie Archwood turned toward the guard. "Can you call her in now?"

The guard signaled to the camera mounted on the wall.

Victor continued to regard his mother. That frizzy hair of hers was more of a problem. He would simply pour a bucket of hot wax over her head. That would smooth her hair.

"Are they treating you all right?" Natalie asked him.

"Yes."

"Are you terribly bored?"

"Not really."

Natalie shook her head in melodramatic sympathy. The guard opened the door and ushered in a good-looking African-American woman who appeared to be in her mid-twenties. She wore a Dodgers baseball cap over chemically straightened hair that was streaked with blond highlights. She came to the table holding a digital recorder and a notebook. She smelled of the outside world, like the breeze and the sun. Victor eyed her curiously.

"Hi, Mr. Archwood," she said, nearly extending her hand and then thinking the better of it. "My name is Andrea Leighton, and I work for Truth TV. It's a cable network that does reality television shows. I am what they call a showrunner. A writer-slash-producer."

Victor nodded, interested—not in her television bull-shit, but in the cinnamon color of her skin and the mint green polish on her fingernails.

His mother bristled with excitement. "They want to do an exposé on you, Vic. To get into the mind of…"

Andrea took up Natalie's slack. "To follow everything from your point of view. Your life in prison while you await trial, the trial itself, and—everything."

"Like what my deepest feelings are as they're giving me the lethal injection?"

Andrea blinked at Victor, unsure if he was being facetious.

"No one's going to be executed here," Natalie said, sneering at the guard.

Victor grinned. Now his mother was acting like the bitch he was familiar with.

Andrea leaned toward him. "Mr. Archwood, can I call you Victor?"

Archwood regarded her with a half smile, amused to find her body so close to his. "You can call me Vic."

"Okay, Vic. This will show the human perspective of someone accused of very serious crimes. Your side of the story. Are you interested?"

Victor deeply breathed in her sun-and-sky scent and wondered if somehow he'd be able to collect all ten of Andrea's shiny fingernails.

"Yes," he answered her truthfully. "I'm interested."

GABRIEL TOOK his father to a park bordering Lake Union. Mount Rainier, still wearing a toupee of white snow, stood stoically in the distance. The outing freed Mrs. McRay to do some shopping and gave Gabriel some quality time with his father. It had been many years since the two of them had spent any time alone together.

"How are you feeling, Dad?"

Mr. McRay gave Gabriel an odd look, as if he were deliberating why his raven-haired companion addressed him as "Dad."

Gabriel felt heaviness in his chest. For many years he

had ignored his parents. In therapy, after he'd realized (*remembered!*) that he had been molested, Gabriel had felt nothing but anger toward his father. He blamed his parents for not seeing the signs of his molestation, for being oblivious.

"Right as rain," Mr. McRay answered guardedly, looking Gabriel over once more.

I'm sorry I missed my chance to reconnect with you, Dad.

Gabriel tried to fill the gap with conversation. "I visited San Francisco a while back. Do you remember San Francisco?"

Mr. McRay nodded. They walked on.

"I went by Golden Gate Park."

I went to the ruins of the Sutro Baths and met a serial killer in the fog. He stabbed me twice.

"I stayed at the Embarcadero."

I walked our old neighborhood and saw the house where I was abused as a child.

Gabriel couldn't think of anything else to say. The heaviness in his chest was apt to break his heart. He hooked his arm through his father's and sighed.

"You're a good boy," his father murmured and patted Gabriel's arm. "You always were."

THAT NIGHT, Gabriel sat on the couch, sandwiched between Liam and Amber who slept on either side of him. His arm was asleep, but he didn't want to disturb the two dreamers. They had been watching a Disney movie, and now the credits were rolling.

Children were a novel concept to Gabriel. His own childhood had been marred, and he'd never felt much at ease around kids. On top of that, Gabriel worried that he wouldn't make it through tonight's movie without some symptom of his damaged psyche rearing its ugly head. Dr. B had warned Gabriel about possible triggers. Triggers were ordinary occurrences that would suddenly remind him of the trauma. Dr. B had discussed the possibility that Gabriel might close down or turn to his anger for protection.

When the kids pulled at his hands and begged him to watch the movie with them, Gabriel had acquiesced, figuring this would be a good test of his strength because —

Andrew Pierce had taken him to children's movies in the theater. He had bought candy and popcorn for Gabriel. People would smile at Andrew, thinking how sweet it was to see this young man looking after a little boy. But Gabriel never smiled. He sat terrified, waiting for Andrew to make his move. And he always made his move—sometimes at the theater, urging Gabriel's hand to touch him, or back at Andrew's house, where the more intense sexual abuse took place. Every bad feeling was experienced, pain, humiliation, degradation, and terror.

Let's not go there, Gabriel told himself. Let's not think about that right now. Think about these two who trust you so implicitly they can fall asleep against you.

Gabriel felt them breathing against him. His original intention had only been to stitch things up with his family. Getting to know Janet's children was an unexpected bonus. Their simple innocence and unconditional love was refreshing water that doused the flames of

Gabriel's burning hurt. It was strange, not being judged by them. He walked around feeling judged by everyone else except Ming.

His arm felt numb. Gabriel stealthily maneuvered his limb from behind his nephew. Leaning forward ever so carefully, Gabriel grabbed the remote control, sat back, and with some relief, switched to a news channel. Liam tossed a bit and then nuzzled up to his uncle once more.

Janet quietly entered in her robe and slippers. She halted upon seeing Gabriel snuggled up with her children.

"Are they bothering you?" she whispered nervously. "Do you want me to take them to bed?"

"No," he said softly. "I'm fine."

And to his surprise, he felt fine. Gabriel regarded the two children nestled against him. "Kids are a new and unusual event for me."

"They adore you."

It was nice to be adored. Not too long ago, Gabriel had thought of himself as a pariah, someone who hung at the fringe of normal society. The adoration of a child inserted him right in the middle of everything that was wholesome and acceptable. Children possessed that kind of magic.

Janet made to pick up Amber.

"Want me to help you put them to bed?" Gabriel asked.

Janet shook her head. "No, I'll take them." She offered him a weak smile. "I'm used to it."

She took Amber in her arms and roused Liam. The

children mumbled in their sleep, but Liam obediently followed his mother down the hall.

On the news, a weatherman projected rain for Seattle. Down south, Los Angeles geared up for a warm summer. Gabriel flipped through the channels and yawned, feeling sleepy himself. He was mulling over whether to call it a night when suddenly his vision caught something on a previous channel, a familiar image. Gabriel flipped backward through the channels and then held his breath in surprise. On the television, Natalie Archwood was being interviewed.

Janet reentered the room and sat at the opposite end of the couch from Gabriel. Wrapping herself in a throw blanket, she noticed her brother's stunned expression.

"What is it?" Janet asked him. "What's the show?"

Gabriel couldn't answer. He had to listen.

On the television show, Natalie was saying, "As a mother, of course it's hard. I worry if he's eating, if he's exercising. I even worry if he's getting enough sunlight. My son is innocent of these terrible crimes, and he will be exonerated."

Gabriel let go of the breath he'd been holding. *Natalie Archwood…*

Natalie hadn't changed much in two years. Gabriel could still sense the shrew lurking inside the woman's inflections, although she was playing the devoted mother for the cameras.

Natalie Archwood, on television.

During the hunt for the Malibu Canyon Murderer, Gabriel had infiltrated the Archwood family, yearning to learn more about his prey; itching to find out how he and

Victor Archwood were connected. The Archwoods were a completely dysfunctional clan, and they'd nearly succeeded in wrapping Gabriel into their web of lunacy.

Natalie Archwood, the mother of a serial killer.

Then Victor Archwood appeared on the screen. The last time Gabriel had seen Archwood, they had been struggling on the balcony of the famed Cliff House in San Francisco. Gabriel absently touched the scar on his arm where Archwood had stabbed him, forever giving Gabriel something to remember him by.

Prison apparently had been easy on Archwood. He still had his frat-boy good looks. He was simply charming as he showed the interviewer around his small cell.

"Who is that?" Janet asked.

"That's Victor Archwood," Gabriel muttered, his eyes glued to the screen.

"Wow, really?" Janet said, leaning forward. "Turn it up."

Reluctantly Gabriel did as he was told. Archwood's voice got louder.

"I've tried to use the time here to educate myself. I already hold a graduate degree in Theater Arts."

Yes, you do, Gabriel thought bitterly. You played several roles to fool your victims.

Gabriel pressed the information button on the remote and saw that Archwood was featured on some new reality television show called *The Dark Mind*.

"Now I'm taking business classes, and I read these kinds of things for fun." On TV, Archwood displayed some art magazines and a copy of Robert Anton Wilson's *Prometheus Rising*.

Archwood smiled onscreen. "I know. It's a bit esoteric, but it feeds the soul."

Souls, Gabriel repeated silently. Archwood is still talking about souls. *You killed people because you claimed to absorb their energy. You wanted to capture their souls.*

"He comes off as normal," Janet observed.

Gabriel jerked his eyes to her. "He's an actor, Janet. It's all an act. Archwood is right where he belongs—in a cage. The question is, how the hell did he get a TV show?"

ANDREA SAT across from Victor in the prison's family visiting room, talking rapidly, flipping her hair back, and gesturing with her hands.

"The taping went really well today," she said enthusiastically. She was excited, turned-on. "You should see all the letters we're getting. People want to meet you. A well-known screenwriter is asking for the rights to your story. Do you have a biographer already? The writer wants to know."

"I'm not all that interesting," Victor lied calmly.

He knew why all this attention was being paid to him. They could feel the energy flowing off him. They wanted to get close to him, like moths to a brilliant flame. Victor's heart swelled with excitement. He had thought he'd been derailed when Gabriel McRay had trounced his plans. He'd been surprised and depressed to find himself stuck in a jail cell, with the prosecutors and the public rallying to destroy him. And then the path suddenly cleared, and Victor realized why he was meant for this bizarre detour of prison. He was becoming famous.

It made sense now and reinforced the knowledge that he was on the conqueror's path. He would stomp through this world like an ancient god, and his power would only continue to grow.

But Victor kept these thoughts to himself, figuring a mask of modesty might serve him better. His innocuous image would keep the prosecutors at bay and turn the public to his side. He would tell people what they wanted to hear until he was far away from incarceration. Victor glanced at Andrea.

And he would keep this girl nearby. She would continue to do more for him.

He settled a gentle gaze on her. "You've been very understanding, Andrea."

He hoped his eyes conveyed a tenderness he didn't feel.

She blushed and smiled. "It's been quite an experience working together. I think you've been misunderstood."

Victor nodded solemnly.

"Did you?" she asked, suddenly expressionless.

"Did I what?"

"Did you kill those people?"

She thinks she's being adept, mused Victor. The Writer-Slash-Producer thought she was catching him off guard.

So cool, aren't we? Shall I act shocked? Indignant? How do you want me to react, Ms. Showrunner?

Andrea kept a poker face and waited. For a cold

moment, Victor wished he'd had his antique trench knife with him. He wanted very much to cut an expression onto Andrea's expressionless face. A dumbass smile, for instance. A smile that would bleed from cheek to cheek. But the knife was gone, down into the watery depths of the Pacific Ocean thanks to Gabriel McRay, the knife along with other certain mementos. *Gifts from my grandfather…*

In his head, Victor heard his grandfather's Russian accent. He heard whispered Russian words, and his insides wanted to compress. Outside, Victor Archwood was the model of composure.

He cracked a Mona Lisa smile for Andrea, leaned back in his chair, and announced lightly, "The killer is out there."

That wasn't a lie exactly. It was simply a vague enough answer to have multiple interpretations. Andrea believed what she wanted to believe and took it to mean that the killer dwelt somewhere other than the room in which she sat.

She was wrong.

Andrea smiled in relief. "You're going to come out on top of this, Vic."

He met her smile. "Of that, I have no doubt."

"ARE YOU WATCHING THIS SHIT?" Gabriel was on the phone with Ming and they were both viewing another episode of *The Dark Mind*.

"This could only happen in LA," Gabriel muttered as

he held his cell phone and tore a frustrated swath across the carpeting in the basement guest room. Seeing Archwood talking amicably onscreen was a slap in his face. It was a slap in the face of seven people moldering in their graves. *Tania Dankowski had been a wife and a mother of a young son.*

On the television, Victor Archwood was giving an introduction into the different types of meals he was afforded.

Patrick Funston had been a college student with a bright future, well loved by his parents. Brian Goldfield had been a movie producer. How would he feel knowing his murderer was becoming a star?

"Turn it off, Gabriel," Ming told him.

Gabriel pointed the remote and turned off the television. He sat down on his pullout bed and glared at the now-black screen of the TV.

"Are you there?" Ming asked gently over the phone.

"I'm here."

Ming kept quiet. They held a silent tribute to the mutual repugnance they felt for Archwood. Neither could speak for a while.

Finally, Ming said, "The trial will be tough, but at least when it's over we can forget about him. He'll be nothing."

"Hopefully he'll be executed," Gabriel said. "In my book, he deserves nothing less."

"He's a young man. Rotting in prison for life would be no picnic for him."

"But he still gets to breathe."

Ming changed the subject. "How's it going with everyone?"

Gabriel welcomed the change, and holding the phone in the crook of his neck, he proceeded to take off his shoes to get comfortable. "It's going. I like Janet's kids. Amber is an angel, and Liam is a devil. Nothing much gets by him." Gabriel dropped his shoes in the closet. "Janet's a bit strange with me. I haven't quite figured her out yet. Her husband Michael is counting the days until I leave."

"Why?"

"My reputation preceded me, I guess," Gabriel offered. "I think I scare him."

"They need to get to know you like I know you."

Gabriel moved to the window and watched the incoming mist shroud the water. "Miss you," he said softly.

"Come home," she begged.

"Soon. How's Ramirez? Dash?"

Dash was the nickname for Michael Starkweather, Gabriel's partner for many years. Detective Starkweather had earned his nickname because he clung diligently to a salt-free diet and carried around the salt substitute Mrs. Dash in his pocket.

"Everyone's fine," Ming told him. "How's your Mom? Please tell her hello from me."

"I will."

Through the window, Gabriel could see the mist edging up the grass toward him. "I always thought they were the enemy," he said. "But now I see them—my dad, so frail. My mother, trying to be strong. I screwed up, Ming. I shut them out."

"You're there now, and that's what counts."

Gabriel said nothing as the mist faced him at the window.

CHAPTER FOUR

M errill Brillstein organized his client's papers in one of the prison's three legal visiting rooms. Truth be told, Victor Archwood gave Brillstein the creeps, but Vic's mother was willing to pay the lawyer's exorbitant fees, so his client was going to get the best defense possible. They brought Archwood into the room, and the young, handsome man sat across from his attorney.

"They treating you all right, Vic?"

Archwood nodded.

"More time out in the yard?"

"Yes." Archwood gave Brillstein a look that said get to the point.

No problem, Brillstein replied to himself, *because the sooner I'm done, the faster I can get away from you.*

Aloud, Brillstein said, "Look, the DA is offering you a deal: life without parole if you admit to the killings of Ronald and Meredith Hall. They'll forget the death penalty. Personally, I say no deal, but I'm obliged to ask you what you want to do."

Archwood reflected on that for a moment and then asked, "Why the Halls?"

"They have strong evidence against you with those two."

"What evidence? The DNA?"

Brillstein shook his head. "The DNA evidence is from another victim altogether, and it's degraded. While the DNA sample doesn't discount you, we can argue that it can't pinpoint you either. I'll call in an expert to defuse that situation, no problem."

"Then what is it?"

"It's the wedding band that was found in the cabin in San Francisco, the ring belonging to Ronald Hall. That's gonna be tougher to get around."

Archwood narrowed his eyes. "Say that again?"

"The ring belonging to the victim Ronald Hall was—" Brillstein put on his reading glasses and read from a paper. "Let's see... Ronald Hall was found next to his wife, Meredith, in their Lexus off a mountain road near Los Angeles. Both had been stabbed numerous times. Their wedding rings were missing. Ronald Hall's ring was later recovered at a burned-out cabin outside San Francisco. This cabin was purported to be the hideout of Victor Archwood."

The defense attorney removed his glasses and then looked up at Archwood for comment.

Archwood seemed confused. "Ronald Hall's ring was found in San Francisco?"

Brillstein nodded.

A small smile crept over Archwood's features. "May I read the report?"

Brillstein handed the report to Archwood and felt a tingle of revulsion when his fingers inadvertently touched his client's hand. What was it about Victor Archwood that made the normally feisty defense attorney want to run for cover? Archwood's good looks were deceiving. His eyes, while an innocent sapphire color, were derelict of emotion. The vacancy had to be masking something toxic. If it were up to Brillstein, he'd say Victor Archwood was completely guilty of hacking seven people to death, but luckily he didn't have to give his opinion. Only the jury's opinion counted, and it was Brillstein's job to create reasonable doubt of his client's guilt. The lawyer felt pretty confident he could, given the sore lack of physical evidence in the prosecution's case.

"So what do I tell them, Vic? If we go to trial, they're going for the death penalty. Do you want to make a plea deal?"

Archwood, reading the report, now wore a treacherous smile that unnerved his attorney. "Definitely not."

GABRIEL THREW his duffle bag into Janet's SUV and bade good-bye to his family. Although Amber and Liam wanted to accompany their uncle to the airport, Michael was firm on them staying home.

"When are you coming back?" Amber held out her arms to Gabriel. He knelt down and received a tight hug.

"Soon." Gabriel couldn't help but glance at Michael, who forced a smile.

"Can we come to your house?" Liam grabbed Gabriel before he could stand up. The little boy seemed truly sad to see his uncle leaving.

Gabriel nodded. "Sure."

"Will you teach me how to shoot?"

Gabriel ruffled his nephew's hair and stood up. "Maybe."

"Pleeease!"

While Liam whined, Gabriel went to Mrs. McRay. Thick strands of gray wove through his mother's black hair, which today she wore loose. After a moment's hesitation, Gabriel raised his hand to smooth an errant lock back into place. He regarded her wistfully.

Mrs. McRay lifted her hands to her son's face and planted a kiss on his cheek. "I'm happy you visited, Son. It means a lot."

Gabriel nodded and then walked over to his father. He put awkward arms around the older man. "Stay well, Dad. Okay?"

Pete McRay pulled away and apathetically patted Gabriel's shoulder.

Ming had warned Gabriel that emotions were often blunted in Alzheimer's patients. Doctors theorized that the lack of empathy might be due to memory loss, as emotions are often associated with memories. Ming advised Gabriel not to take it personally. That, however, was easier said than done.

Gabriel went over to his brother-in-law and extended his hand. "Thanks for everything."

Michael shook it—hard. "Good luck with the trial."

～

A FEW HOURS LATER, as purple dusk was settling over the ocean, Gabriel entered his apartment in Santa Monica, one of the last rent-controlled places on Bay Street. After being in Janet's large house, his apartment seemed dingy and confining to him.

Gabriel unpacked his duffle bag and went into the kitchen. He opened his nearly empty refrigerator and took out one of two beers waiting inside. The absence of children's laughter was noticeable, and Gabriel felt a void opening in his soul.

Is this loneliness?

Depressed, he sat on his worn couch and surveyed his surroundings. His apartment had always been a safe haven for him, only now it felt like a musty cave where some hibernating animal had slept. Had he lived his life in hibernation? Certainly Gabriel had spent most of his waking hours either being in hell or working to pull himself out of it.

His phone rang, cutting the silence, and Gabriel eagerly answered it.

"Hello?"

"Hi, Stranger," Ming said. "Want company?"

"Yeah, I'd love some company." His eyes traveled toward his kitchen. "Give me a half hour so I can go get us some edibles."

"You just got home. Leave the marketing to me."

· · ·

MING CAME OVER AN HOUR LATER, toting a bag of groceries.

"You didn't have to do this," Gabriel said, taking the bag from her.

"I have selfish motives." She followed him into the kitchen. "I was hoping you'd make us dinner. If you're too tired, we can go out."

"I'm okay," Gabriel said as he began unpacking the bag. "Hey, how crappy do you think this place is?"

"It's great. It's a couple of blocks from the beach, and you love the water."

Gabriel pulled out a package of bacon from the bag and set it on the counter. "But it's pretty crappy, right?"

Ming came up behind him and wrapped her arms around his waist. "It's an old apartment, Gabe. Don't pick on it." She purred against him, loving the familiar feeling of his muscular body. "Oh, I missed you. You feel good."

Gabriel pivoted in her arms, holding a can of lima beans in one hand and two tins of sardines in the other. "What are these for?"

"I was hungry, so I pulled a bunch of random things off the shelves."

Amused, Gabriel placed the items down on the counter and draped his arms about his girlfriend. "We'd better go out. I'm not sure I can make anything with what you bought."

Ming smiled. "Oh, that doesn't sound like the chef I know. Come on and show me how you kick culinary ass."

Gabriel looked over his shoulder at the array of odd ingredients. For some reason, he didn't feel connected to his kitchen, much less his apartment. He didn't know why.

But they were hungry and it was getting late, so Gabriel mentally kicked himself into gear.

After searching his pantry for possible ingredients, Gabriel pulled out a bag of flour, a random onion, and a package of brown sugar. As Ming observed with some wonderment, Gabriel fried a few pieces of the bacon and then cooked the can of lima beans with some brown sugar and chopped onion. He mixed them together then put the dish aside. Taking up the last bottle in his fridge, he whisked a half cupful of beer into a portion of flour, and then added some salt. He instructed Ming to drain the sardines and pat them dry. Ming, having no problem playing sous-chef, did as she was told and then cut a lime into wedges at Gabriel's direction.

Gabriel dredged the sardines into the flour mixture and fried them along with the lime wedges. He rolled two pieces of parchment paper into cones and placed the sardines and lime wedges inside like French fries.

He put the cones on two plates along with a helping of the lima bean and bacon dish. "I wouldn't say it's the healthiest of meals," he told Ming. "But it'll work if you're hungry."

"You are a genius." Ming eyed him with rapture. "What would I do without you?"

Gabriel winked at her as he handed her a plate. "Probably starve."

∾

AFTER DINNER, Ming volunteered to clean up while Gabriel took a shower. When he came out wearing jeans but no shirt, he found her sitting on the couch watching television. He watched her from the doorway, feeling grateful for the company.

He dropped down next to her on the couch.

"There's nothing on," she commented as she changed the channels.

It was a warm evening, and Ming wore a loose, sleeveless T-shirt over leggings. She was also braless. As she lifted her arm to point the remote control, Gabriel was afforded a nice view of the side of her breast. He must have been gazing a bit too contentedly because Ming caught him.

"Are you looking at my boob?"

"Well," Gabriel admitted, "it's kind of right out there."

Ming leaned against her boyfriend, putting her face close to his. Gabriel could feel the twin bulges of her breasts and the growing pressure in his own jeans.

"Does that bother you?" she asked invitingly.

"It doesn't bother me," Gabriel said. "Except that every other guy can see the package."

"Uh-oh." Ming let her hand trek across his bare chest down to his zipper. "Are you getting possessive of me?"

Gabriel shrugged, enjoying the path her hand was taking.

Ming pretended to be shocked at what she felt in his pants. "What is this? Did you forget to put your gun away, Detective?"

He smiled.

Ming gently kissed his neck. "I've never seen you possessive before. I kind of like it."

Gabriel half heard her. She had freed him from his jeans, and her stroking made him forget what they were talking about. He wrapped his hand around her breast and used his other hand to press her body to his. He'd missed her. He'd missed this. He slipped one hand into her leggings and groaned with longing when his fingers met wetness.

The phone rang.

He ignored it. He was too busy getting turned on by Ming's body, her quick sighs, and the movement of her hand.

The answering machine clicked on, and the voice of Lieutenant Miguel Ramirez boomed. "Pick up, McRay. I know you're home."

Gabriel swore under his breath.

"Don't move," Ming pleaded.

"I'm waiting, McRay," said the voice on the machine. "This is important."

With an angry sigh, Ming pulled away and sat back against the cushions. She grabbed the remote. Gabriel hoisted himself off the couch and swiped up the phone.

"Yes, Lieutenant," he said curtly.

"Oh, hey, McRay. What's up?" Ramirez asked innocently. "Did I interrupt something? Are you having a session?"

His superior was making a teasing reference to Gabriel's appointments with his psychiatrist.

"Actually I am in therapy right now." Gabriel grinned at Ming. She frowned, still in a huff.

There was a moment of confused silence on Ramirez's end. Perhaps he was wondering if Gabriel's psychologist actually did make house calls.

"Whatever," Ramirez finally muttered. "Did you have a nice vacation?"

"Yes, thank you."

"You don't sound like you had a nice vacation. You sound pissed off."

"Miguel..."

"Listen, you're on the Pennington case. That should make you happy. You get to work with your *novia*."

Novia meaning girlfriend. Girlfriend meaning Ming. Ramirez was baiting him, but Gabriel didn't bite. "I'll get right on it tomorrow, sir."

"Yeah, okay." Ramirez sounded a little disappointed that he didn't get a rise out of Gabriel. "Go back to your therapy session."

Gabriel hung up and returned to Ming.

CHAPTER FIVE

The following morning, Gabriel drove to the homicide bureau and saw the Pennington file waiting for him on his desk. Ramirez wasn't around, and Gabriel took that as a sign it would be a good day. Planting himself in his cubicle, he began to study the case file.

The first thing he did was read the incident report from the first responder. The face page of the report consisted of the reporting number of the uniformed patrolman who had been called to the scene, plus the date, location, and time when he first came upon the body of April Pennington. The second page contained the narrative, which described the circumstances of the incident and the brief interview held between the patrol officer and April's live-in boyfriend, a man who identified himself as Mr. Todd King.

Mr. King readily admitted that both he and April had been habitual drug users, although he claimed to have rehabilitated himself and was no longer using. According to the police report, Mr. King agreed to a drug test and he came out clean. A small amount of cocaine was discovered near the dead girl along with a used syringe. Both had been bagged for evidence. A further search of the premises, wisely including the trash bins, did not produce any further drug paraphernalia.

Gabriel then reviewed the supplemental reports, which included the onsite coroner's observations.

When a coroner is called to the scene of a death, the coroner takes possession of the body. Not only in the literal sense, but figuratively speaking as well. The body and everything around it is at the coroner's disposal. He or she has the freedom to photograph whatever seems important at the time. The coroner who took command over April Pennington's body had photographed all the rooms of the dead woman's home.

Gabriel studied one particular photo of the kitchen. Pots and pans filled the sink, and he saw a small mess on the counter where food had spilled. While a kitchen mess isn't unusual, the metal pileup was in stark contrast to the orderliness of the rest of the house, even the bedroom where the young lady was found.

Thinking of his own culinary exploits, Gabriel made a couple of notes to follow up. He then perused Ming's pathology report, which didn't show anything unusual. She had ordered toxicology testing for drugs of abuse, and Gabriel knew those results wouldn't be back for a few weeks.

"Hey, Big Guy."

Gabriel heard a familiar voice behind him and turned

to see Dash. Tall and reedy, wearing a sport coat that seemed to drip over him and a tie that couldn't hide his profound Adam's apple, Michael "Dash" Starkweather held a steaming cup of coffee out to his partner.

Gabriel took it gratefully. "Thanks."

Dash grabbed the chair from his own cubicle and rolled it over to Gabriel's. Sitting down, he sipped from his own cup.

"How was Seattle?"

"Worth it." Gabriel did not elaborate further.

Dash knew better than to grill Gabriel, so he let the two-word answer suffice. He leaned over to view the file on Gabriel's desk.

"Pennington girl," Dash said. "Looks pretty cut-and-dried to me."

"Me too."

Dash slurped his coffee and spilled some on his jacket. "Shit." He wiped at the stain with his coat sleeve. "Well, we'll see what her boyfriend has to say. Wanna go bother him this afternoon?"

"Tomorrow morning," Gabriel said, a bit penitent. "I've got an appointment later."

Again, Dash didn't question him further. He knew very well with whom Gabriel had his appointment.

DR. RAYMOND BERKOWITZ, also known as Dr. B, welcomed his patient with a warm handshake. Gabriel had booked this appointment at the same time he'd booked his plane reservation to Seattle, figuring that a family reunion might drive him straight back into therapy. Wondering how his patient had fared, Dr. B delved right into the heart of the matter.

"So," the psychiatrist said, "You faced the whole family in one sitting. How did that go?"

Gabriel poured himself a glass of water from a ready pitcher. He wasn't thirsty, but getting a glass of water had become a comfortable routine with him to break the ice.

"A little strange."

"I'm sure it was."

As a psychiatrist, Dr. B was unusual in two ways. First, he subscribed to the School of Individual Psychology developed by Alfred Adler. Since Adler believed the analyst should not be an authority figure to the patient, Dr. B sat next to his patient as if they were old pals. Secondly, as a psychiatrist in today's world, he was expected to limit his career to prescribing medications, but Dr. B enjoyed being a therapist to his patients too much to let that part of his practice go.

"You've made great progress, Gabe. I hope you acknowledge that. You initiated this move to go forward. Tell me, did you feel like you recaptured a bit of your childhood by seeing your family?"

Gabriel watched the water spill into the glass. "So many memories, good ones, came up."

"You stayed with your sister. How did that go?" Dr. B asked.

Gabriel broke into a pensive grin as he took a seat in his usual chair. "I think Janet is happy I'm no longer darkening her doorstep."

"Explain."

"She and her husband think I'm... Unstable."

"Did anything particular happen this time to make them think that?"

"No," Gabriel answered. "But they know my history. My suspension, et cetera."

"Do they know that you were molested?"

Gabriel winced slightly. He always did whenever his issues were verbalized out loud. The temptation to keep his secret quiet, to forget it ever happened, hung at every turn of the road in his recovery. It still shamed him. Dr. B squashed that temptation every session by talking openly and plainly about what had happened.

Dr. B always gets right to the point, but it's a point that never fails to stab.

"My sister knows. I told her."

"How did she react?"

"Concerned. Then weird."

"And how do you think you ought to tackle that?"

Gabriel shrugged. "I don't know. My sister's opinion matters because I think I'd like to get to know her kids better."

"That's something new. You never talked much about your niece and nephew before."

"I didn't know much about them." Gabriel watched the second hand of the wooden clock perched on Dr. B's desk turn in a slow, smooth circle. "I think the thing that most struck me on this trip was that I wasn't angry with any of them. I thought I'd be, but I wasn't."

"That's wonderful," Dr. B said. Although Gabriel's molestation had happened when he was a child, he still carried what he perceived as his parent's betrayal around with him. It weighed upon him like any piece of heavy baggage would. This trip was meant to reestablish trust with his family. This trip was to help leave that baggage behind.

"Were you able to talk more easily with your mother?"

"Yeah. Ma is trying to..." Gabriel searched for the words and looked to Dr. B for help.

"To give you a comfort zone?" Dr. B finished for him.

"Exactly."

"It's very easy for a parent of an abused person to crawl into their own defenses," Dr. B explained. "They can intellectualize the abuse, overprotect and smother the child, or simply shut the subject out. With any of those scenarios, the abused person is left feeling unsupported. In your case, however, it sounds like your mother is doing all the right things."

Gabriel stared mutely into his glass of water. "She's upset about what happened. I know that. I also know she blames herself for not seeing the signs."

"With boys people rarely see the signs, " Dr. B said. "When people see a girl in distress they immediately consider the possibility of sexual victimization. And granted, females do make up the larger proportion of victims. Your mother and father reacted the way most people do with males. When a boy is seen as oppositional —defiant, hyperactive, or having some sort of disruptive behavioral problem, nobody thinks that the male child is suffering from a sexual trauma."

Gabriel gave his therapist a questioning look.

Dr. B took the cue. "It's because males are supposed

to like and initiate sex, no matter what the form. But you and I know that any kind of coerced sex, even coerced sex where the victim experiences arousal, is abusive."

Gabriel formed a tent with his hands and pressed his fingers together. "I don't want to be a living symbol of someone else's guilt. I don't like that she feels bad for me."

"She has a right to her feelings, and it will be up to her to work them out. What you need to do is concentrate on the fact that your mother is making the effort to encourage you to trust in her again."

Gabriel waved it off. "I'm a grown man. It shouldn't matter."

Dr. B smiled and sat back in his chair. "You have unresolved issues, Gabe. Unfortunately, we age, but our issues never grow old."

TERMINAL ISLAND'S north yard was where the inmates played handball and basketball. Sergio Mendoza sat with his friend Victor Archwood, watching the other men play sports but not participating. Vic was allowed only a limited amount of time in the yard, and he didn't want to waste it playing games. He preferred to talk instead. Next to Sergio was a stack of magazines, and today Vic was introducing him to *Architectural Digest*.

Sergio liked hanging out with the serial killer because most of the other inmates considered Vic too crazy to mess with. Plus the guards gave Vic more protection than normal because he was famous. By sticking close to Vic, Sergio kept himself safe.

Sergio was a Guatemalan, and while many figured he was in for a gang-related crime, nothing could be further from the truth. Sergio was, in fact, a computer whiz. He was serving twenty months of his forty-month sentence in federal prison for one count of conspiracy to commit computer fraud and five counts of failure to file a U.S. income tax return. Sergio had infected computers with a software program that forced their modems to dial premium telephone numbers that he himself had rented. The phone companies charged the "callers" for added expenses on top of standard connection fees and then sent a portion of those expenses to Sergio. It had been a handy scheme with Sergio earning a sizeable income until the Feds had closed in.

T.I. was a nice prison by most standards. Sergio would have never encountered someone like Victor Archwood except that Vic's lawyer had worked the system hard enough to keep his client here while awaiting trial. For an alleged killer, Vic came off as quiet, calm, and confident. He carried that confidence without the forced bravado of some of the other inmates. It was in the intelligence behind Vic's eyes and in the steadiness of his walk. Vic didn't seem to be afraid of anything. Sergio, on the other hand, was scared shitless of prison. He might be called a *maricón*, but he wasn't dumb. He made the bold move of engaging the serial killer, and to his surprise, Victor Archwood had been willing to be his friend.

A pharmacist had briefly joined their small group. Vic had sought out his company. The pharmacist, a portly fellow with dark greasy hair and a French-looking pencil mustache, had been a Beverly Hills big shot before he got busted. Seems he had given out too many prescription medications to celebrities in exchange for autographs and party passes. Before the pharmacist was paroled, he, Vic, and Sergio had formed an unlikely trio. Now, only the two of them remained, and Sergio himself would get paroled soon.

This made Sergio feel a little sorry for Vic, and he paid extra attention to his friend. Today, with the fresh sea air breezing in around them from the port, Sergio listened intently as Vic tried to cultivate him by pointing out the various styles of homes in the magazine. That's another thing Sergio admired about Victor Archwood. The man always tried to improve himself and possessed a mind like a sponge. Sergio was smart, but even he couldn't keep track of everything Vic and the pharmacist had talked about.

"If I had the opportunity, I would build modern," Vic told him. "I like a clean, linear look. What about you? What's your dream house like?"

"Fucking big," Sergio told him. "Hey, when I get out, I'll send you money—keep you in good shape, you know what I mean?"

"I appreciate that," his friend told him. "But I'll be getting out about the same time as you."

Sergio didn't comment and pretended to be interested in the magazine. The word going around had it that Victor Archwood would end up on death row in San Quentin. It made Sergio a little sad to think his friend was so naively optimistic.

CHAPTER SIX

G abriel and Dash drove to Triunfo Canyon and the small, developed community nestled within the hills to interview April Pennington's live-in boyfriend, Todd King. The detectives knocked on the door of a Mediterranean-styled villa that seemed a carbon copy of the rest of the neighborhood houses. A man in his early thirties, dark-eyed, closely cropped thinning hair, answered the door.

"Mr. King?" Gabriel asked.

The man nodded but did not reply.

"Thanks for seeing us," Dash chimed in and then introduced himself and Gabriel. The two investigators displayed their identification.

The man led them into a tidy house adorned with African art. Colorful textiles hung from the walls, and homemade baskets and woodcarvings were neatly placed along shelves. Dash commented on the art and asked Mr. King where he'd gotten the pieces.

"I picked those up in Somalia."

"What were you doing there?" Gabriel asked him.

"You're not a pirate, are you, Todd?" Dash joked.

The younger man did not appear amused. "Please address me as Mr. King."

Gabriel and Dash exchanged glances. Dash cocked his head in apology. Mr. King bade them sit down.

"Actually," he said with a lighter tone, "I'm with a charity group that brings medical supplies to the indigenous people."

"That must be very rewarding," Dash commented. "Do you speak the language?"

"I speak a few words," Mr. King answered. "But my contacts speak English, so we can converse pretty easily."

"They learn a little about your culture," Dash said. "You learn about theirs?"

Mr. King nodded and looked at his wristwatch. Gabriel noted that the wristwatch was Swiss made and expensive. The art, the Swiss-made watch... Gabriel observed the man himself. Mr. King appeared very clean-cut, wearing a snappy dress shirt with the sleeves casually rolled up. The consummate yuppie. But Gabriel could see the edge of a very colorful tattoo peeking out from under one forearm. Mr. King, apparently aware that Gabriel scrutinized him, pulled his sleeve down and covered his skin art. Mr. King, Gabriel realized, was a man who had some high ideas about himself. Gabriel wondered where drug-addled April fit into her boyfriend's lofty self-image.

"The reason we're here," Gabriel told him, "is that it's standard procedure to investigate a death that isn't from natural causes. You understand, don't you, Mr. King?"

Gabriel made sure he put an emphasis on the royal word.

"Of course," the man assured him. "How can I help?"

"Tell us about your relationship with April," Dash prompted.

"We met in high school, and we were boyfriend and girlfriend."

"Long relationship," Dash mused aloud.

Mr. King looked at his watch again. "Yeah."

"And you two did drugs together?" Gabriel asked.

Caught off guard, natty Mr. King went wide-eyed. Gabriel grinned to himself. This was why he and Dash were copasetic. Dash played good cop to Gabriel's more brusque approach. The two of them fell into it naturally.

Mr. King answered nervously, "We both went to rehab. It worked for me, but April didn't last long before she lapsed into the life again."

The two detectives nodded sympathetically.

"It was my traveling," Mr. King explained, his tone ringing with regret. "I blame myself for leaving her alone with nothing to do but... You have to understand, it's not easy living with an addict, with someone who fights your sobriety. She wanted me to party with her. Honestly, I liked getting away from her." He corrected himself. "From *here*."

Mr. King hung his head and looked down... at his Swiss wristwatch.

"Which of you did the cooking?" Gabriel asked.

Mr. King looked up at Gabriel, perplexed. "What?"

"Who liked making the meals? You or April?"

The man gave Gabriel a strange look. "Neither of us is much of a cook. We mostly did takeout."

Gabriel nodded thoughtfully.

Dash asked, "Is there anything else you'd like to tell us about April?"

Mr. King shook his head. "I had just come home from abroad. We'd had another one of our fights. I slept in the guest bedroom. In the morning, she never came out of our room. I should have looked in on her, I know."

Gabriel and Dash made no comment. Everything Mr. King told them was already in the initial police report. His story hadn't changed. Dash stood up and made ready to leave.

"Thank you, Mr. King."

The other man rose from his chair. Gabriel joined them, and the three men walked to the front door.

On the way there, Gabriel glanced inside the kitchen, which he saw was orderly and sparkling clean.

OUTSIDE, Dash hitched up his pants and squinted into the sunlight. "Cut-and-dried."

"He was a little affected though, wasn't he?" Gabriel opened the door to their service car.

"How do you mean?"

"I don't know." Gabriel also squinted, less from the bright light and more from the memory of their interview. "I didn't really buy his brand of remorse."

"Hey," Dash said. "He admitted that he didn't get along with his girl real well. Maybe he's not sorry she's gone. Look, we know what she used. It was found on her. And he was clean as a whistle when the black-and-whites showed up."

"True," Gabriel admitted.

Dash took a seat in the car. "We've got bigger fish to fry, Partner. Let this one go."

THE BIGGER FISH to fry turned out to be the pretrial meeting of the People versus Victor Archwood. Gabriel and Dash returned to the homicide bureau in Commerce. There, they joined the rest of those who worked the Malibu Canyon Murder case to confer with the district attorney.

Ramirez idled alone at the table in the conference room as no one else had arrived yet. The two detectives sat across from him and took the opportunity to update their superior on the Pennington case.

"All right," Ramirez told them when they were finished. "Just write up your reports, and that will be that. Dash, I want you to assist Rick Frasier on a triple murder he's working on. You can get the details from him after the meeting."

Dash nodded and then excused himself for a getaway to the men's room.

Alone with Ramirez, Gabriel asked, "What am I gonna work on?"

"Nothing for now."

Gabriel hadn't expected that reply. "You're not giving me anything other than the Pennington case?"

"No." Ramirez ignored the smoke-free policy by pulling a pack of Winstons out of his coat pocket and lighting up.

Gabriel kept a steady eye on his superior. "Did the homicide rate go down since my vacation?"

Ramirez took a deep drag on the cigarette and looked at Gabriel. "Take it easy during the trial, *cabron*."

"What does that mean?"

"Don't get all hot and bothered."

Gabriel shook his head in disbelief. "You think I'm made of glass? Look, I'm not going to break because of this trial, Lieutenant. Is that what you're thinking?"

In answer, Ramirez took another puff on his cigarette.

Gabriel sat back, frustrated.

Ramirez wants me to "take it easy." My sister thinks I'm teetering on insanity. Just how badly do I come across?

Just then Dr. Berkowitz, Rick Frasier, and Dash tumbled noisily into the room.

Gabriel made a subtle turn toward Ramirez and muttered, "This conversation is not over."

Ramirez ignored him and stood to welcome his visitors.

Upon seeing Gabriel, Rick Frasier headed over and warmly shook his hand. Rick had been a rookie detective back when he worked the Malibu Canyon Murder case. Quite a few homicides later, Rick was now a practiced investigator. The others joked about Rick because he dressed preppie and blow-dried his hair. Today he wore a pink gingham button-down shirt under a clubhouse blazer along with chino pants over Sperry Topsiders.

Gabriel couldn't help but grin as he greeted Rick along with the others.

Dr. B also shook Gabriel's hand in a friendly hello but left his role as Gabriel's therapist outside the room. Today they were co-workers. Dr. B had profiled the Malibu Canyon Murderer.

Deputy District Attorney Donavon Thorne entered, toting a briefcase. Theatrical and smooth talking, Thorne was the darling of the DA's office. Everyone had at one time or the other, worked with the DA's office, so nobody was a stranger. Still, they shook hands and made introductions.

Ming entered the room, having traded her scrubs for a sensible work skirt and blouse. She moved to reach over and kiss Gabriel, but then caught herself. She sent a radiant smile his way as she took the seat next to him. He let his hand brush against her thigh in acknowledgment, but then did them both a favor by keeping a professional distance.

Thorne addressed his witnesses. "Now most of you have had ample experience in the courtroom. You know how to dress; you know how to handle yourself in front of a jury. Detective Frasier..." Thorne turned to the preppie investigator. "We'll call on you first to give the jury an insider's view of the murder scenes—the bloody Russian words scrawled on the windshields, the burning cars... I'd like you to cement the horror of the crime scenes in their minds. Now Detective Starkweather..."

Dash came to attention.

"I'll be asking you more police-procedural-type questions to show the groundwork of the investigation; that all the i's were dotted and the t's were crossed."

Dash cleared his throat nervously and then nodded. He appeared somewhat distressed. Gabriel, knowing his partner well, looked at Dash in concern. He wondered if Dash had something else on his mind besides the trial. He was about to quietly ask after it, but then Thorne addressed him.

"Detective McRay, I don't need to tell you that much of this case hangs on your testimony. Because of your past relationship with the defendant, no doubt the defense is going to try to impeach you as a witness. Unfortunately, during the pretrial motions, Judge Durante decided to allow into evidence your psychiatric history and your termination due to excessive force because both have already been made public. I guarantee that it's going to get very ugly for you. Merrill Brillstein is a pit bull, and you'll have to practice a lot of self-control to look upright in the jury's eyes."

"In other words," Ramirez interjected, "Don't be your usual self."

"I get it, Lieutenant," Gabriel told him.

"Don't fuck this up, McRay," Ramirez warned.

"Miguel..." Dr. B quietly admonished from his seat.

Gabriel shook his head. The trial for Victor Archwood hadn't even begun, but Gabriel was already and forever being judged.

CHAPTER SEVEN

O n the steps outside the downtown courthouse, a female news reporter with a Brazilian blowout and full cleavage stood in front of a camera, holding a microphone to her Restylane-puffed lips.

"Here we are at the long-anticipated criminal trial of accused serial killer Victor Archwood." She glanced over her shoulder and then turned to face the camera once again. "You can see the crowd of people waiting in line wanting to be among the few who will get to sit inside the courtroom to hear the opening statements."

INSIDE THE COURTROOM, the judge had allowed the media full reign, so cameras lined the walls. Andrea Leighton, the producer of Archwood's reality TV show, was being interviewed. She tucked her hair with its golden streaks under her trademark Dodgers baseball cap and proclaimed Archwood's innocence.

On the other side of the courtroom, the victim's relatives and friends talked of closure and justice for their loved ones. Imogene Goldfield, the ex-wife of the murdered movie producer, made sure she was in full view of the camera lens.

Gabriel sat as far away from the media frenzy as he could. Ming sat next to him, being uncharacteristically quiet. Gabriel put a protective hand over hers. She gave him a brief but grateful smile.

Sonia Archwood, the killer's sister, walked into Gabriel's line of sight. The big girl had gained even more weight since he had last seen her. She lumbered toward her seat, which was right next to her mother's.

Natalie Archwood, dressed in a tailored skirt and jacket, sat stoically as she gazed at the empty defense table. Neither mother nor daughter said a word to each other.

Then the bailiff entered and demanded quiet. The doors were closed, and Donovan Thorne took his place among his fellow prosecutors. Merrill Brillstein, the defense counsel, waited with his assistants for his client to arrive. Within moments, Victor Archwood was led into the courtroom and was seated beside his lawyer.

Gabriel craned his neck to get a glimpse of Archwood but could only make out tufts of blond hair and the shoulder portion of a freshly pressed dark gray suit.

They should bring him in splattered in blood, Gabriel thought dolefully. That's more his style.

"All rise for the Honorable Judge Elgin Durante," the bailiff announced.

Everybody stood. The judge, a swarthy, large fellow

under his black robe, greeted the court and spoke briefly. Soon afterward, the entire assembly rose again as the twelve jurors made their entrance and took their seats.

The judge's instructions to the courtroom were lost on Gabriel. His mind wandered back through time, when he was running two parallel investigations, the first searching his mind to remember something he was terrified to recall and the second searching the Santa Monica Mountains to capture the man standing serenely before the court today.

Hunting Victor Archwood had pried open the locked doors of Gabriel's mind, forcing him to remember that he had been molested as a child. In a strange way, he owed his recovery to Archwood.

He felt a nudge and looked at Ming. She was nodding toward the front of the room. Donovan Thorne, the prosecutor, confidently approached the jury box. After greeting and thanking the jurors, Thorne began his opening statement.

"The People will show how two summers ago Victor Archwood went on a killing spree in the Santa Monica Mountains to fulfill a warped fantasy. A fantasy in which Mr. Archwood imagined he could capture the souls of people by cutting holes into their chakras—known in East Indian practice as the spiritual power points along the body."

"As bizarre as that sounds, we will hear from Mr. Archwood's own family as to how diligently the defendant believed in this theory of trapping souls. Then we will show you how the horrible wounds on each victim clearly correspond to these chakra points."

Thorne paused for a moment, allowing the jury members to absorb his words as he looked each one in the eye.

"You will also learn how Mr. Archwood lured the homicide investigation team right to him, first by leaving notes on his victims' bodies addressed to the lead investigator of the case, then by leaving a vital clue in a tackle box filled with mementos belonging to the victims. This clue was a small, yellow membership card to a theater club at the University of California at Berkeley, the very university that Mr. Archwood himself attended. When the investigation moved north to San Francisco, Victor Archwood then tried to fake his own suicide. He pulled out his own tooth and left it near the body of a badly burned corpse in his hideout."

"But Mr. Archwood left yet another valuable clue at his hideout—something that serves as irrefutable evidence of his guilt: a gold wedding ring belonging to one of the victims." The prosecutor solemnly regarded the jury. "Even after staging his own death, Mr. Archwood could not deny his bloodlust. He kidnapped the forensic medical examiner who is fortunately here with us today and who will provide eyewitness testimony. Mr. Archwood then used her as bait to lure the lead investigator to him. But why? Why leave notes for this investigator? Why bait him to meet? Well, Mr. Archwood confessed that very reason when he finally met the investigator face-to-face. According to Mr. Archwood, the investigator was to receive the final chakra cut. Victor Archwood attempted to murder the detective. Thankfully, his attempt failed.

"Eyewitness testimony, a ring belonging to a victim found in Mr. Archwood's hideout, a face-to-face attempt on the case detective's life—ladies and gentlemen, we will prove to you beyond all reasonable doubt that the Malibu Canyon Murderer is sitting right here in this courtroom." Thorne pointed to the defense table and added dramatically, "And that he is Victor Archwood."

MING AND GABRIEL EXCHANGED GLANCES. The prosecution was coming off strong. Both of them felt a twinge of hope that the trial would be over quickly. The defense counsel, Merrill Brillstein stood up and walked over to the jury. He began his opening statement in a soft voice.

"Ladies and gentlemen, my opening statement is very brief. Suffice it to say that the defense will prove that the Sheriff's Department went on a vicious rampage against my client, tracking him down, harassing his family, and all this based upon the word of a disturbed lead investigator under psychiatric care."

Brillstein allowed his voice to rise. "A lead investigator who then convinced his police department, who were desperate to capture a suspect, that Victor Archwood was their man. I will show you how this selfsame police department used the vilest and most corrupt tactics to frame Mr. Archwood, and that they have nothing, nothing that ties Victor Archwood to any of these heinous murders!"

Brillstein went calm again. "Ladies and gentlemen, I assure you that by closing remarks it will become clear to you that Victor Archwood has been falsely accused and is, in fact, an innocent man."

POWERFUL WORDS in Archwood's defense, although the jury did not look so convinced. Gabriel, however, was unsettled. The disturbed lead investigator, of course, was he. Gabriel wondered how well he was going to fare throughout this ordeal.

WHILE THE TRIAL could dominate the headlines on the news, Gabriel had no intention of letting it command his life. He wanted to show Ramirez that he didn't need to "take it easy," and he made sure he was at his desk in Commerce as much as time would allow.

Being at work kept him out of his apartment. Ever since he'd been with his family in Seattle, Gabriel seemed to notice every flaw in his lifestyle. There was the matter of his old Celica, truly a relic of a car—dented and old. Why had he never gotten a new car? And his apartment, worn and tired-looking. Gabriel began noticing how the other guys in his department lived. Anyone his age seemed to have a proper home and a family. This made Gabriel feel somewhat inadequate, and he knew that feeling negative about himself wouldn't help him in facing Victor Archwood's attorney. He silently hoped for something else to concentrate on. A couple of days into the trial, Gabriel got his wish.

It came in the form of a phone call he received at

work. The woman on the line claimed to be April Pennington's estranged sister. She gave her name as Wendy Pennington and told Gabriel that she and April had reunited recently.

"I was shocked to hear about her overdose," Wendy said over the phone.

"I understand," Gabriel told her gently. "It's terrible to lose a loved one."

"No. I mean I was shocked about her overdosing because April stopped taking drugs."

Gabriel paused a moment and then said, "Her boyfriend told us that they had both gone to rehab, but unfortunately April started using again. Perhaps she kept that from you."

"No," the woman insisted. "She was not doing drugs anymore, Detective McRay. I promise you. I saw her, I spoke to her. She was clean. I want you to look into this further."

"Ma'am..."

"You have to help me clear her name. My family thinks April died an addict, but she wasn't on drugs!"

Gabriel felt sorry for the woman. He had been estranged from his own father and lost his dad to a disease before he could reconnect with him. Wendy Pennington had only just reconnected with a long lost sister only to lose her permanently once again. It made sense that she was heartbroken.

He asked Wendy to hold on and then searched for April's file. He and Dash were about to close it out.

When Gabriel returned to his desk, he thumbed through the various papers in the folder. Toxicology had come back and reported the definite presence of cocaine in both the femoral and heart blood.

"She had drugs in her system," he told April's sister when he got back on the phone. "I have the toxicology report from the postmortem exam right in front of me."

Wendy began to sob. "That's impossible!"

Gabriel patiently remained on the line, giving the sister time to cry out her frustration. When her sobs reduced to sniffles, Gabriel spoke. "I'm sorry, Miss Pennington."

"She told me she wasn't doing drugs anymore."

"Then take comfort in the fact that she cared about what you thought of her," he replied.

It was the most honest response he could think of.

After his conversation with April's sister ended, Gabriel reread the toxicology report. Wendy seemed pretty firm on the fact that her sister had rehabilitated. Still, it was there in black and white. The presence of cocaine was in April's body. As Gabriel read on, however, he learned that the drug appeared to be at an insufficient level to cause death. Gabriel cocked an eyebrow at that, but then read Ming's notation that with persistent drug use the heart reacts more erratically than does a normal, healthy heart.

Help me clear her name.

Underneath Ming's report, the corner of a photograph peeked out. Gabriel tugged at the edge and saw once again the picture of the kitchen with its pots and pans in disarray. It reminded him of the partially hidden tattoo on Mr. King's arm and how it was a telltale sign of a life lived differently.

CHAPTER EIGHT

When the court convened to hear the presentation of evidence, prosecutor Donovan Thorne kept to his word by calling Rick Frasier to take the stand first. Rick imparted to the jury the sordid details of the murder scenes. He explained how the first victim, Ted Brody, was discovered burning in his handyman's truck. How Russian words that spelled out "souls" were written in his blood on the truck's windows. How a couple of weeks later the fire department discovered yet another burning vehicle with a body inside. This was the body of Tania Dankowski.

Rick did well, and Gabriel could see that the jury enjoyed both looking and listening to the young man. Rick looked more like a member of an exclusive country club than a seasoned homicide detective, so with him illuminating the gory details behind the crimes, the point was truly driven home for the jury members.

The defense attorney did not cross-examine Rick.

Gabriel figured that was a smooth move on Brillstein's part as no one was refuting the fact that these crimes were committed.

Next, a jittery college student named Marie Engstrom was called to the stand. Gabriel remembered her as the witness who had discovered the body of Ted Brody and was able to describe for the jury what the photos of the burned truck could not—the bloodied foreign words streaking the windshield, the dead man with his mouth stuck open in a horrified "O." How the lap of his pants was a pool of blood. How the smoke that filled his truck's cab soon obliterated the victim from her view and then how the entire truck caught fire.

Some of the jury members shook their heads at her descriptions, but again defense counsel Brillstein stayed quiet, biding his time.

Thorne then called Dr. Ming Li as an expert witness, as the chief medical examiner.

Ming clinically discussed her findings from the autopsies of the victims. How the wounds were literally dug into points along the bodies that appeared to be traveling upward with each successive victim. Her descriptions started at the base of Ted Brody's spine, then in Tania Dankowski's womb, then the mutilation of Brian Goldfield's solar plexus, in Patrick Funston's heart, Meredith Hall's throat, and ending with a hole cut like a third eye in Ronald Hall's forehead.

Autopsy photos were shown to the jury, turning some of them green in the face. In this capable role, Ming's testimony was flawless. But she did not look once at

Victor Archwood. She purposely averted her eyes from going anywhere in his direction.

AFTER THE LUNCH BREAK, the prosecution called up a weapons expert. According to forensic testing, the weapon used was described as a nonserrated blade at least six inches long with a quillon or guard—something found in antique military trench knives. One of the victims, Adam Parraco, had not been cut. He had been shot instead. Based upon the spent cartridges, ballistics suspected the weapon used was an antique Nagant revolver.

Gabriel risked a look at Brillstein; sure the defense would climb all over this one because neither weapon had been recovered. Gabriel had been the last person to see the knife—right after Archwood had stabbed him with it. And Gabriel had seen the gun too, just before he had flung both himself and Archwood into the Pacific Ocean. The water had been freezing, and he was bleeding, but if Gabriel had stayed on that balcony with Archwood, he would not be in this courtroom today.

Again Brillstein declined to cross-examine the weapons expert. Apparently, no one would contend the gruesome mutilation of the victims, nor argue over what weapons were used to inflict the damage.

Then Prosecutor Thorne announced, "The People would next like to call Ms. Sonia Archwood to the stand."

Sonia swayed and heaved down the aisle. Pity flashed through Gabriel upon seeing her. He remembered her as the most vulnerable of the Archwood clan, finding her solace in food and burdened by innumerable physical ailments, real or imagined. Sonia was sworn in and hefted her bulk into the witness seat.

"Ms. Archwood," the prosecutor began, "Can you tell us how you are related to the defendant?"

Sonia nodded toward Victor. "He's my brother."

"And to your knowledge," Thorne asked, "Did your brother own both an antique Camillus trench knife and an 1895 Nagant revolver?"

"I don't know what they were called, but I do know Grandpa gave Vic a knife and an old gun that he'd gotten in a trade at the end of World War II."

"So your grandfather possessed antique military weapons which he gave to the defendant."

"Yeah."

Thorne crossed his arms. "I understand that your grandmother lived with your family after your grandfather passed away. Could you tell the jury what your grandmother liked to discuss with Victor?"

Sonia rolled her eyes and shook her head. "She told him that a person could capture other people's souls. She was a complete nutca—"

"Thank you, Ms. Archwood." To the judge, Thorne stated, "No further questions."

Merrill Brillstein refrained from cross-examination and remained expressionless. Victor Archwood, however, watched his sister with obvious disgust as she slowly made her way back to her seat.

The prosecutor kept up the tempo by producing a

large and colorful chart that was entitled The Seven Chakras.

"I would like to educate the jury on the chakras," Thorne explained, "as they do have significance in this case."

The counsel called up a Hindu yogi of some repute in the Los Angeles area. The yogi tried his best to give credence to the chakras. He pointed out that Hinduism is the third largest religion in the world, and there are over one billion Hindus worldwide, many who believe in the power of the chakras. The yogi explained that the chakras are portals or focal points for the transmission of energy or "prana." Attention paid to these chakras might actually heal a person of physical or mental woes. The yogi pointed out each chakra on the chart.

Gabriel studied the jury members hopefully. You didn't have to be smart to see that the position of six chakras coincided exactly with the location of the wounds on the victims. The only chakra point that was unaccounted for, in regards to the victims, was the spiritually highest seventh chakra—the crown chakra that lay on the top of the skull. Archwood had reserved the mutilation of that particular chakra point for Gabriel.

When the yogi had finished giving his testimony for the prosecution, the judge looked questioningly at defense counsel Merrill Brillstein, who announced, "No questions, Your Honor."

The court recessed for the weekend.

ALTHOUGH HE WAS TIRED, Gabriel drove back to Commerce, sat at his desk, and scanned the photo of Mr. King's kitchen into his laptop. He then increased the size of it. The more he enlarged the photo, the blurrier it became, but he wanted to see what the spillage on the kitchen counter was. It looked like bits of dark chocolate to him.

Gabriel rubbed his thumb against his lips, thinking as he studied the photograph. The dark granules might have also been coffee grounds, but they looked soft. As an investigator, Gabriel was alert to anything that stood out. Nervous-looking messes in otherwise-neat houses stood out. Nervous-looking messes hanging around a death definitely stood out.

He reached for the phone and called Ming's cell phone.

"I looked at your deputy's photos again today," Gabriel said once Ming got on the line.

"Are you back at work?" she asked. "Wow, you're my hero. I went straight home. I'd had enough. Being in the same room with Archwood gives me the creeps."

"Totally understandable," Gabriel agreed. "He is a creep."

"So what were you saying about photos?"

Gabriel leaned back in his chair. "I think you ought to run a complete toxicology on the Pennington girl."

"Why?" Ming asked surprised. Complete toxicology panels were expensive and not done unless specifically requested.

"Just to put my curiosity to rest," Gabriel told her.

"Someone who doesn't cook was cooking something in the kitchen the day April died."

"She didn't have any signs of poisoning, Gabe."

"I know, but it's bugging me. Can you do it?"

"If you say so I'll do it." Ming's voice then turned coy. "Any chance you're up for another night of feeding our libidos?"

Gabriel smiled and rocked in the chair. "I'm always up for that."

"What are you doing tonight?"

"Tonight I'm meeting a hot mama back at my place."

He sensed Ming pause.

"She's got long dark hair," Gabriel continued. "And sometimes she doesn't wear a bra."

"You're not gonna let that one go, are you?"

"Nope."

"See you at seven, hero."

MING WAS an exotic blend of her Asian father and Mexican mother. That long dark hair lay lushly over the pillows of his bed as Gabriel reveled in her light mocha skin. Her beautiful almond-shaped eyes regarded Gabriel as he feasted on her, and they soon closed as she moaned and trembled against him in her ecstasy. He pulled her underneath him and, feeling his way with his fingers, moved into her. The rhythm of their lovemaking rocked the bed, and she felt so warm, so good, that it wasn't long before Gabriel repeatedly hitched hard against her in his own pleasurable release.

When the room went silent except for sighing, Gabriel collapsed on the sheets next to her and put an exhausted hand over his eyes. "I'm baked. The trial, work, and *you*."

Ming rested her chin on his firm chest, and he tucked an arm around her.

They rested like that for a moment, and Gabriel might have dozed off when Ming blew a raspberry on his stomach.

"Don't go to sleep. Let's talk."

He patted her shoulder and closed his eyes. "Rest," he murmured.

"I'm not tired," she whined.

Gabriel pulled her closer but kept his eyes closed.

"Don't go to sleep!" Ming nudged him. "I'll sing. You won't be able to sleep through my singing."

He didn't respond, so Ming began to sing, "Mary had a little lamb, little lamb, little lamb…"

Gabriel's face cracked into a smile. Ming was completely off-key.

"Mary had a little lamb…"

Gabriel rubbed his weary eyes, smiling and groaning at the same time. Suddenly he lurched upward as Ming squealed in expectation and protectively raised the covers to her shoulders. Gabriel moved menacingly toward her. "All right, mouth, you got me up."

Gabriel shot out an arm and began tickling Ming through the sheet, under her arms, her sides… She giggled as she thrashed, trying to avoid his frenetic fingers.

"Sing," Gabriel said, laughing. He held her down with

his other hand and kept tickling her. "Why aren't you singing?

Ming finally yelled, "Stop!"

He didn't. Ming twisted with laughter. Gabriel, feeling hot for her again, was about to rip the sheet away from her body, when they heard a muffled pounding on the ceiling that arrested their movements. Mrs. Littman upstairs was pounding a broom against her floor.

Ming clasped a hand over her mouth, stared at Gabriel in surprise, and then burst out giggling. Gabriel, however, stared open-mouthed at the ceiling. He was indignant at the intrusion.

"How much did she hear?" he whispered to his laughing companion.

No one, not even old Mrs. Littman, should be intruding upon his most private moments, Gabriel thought. How could he explain to Ming that an invasion of any kind, even accidental or innocent, brought a low, sick feeling to his gut?

"This sucks," Gabriel said, still looking at the ceiling. "We need privacy."

"Oh, don't worry about it," Ming said, putting an admiring hand on his strong bicep.

Gabriel shook his head as he hoisted himself up and pulled on his pants. "I need a real place. I'm going to look for one this week."

"Come back here!" Ming begged, but it was apparent their lovemaking was over. Ming pouted, sat up, and smoothed her mussed tresses. "Are you sure you want to give up rent control? It's hard to find."

"I've been living here for years. Most of the guys at work have real homes, and I live like a pig."

"I wouldn't say that," Ming commented as she reached for her bra. "And real estate around here is very expensive."

That miffed Gabriel. "I've saved money. What do you think I've done with my salary all these years?"

Ming rose from the bed. "Why don't you get a new car instead?"

She opened Gabriel's closet to adjust her clothes in the cheap, narrow mirror hanging inside the door.

"Maybe I will. Maybe I'll get a new place and a new car."

Ming raised her eyebrows in the mirror. "Just don't get a new girl."

Gabriel playfully slapped her fanny. "Come on. I'll make you some fried sardines."

CHAPTER NINE

"So you want to up your lifestyle."

Gabriel sat in his usual chair across from Dr. B and nodded. Although it was Saturday, Dr. B and Gabriel decided to meet because most every day now was taken up by the trial.

"I think that's a positive sign of your recovery, Gabe. You want to take chances and move on from what's comfortable. Your apartment is where you've always felt safe."

"Well, it's a shithole," Gabriel told him.

Dr. B laughed. "I've been to your place. It's not that bad."

"It's bad. I mean, Ming and I were doing it—" Gabriel caught himself. "She was on my couch, and it's totally threadbare. And the lady upstairs hears everything that goes on in my bedroom. That... That is not acceptable."

Dr. B sobered, sensing Gabriel's discomfort. "Of

course not. How is your relationship going with Ming, by the way? From a sexual standpoint."

Gabriel looked away, a bit embarrassed. "Jesus, you get right to it. You and she have that in common, you know."

"I knew there was something about Ming I admired." Dr. B rose to get a glass of water. "You don't experience any kind of dysfunction? No more sexual aversion?"

A couple of years ago, Gabriel would have had to admit to having dysfunction. Oh, he knew how to go through the motions of having sex, but he had felt empty inside. He couldn't enjoy it. He didn't know how. His coldness had cost him his marriage because his ex-wife, Sheryl, knew he was playacting in the bedroom.

Dr. B gestured the water pitcher toward Gabriel, who shook his head.

Ming brought levity to the relationship. She didn't judge him. She had given Gabriel room to get comfortable at his own pace and view sex as healthy rather than shameful—a legacy left to him by Andrew Pierce. Now Gabriel couldn't get enough of Ming.

He did go overboard one time. He'd almost gotten addicted to sex—and with the wrong woman too. That had been a nasty patch in his blossoming relationship with Ming, but the two of them had worked through it.

"I wish I wasn't so clumsy with all this," he said quietly.

"Do you honestly think Ming would call you clumsy?"

Gabriel thought about their mutual orgasm last night. "No, I guess she wouldn't."

"Then do yourself a favor and don't berate yourself. You don't deserve it."

Dr. B returned to his chair, balancing a full water glass.

"Learning to care for Ming and trusting her is one of the most difficult things I've ever done," Gabriel confessed.

"But you have learned, and you do care," Dr. B told him. "And you are quite confident in your masculinity."

Gabriel's jet blue eyes found Dr. B's. "Why wouldn't I be?"

"Well, sexual abuse poses a major threat to a male's sense of masculinity. Males, in general, have been socialized from early childhood to hide physical and emotional vulnerability. What we do here, I know, is very challenging for you. For any man."

Gabriel made no reply.

Dr. B regarded his patient good-naturedly, although he was quite aware of the frown that Gabriel now wore. The psychiatrist plowed forward, willing to take his chances. "The abuse itself rendered you powerless—a victim. Feelings of helplessness, of victimization, are nearly intolerable to males. Society demands that men be strong and assertive. This would help explain your problems with excessive force on the job. The victimization made you feel powerless, so you gave yourself a temporary sense of power by overpowering others. What I'm saying, Gabe, is that for you to be so well adjusted in your masculinity now is remarkable. You should be happy with this progress."

Again Gabriel remained silent, but his demeanor had darkened noticeably.

"What is it?" Dr. B asked.

"I'm a little pissed off at your comments," Gabriel told him angrily. "I've been fine, right? Making progress, as you say. And then you have to bring up something that doesn't even apply. Why did you do that?"

"Everything applies, Gabe. And if you're feeling irritated by the subject of your masculinity, then an issue still exists under the surface."

"There wasn't an issue until you brought it up."

"I may have brought it up, but you're bothered by it. Why?"

Gabriel rose from his chair.

"Where are you going?" Dr. B asked.

"To get some fresh air," Gabriel answered abruptly. "This room feels stifling right now."

DR. B's words kept buzzing around Gabriel's head like a pesky mosquito. And like a mosquito, the words threatened to settle upon him and draw blood. Dr. B was always doing that, throwing psychological barbs at Gabriel, hoping one would puncture through. Then both Gabriel and his therapist would have to carefully pick it out until the barb no longer stung.

He does it on purpose, I know. Why do I continue to go through this torture?

The weekend beckoned. Gabriel welcomed the break from both the trial and Dr. B. Desiring to do something fun, he called Dash and asked if he wanted to bring his wife, Eve, to a food-truck festival going on in Santa Monica.

Gabriel invited Ming, of course, and the two couples sampled various delicacies as they promenaded up and down a quadrant of cordoned-off city streets lined with food trucks. The carefree feeling of summer combined with the ocean air put the memory of Gabriel's last session with Dr. B to rest. After perusing the various menus plastered on the side of each truck, Gabriel settled on Mexican egg rolls from an Asian/Mexican-food food vendor. He joined Ming, who was standing in line at a barbeque truck, waiting for a pulled pork sandwich.

Gabriel held up the eggroll to her mouth for her to try.

"It's yummy," she declared after taking a bite.

He winked at her. "It reminds me of you—fusion!"

Ming elbowed him, and then offered him a bite of her sandwich. Sauce dribbled down Gabriel's chin, and he wiped his mouth with the back of his hand.

"It's good," he said, chewing—shrugging his shoulders. "Not the best I've ever had, but it's all right."

"Let's try the Louisiana cooking next," Ming said. Taking hold of his sleeve, she led him through the crowd to a pink-painted truck with a picture of a crawdad wearing a chef's hat.

Dash had more trouble. He went from truck to truck, asking what ingredients they used. He finally settled on a falafel plate but ate only the salad.

The four of them sat on an available bus bench and

ate their meals in silence. Gabriel noticed that Dash was unusually quiet.

"Something bothering you, Dash?" he asked his partner.

"I guess we're both on the stand Monday morning," Dash stated, as he stabbed and broke a falafel to bits.

Gabriel watched him, perplexed by the man's apparent worry. The two of them had worked many cases together and had often testified in court. Dash was always cool and unruffled when giving testimony.

Eve shrugged her shoulders at Gabriel. She too noticed that her husband was in a bit of a funk. Eve was a trim, bespectacled woman who sported bangs over her honey-blond hair. She'd been a cheerleader in high school and college and had never retired her peppiness. Eve was well used to her husband's finicky eating habits, his aversion to germs, and his worry over heart attacks. She took everything lightly and prepared his limited menu of meals and weathered his eccentricities without complaint. She was a good wife, a good person, and Gabriel liked her a lot. During his bad times, Eve and Dash would be frequent dinner guests to Gabriel's apartment, and both of them knew how to bring him out of his dark moods.

The abuse itself rendered you powerless

Gabriel swatted the thought away.

"He's been like this since the trial started," Eve told Gabriel.

"Been like what?" Dash turned to her with annoyance.

"You've been edgy," Eve told her husband and then grinned at Gabriel. "Edgier than normal."

"You've got nothing to worry about," Gabriel assured him.

Dash stuck a forkful of salad into his mouth and made a face at both Eve and Gabriel.

"That's mature," Eve laughed.

"Are you ready?" Ming asked Gabriel.

"As ready as I'll ever be." Gabriel tossed his plate into a trashcan. "Let's not talk about it."

"Fine," Ming agreed. "Let's talk about how we'll spend the rest of the weekend."

"I know how I'm spending my weekend." Gabriel tried to suppress a proud smile. "I'm going to look at open houses."

A short laugh burst from Dash. "Get out... You? You've taken root in that apartment."

"I know," Gabriel said. "That's why it's time to uproot. Gotta grow somewhere else now."

"About time, my friend." Dash held out his closed fist, knuckles out, and Gabriel gave him a confident fist bump.

Gabriel then looked over at Ming. She was grinning too, but her smile looked fake, plastered onto her face. Her eyes looked as worried as Dash's.

SUNDAY AFTERNOON, Gabriel met Ming at a little Venice cafe on Abbot Kinney. He still wasn't finished working with his Realtor, but he needed the break. His head was spinning.

He tossed a stack of flyers onto the table where Ming sat waiting for him.

"I thought I had a lot of money saved," Gabriel told her as he took a seat. "But even the condos are expensive. Today I saw a two-bedroom bungalow for over $750,000. Can you believe that? I'm trying to find a short sale or a fixer-upper."

"Like you've got time for a fixer-upper." Ming motioned the waitress over and ordered a black coffee for Gabriel and a chai latte for herself.

"I'm going to bug Ramirez for a pay raise," Gabriel said, more to himself. "You know, life was a lot more affordable when I was messed up."

"Gabriel," Ming began. "I have to talk to you."

He rifled through the flyers. "I think I'm gonna have to move out of the city if I want a decent house."

Ming cleared her throat. "I have an idea…"

"I'd hate to give up the beach, though."

"Gabriel!" She stopped him.

He looked across the table at her.

"I've been thinking."

"Uh-oh…" he said in mock fear and then grinned.

"You should move in with me."

Gabriel felt the smile fade from his face.

"I have this big house," she explained. "I live by myself. It makes sense, doesn't it?"

The waitress brought their drinks, but neither Gabriel nor Ming touched them. The steam wafted between the couple, creating a vaporous barrier.

Of course it makes sense, Gabriel thought. Ming had a gorgeous home in Los Feliz near Griffith Park. It was an old Hollywood Spanish colonial, big enough for two families, with wrought-iron chandeliers and Mexican tile work. The Mexican tile work represented a silent homage to Ming's masked Latina heritage. The rest of the house served as Ming's testimony to her status as a successful career woman. At one time, Gabriel had resented her success. It had intimidated him, but that had faded away like all their other challenges. He and Ming hung out together practically all the time now. Moving in with her was a logical step.

Except that it felt wrong.

Why is it that every time you're on a roll, marching confidently on what you feel is the right path, some obstacle rolls in the way and trips you up?

Some sort of cosmic litmus test, Gabriel supposed wearily.

Ming appeared hurt. "Why are you looking at me like that? It's not such a far-fetched idea, is it?"

"I don't know, Ming," Gabriel said.

"What's the problem?" She pressed.

He took a deep breath.

Vacillating again. Feeling insecure. Just like in the bad old days. Dammit! Why did Dr. B have to open his mouth?

"Gabriel?"

He spoke slowly, trying to articulate the right words even as his emotions intercepted them. "It's only that I feel like I need to better myself. Do you understand?"

"No," Ming answered tersely. "I thought we were boyfriend and girlfriend."

LAURIE STEVENS

"We are, but I can't move in with you."

"Why not?"

"It's your place. I need to… build a new life."

"What exactly does that mean?" Ming frowned. "Am I not part of your new life?"

"Of course you're part of it." Gabriel ran a hand through his hair. "I don't how to explain it."

Ming was getting angry. "I thought this would be the obvious plan of action."

Gabriel shook his head. "I need time, Ming."

"You need time." Her expression went steely. "Well, look what taking too much time with your father cost you."

A cloud fell over Gabriel's features, and Ming knew she'd gone too far. "I'm sorry. I shouldn't have said that. It's just that you're being silly!"

Gabriel pulled out his wallet.

"Don't leave," Ming pleaded.

He threw a few dollars on the table to cover their drinks. He collected his real estate comps and stood up.

"That was low," Gabriel told her and headed for the door.

CHAPTER TEN

The next morning, Gabriel showed up to the courthouse early to have a quick briefing with Ramirez, Dash, and Donovan Thorne. Once again he found his diminutive lieutenant alone in one of the antechambers as the other two men had yet to arrive.

Ramirez took one look at Gabriel and said, "Sit down, McRay. How was your weekend?"

Gabriel took a seat. "Good."

"So tell me why you look like someone ran over your poodle."

"I'm fine."

"Come on," Ramirez coaxed. "You can tell me. I'm a friend."

"You're a friend?"

"Face it, McRay. You don't have many friends. Be grateful for what you got."

Gabriel shook his head.

"Come on! You can pretend I'm Dr. B."

Gabriel was unsure if he could stomach Ramirez's quirky brand of humor right now. Maybe he should leave the room.

"I can tighten that loose screw in your head as good as anybody," Ramirez winked at him. "Come on. It's Dr. Li, isn't it? You two are having problems?" Ramirez shook a cigarette out of his pack.

Gabriel turned toward his superior. "Well, she wants to take some steps forward in the relationship, which I don't think I'm ready for, and I..." Gabriel trailed off as he watched Ramirez yawn widely. "God, am I boring you?"

Ramirez nodded. "Yeah, let's cut the bullshit."

Gabriel rolled his eyes and waited.

Ramirez lit up and shook out the match. "Here's my advice. Kiss Dr. Li's ass as much as possible. She's way out of your league, so if I was you, I would do anything to keep her."

Gabriel stared dully at his superior. "Thanks for the advice."

"No problem." Ramirez dragged on his cigarette. "See how easy that was? Feel better?"

"No."

"That's because you're messed up in the head, McRay." Ramirez waved his cigarette around. "But anytime you want to talk, I'm available."

THE BRIEFING DID nothing for Gabriel except give

Thorne and Ramirez one more opportunity to warn him not to screw up. He knew why they were concerned. Much of Gabriel's personal life was going to be attacked—his past relationship with the defendant, his record of excessive force. Still, their continual reminders and unwanted advice were only making Gabriel more stressed out.

He took his seat next to Dash in the courtroom and fidgeted nervously until he noticed that Dash appeared more distressed than he. Perhaps Dash was having troubles with Eve.

"Everything all right?" Gabriel asked him.

His normally emotive friend made no reply.

Ming entered the courtroom and looked around for Gabriel. She spotted him and waved at him briefly, a gesture filled with apology. He cocked his head toward the seat next to him, indicating that she should come over. He knew Ming too well to hold a grudge against one stupid comment.

"Hi," she said carefully.

Gabriel stood to greet her.

"Do you hate me?" she whispered.

"Never," Gabriel told her.

The two of them sat down. Ming leaned over and patted Dash's arm. He nodded a hello to her. Then the judge took his seat, followed by the jury.

AFTER THE CALL TO ORDER, Thorne called Dash up to the witness stand to be sworn in.

Dash was introduced to the jury and asked how he

was related to the case. Dash explained his role as one of the lead investigators.

"Detective Starkweather," the prosecutor said. "Can you tell us what you found at the crime scene of Adam Parraco and Brian Goldfield?

"We discovered that their car had been set on fire."

"Had you seen this prior?"

"Yes, which in my opinion made this the MO of the murderer. Each victim's car was set afire."

"Was something different about the Goldfield/Parraco vehicle fire?"

"Yes," Dash replied and glanced at Archwood, who was busy weaving a pencil through his fingers. "This time the victim's bodies were discovered in the trunk of the car, which had protected them somewhat. We wondered why the killer had trunked the victims this time around."

"And in your opinion, why do you think the suspect placed the bodies in the trunk this time?"

"The suspect left something on Mr. Goldfield's body, which, in my opinion, he did not want to burn."

"What did he leave?"

"A note"—This time Dash looked directly at Gabriel —"addressed to Detective McRay."

"And what did this note say?"

Dash gazed sympathetically at Gabriel. "It said 'We are one.'"

The jury also looked over at Gabriel. He forced a poker face and kept his own eyes on Donovan Thorne. The prosecutor then thanked Dash for his testimony. The judge looked over at Brillstein, but the defense chose not to cross-examine Dash.

"You did fine," Gabriel assured his partner when Dash returned to his seat.

Dash mumbled, "Thanks."

Thorne addressed the court. "The People call Detective Sergeant Gabriel McRay."

For the first time in two years, Gabriel stood within a few feet of Victor Archwood. After Archwood had been arrested, it was Dash who had made the initial trips to interview their prisoner. Gabriel had been on bed rest, recovering from the stabbings he had received.

As he took the stand, Gabriel made sure he looked Archwood straight in the eye. At that, the blond man hid a small smile and perused some papers on the table before him.

Gabriel put his left hand on the Bible and raised his right hand.

"You do solemnly state that the testimony you may give in the cause now pending before this court shall be the truth, the whole truth, and nothing but the truth, so help you God."

"I do."

Thorne moved over to him. "Detective McRay, you are a homicide investigator with the Los Angeles County Sheriff's Department. The LASD has jurisdiction over the Santa Monica Mountain parkland along with the areas outlying the city proper, correct?"

"Yes."

"You were not originally assigned to the Malibu Canyon Murder case, were you, Detective McRay?"

"No."

"Tell us in your own words why you were brought on the case?"

"Because Mr. Archwood left notes on the victims' bodies addressed to me."

"Objection, Your Honor! The witness assumes facts not in evidence."

The previously silent defense had been waiting to sink its teeth into Gabriel. The teeth were now bared and would prove very sharp.

"Sustained," Judge Durante agreed.

Gabriel nodded once at the judge and said, "I was brought onto the case because the suspect left notes addressed to me, and my superiors felt there might be a connection—that he might know me."

Thorne moved to the jury box. "Please turn your attention to Exhibits 1 through 5. You can see that the suspect has addressed these notes specifically to Detective McRay."

Enlargements of the notes were displayed on a screen for the jury. The words swam before Gabriel's eyes and blurred into one continuous accusation:

We are one—You are a Great Pretender—Take heart, I know who you really are—You are moving away from everything you know —The young ones tempt you, don't they?

Nearly two years had passed since Gabriel had seen these notes, their eerie messages now enlarged and displayed publicly. He remembered the Santa Ana wind blowing warmly around his face and the smell of fire. He would always equate these notes with burning cars and burning questions.

The prosecutor's voice broke Gabriel out of his reverie. "You can see one particular note reads, 'Take heart, I know who you really are.'" Thorne leaned toward Gabriel. "Did this make you assume that the suspect knew you?"

"Yes."

"What led you to believe the suspect was a theater student, Detective McRay?"

"We found a clue in his trophy box."

Again, Gabriel glanced at Archwood, but the younger man's gaze still lay on the papers before him.

"What do you mean by a trophy box?" Thorne asked.

"It was a fishing-tackle box, and inside were items belonging to the victims. The items were found in all the small compartments inside the tackle box. It's not unusual for murderers to keep personal tokens of their victims. These were his trophies."

Another glance at Archwood. This time Archwood met Gabriel's eyes. The prosecutor deftly blocked Archwood's view, standing between him and Gabriel.

"I would now like to turn the jury's attention to People's exhibits number 27 and number 28, the fishing-tackle box." Thorne directed a pointer to the projected images of the exhibits.

"Exhibit number 27 is a photograph showing the tackle box closed, and Exhibit number 28 shows the box open, displaying all the individual compartments filled with the various mementos. Can you give us a brief description of the items found in there?"

"Detective Starkweather and I found the victims' rings. We found Tania Dankowski's earring, with part of her ear still attached. We found a gold cross belonging to Patrick Funston."

The prosecutor then laboriously went through the small items in their envelopes. They were mere exhibits now, no longer tokens of love and personal expression. Separated from their deceased owners, the pieces had lost their talisman-like meanings.

Thorne pointed to the screen, where photos of the individual items were projected, and asked Gabriel, "Besides the trophies, as you call them, what else did you find in the fishing-tackle box?"

"A lead."

"What sort of lead?"

"I found a Thespian card from the University of California at Berkeley."

"What is a Thespian?"

"From what I learned, if someone participates in the theater for enough hours, he is then considered a Thespian."

"So this was some sort of membership card?"

"Yes."

"Was there a name on the card?"

"No, the name had been cut out."

"Could this card have belonged to one of the victims, perhaps?"

Gabriel shook his head. "No, we checked that out."

District Attorney Thorne then turned to the jury. "So the killer left a clue, something that belonged to him, not to the victims." He turned back to Gabriel. "You subsequently researched a list of theater students from UC

Berkeley. When you perused that list, you recognized a name, someone who knew you."

"Objection!" Brillstein cried. "Leading!"

"Sustained," Judge Durante said. "Rephrase, please."

Thorne nodded. "Did you see a name on the list of someone familiar to you?"

"Yes," Gabriel answered.

"That someone is Victor Archwood, correct?"

"Yes."

"After you realized that you knew him, what happened?"

"I knew he was someone who might have a vendetta against me." Gabriel again looked at Victor Archwood. The defendant's sapphire-colored eyes coolly appraised him.

Brillstein shook his head, about to shout out an objection, but Judge Durante interrupted him by addressing Donovan Thorne. "Counsel, approach the bench."

When Thorne stood near, Judge Durante asked him, "Where are you heading with this line of questioning? A vendetta against Detective McRay is not relevant to finding the defendant guilty of murder."

Thorne was undaunted. "Please, Your Honor, as I mentioned in my opening statement, I want to establish a motive for the defendant to target Detective McRay as the final chakra victim. I don't have to remind the court that chakras are inextricably linked to all the victims."

The judge reflected on this and then gave Thorne permission to continue.

The prosecutor turned back to Gabriel. "Detective McRay, tell us how you knew Victor Archwood?"

"I babysat him when I was a teenager."

The jury members exchanged glances. The cameras rolled.

"Did something happen that, in your opinion, would give Mr. Archwood a reason to torment you?"

"At first, I thought it was because I had beaten the defendant when he was a child." There were a couple of gasps in the courtroom, and Gabriel paused a moment. Then he said, "But apparently, the defendant's mother, Natalie Archwood, told Vic a lie about me after I had moved away from the neighborhood."

"Vic meaning Mr. Archwood?"

"Yes. That's what I used to call him. That's what everyone who knew him called him."

"What was this lie?"

"She told Vic I had sexually abused him."

A murmur ran through the courtroom. Gabriel once again glanced toward the defense table. Victor Archwood was giving him a deadeye stare.

"How did you find out about this?" Thorne asked.

"Mrs. Archwood admitted it to me during the course of the investigation." Gabriel caught Natalie seated in the courtroom with her arms crossed. She glared at him in cold fury.

"Were others present to this admission?"

"Yes, members of the San Francisco PD; in particular, Detective Sergeant Kroll."

"What exactly did Natalie Archwood admit to you?"

"She told me that she had lied to Vic for many years, telling him that I had molested him when he was a little boy."

"Did she say why she lied about you?"

"Yes," Gabriel answered. "She told me she lied to Vic because she didn't want him to know the truth. She wanted to prevent him from recalling the person who had truly abused him. She did not want Vic to remember his grandfather in a bad way."

Gabriel looked over at Archwood, searching for a little boy's features imprinted on the killer's face. In return, Archwood fixed a reptilian gaze upon Gabriel. Unnerved, Gabriel looked away. The little boy who had once adored his babysitter had long ago disappeared.

"From what you are saying, Mr. Archwood was told from an early age that you hurt him, that you molested him," Thorne said. "In fact, we could say his entire life was overshadowed by this lie."

The prosecutor looked at the jury to make sure they were enthralled by his performance. They were. He looked back at Gabriel and added solemnly, "And gave the defendant a lifelong motivation to seek revenge on you."

Thorne's eyes stayed on Gabriel for a moment for dramatic effect, and then he said, "Detective McRay, you have a scar on your side and on your arm from two stab wounds, correct?"

"Yes."

"How did you get these stab wounds?"

"When I finally confronted the defendant face-to-face, he stabbed me."

"Tell us the details behind this confrontation."

"Dr. Li had been kidnapped, and I received a note that told me I'd better remember where Vic and I used to hang out when he was little. Otherwise, Dr. Li was going to die. I found Ming—Dr. Li—buried alive at the Sutro Bath ruins."

Gabriel glanced at Ming who gave him a wild, teary-eyed look, then immediately dropped her gaze to her hands, which were folded in her lap.

Gabriel continued in a calm voice. "After we got her some help, and then I went looking for Vic. I found him at the Cliff House."

"And what is the Cliff House?"

"It's a seaside restaurant not far from the ruins. It was late at night, and the place was closed."

"And what happened?"

"Vic had the Nagant revolver with him and the Camillus knife. He told me he was going to possess my soul by carving the final chakra into my head."

Some members of the jury gasped. The prosecutor nodded for Gabriel to continue.

"He told me I would die, but live through him. Then I brought up the subject of his grandfather. I told him about his mother's lie." Gabriel viewed Archwood, who was motionless, staring back at him. "I told him it was his grandfather who had betrayed him—who had hurt him."

"And what did Victor Archwood do then?"

Gabriel looked back at the prosecutor. "He told me not to talk about his family, and he stabbed me in the arm. I pulled out the blade, and we began to fight. He produced the gun, and I can't quite recall, but I believe I lost the knife by trying to get the gun from him. Some-how, he retrieved the knife because he stabbed me in the side. I pushed him over the rail and we both fell into the ocean."

"And then what happened?"

"From there, we were both rescued."

"Thank you." Thorne looked at Judge Durante. "No further questions."

The judge addressed Merrill Brillstein, "Does counsel wish to cross-examine this witness?"

"Yes, Your Honor."

THE JURY WATCHED with interest as Brillstein sauntered toward Gabriel. Up until now, the defense had taken a lax role in the trial. The jury members were waiting for some fireworks. They would get them now.

"Let's take this step by step, Detective McRay," Brillstein began. "Regarding these notes, People's Exhibits 1 through 5, you felt it was someone from your past writing them because they were addressed to you personally. Is that correct?"

"Yes."

"But didn't your name make the newspapers and television news on numerous occasions?"

"Yes."

"Enlighten us as to why your name made the news."

"I was the lead investigator on the case."

Brillstein smiled condescendingly. "Before that. Why did your name appear in the media before you were assigned to this case?"

Gabriel took a deep breath. *Here it goes.*

"I was having some issues within the department."

"Issues?" Brillstein raised his eyebrows. "Were you not on suspension for throttling a fifteen-year-old child?"

Gabriel's mouth stayed quiet, but inside he justified himself. *He came at me with a knife.*

Judge Durante leaned toward Gabriel. "Please answer the question, Detective."

"Yes, I was on suspension."

"And after you came back to the homicide bureau, weren't you then terminated after knocking down a grandmother, who subsequently sued the city and won five million dollars?"

She called me a cop-pig, and the shotgun behind her was in full view.

Aloud, Gabriel replied, "Yes, I was terminated."

"Given your"—The defense counsel cleared his throat for impact, —"notoriety, why did you think it was someone from your past who was writing these notes to you as opposed to some random member of the populace who wanted to share the attention?"

"I didn't think it was anyone I knew until I saw Victor Archwood's name on the list of theater students from UC Berkeley."

"Yes," Brillstein mused, nodding. "That brings us to the next order of business, the Thespian membership card. Just to refresh my memory..." Brillstein gently scratched the side of his face in contemplation. "This caused you to order lists of theater students, past and present, from UC Berkeley. Is that correct?"

"Yes."

"And you recognized a name?"

"Yes."

"Hmm. So you recognized a name from a large and famous university near the place where you grew up. You are from the Bay Area, aren't you, Detective McRay?"

"Yes."

"Well, chances are you'd recognize someone from your past that attended that university. Were you not inspecting a list that went back ten years?"

"I was."

"Ten years is a long time." Brillstein looked at the jury, and said, "I'm sure if I perused student names from colleges near to where I grew up, I'd recognize a name." Brillstein paused and then turned back to Gabriel. "So you decided that this was the name of the Malibu Canyon Murderer."

"I object!" cried Thorne. "Defense counsel is testifying."

"Sustained," Judge Durante said. "The court will strike that from the record."

Brillstein nodded. "Detective McRay, did you have any physical evidence that connected the name on that list to the Malibu Canyon Murderer?"

"No, but I—"

"No," Brillstein interrupted and then pursed his lips. He turned around and faced the jury. "No physical evidence. Only Detective McRay's word that a child he once babysat is now a murderer. Only the word of a detective undergoing psychiatric care—"

"Objection!" cried Thorne. "Badgering!"

"—and you still are undergoing psychiatric care, am I right, Detective McRay? How is that anger management going?"

"Objection! Defense counsel is badgering the witness!"

"Sustained." The judge gave Brillstein a warning look. "Counsel, approach the bench."

Gabriel forced himself to appear calm, although he knew all eyes were trying to penetrate him. Meanwhile, both Brillstein and Thorne moved over to the judge.

"Your Honor," Brillstein began, "It is exactly Detective McRay's anger management issues that fuel his vendetta against my client."

Judge Durante regarded Brillstein in exasperation. "Now Detective McRay has a vendetta?"

"This is ridiculous," Thorne chimed in.

The judge shook his head tiredly, glanced at a large wall clock, and then addressed the courtroom. "I think we are going to adjourn for the day. We will continue with the defense's cross-examination of Detective Sergeant McRay at 9:00 a.m. tomorrow morning."

Judge Durante rose from his seat and exited.

Gabriel, weary and angry, exited the witness stand and was stopped by Donavon Thorne.

"Are you okay? Do you want me to ask for a continuance?"

"No," Gabriel told him. "I want to get this over with."

"Don't let him get you upset. That's what he's trying to do."

Gabriel nodded curtly and left the courtroom.

CHAPTER ELEVEN

That very evening, a realtor showed Gabriel a dejected little house a few blocks from the beach. She explained it was a two bedroom, one bathroom place with a small yard. The grass out front was dead, the garage door looked like it would crumble if pushed too hard, and the asphalt on the driveway was cracked and jutted up in places like small hills.

Upon first entering the house, Gabriel felt like he was walking into his own apartment with the hollow pressboard doors, the warped vinyl flooring in the kitchen, the stained carpeting in the rooms, and the overall musty smell which permeated the place.

"You can steal this for $500,000.00," said the realtor, who was a gum-smacking, high-strung brunette named Sandy.

Gabriel gave her incredulous look. "It's a steal at a half million?"

"Absolutely."

Gabriel peered out at the backyard. The wooden border fence was falling over at places. Ripped blue tarpaulin hung from the patio overhang, which Gabriel could see had dry rot.

"What kind of animal lived here?" Gabriel asked, kidding, but only halfway.

"The owner went upside down on his mortgage, which was with a private lender," Sandy explained. "That lender is highly motivated to sell and happens to be a friend of a friend. That's how I found out about this. Short escrow, bought as is. Gabriel, if you want it, we've got to act now."

Gabriel could smell the ocean as the breeze lifted his dark hair. He felt the instant tranquility he used to get when he'd return to his "cave" after a particularly brutal workday. Gabriel surveyed the damage. A large down payment on this place would pretty much kill everything he had saved, but then he wouldn't have a huge mortgage. It had been a long time since he had rolled up his sleeves and performed any kind of home repair, but Gabriel figured he was up to the task.

"Let's write an offer," he said.

HE RETURNED to his apartment to hear his telephone ringing. The caller was identified as his sister. Gabriel picked up.

"Hi, Janet," he said as he squirmed out of his coat. It had been too long a day, and his stomach was empty and unsettled from Brillstein's questions and the fact that he had just committed to buying a house.

A tear-down…

"How's the trial going?" Janet asked. "I've been watching you on TV."

Gabriel kicked off his shoes. "Oh, yeah?"

"Yeah. You held up well today. But it must be hard being on that witness stand."

"It's okay." He moved into his kitchen and opened the refrigerator. Empty. He'd forgotten to go grocery shopping again. What was the matter with him?

"Listen, the kids are driving me crazy," Janet said. "They really want to come down this summer to stay with you. All I hear about is Uncle Gabe and Disneyland. What do you think?"

Gabriel paused. "They want to stay with me?"

"I told them it would be too much trouble—"

"No," Gabriel interrupted. "It's no trouble."

He cast his eyes around his apartment.

If Janet saw this, she'd definitely label me the creepy uncle.

He thought about the house he'd just seen.

"When?" Gabriel asked Janet.

"August?"

"I can do that," he answered before he could stop himself.

"Awesome," Janet said, but her voice didn't sound very enthusiastic. "Can I ask you a question?"

"Sure." Gabriel flopped down on his couch and, lying back, rubbed his temples, exhausted.

"One of those notes that the killer wrote you —'the

young ones tempt you'—what did Victor Archwood mean by that?"

"What do you mean, what did he mean? He's a freak, Janet."

"Well, it's an unusual thing to say."

"It's not unusual if he thought I was a child molester, which is what his mother drilled into his head." Gabriel paused. "Why are you asking?"

Janet fell silent for a moment and then said, "No reason."

Sure…

"How's Dad?" Gabriel changed the subject.

"The same."

"Did he ask about me at all, you know, after I left?"

"No." Janet seemed to sense Gabriel's disappointment, and she quickly added, "But he doesn't ask after anyone anymore. He remembers strange things like the shoe store. The other day he asked me what shoes had come into stock and if I'd put them out on the displays yet." She sighed over the phone. "It's heartbreaking, Gabe, but what are we supposed to do?"

Gabriel couldn't reply. *Dad's back at the shoe store. He's gone back in time. He's boarded the Alzheimer's train with a one-way ticket. Destination: Oblivion.*

"He's getting the best care possible," Janet said, filling in for her brother's silence. "Mom's got him in a day facility, and they stimulate him as much as possible. Sometimes the medicine kicks in, and he's like his old self."

His old self, Gabriel thought mournfully. *I can barely remember Dad's old self.*

THE FOLLOWING DAY Merrill Brillstein continued with his cross-examination of Gabriel, who hadn't slept much the night before. Thoughts of his father's loss of brain cells, his impulsive home buy, and Janet's concern over Archwood's notes had given Gabriel a bad case of insomnia.

Tired as he was, Gabriel made sure to sit upright in his chair and appear as strong and confident as possible.

"Tell us about this alleged face-to-face meeting you had with Mr. Archwood," Brillstein asked Gabriel. "Where did it take place?"

"He confronted me on the balcony of the Cliff House."

"The Cliff House being the seaside restaurant in San Francisco."

"Yes."

"You claim to have met the defendant on a balcony of the Cliff House. What was the alleged confession again?"

Alleged...

Gabriel didn't mince words. "That he planned to carve a hole into my highest chakra, that being my skull."

"Did anyone else witness this alleged confession?"

"No."

"No," Brillstein repeated. "And the so-called murder weapon, the antique Camillus trench knife, where is it?"

"It fell into the ocean."

"And in your testimony yesterday you claimed your assailant also had a gun, the Nagant revolver." Brillstein smiled at the jury. "Was this not a veritable juggling act with so many weapons?" He turned back to Gabriel with a sneer. "Where is the gun?"

"In the ocean," Gabriel replied in a low voice. His weariness had caught up to him, and the anger percolated in his chest.

Brillstein gaped at Gabriel in disbelief. "Both weapons fell into the ocean?" He then turned to the jury and shrugged. "It's a little bit difficult to prove Mr. Archwood had them, isn't it?"

Gabriel couldn't hold back, and he yelled: "He had them. He'd gotten them from his grandfather who was in the military. He stabbed me with the knife! I've got the scar right here..." Gabriel stood up and began pushing up his coat sleeve.

Judge Durante turned toward Gabriel. "Detective McRay, you will only answer the questions put to you."

Gabriel saw Ramirez shake his head warningly from the audience, and closer still, Victor Archwood viewed Gabriel with intense interest. Gabriel avoided eye contact with the television cameras, whose black lenses ogled him mercilessly.

"Please sit down, Detective McRay," the judge ordered.

Gabriel took a deep breath. He straightened his coat sleeve and sat back down.

"Detective McRay," Brillstein began again. "During the Malibu Canyon murder investigation, were you seeing a psychiatrist for the treatment of memory lapses?"

Gabriel glared at the defense counsel and silently

talked himself down from grabbing Brillstein by the collar.

"The witness refuses to answer the question," Brillstein stated haughtily.

"Yes," Gabriel hissed through clenched teeth.

"These memory lapses are also known as fugue states. Am I right, Detective?"

"Yes."

"So the jury can fully understand, a fugue state can be described as an altered state of consciousness in which a person may move about and even speak but is not fully aware. Couldn't we describe your condition as such at the time of the investigation, Detective?"

"Objection!" Thorne called out.

"Overruled," said Judge Durante.

Brillstein crossed his arms and looked at Gabriel. "Were you suffering from fugue states at the time of the investigation?"

Having no other choice, Gabriel spoke the truth. "I was."

"No further questions, Your Honor."

Gently as he could, the judge addressed Gabriel. "You may step down, Detective McRay."

As Gabriel walked by him, Victor Archwood leaned forward, as if he were making a subtle invitation to engage Gabriel in conversation. Gabriel wanted nothing more than to grab Archwood by the hair and slam his face onto the desk, but he fought that urge too.

∿

THE COURT BROKE for the weekend, and Ming came over to help Gabriel hold a garage sale. The sun shone merrily on all his furnishings, which were displayed at the front of his building. Gabriel put everything up for sale except his cookware and his couch. Ming convinced him that the sofa, with its pullout mattress, had good bones and needed only to be reupholstered.

Although Gabriel was aware he could use some of the other furniture in his new home, he didn't want to. He wanted to divorce himself from everything in the past, including his self-doubts and his fears. His new house would reflect the new man he was becoming.

A quick glance over his inventory caused him to see one item he did not want to part with. Ming must have found it when they were packing up his place and had placed it for sale, not realizing the provenance it carried for Gabriel. He strode over and swept up the object in his fist.

It was a hollow brass egg that opened like a box. Hand-painted in pretty pastel Easter colors, the egg was inscribed with Russian words in gold lettering. The hand-crafted heirloom belonged to Victor Archwood.

Vic's grandfather had made it for him, the same one who had abused him.

Gabriel had discovered the egg buried outside Natalie Archwood's home in San Francisco. Vic had supposedly committed suicide, and the case was closed. Gabriel, however, still yearned to find the missing puzzle pieces of his memory. He had no one to help him put his past together. His molester was dead, and Gabriel had not been on speaking terms with his own family.

Recklessly, he had gone looking for answers at the Archwood home. Vic, after all, had been part of Gabriel's past. When Natalie put her house up for sale, Gabriel pretended to be a prospective buyer. Buried under the rotted floor of a decrepit shed in the backyard, he had found the Easter egg along with two other handcrafted boxes.

That fateful night at the Cliff House when he went face-to-face with Victor Archwood, Gabriel had flung two of the boxes into the ocean. Why he had kept the egg, he didn't know. Perhaps it was because he had something on the killer, a link to Archwood's Achilles' heel. Gabriel clearly remembered Archwood's violent reaction upon seeing his grandfather's gifts unearthed, brought back to the surface to feed off him like soul-sucking ghouls.

"Gabe!"

Gabriel looked up to see Ming holding up a useless print of a still life that had hung in his bedroom. A matronly woman stood next to Ming, apparently waiting to buy it.

"Are you sure you don't want this for your new place?" Ming asked.

"Sell everything," Gabriel told her and pocketed the brass egg.

CHAPTER TWELVE

Monday morning came, and as Janet folded laundry in her Seattle home, she watched the court proceedings on television.

More forensic experts were called to the stand. DNA scientist Anthony Hamilton gave his testimony. The DNA from a semen stain found on the pant leg of one of the victims matched the DNA from a swabbed sample taken from Victor Archwood at the time of his arrest. Thorne asked Hamilton if this could tie Victor Archwood directly to the murder victims. Hamilton was of the opinion that it did.

Prosecutor Donovan Thorne next called up Natalie Archwood.

Natalie scowled at the prosecutor and took her time walking to the witness stand.

"Let the court show that Mrs. Archwood is an adverse witness," Thorne commented as she drew near. When she was sworn in, Thorne addressed her.

"Do you admit that you lied to your son, Victor Archwood, by telling him that Gabriel McRay had sexually abused him?"

Natalie refused to answer.

Judge Durante looked at Natalie. "You are under oath, ma'am."

Thorne got into Natalie's face. "Do you admit that you continually lied to your son, Victor Archwood, in telling him Detective McRay had sexually molested him?"

Natalie hissed at the prosecutor. "Yes."

Thorne grinned at Natalie. "No further questions."

Off and on, the camera would pan to Gabriel sitting in the audience. His shoulders were tense, and his lips were closed in a tight line.

WATCHING HIM ON TELEVISION, Janet wondered how her brother was doing. When he had been a guest at her home, she had seen nothing of the short-tempered "bad" cop he was reputed to be. Instead, Gabriel had been a polite visitor. Seated next to Gabriel was an attractive Asian woman. Janet knew this woman to be Dr. Ming Li, a pathologist who had made quite a name for herself in her field. Janet also knew that Ming was Gabriel's girlfriend.

Janet was curious about the attraction Ming felt for Gabriel. Miss Super Successful could probably have had her pick of professionals, so why go for Janet's troubled brother?

Janet herself had gone to the University of Washington where she had every intention of obtaining a pre-medical degree. Of course, her marriage to Michael had permanently postponed that plan. It wasn't that her husband objected to her going forward. It's just that the prospect of medical school, then a residency, seemed like a huge commitment. Besides, Janet had wanted to have a baby.

Her parents had been especially thrilled by the prospect of a grandchild, and Janet had been eager to grab their attention.

Janet folded her husband's shirt and once again glanced up at the television to catch a glimpse of Dr. Ming Li. The famous pathologist looked nothing like the confident career woman she was purported to be. In fact, she appeared to be petrified.

IN THE LOS ANGELES COURTROOM, Donovan Thorne called up Ming to deliver her eyewitness testimony. Ming approached the bench with trepidation. She was no longer functioning as a medical professional, maintaining her professional distance from the catastrophe. She was a witness now, a victim of catastrophe herself. Her knees were nearly knocking as she took her seat in the witness stand.

"Dr. Li," Thorne began, "you were summoned up to San Francisco to aid in the investigation. Why?"

"Because I was familiar with the case, having performed autopsies on all the victims in Los Angeles."

"And what happened to you at the lab on the night of October 19th?"

"It was after hours; the place was empty except for me and Taylor, the janitor. After Taylor said goodnight, I waited around for a fax to come. A little later, I heard noises, so I looked out the office door and saw a janitor mopping the floor. I was a little surprised because I thought Taylor had left. The janitor turned around, and I saw it wasn't Taylor."

"Then what happened?"

"The man hit me, and I blacked out."

"Is the person who struck you in this courtroom?"

"Yes."

"Could you point him out to us, please?"

Ming licked her lips, averted her eyes, and pointed to Victor Archwood.

"What happened after you were struck?"

"I woke up to find myself halfway buried in the ground." Ming kept her eyes on her folded hands. "I didn't know where I was or how I'd gotten there. When I was fully awake, some sort of pipe was shoved into my mouth. I heard a man say that I should pray for Detective McRay to find me."

"And then?"

Ming swallowed and raised her eyes. She searched for Gabriel's face in the courtroom and found him. He gave her a reassuring nod.

"The man covered me with sand. I could breathe through the pipe, but I was completely buried."

Thorne nodded sympathetically to Ming. "Thank you,

Dr. Li." To the judge, he added, "No further questions, Your Honor."

BRILLSTEIN CALMLY APPROACHED Ming for cross-examination.

"Dr. Li, you have been a reliable forensic expert in how many court cases would you say?"

"Many. I can't give you an exact number without looking—"

"That won't be necessary," Brillstein politely interrupted. "But wouldn't you agree that you can be counted on to be quite thorough and professional in your forensic testimonies?"

"Yes."

Brillstein gave her a Cheshire-cat grin. "Not too many details get by you, do they?"

"No," Ming answered warily, unsure of Brillstein's plan of attack.

"That's exactly your reputation: precise and thorough. Now could you tell me honestly, Dr. Li, and remember you are under oath, what exactly did your kidnapper look like?"

"It was Victor Arch—"

"Ahhh…" Brillstein interrupted by waving a finger in front of her face. "I did not ask you to name anyone. I am asking you, as a professional with a sharp forensic eye, to tell me exactly what your assailant looked like as you recall from memory. No artist sketches were ever submitted into evidence. Didn't anyone ask you what your assailant looked like?"

"No, because he left a note for Detective McRay who saw him right after I was taken, and—"

Brillstein interrupted. "I find it bothersome that no one asked you what your attacker looked like. Well, I'm asking you now. Describe him to me." Brillstein blocked Ming's view of Archwood.

Ming met Brillstein's eyes defiantly. "He had blond hair."

"And?"

"He was dressed as a janitor."

"And?"

"He told me to pray for Gabriel to find me and—"

"I didn't ask you what he said. I'm asking you what he looked like."

"Objection!" cried Donovan Thorne. "Badgering the witness!"

Judge Durante nodded. "Sustained."

"Dr. Li," Brillstein continued, "you told police that your assailant hit you and caused you to black out. Besides the blond hair and a janitor's uniform, did you notice any distinguishable features of your assailant?"

Ming tried to look at Archwood, but Brillstein again blocked her view. "Please look at me and not the defendant and describe the man who attacked you that night!"

Ming seemed at a loss for words. Out in the audience, Gabriel loosened his tie in frustration. He was getting steamed.

"Dr. Li?" The judge asked.

"How about when you were being buried alive?" Brillstein asked, quickly trading in politeness for exasperation. "Did you see your assailant's face then?"

Ming's shoulders fell. "No."

"Can you, in all honesty, as a professional with an eye for details, give us a description of your assailant?"

Ming remained silent.

"Please answer the question. Can you describe what your assailant looked like?"

Ming looked desperately at Gabriel and then gave her only honest answer. "No, I cannot."

"No more questions, Your Honor," Brillstein said.

As he passed by Donovan Thorne, the defense counsel whispered, "Do you have anything solid to nail on my client?"

NONPLUSSED, ignoring Brillstein's jab, the prosecutor stood up. "The People call Special Agent Ralph Tenant of the Federal Bureau of Investigation."

Tenant's usual ruddy complexion was a shade rosier today under his white hair. He was a bulky, tough Fed who wasn't at all happy with Brillstein's tactics. Tenant gave the defense counsel a dark look on his way to the stand. When his eyes alighted on the defendant, he gave Archwood an even blacker look.

Once the FBI agent was sworn in, Thorne addressed him. "Special Agent Tenant, you joined the investigation when it headed up to San Francisco, correct?"

"Yes."

"Give us a brief background on that."

"The investigation had moved north so that the Los Angeles homicide team could follow up on the Berkeley theater clue. At that time, Natalie Archwood, the defendant's mother, told us she would cooperate with authorities. She came into the PD headquarters where the investigation was temporarily housed, and she told me that her son had called her, sounding despondent."

Thorne elucidated for the jury. "Victor Archwood sounded despondent."

"That is correct."

"Go on."

"Mrs. Archwood told us that Victor was staying at a cabin in Muir Woods. She gave us the address, and we moved in on it."

"And what did you find when you got there?"

"The cabin was on fire," Tenant replied. "Inside was the body of a man. He had apparently shot himself in the mouth."

"I'd like to present Exhibit 29, a photograph of this badly burned corpse. The People will later call a forensic odontologist to educate us as to the effects of shotgun blasts to the mouth, but for now, please continue, Agent Tenant."

"Well, due to the bad condition of the body, we couldn't readily identify him. We found a tooth with a gold inlay. The tooth matched Victor Archwood's dental records. We assumed Mr. Archwood had committed suicide."

Thorne cocked his head at Agent Tenant. "But there was a problem with that corpse, am I right?"

"There sure was," Tenant replied eagerly. "DNA testing proved that the corpse was not Victor Archwood."

"*Not* Victor Archwood," the prosecutor enunciated for the jury. "Hmm. Do you have an opinion, Agent

Tenant, as to why the suspect would fake his own suicide?"

"In my opinion, we were getting too close to him." Tenant took a moment to frown at the defendant. "He faked his own death to throw us off track."

"And did the forensics report come to any conclusion as to whether or not that shotgun wound was self-inflicted?"

"The tests were inconclusive. Homicide or suicide—it could have gone either way."

Thorne nodded. "I see, but could it have been a homicide?"

"That possibility is currently being investigated," Tenant answered.

"Okay. What else did you find at the cabin?"

"We found the wedding ring belonging to Ronald Hall."

"Ronald Hall being one of the Malibu Canyon Murder victims."

"That's correct."

"People's Exhibit 31 is the ring belonging to victim Ronald Hall. No further questions, Your Honor."

BRILLSTEIN APPROACHED TENANT FOR CROSS-EXAMINATION, looking like the cat that ate the canary. "Agent Tenant, did you say this cabin in Muir Woods was supposed to be a hideout of sorts?"

"The defendant's mother referred to it as Mr. Archwood's hideout."

"All right. Did you ever see my client there?"

"No, but we found a body we assumed was his."

"But DNA testing proved that it was not, correct?"

"Correct."

"Whose body was it?"

Tenant took a big breath. "Unidentified. Nothing has come up in missing persons. We assume this was a homeless male."

"So many assumptions in this case. And yet no hard evidence."

Tenant defiantly stuck his chin out at the defense counsel. "We found Archwood's tooth at the scene. Obviously, he wanted it to look like he'd committed suicide."

"Really?" Brillstein countered. "My client's tooth was found there. Can a tooth pull the trigger of a shotgun?"

Chuckles erupted from the jury box.

Brillstein smiled too. "So my client might have visited this cabin on occasion, and one time he lost a tooth with a gold inlay. Okay. So then a homeless man comes along and commits suicide. You find my client's tooth, and all of a sudden, he's a serial killer."

"The homeless man didn't own Ronald Hall's ring!" Tenant nearly roared.

Brillstein wasn't put off. In fact, he regarded Agent Tenant calmly for a long moment and then asked, "How d'ya know?"

Brillstein looked at the judge. "No further questions, Your Honor."

Judge Durante nodded at Agent Tenant. "Thank you. You are excused."

THE DAYS WORE ON. Escrow closed on Gabriel's new home. When he wasn't in court, Gabriel immersed himself in renovating the place. Laborers helped him patch plaster, paint, and hang new doors. New appliances were ordered. The old, stained carpeting was torn out and wood flooring took its place. Brand new carpet graced the second bedroom because Gabriel wanted to make the room as welcoming for guests as possible.

He mused over what sort of furniture he should buy. Beds for that second room were an impractical choice, as Gabriel would not always be entertaining. Ming came up with the perfect solution one weekend when they were hunting for furniture. She came across a roomy armchair that pulled out into a nice-sized twin bed.

"I'll buy two of them," Gabriel commented as he inspected the chair in the showroom. "Then the kids will have their own beds."

"And when the room isn't being used for guests," Ming added, "it will be a cozy study for you."

"What would I do without you?" He gave her a quick kiss and then wrote out another check.

Ming nodded acquiescently but kept her opinions to herself. She watched Gabriel spend more and more of his hard earned cash and wondered why he didn't want to live with her.

"THERE'S a Wendy Pennington here to see you, Detective."

Gabriel sat at his desk typing an e-mail to Ramirez,

hassling him for a case to work. It was late in the afternoon, well after five p.m., and Gabriel hadn't expected any visitors. As the clerk walked back toward the lobby area, Gabriel peered out of his cubicle to see a thin woman looking his way.

He leaned behind the gray textured wall and sighed.

Some people don't quit, he thought.

Okay, let's get this over with.

He got to his feet and walked over to the woman. Wendy Pennington was a bony woman with hazardous features. She had the sallow-looking skin and brittleness of someone who had experienced one too many hard knocks. Her hair might have been a dirty blond but was ragged enough to pass for gray. Gabriel wondered if the same thing that had turned April into a drug addict had contributed to Wendy getting old before her time.

"You wanted to see me, Miss Pennington?"

He did not invite her over to sit at his cubicle. He was going to make this meeting brief.

"I wanted to know how my sister's case is coming along."

"We're about to close it, Miss Pennington."

"No fucking way." April's sister shook her head vehemently and rummaged through her overly large purse.

She had nicotine stains on her fingers, so Gabriel calmly surmised she was searching for cigarettes and not for a gun to settle things the old-fashioned way.

Wendy Pennington then seemed to remember things like no-smoking policies and the appropriate language to use in front of a cop and promptly let her purse drop to her hip.

"I asked you to look into this further," she said sullenly.

Gabriel didn't tell her about the additional toxicology testing that he had asked to be performed, but he did say, "I'm making sure that what we're taking as fact is indeed the way it happened."

Wendy sighed, and Gabriel could smell expired cigarette smoke.

"What about Todd?" she threw at him. "What's his explanation?"

"You don't talk to Mr. King?"

"He thinks our family is trash. He treated April like trash until he wanted her to sign the papers. Then he was just as sweet as can be. She actually thought he had changed and things would be like they were before. Poor kid."

Gabriel cleared his throat. "What papers?"

He had a hunch as to what kind of papers Mr. King would ask his girlfriend to sign but wanted to hear it from Wendy anyhow.

The bony woman grimaced at him and said in a voice made harsh with smoke, "What kind do you think, Detective McRay? The kind where he gets money if she croaks. A life insurance policy, of course."

CHAPTER THIRTEEN

G abriel sat in the courtroom preoccupied, thinking about April Pennington and Mr. Todd King. As the defense presented its evidence, he could barely concentrate on the proceedings. A life insurance policy changed the whole dynamic of the Pennington case. Now a motive existed behind April's death.

He leaned closer to Ming, who was sitting next to him as usual. He whispered in her ear. "I'm going to have that syringe she was using fingerprinted."

Ming, who had been watching the trial, looked confused. "What? Whose syringe?"

"April Pennington's syringe. I want to know whose prints are on it."

"Forget about it," Ming said.

"But he took out a life insurance policy on her."

"Who?"

"Her boyfriend, Mr. King."

Ming rolled her eyes, exasperated—more from being

uneasy due to the trial and less from Gabriel's thoroughness. "There are no physical signs of homicide. Not a one."

Ramirez, sitting behind them, tapped Gabriel on the shoulder. He put his finger to his lips and then pointed to the witness stand.

Gabriel took the cue and stopped talking. He sat back and watched as a renowned genetic scientist was called as an expert witness.

The scientist countered the People's expert by claiming that the DNA found on a victim's pant leg had been burned and was therefore too degraded to make a positive match to any one suspect. While the genetic markers didn't exclude Victor Archwood, the sample could not positively identify him either.

The dry testimony of the scientist became boring after a while, but things perked up again when the defense called Vic's sister Sonia to the stand.

The big girl wore a huge smile as if she'd been called up to be a contestant on a game show.

"Miss Archwood," Brillstein began. "Or should I use your married name?"

Sonia snorted. "I divorced that jack-hole. Use my maiden name."

"Very well." Brillstein glanced at the jury to see if they were up for riding The Sonia Joke. They were.

"Ms. Archwood, to your knowledge did Victor ever mention chakras?"

"Say what?"

"Chakras."

"No." Big smile again for the audience.

"To your knowledge did he ever show an interest in East Indian beliefs?"

"No."

"Did he have books or anything remotely related to the chakras?"

"No."

"Did your grandmother, who allegedly educated Mr. Archwood in the process of quote/unquote 'capturing souls'—did she ever mention or have in her possession anything to do with chakras?"

"No."

"Hinduism?"

"No." Sonia giggled. This was too fun.

"East Indian practices?"

"Dude," she began, playing right into Brillstein's hands, "her idea of world travel was going from the bed to the toilet, okay?"

The jury laughed. Sonia laughed.

Brillstein nodded happily. "Thank you, Sonia."

Sitting in the audience, Gabriel sighed. Brillstein was looking like a regular good guy, and that was bad. The jury was not offended by him, and in one smart maneuver, he'd used Sonia to not only throw water on the link between Victor Archwood and the chakras, but also to gather the jury members over to his side by poking fun at her—a key witness for the prosecution.

During cross-examination, Thorne tried to get Sonia back on the "capturing souls" track, but that engine had lost its steam, as far the jury was concerned. Mentally, they had moved on. In fact, they seemed rather disappointed that Thorne wasn't using the big girl for amusement as Brillstein had. Dejectedly, Thorne told the judge he had no more questions.

FOR HIS FINAL WITNESS, the defense attorney called up arson investigator Paul Vacher. Gabriel was surprised. He hadn't been aware that the defense was calling up one of his own comrades at the LASD.

Once Vacher was sworn in, Brillstein wasted no time.

"Investigator Vacher, in your capacity as an arson investigator, you were called in to recover evidence at the Los Angeles apartment of the Malibu Canyon Murderer. During your search for evidence, you found a fishing-tackle box, correct?"

"Yes."

"As the prosecution already mentioned, this tackle box held various personal items belonging to the victims."

It wasn't a question, but Brillstein waited for Vacher to give a response. The arson investigator nodded in agreement.

Brillstein then continued. "The defense would turn the jury's attention back to People's Exhibit number 28, which is the fishing-tackle box shown open. We can see the many items that belonged to the victims, just as they were found in their individual compartments. Did you take this photo, Investigator Vacher?"

"No," Vacher said with some surprise. "Apparently one of my deputies did."

"Did you know this photo was taken?"

"I did not. I myself took photos of all the items individually as they were entered into evidence. I wasn't aware of this one."

Brillstein took a metal rod and pointed to the compartment containing Meredith Hall's wedding band and Ted Brody's ring. "When were these rings entered into evidence?"

"The day that we found them," Vacher replied.

"The day that you found them. That would have occurred well before the investigation moved north to San Francisco, am I correct?"

"Of course."

"Good. And could you tell us, when an item is entered into evidence, where is it stored?"

Vacher looked with concern at Donovan Thorne who, like him, wondered where this was going.

"In the evidence room," Vacher answered. "All items are counted and verified by the impounding officer. The rings, being considered valuable, would have additionally been tagged and put into an evidence locker."

"Can anybody walk into an evidence room? Is it open to the public?"

"Of course not," Vacher told him. "All property is secured, and no one is allowed entry without the evidence officer being present."

"Who then is allowed access to this evidence?"

"The investigating officers."

"I see." Brillstein paused. "Let's back up. You stated that when these rings were entered into evidence they were photographed by you separately. The defense would like to show Exhibits 1 and 2, a photograph of Ted Brody's ring and a photo of Meredith Hall's wedding band as they were entered into evidence. You took these photos, correct?

"Correct."

"Where is Ronald Hall's wedding band?"

"It wasn't there. It was later found at a cabin in—"

"Again I direct your attention back to People's Exhibit number 28, the photograph, taken by your deputy, which is exactly how the tackle box looked when it was first recovered."

All eyes returned to the photograph. Brillstein then produced a poster-sized enlargement of the same photograph.

"I would like to show an enlargement of this photo. We will focus on the rings in their tackle-box compartment."

Gabriel's trained eyes went wide, and he nearly stood up in his seat. Ming looked at him in concern and whispered, "What is it?"

He couldn't answer. He felt a twinge of panic reverberate through his body as he stared hard at the photograph.

Brillstein pulled out another poster of an even greater enlargement. "Now let's look even closer at the same photo. Investigator Vacher, will you count for the court how many rings you see in that compartment?"

"Three," Vacher said in surprise.

"Three. And yet only two rings were counted into evidence and photographed by you. Now let's enlarge the enlargement." Brillstein pulled out a poster of an even closer view. "Tell me, can you see that third ring now visible behind the other two? And can you make out the "R" inside that third ring?"

A collective gasp went through the courtroom.

Vacher couldn't seem to speak, so Brillstein answered for him.

"I would like to call the jury's attention back to People's Exhibit number 31. The ring belonging to Ronald Hall that was found in the cabin outside San Francisco."

He directed the pointer to the curving initials, RH, which were clearly inscribed inside the wedding band of the San Francisco photo. He then pointed to an identical curving letter R that was visible in the partially hidden ring in the tackle box photo from Los Angeles.

Brillstein rocked back and forth on his heels. "I'm assuming Ronald Hall did not die with two identical wedding bands on his finger. So tell me, Investigator Vacher, how does a ring photographed as evidence in Los Angeles make its way up to a San Francisco crime scene?"

In growing desperation, Gabriel looked at Dash for an explanation; but his partner was now hanging his head, staring at the floor.

No, this didn't... You wouldn't have...

"I'll tell you how that ring got up to San Francisco," Brillstein offered. "The very people that entered it into evidence right here in L.A. dropped it there to frame my client! No one else is allowed to handle evidence. Am I right, Investigator Vacher? Isn't that what you said?"

Vacher nodded, studying the photo, spellbound.

"Please answer yes or no."

"Yes."

"And who would have had access to this tackle box with all the items still inside before you had processed and photographed them into evidence?"

"Detectives Starkweather and McRay."

"No further questions, Your Honor. The defense rests."

DONOVAN THORNE, chewing his lower lip, shuffled to the witness stand, hoping to deflect the fallout from Brillstein's dropped bomb.

"Investigator Vacher," he began, flustered. "When you entered the rings into evidence, you saw only two rings—Ted Brody's and Meredith Hall's, correct?"

"That's correct," Vacher replied eagerly.

"Do you recall ever seeing a third ring along with the other two at any time?"

"I-I can't remember." Vacher began growing visibly nervous. "We had everything out on a table, and I hadn't begun itemizing everything yet. I didn't know that my deputy took that picture of the tackle box when it first came in."

Thorne pressed him. "But do you ever recall seeing a third ring in that compartment along with the other two?"

"No."

"No more questions," Thorne said as beads of perspiration streamed down his elegant face.

Gabriel sat like a stone, unable to move a muscle. He was aware that next to him, Dash was the polar opposite

—fidgeting in his seat, unable to get comfortable. On Gabriel's other side, Ming was quiet, hardly breathing.

Gabriel forced his head to turn slightly and saw Victor Archwood staring at him. Although the killer's face was calm and expressionless, Archwood's eyes bore intently through Gabriel.

CHAPTER FOURTEEN

During closing remarks, it was plain that the usually confident Donovan Thorne was off-kilter. Even so, he reiterated for the jury all the points he'd made during his presentation of evidence.

"The dead cannot speak," he said. "And yet they are here with us through their pictures, through the description of their wounds, and through their personal items. They are crying out to you for justice. The defense's claim regarding the ring belonging to Ronald Hall pales in importance when compared to the evidence we have already presented. We have a DNA sample that our reliable expert witness swears is a match to the defendant. And we have, above all, Detective McRay's eyewitness account of a deranged killer confronting him, wanting to murder him in the same manner in which all the victims were killed. We have also established the motive for this attack: Mr. Archwood's lifelong vendetta against Detective McRay.

"Ladies and gentlemen, on behalf of the People of the State of California, because we have proven beyond a reasonable doubt that the defendant committed these murders, we ask you to find the defendant guilty of murder in the first degree of Ronald Hall, Meredith Hall, Patrick Funston, Tania Dankowsi, Ted Brody, Adam Parraco, and Brian Goldfield. You must answer their cries for justice."

Defense counsel Brillstein took the floor and began his closing remarks.

"The People are accusing us of taking liberties with evidence. These aren't mere claims we are making in regards to Ronald Hall's wedding ring. We didn't Photoshop a third ring into that enlargement of the fishing-tackle box. We didn't tamper with evidence, but there has been a travesty of evidence tampering revealed in this courtroom. Who dropped Ronald Hall's ring at the crime scene in San Francisco? We may never know. But we do know that that ring was removed from a box already in the possession of investigators. Since no other solid evidence against the defendant existed, the Sheriff's Department decided to plant evidence so they could arrest Mr. Archwood. In fact, the testimonies of Detectives McRay and Starkweather should be stricken altogether and totally disregarded. Detective McRay's eyewitness account smacks of conspiracy and a lack of mental competency.

"Ladies and gentlemen, if after hearing all this you have reasonable doubt, then Victor Archwood must have an acquittal. I believe there is much doubt about Mr. Archwood's guilt here today. The truth is what we are seeking. The evidence is what you must deliberate on. I believe the truth will clearly stand out for you and will convince you once and for all that Victor Archwood is a wronged man, wrongly accused. The fate of an innocent man is in your hands."

JURY DELIBERATION CREATED a trial of sorts for Gabriel and Ming, who went about their business in a tensely subdued manner. Gabriel kept telling himself that some sort of mistake had been made, that the issue regarding Ronald Hall's wedding ring was a defense ploy and nothing more. Time and again, he mulled over the old details of the case. He tried to puzzle it out, tried to recall when and where a *faux pas* might have occurred. What stone had he left unturned?

He purposely avoided speaking of it to Dash. Although Gabriel worried unendingly about the matter, he wanted to believe that an accident had somehow transpired; just an accident that would have no bearing on the jury's verdict. He kept himself occupied by packing up what was left in his apartment and putting the finishing touches on his new house. Gabriel performed these tasks like an automaton—numb and robot-like.

He clung to his work, the only space where he felt safe. On the third day of jury deliberation, he headed to the chemical-processing lab on the third floor of the LASD's new Forensic Science Center, an all-encompassing testing center on the campus of Cal State Los Angeles.

He intended to find out whose fingerprints were on the syringe that April Pennington used the last day she drew breath. Ming had told him he was wasting his time. Gabriel didn't care. He needed something else to think about, and since Ramirez hadn't given him anything else to chew on, he was going to eat and drink this case.

The syringe was now ensconced in a Syringe Protection/Collection Kit, which was a clear plastic tube that contained a special insert to capture liquids and secure the needle. Not only designed to protect the evidence inside, it also shielded the police and crime lab personnel from any blood-borne diseases that might be hanging around.

When Roland Hillenbrand, the fingerprint criminologist, received the tube from Gabriel, he broke the evidence seal with its biohazard symbols and shrugged.

"They're going to be partial," he warned Gabriel as he studied the syringe. "The barrel size will determine how much of the prints will be shown, but I can almost assure you there's not gonna be enough pattern to use in a court of law."

Roland's eyes alighted on Gabriel momentarily, and then he went back to examining the evidence. Obviously, Gabriel surmised, Roland was following the Victor Archwood trial and was worried about the outcome.

He and everybody else.

The criminologist continued, "But I think I can pull enough off here to assist you in identifying a suspect. We'll try cyanoacrylate fuming. If Super Glue does the job, then I'll have something for you in about two hours. Good enough?"

"Good enough," Gabriel replied and thanked him.

GABRIEL RETURNED to Commerce to wait for Roland's call. Dash sat in his cubicle next to Gabriel's.

"Hey," he heard Dash call in greeting.

"Hey," Gabriel echoed back hollowly.

Totally awkward. I need to talk to him.

But Gabriel didn't speak. He shuffled papers on his desk and silently cussed out Ramirez for thinking him too weak to handle his job along with a trial.

When the fingerprint analysis call came in, the results were not startling. Only April's prints were found on the syringe that had administered her death dose.

"How about the position of the prints?" Gabriel pressed Roland over the phone. He saw Dash's head poke around the wall dividing them. "Could she have been coerced somehow?"

"What are you doing?" Dash whispered to Gabriel.

Gabriel didn't answer. On the telephone, Roland said he saw nothing unusual about the pattern of the prints. Nothing that would indicate an abnormal hold on the syringe.

"So the dose was self-inflicted."

Objection! Testifying!

Gabriel put a hand to his forehead. "Is that your opinion?"

Dash stood up and fully entered the cubicle. "Gabe?

What's going on?"

Gabriel relented and ended the call with the criminologist. Only then did he look at his partner, who now stood over him.

"The case is closed," Dash said.

"There's an insurance policy."

"So?"

"So maybe he held a gun to her head and forced her to inject herself." Anger seeped into Gabriel's words.

"Way ahead of you, man," Dash told him evenly. "I checked out Mr. King, and there are no firearms registered to either him or April Pennington."

Gabriel rose and faced the other man eye to eye. "Maybe he's hiding one. Maybe he's got secrets."

Dash swallowed, and his Adam's apple bobbed nervously in his throat. "Gabe, if His Majesty truly wanted to kill April, he would have made sure she gave herself a lethal dose. There wasn't enough coke in her to cause death. Her heart had problems from habitual drug use, and she mainlined one too many times. Why can't you... Why can't you let it lie?"

"Did you plant that ring?" Gabriel asked in a low, ominous voice.

Dash stared back at Gabriel without blinking. The space between the two partners stood silent and still.

"How can you ask that?" Dash said finally. "You were with me the entire time we examined the tackle box. Don't you remember?"

Gabriel backed off, suddenly feeling drained. He ran a trembling hand through his dark hair and shook his head. "Honestly, I don't."

CHAPTER FIFTEEN

"Ladies and gentlemen, the jury has reached a verdict."

The courtroom was filled with an atmosphere thick with the breath, sweat, and tension of those with everything to gain and everything to lose.

Judge Durante addressed them all. "Mr. Archwood is present before the court with his counsel, Mr. Brillstein. The People are represented by Mr. Thorne."

Gabriel, Ramirez, Ming, Dash, and even Dr. B were present, holding their breaths as the judge went through the protocol, first asking the clerk, "Mrs. Spaulding, do you have the envelope with the sealed jury verdict?"

The clerk confirmed that she did, and she handed the envelope to the court deputy who was then instructed to give it to the jury foreperson for validation. Gabriel watched the proceedings with a fluttering heart.

"Madam Foreperson," relayed the judge. "Would you

please open the envelope and check the condition of the verdict forms?"

When she checked them and assured the court the verdict forms were in order, they were handed back to the clerk.

Judge Durante addressed the audience members and television cameras. "I will caution the audience members during the reading of these verdicts to remain calm. We will not have these proceedings disrupted." He then turned his attention to the defense table. "Mr. Archwood, would you please stand and face the jury?"

Archwood stood up tall with Brillstein at his side.

The clerk read, "The Superior Court of California, County of Los Angeles in the matter of the State of California versus Victor Archwood: We the jury in the above-entitled action find the defendant, Victor Archwood, not guilty in the crime of murder in violation of penal code section 187A—"

A rush of gasps and murmurs rolled through the courtroom. Patrick Funston's mother began a loud mewling. Andrea Leighton blurted out a quick and happy, "Yes!"

The clerk continued, "— a felony upon Ronald Hall, a human being as charged in Count One of the Information. The Superior Court of California, County of Los Angeles in the matter of the State of California versus Victor Archwood. We the jury in the above-entitled action find the defendant, Victor Archwood, not guilty—"

No, thought Gabriel. *This is a dream. A nightmare...*

"—a felony upon Meredith Hall, a human being as charged in Count Two of the Information."

The clerk's voice droned like a metronome as she read through all the counts, through all the murder victims. With each "not guilty" verdict, Gabriel felt the pit in his stomach growing into a black abyss. Pain flared through his hand, and when he looked down, he saw Ming's fingernails digging into his flesh. Gabriel met her ebony eyes and saw tears pooling there. She seemed as if she wanted to speak but could not. Gabriel couldn't formulate words either

Because they can't be letting him off...

"We the jury in the above-entitled action further find the special circumstance the defendant, Victor Archwood, has in this case of being convicted of at least one crime of murder of the first degree and one or more crimes of murder of the first or second degree to be not true."

Ramirez had his eyes closed and sat in his seat muttering swear words in Spanish. Special Agent Ralph Tenant was shaking his head so hard his jowls were dancing.

The judge turned to the jury. "Ladies and Gentlemen of the jury, is this your verdict, so say one, so say you all?

Madame Foreperson answered. "Yes, Your Honor."

Brillstein kept his hand on Archwood's back, but his face was shining in victory.

The judge proceeded to thank the jury and dismissed them. He then turned to the courtroom.

"The defendant, having been acquitted of all charges, is ordered transported to an appropriate Sheriff's facility and released forthwith. We'll stand to recess."

The judge hit his gavel once and exited.

Andrea, his mother, and Sonia, immediately

surrounded Victor Archwood. Brillstein gave his client a big hug for the cameras. Through the crowd, Archwood met Gabriel's eyes and winked. Gabriel, sickened, looked away, and with Ming clutching him, they walked rapidly out of the courtroom.

ON THE STEPS of the courthouse, under a bright and winking sun, Gabriel and Ming watched the press interview Brillstein, who was happily soaking up the limelight. When Brillstein jauntily made his way down the steps, Gabriel walked over to him and caught the defense counsel by the sleeve.

"You don't know what you've done," Gabriel told him. "You've set a maniacal killer loose."

"I didn't set him loose," Brillstein retorted. "You and your partner did."

The attorney abruptly pulled his arm away and strode off.

Gabriel went numb and walked on unsteady feet back to Ming.

THE FEELING around the homicide bureau was gloomy. The acquittal had thrown a dark shadow over the entire department, and everyone from the chief to the mayor wanted an explanation. While there was no proof that Gabriel or Dash had carried Ronald Hall's ring with them to San Francisco, most people believed one of them did it.

Gabriel was the most likely candidate because it was he who had led them to Victor Archwood in the first place. Unfortunately for Gabriel, he was simply in too much shock over the verdict to defend himself from allegations. The rumors were festering, about to erupt like a bad infection, and just when it seemed the media was about to crucify Gabriel, Dash came forward and told Ramirez he wanted to meet in private.

Ramirez allowed Gabriel to attend the meeting.

"I'm not admitting to anything," Dash announced, unable to meet either man's eye. "But I'll say that Gabriel had nothing to do with it and no knowledge of it."

"Why, Dash?" Gabriel asked, bewildered.

"Partner, your memory was sketchy at best back then. We didn't have much of a case, and you and I both knew Archwood was guilty as hell." Dash sighed at the distant memory. "Vacher said the rings hadn't been photographed yet. The ring wasn't supposed to be missed."

The three men were silent for a moment, and then Ramirez finally spoke. "McRay, you can go now."

"I'd rather not."

"You can go!" Ramirez barked, visibly upset. He gestured angrily to the door.

Gabriel looked at his partner once more. He wanted to say something to Dash, anything, only nothing came to mind.

WHEN GABRIEL RETURNED HOME, his apartment had an alien, empty look with the moving boxes piled in the middle of the living room. In his kitchen, the epicenter of his culinary adventures, half-open cabinet doors revealed dark and empty shelves. Except for the couch, all his furniture had been sold, donated or trashed. The place looked desolate, devoid of life, perfectly mirroring Gabriel's current emotional state.

How many times had Dash and his wife Eve come here for dinner? How many times had Gabriel sat in this very room as the ocean breeze wafted in through the windows to calm him while he pored over his case notes?

Everything familiar to Gabriel was gone. Everything had changed, and he feared the future, which suddenly loomed before him like a black hole that threatened to suck him into oblivion. A future with a liberated serial killer and his partner, his friend...

Gabriel sat dismally on one of the moving boxes and let the ghosts of his memories wrap their starving arms around him as the daylight receded and darkness crept into his barren home.

CHAPTER SIXTEEN

Excerpt from an article in the Los Angeles Times:

Defense attorney, Merrill Brillstein has sued the Sheriff's Department for damages on behalf of his client, Victor Archwood. The county has settled the lawsuit for an undisclosed amount.

EXCERPT FROM AN ENTERTAINMENT INDUSTRY PRESS RELEASE:

A new season of *The Dark Mind* premieres Sunday!

Victor Archwood's reality TV show is revving with new life since his acquittal. A film production company has bought the rights to his story for what is rumored to be well over a million dollars.

Meanwhile, Mr. Archwood is receiving rave reviews in the stage play *Anything Goes* and is also lecturing at various local colleges and participating in panel discussions regarding the judicial system as "The Wronged Man —Wrongly Accused."

On a more personal note, Mr. Archwood has been seen about town with reality television producer, Andrea Leighton, and has bought a house in the Santa Monica Mountains, which he is reportedly refurbishing into his dream home.

~

"WE'VE GOT A PROBLEM, MR. ARCHWOOD."

Victor was at his property in the mountains, observing the reconstruction of his home. Nearly nothing was left of the original house and all his changes and additions were being implemented in a very timely fashion. He could well afford his contractor's prompt attention.

"Mr. Archwood?"

A geologist approached Vic, wiping sweat from his brow with a worn bandana.

"You can't build that cabana where you want it," the geologist said and pointed to the edge of the backyard, which dropped off sharply to the canyon below.

The view was beautiful from the back. The blue horizon of the Pacific Ocean stretched out before them, framed by the hazy vista of the city to their left and the gentle curve of the hills to their right.

"I dug some test pits," the geologist said, "and that's a slide area. In fact, I would put caissons along that whole edge. It's that unstable."

Victor digested this news with a frown. He told the

geologist he would stop work on the cabana and promised he would give the caissons some thought.

No wonder the home had gone so cheap, Victor said to himself. The land had geological problems. Victor, however, had every intention of building the cabana at that location. He'd just do it after the inspections were through.

He saw a car pulling up the long driveway. As the car approached in a cloud of remodeling dust, Victor was astonished to see his mother behind the wheel. He excused himself from the geologist and went over to her car.

"What are you doing here?"

"Nice way to greet your mother," Natalie said as she exited the car.

"I didn't know you were coming back into town."

She surveyed the men at work. "I wanted to see your house."

"As you can tell, it's not ready for viewing yet."

The skinny older woman shrugged and walked toward the edge of the property. "Wow, what a view!"

Victor followed her, curious as to why his mother had returned to the Southland. He was anxious to get her gone again.

Natalie came to a stop on the precise location of the proposed cabana and looked out at the ocean in the distance.

"I thought we could visit for a couple of days, Vic," she said. "You know, celebrate your freedom."

Realization hit Victor, and he crossed his arms and waited.

Natalie took in the view. "I would think you'd want to thank me for saving your ass."

Archwood shook his head and thought,

Bitch...

"Do you have any idea how much I had to pay that Jew lawyer?"

Vic grinned. *A bitch and a bigot to boot...*

"Okay, Mother," he said. "Why don't you come over for dinner tonight? We can discuss your financial situation, and you can meet my girlfriend."

Natalie turned and regarded her son with wicked amusement. "You have a girlfriend?"

She stood precariously close to the cliff's edge, and Victor visualized pushing her over. He would enjoy hearing the sounds her body made as it cracked on the rocks below. He placed a hand on his mother's back, but then steered her toward the safety of her car.

"I'm staying at the Chateau Marmont," he told her. "We'll have dinner in my suite."

"Your suite?" Natalie echoed and then scowled at him. "Little Lord Fauntleroy. Aren't you the fancy one?" She took a seat in her car and added, "Better save some of that cash, Vic."

MING SAT in her office at L.A. County General and read through the toxicology report on Ms. Pennington, the young chestnut-haired woman. A trace amount of the chemical ouabain was found in the dead girl's ocular fluid. Silently congratulating herself on having that eye jelly extracted, Ming turned toward her computer to research the chemical and then noticed that the building was too quiet.

Feeling fingers of panic creep into her solar plexus, Ming left her desk and peeked out her door to make sure that the morgue assistants were still around. They were. Geoffrey gave her a pleasant smile from where he worked. Reassured by the sound of human conversation, Ming returned to her desk.

She didn't like being alone anymore. Victor Archwood roamed free in the same city, and Ming fought the temptation to lock her office door. She quickly accessed the Internet to try to forget about Archwood.

She found that ouabain had been used at one time to stimulate the heart muscle in medical procedures. It was the principal chemical in a plant compound called Acokanthera. This genus contained cardiac glycosides that slowed the heart rate yet increased cardiac output. Humans with heart problems sometimes had a higher amount of ouabain in their systems naturally.

Ming gazed at the monitor. That would prove that April Pennington had prior heart problems and the cocaine had aggravated her condition.

Final proof of the girl's untimely demise—overdose, not homicide. A trace amount of antihistamines were also found in April's blood. These were common enough. Anyone with hay fever or allergies took antihistamines.

Well, that was that. Gabriel's mind could be put to rest, and perhaps now Ramirez would give him a new case to work.

Ming hoped the assignment would come soon. Like

her, Gabriel found solace in his work. He had been felled by Archwood's acquittal and Dash's admission of planting evidence. Ming knew how badly he needed to get his mind off both.

She glanced at her watch and smiled in relief—time to leave. Gabriel was christening his new kitchen tonight, promising to make her one of his wonderful gourmet meals. The thought of them doing something familiar together gave her hope that they could put all this unpleasantness behind them. Even more, Ming simply felt safer around Gabriel. She quickly organized her report and readied herself to leave.

GABRIEL OPENED his front door and saw Ming holding a wrapped present.

"Happy homeownership!" she said and planted a kiss on his lips. She handed him the present as she entered a living room that still smelled of fresh paint and sawed wood.

Gabriel shook the present near his ear. "Ming, you've got to stop doing this. You've been generous enough."

"Stop complaining and attach it to your TV."

Gabriel smiled as he tore off the wrapping. Ming couldn't keep a secret to save her life. As the wrapping fell away, he saw a small black box.

"You can get wireless Internet on your television now," Ming told him. "We can get movies and play games. You can also download dozens of apps with this."

Gabriel kept the smile pasted on his face to please her. "This is great."

Ming's own face fell a little. Gabriel was as bad at acting as Ming was at keeping secrets. She supposed he wasn't in the mood for 'dozens of apps.'

Ming sniffed the air. She could only smell paint, not the fragrance of cooked food.

"You're not cooking?"

"I hope you don't mind," Gabriel told her as he put the box down. "We'll celebrate when the place is completely done. I don't even have a dining table yet."

Ming nodded, feeling out of sorts.

"I have something for you." Gabriel dug in the pocket of his jeans. "Hold out your hand."

She held out her hand, and an unexpected flutter of anticipation ran through her. For a moment, one quick moment, Ming thought Gabriel might present her with an engagement ring. He wore a secretive smile that played at the corners of his mouth, and his fingers trembled nervously as they searched his pocket for the gift. Ming tried to keep a straight face, surprised to find she was beyond excited at the prospect of marriage.

Gabriel dropped a key into her waiting palm.

Ming eyed the house key, not quite what she was hoping for, but she grinned anyhow. "Hey, I can enter the man cave!"

"Anytime."

Ming closed her fingers around the key. "Are you sure? I mean, I know you want space to build a new—"

Gabriel pulled her into his arms. "I'm sure."

She loved the way his arms felt around her, and Ming nearly pitied herself that she wanted him so badly.

"I'm sorry about dinner," he told her, nuzzling his chin against the top of her head. "I just can't seem to find my footing lately."

"I know," Ming assured him and sighed against Gabriel's chest, comforted to be in the place she felt the safest.

ACROSS THE CITY in West Hollywood, at the castle-like Chateau Marmont Hotel, Natalie Archwood knocked twice on Victor's suite. Her handsome son opened the door, allowing her to enter.

"Hello, Mother."

Natalie gave him a prim nod and sauntered in like a diva, sweeping past him and surveying the parlor with an approving look.

"The food should arrive any minute," Victor said and gestured his mother toward a white cloth-covered table in the middle of the room.

"Are you trying to rush me out already? Why don't you get me a drink?"

Victor went over to a small wine rack as Natalie took a seat at the table. He pulled out the cheapest bottle. No sense wasting a good one. He uncorked the bottle and poured the wine into a ready glass.

"Don't you have anything stronger? No vodka?" Natalie asked from the table.

"Just wine," he replied.

"For a Mr. Fancypants, you sure as shit don't know how to stock a bar."

Victor set down the bottle a bit too hard and then turned toward his mother. Just then Andrea Leighton strode in from the bedroom. The girl wore a sequined baseball jersey and tight black jeans. Her streaked hair was tucked as usual under her baseball cap.

"Hi!" she said to Natalie, giving her a little wave.

"You remember Andrea, don't you?" Victor handed his mother the glass and then went over to the girl.

"Of course," Natalie said as she rose from her chair in greeting. "The show's producer."

Natalie beamed at them until Victor tilted Andrea's face up to his and gave her a passionate open-mouthed kiss, leaving his mother dangling before them. Andrea, embarrassed, squirmed in his arms, but Victor held her tightly, lovingly, allowing his mother to absorb it all. Finally, he released his girlfriend.

"I'll call room service to check on the food," Andrea said, somewhat ashamed, and she escaped back into the bedroom.

Natalie Archwood looked momentarily disgusted and then masked her features behind a smirk. She turned toward her son.

"I know what you're doing. You've got a black girl-friend because you think it's going to shock me. Well, it doesn't." Natalie smoothed her frizzy hair and took her seat, once again the cool, collected grande dame. "I know you, Vic, better than you know yourself. I know you don't like that girl."

"I don't?"

Natalie shook her head. "No. I'm your mother, after all. I can read you like a book. You're damaged. It's not your fault, but you're damaged." Natalie took a delicate sip of wine and smiled sweetly. "And I'm sure it's affected your sex life."

Victor glared at her. "If I'm damaged, it's because I've inherited your genes."

"Go ahead," Natalie retorted. "Be angry with me. Only give me some money. It's because of me you got your stupid show in the first place. It's because of me you got the best lawyer in town. And how do you repay me? By building yourself a mansion. That's gratitude for you. Well, you're not half the man you think you are, Mr. Fancypants."

Victor stared at his mother, wondering how he'd gotten the rotten luck to be birthed by such a creature. Maybe he should just write her a check and show her the door. His energy was stifled by her presence. She diminished his power.

Looking at the gaudy crimson lipstick stain she was leaving on his wine glass, a sudden urge came over Victor.

"Did you lie to me?" he asked his mother.

Natalie took a swallow of wine and wouldn't meet his eyes. "About what?"

"About Gabriel McRay."

For years the very core of Victor had sickened to know that his idol, Gabriel, had used him like a sex toy. His memories of Gabriel had always been so wholesome, the one bright light in an otherwise dreary existence. He'd had a father who had continually beat him and then abandoned him to the sole care of this demonic witch, his mother.

Then one day, Gabriel McRay had come along, a somewhat lonely teenager, and fast became Victor's savior.

It was Gabriel who had held his hand when they walked along the city streets. It was Gabriel who treated Vic tenderly, showing the little boy the only affection he ever received. Gabriel would ask Vic what he would like for lunch, and he'd make it for him without complaint. Gabriel once taught Vic how to make a homemade fishing rod out of a common stick and some fishing line. They went to Stow Lake to fish for oriental carp, knowing they couldn't catch any, but enjoying the attempt just the same. Gabriel had tried to impart his love of nature on little Vic. Oftentimes, they would explore Golden Gate Park, collecting pinecones or feeding the ducks in the ponds. They would sit on a bench and watch those ducks, marveling in bittersweet moments how protective ducks were over their young.

And when the tears came unbidden and without cause, it was Gabriel who hugged him. Gabriel would never call Vic a baby or make fun of him. He would only smooth the little boy's golden hair, and tell him that he did matter and that he was important, and that if nobody else loved him, then Gabriel did.

For so many years, Natalie continually assured Victor that the older boy had taken liberties with him.

Yes, we'll call it that. Liberties.

But if Gabriel hadn't done what his mother claimed he did, then could it... might it...

Dedushka, you wouldn't hurt me, would you?

He heard his grandfather's soft Russian words and felt so knotted up inside that, for a moment, Victor thought he might keel over onto the white tablecloth.

"I didn't lie to you," Natalie answered him firmly. "McRay is insane. Everybody knows that. He coerced me; that's what he did. He made me say that Papa hurt you. But it was McRay that hurt you. He's a violent and terrible man."

She lifted the glass to her lips where it hovered, waiting. "McRay wanted to connect you to those killings, and he found a way to do it, by threatening me and making me say I lied to you."

She drank deeply from the glass, polishing off the wine. Keeping her eyes pinned on the tablecloth, she waved the empty glass at her son. "Got any more of this?"

CHAPTER SEVENTEEN

Janet would arrive soon with the kids, and Gabriel was in a hurry to finish his home. Ming had come over to help him and now they were trying to find where to place the one survivor of his garage sale, his living room couch.

"This is breaking my back," Ming told Gabriel as they pushed the newly upholstered couch across the floor. "Can't Janet stay at my place?"

"No." Gabriel gave one final push and surveyed the position of the couch. "Do you think I should buy a privacy screen for her?"

"Gabriel, you're sure making a big effort here. They're only staying one week."

"Well, they'll come down again. And there's my mother and..." he paused. "Do you think my father could travel?"

Ming shook her head sympathetically. "I think it's

better to keep him in familiar surroundings." Upon sensing Gabriel's disappointment, she added, "But what do I know?"

She crossed the floor and put her arms over her boyfriend's shoulders. "Why don't you save some of the money you're spending, and buy airline tickets to visit him?"

Gabriel nodded and rested his hands gently on her arms. "Part of the plan. But Ramirez has got to give me a case soon or I'm gonna wonder if I have a job."

His broad shoulders fell slightly, and Ming knew that the subject of work was reminding him of Dash.

Gabriel pulled away from Ming and sat on the couch, which still smelled pertly of new fabric. "Dash was my partner for over ten years. How can I work without him? He was the good one, the one who knew how to talk to people. I can't believe he's sitting in a cell. How did this happen?"

"Dash made a terrible mistake." Ming took a seat next to him and wove her fingers through Gabriel's. "Should we be worried? Do you think Archwood will come after us?"

Gabriel regarded their entwined hands. Ming knew her boyfriend would put aside his own problems if he thought she was vulnerable.

"I will kill that bastard if he gets anywhere near you again."

"Don't say that." Ming leaned over and kissed the threat from Gabriel's lips, even though he said exactly what she wanted him to say.

The following day, Gabriel decided to visit Dash at the lockup downtown. He watched sorrowfully as his partner was brought into the visiting room like an ordinary criminal. Dash had been given twenty months, but he would be eligible for parole in ten.

"It's not such a long time," Gabriel assured him, trying to be upbeat. "It'll fly by, and then all this will be behind you."

This terrible mistake.

Dash was perusing a book on heart health that he'd asked Gabriel to bring him. "Yeah, this will be behind me. But what kind of future will I have?"

"We'll cross that bridge when we get to it." Even as Gabriel said it, he knew he sounded weak. He observed Dash wearing prison coveralls and swallowed uncomfortably. "Can I bring you anything else? I mean, how're you getting along with the food?"

"It's being taken care of." Dash reached into his pocket and, with a brave smile, displayed his ever-ready seasoning bottle. Too soon the smile faded, and he said, "'I'm sorry, Gabe. I really blew it."

"I'll write the bureau on your behalf," Gabriel said too quickly. He didn't even know if he would keep that promise. He wasn't sure what he could write.

After an awkward bit of surface conversation, Gabriel made his goodbyes. Visiting Dash in prison felt surreal. His partner should have been walking out the door with him, discussing their current case. Instead, Gabriel left his best friend at the county lockup with only sorrow accompanying him out the door.

In Lieutenant Ramirez's office, Gabriel perused Ming's report on April Pennington.

"A drug addict with cardiac arrest," Ramirez commented as he watched Gabriel read. "Okay to close it out?"

"Yeah," Gabriel told him. "Toxicology came back clean of obvious poisons." He thought about April's worn-looking sister. "The sister won't like it. She's pretty convinced Mr. King had something to do with April's demise."

Ramirez closed the file. "Nobody likes an untimely death. But it is what it is."

That was a common saying around the LASD. "It is what it is." Many times investigators felt the need to read more into a situation than it necessitated.

Gabriel fidgeted a bit and sighed audibly. Ramirez looked up at him from the file.

"Yes, McRay?"

"How long do you think it will it be until you can reinstate Dash?"

"I don't know that we will be reinstating Detective Starkweather."

Gabriel figured as much, but it hurt to hear it all the same. This was also the first time he had ever heard Ramirez refer to Dash by his title and last name.

"I'm assigning you a new partner," Ramirez told him.

That hurt too, but Gabriel didn't let it show.

"Rick?" he suggested to Ramirez.

Rick Frasier seemed the most likely candidate since he and Gabriel had already worked together on the Malibu Canyon Murder case. Preppie Rick's youthful enthusiasm might be a good match against Gabriel's more old school, seasoned personality.

Ramirez shook his head. "Jonelle Williams."

"What?" Gabriel asked in surprise.

Jonelle had been in the Sex Crimes division and had deftly played politics in order to wrangle a transfer to the homicide bureau. Gabriel knew her from his investigation of the Tara Samuels case, and the two of them did not get along.

"You're not bigoted, are you McRay?"

Jonelle was African-American.

"No, but she can't stand me."

"Well, you're going to have to stand each other from now on." Ramirez reached into his shirt pocket for his Winstons. "I suggest you start getting to know your new partner today."

"Where is she?"

"On her way to the evidence-handling seminar that you're supposed to be in."

Gabriel looked at his watch and groaned.

"You didn't think I'd let you skip that, did you?"

"No," Gabriel said as he picked up his jacket.

It is what it is.

"You might as well know, McRay. Detective Williams is taking over Dash's desk."

Gabriel gazed steadily at his superior. "That's a little raw, isn't it?"

"Someone has to sit at that desk, McRay. I'm not going to keep it as a shrine to someone who fucked us over."

"He was trying to help."

Ramirez shoved a cigarette in his mouth and lit up. "Is that what you think?"

"It's what Dash thought."

"Yeah, he sure helped," Ramirez said, blowing out smoke. "He helped Archwood go free. Now go shake hands with your new partner."

As Gabriel spoke with Ramirez in Commerce, a woman knocked on the departmental psychiatrist's door over in Monterey Park. She was a tall redhead, wearing slightly too much makeup. One arm was covered in tattoos like a sleeve and needle marks littered her other arm.

"I want to make an appointment with Dr. Berkowitz," she told the psychiatrist's assistant.

The assistant was eating a turkey sandwich at her desk and discreetly hid it when she spoke. "Well, he isn't in private practice anymore. He mostly works within the police department."

The redhead's shoulders slumped. "Oh, I see."

The assistant wiped her mouth with a napkin and observed how disappointed the other woman was. "He does take some civilian patients on occasion. But you'd have to talk to him about it."

"Can I ask a few questions about him first regarding privacy?"

"Of course."

The redhead cleared her throat self-consciously. "Where does he keep his records, his case files? Here? In the police station?" The redhead hid her needle-marked arm behind her.

The assistant caught her drift.

"Oh no," she assured the other woman. "He keeps his files offsite."

"Then he has another office that I could go to that's— not here?" the redhead asked hopefully.

The assistant shook her head and lowered her voice. "He doesn't have a separate office. His files are kept at his home. So you don't have to worry about a thing."

The redhead nodded gratefully. "Thank you."

"Do you want an appointment to chat with Dr. B?"

"I'll get back to you on that."

The redhead turned away and exited the office. Shrugging, the assistant went back to her sandwich.

ONCE THE REDHEAD was out in the parking lot, she got inside a new BMW and drove out into the street. As she drove, she pulled off her red-haired wig and rubbed off the fake drug "tracks" she'd painted on that morning. She rolled the thin mesh tattoo sleeve off her other arm. By the time she reached the first traffic light, the redhead was transformed back into Victor Archwood, save for some mascara and the harsh blue eye shadow he'd brushed on above his eyes.

GABRIEL ARRIVED five minutes late to the mandatory class on evidence handling. The evidence-planting scandal had caused such a storm throughout the Sheriff's Department that every known bureaucrat was using it to flex muscle and make a good show for the voters. That meant that the homicide bureau was littered with pamphlets on proper police procedures and various protocols. It also meant that the officers were made to sign dozens of legal documents and sit through U.S. Department of Justice seminars like this one. The bureaucracy was ponderous, and everyone was going to feel the weight.

Jonelle Williams had saved a seat for Gabriel. He tried not to look her over as he sat down next to her, but he did regard her—she was his new partner, after all. Jonelle met his appraisal with a somewhat haughty, defensive expression on her face. Gabriel figured she had her preconceived notions of the average white male cop, and although he did not consider himself bigoted, he was not going to be overly polite just to appease Jonelle's automatic assumption of racism.

He did thank her for saving the seat though, and her defensive posture dissolved a little.

As Gabriel listened to the moderator drone on and on, he felt like he was in high school again. How many cases had he worked on? It was humiliating to sit here with his thumb up his ass when he could have a real case that needed his attention.

"Let's review the principles, policies, and procedures," the moderator said. "Principle One: the handling of evidence is one of the most important factors of the investigation."

Bored, Gabriel thumbed through the pamphlet that was given to every attendee. He quickly realized that the moderator was following the pamphlet word for word. The information contained within was nothing Gabriel didn't already know. He looked over at Jonelle. Her plus-sized figure filled the seat as she listened intently and took careful notes.

"Policy," the moderator continued. "Our policy is that the team member shall ensure the effective collection, preservation, packaging, and transport of evidence."

Gabriel rolled his eyes. Criminals like Archwood could get away with murder while everyone else ran with their tail between their legs, trying to emulate Dudley Do-Right.

By the time the seminar was over, traces of Gabriel's old anger began surfacing again; only this time, he didn't fight it. He let it creep right in and settle comfortably in his body.

"How're you holding up?" Jonelle asked as they exited the class.

"Fine," was his noncommittal answer.

Jonelle paused to remove her jacket in the warm air. The Santa Ana breeze drifted up and rippled at her blouse. She was a buxom woman, not fat, but big. Her hair was wavy, and she wore it loose to her wide shoulders. "So I guess we'll be workin' together."

"I guess." Gabriel surveyed Jonelle once more, trying to imagine how agile she'd be if confronted with a violent suspect.

Jonelle donned a pair of Oakley sunglasses and looked back at Gabriel. At least, he supposed she was eyeballing him through her dark lenses.

"One thing I stick by," she finally said as the sun glinted off a gold bicuspid in her mouth. "Our case information is going to be clear, concise, and well documented. We can't forget to note any of our observations or actions."

Gabriel took a controlled breath. Jonelle was more than playing by the book. She was the book, and it was all Victor Archwood's fault.

She continued. "I don't take chances on being wrong. I will carefully evaluate search-and-seizure issues to determine the necessity of obtaining a search warrant. I follow all protocols regarding tagging and bagging evidence."

The anger flared, and Gabriel barked at her. "I've been in law enforcement for twenty fucking years, Jonelle. I don't need you or any asinine class to remind me how to do my job."

"Is that a fact?" she asked, and the haughtiness was back, on her features and in her voice. "Well, it seems the job you did landed us both into the 'asinine' class."

Touché.

Gabriel kept his eyes on her. Finally, he nodded. "I'm

not the enemy. If you treat me like one, it's going to get in the way."

His cell phone rang, and he answered it. "McRay."

"Uncle Gabe?"

That brought a smile to Gabriel's face. "Hey, Liam. What are you doing?"

"Calling you!" his nephew replied, as if Gabriel had asked a stupid question. "Where are you right now?"

"I'm working." Gabriel glanced at Jonelle. "Are you excited to come see me?"

"Yeah! I can't wait!"

Gabriel heard Janet in the background, saying something about taking too much of Gabriel's time.

"Tell your mom it's okay." Gabriel could hear Liam arguing with his mother.

Finally Liam returned to the line, flustered. "I gotta go, Uncle Gabe."

"Bye, Liam."

But the line had already been disconnected. Gabriel returned his phone to his pocket.

"You got a kid?" Jonelle asked.

"My nephew," Gabriel told her. "My sister is bringing him and my niece here for a visit."

"How old is your nephew?"

"Nine."

"I got a ten-year-old. Name's Trevor." She pulled out her phone, moved her fingers swiftly over the screen, and then held it out. On the phone Gabriel saw a bright-eyed, good-looking boy holding a skateboard.

"Looks like a nice kid," he told Jonelle and then smirked at her. "Must take after his father."

The corners of Jonelle's mouth turned down until she realized Gabriel was kidding.

"Very funny," she commented as she put away her phone. "But if you knew his daddy, you wouldn't want Trevor taking after him."

Gabriel didn't question his new partner further about her personal life. It wasn't necessary. The ice between them had been broken.

CHAPTER EIGHTEEN

G abriel waited on a chair outside Dr. B's office and thumbed through a magazine. He never read celebrity rags, but this was the only periodical available. He was bored, eyed his wristwatch, and then continued turning the pages. On a page entitled "About the Town," he saw a photo of Victor Archwood preening for the cameras. Holding his hand was a pretty African American girl.

Shaking his head, Gabriel read the brief paragraph and learned that Archwood was starring in a play and receiving rave reviews. The article also mentioned that Archwood was remodeling a property in the "mountains outside of Los Angeles," building his dream home. He was also constructing a home for his mother Natalie in Burlingame, a tony suburb of San Francisco.

Just a gem of a guy, Gabriel thought derisively. It infuriated him that he'd put his life on the line to capture the

Malibu Canyon Murderer, only to find the killer free and of all the uncanny things, popular.

DR. B POKED his head out the door and greeted Gabriel warmly. "Come on in, stranger."

Gabriel brought the magazine in with him.

"Sorry, I made you wait," Dr. B said, "I was on the phone with Isaac."

Isaac was Dr. B's son, and Gabriel knew how much his therapist liked being a father. Dr. B poured two glasses of water and handed one to Gabriel.

"I figure we've got much to talk about. It's been a while since we last met." Dr. B took a seat in his chair. "Maybe we should discuss what happened at the trial."

Fuming, Gabriel shoved the article under Dr. B's nose. "This is what happened at the trial,"

Dr. B read the article and Gabriel saw his shoulders stiffen. "You have a right to feel frustrated."

"Don't people realize who he is?" Gabriel stabbed an angry finger on the magazine's glossy page. "What he's about? He killed seven people!"

"The public doesn't see Victor Archwood as a guilty man," Dr. B replied. "They see a good-looking, charismatic guy whose infamy only adds to his mystique."

"Building his dream home," Gabriel sneered in sarcasm. "Building it in the mountains where he butchered his victims. How could they acquit him? They saw the autopsy photos. They know what he did to those people. What kind of justice system do we have?"

"We have the best judicial system in the world."

"The hell we do."

"We do," Dr. B assured Gabriel, although his tense shoulders told a different story. "The jury had reasonable doubt, and that's the end of it. And you know why he was acquitted."

Gabriel knew.

Dr. B took a sip of water and regarded his patient. "Is there a reason you haven't brought up Dash?"

"Why would I?"

"Well, we're talking about the acquittal..."

Gabriel sat in his usual armchair and thought about seeing his best friend in a prison uniform, knowing his career lay in ruins.

Dr. B cocked his head at his patient. "What are you thinking?"

"I'm thinking it sucks. There's no other word for it."

"Archwood isn't doing anything unexpected," Dr. B said. "Playing up to the media, suing the city for money. It stinks, but it's no surprise, is it?"

"I guess not."

"You are angry with him, but could some of that anger be misplaced?"

"Misplaced?" Gabriel asked testily. "Are you kidding?"

Dr. B regarded Gabriel with his luminous brown eyes, made slightly bigger by his lenses. "Are you sure you haven't made Dash into another one of Archwood's victims?"

Gabriel glared back at the psychiatrist. "Let me tell you something. Everyone in this city is a potential victim of Victor Archwood now that he's free. He's nuts,

Raymond; and on top of that, he knows how to hold a grudge."

GABRIEL DROVE BACK TO COMMERCE, angry and unable to vent. That photo of Archwood smiling, tipping an imaginary hat to the paparazzi... The frustration sizzled in in his belly. Archwood was building a house?

Not one, but two...

Gnawing at his lower lip, Gabriel entered the bureau and stormed into Ramirez's office.

"I want to get a brief detail to track Victor Archwood," Gabriel announced to his superior.

"Damn, McRay, you really do need a psychologist."

"He's bound to crack," Gabriel told him. "He can't keep up the facade of a law-abiding citizen for too long."

Ramirez sat behind his desk, a stern look sweeping over his features. He was of mixed blood, part *indigeno de Mexico*, with an aquiline nose, dark eyes, and darker hair.

"McRay," he began, "Don't act stupid. Every cop in this place would like nothing better than to see that *pendejo* fall down and die, but we can't touch him. It's bad enough we're dealing with this shit..." Ramirez held up a protocol pamphlet regarding tagging and bagging items in the evidence room. "What I don't need is Archwood filing a harassment lawsuit too. You stay away from him."

Gabriel shook his head.

"I'm not asking you, McRay," his lieutenant told him. "I'm telling you. Leave Archwood alone."

With one last resentful look toward Ramirez, Gabriel exited the office.

HIS OLD PARTNER rotted in jail. His new partner seemed like a bitch, and Archwood was a free man with celebrity status and a cute girlfriend. Somehow the world was turning on a bizarre axis, and Gabriel feared he might fall off the edge.

As he headed toward his desk, he saw Wendy Pennington waiting in the lobby area. Gabriel considered ducking away but was too late. The woman had spied him and now strode over.

"I thought you were going to follow up on my sister's death. Isn't that your job?"

He kept walking, but the woman remained glued to his side.

"My job is to investigate homicides, Miss Pennington. Now, I am truly sorry for your loss, but your sister OD'd."

"Todd killed her."

"There's no indication of that."

"He did it."

Gabriel took a seat at his desk. "Alright. How?"

"That's fucking your job to find out how, not mine."

Gabriel felt his blood boil. This woman was preventing him from getting on the computer and buying theater tickets. Despite Ramirez's warning, Gabriel planned on watching Victor Archwood in action tonight, and he did not need this wasted-looking female talking to him about how to perform his job.

"The case is closed, Miss Pennington."

She huffed and threw her purse over her shoulder. "Well, you're just one more useless cop, aren't you?"

"Thank you," he said as he opened his laptop.

"She was clean!" she yelled into his face. "She did not OD!"

Gabriel looked up at April's sister and tried to keep his tone calm. "It is what it is."

Wendy Pennington regarded him through red-rimmed eyes, her irises black holes in their yellowed whites. Her lips, chapped and bloodless, and her messy hair gave her the appearance of a homeless bag lady. Behind the rough-hewn street exterior, Gabriel read a lost hope, one more slam from an unkind world.

And he'd been the one to deliver the blow.

Starring Victor Archwood.

Gabriel grimaced as he read the program. He sat in a seat in the Pantages Theatre, waiting for the musical, *Anything Goes*, to begin.

I must be in some parallel universe, Gabriel thought. An upside-down world where killers turn into celebrities and cops go to prison.

Could some of your anger be misplaced?

Who cares? Gabriel silently answered Dr. B's question. The lights went down then, and the orchestra began to play the overture.

A couple of songs later, Gabriel's nemesis took the stage, singing and dancing as Billy Crocker. One couldn't argue against the blond man's talent; only Gabriel recalled how talented Archwood had been with a knife.

Through each scene, through both acts, Archwood seemed as if he hadn't a care in the world. Worst of all, the audience seemed to adore him. Once or twice, Gabriel imagined he saw Archwood's eyes alight on him, and it made his skin crawl. Of course, it was impossible that a performer could focus on a particular audience member in the big venue. Still, Gabriel desired only to see and not be seen, so he hunkered low into his seat.

At the end of Act One, a middle-aged woman sitting next to Gabriel clapped euphorically and exclaimed out loud, "Go, Victor! Yeah!"

The woman abruptly quit clapping when she happened to catch Gabriel glaring at her with fiery eyes.

During intermission, Gabriel stood sullenly near the bar and nursed a whiskey. He overheard a young couple mention Archwood's name.

"It's amazing how productive he's being with his life," the woman said.

"I know," her companion agreed. "Not everybody can get over being screwed by the police."

By the time the character of Reno Sweeney broke into "Blow, Gabriel, Blow," Gabriel truly was about to blow. He refused to stand by while a serial killer took bows amidst applause. Wishing he hadn't come, Gabriel left the theater before the curtain call.

HE RETURNED to his new home and promptly slammed his car keys down upon the kitchen counter. Irritated as hell, he stormed across his living room with a raised fist, wanting nothing more than to punch a hole into the drywall and vent his pent-up rage.

A voice of reason, stronger than his anger, halted him a foot before he hit his mark. Gabriel slowly uncurled his fist and placed his palm upon the wall. After a moment, he rested his forehead against the cool plaster.

What would Liam and Amber think of their uncle acting like a child himself? He was now a sane and rational man who no longer used his fists to express himself. Taking a deep breath, Gabriel moved away from the wall and retreated to his bedroom.

Did you really want to damage your new house—the expression of a new self?

Of course he didn't want to damage his house. This was good, Gabriel told himself. He was angry, but he was handling it.

And Archwood is building not one, but two houses.

I'm *handling* it, Gabriel reminded himself and wondered if he should take a sleeping pill. No, he hated the thought of using drugs to appease his frustrations. But the thought of Victor Archwood as a man-about-town made Gabriel seethe. He knew he wouldn't be able to handle it for very long.

THE FOLLOWING EVENING the source of Gabriel's

frustration, Victor Archwood, dabbed on some tanning makeup, which instantly darkened his normally pale skin. He covered his light blue eyes with brown contact lenses and then used mascara to blacken his eyebrows and lashes. Finally, he donned a wig of short black hair. Peeling off his shirt, he strapped a thick pad over his abdomen, making his normally flat stomach look paunchy. Over this, he donned a cheap white shirt and a black vest. Viewing himself in the mirror, he winked at his reflection and then headed out the door.

He drove to the Meatery, an old-time steak restaurant on Pico Boulevard. It was a favorite haunt of Dr. Raymond Berkowitz, better known as Dr. B. In fact, the doctor and his wife had a standing reservation every other Saturday night at the Meatery. A creature of habit, Dr. B was incredibly easy to track.

Victor waited in the shadows of the parking lot, and without fail, Dr. B pulled up in his Prius. The psychiatrist handed his keys to the valet, who then drove off with the car. Thankfully the Meatery was a popular place, and one car after another lined up for valet parking, keeping the valets too busy to notice a stranger among them.

Vic waited for an opportune moment and then plucked Dr. B's keys from the valet rack. As he'd hoped, there were at least three keys on the ring—one of them had to be a house key.

Vic jogged over to the parked Prius, unlocked the car, and opened the glove box. The registration and proof of insurance were inside. Tailing Dr. B had shown Vic what neighborhood the doctor lived in—a nice gated community—but Vic needed the exact house number. He made note of the address and relocked the car. He glanced behind him toward the restaurant.

Dr. B usually spent a good two hours at the Meatery, but Vic would waste no time. He hopped into his own car and drove directly to the good doctor's home.

Getting past the security at the guard gate was no problem. Vic had simply called the gate beforehand, impersonated the doctor, and instructed the guards to permit a Miguel Ramirez to enter. Vic had created a passable ID for the night, but security didn't even ask for identification.

They let "Ramirez" right in.

Victor parked a little way down from the Berkowitz home and then, after making sure no snooping neighbors were about, he donned a pair of latex gloves and then opened the front door with the key. He searched around and entered a room filled with books and a desk. Vic sat down and accessed Dr. B's computer.

The database where Dr. B stored his patient files was password protected. Following Sergio's instructions, Victor inserted a USB flash drive and ran a password cracking software called Cracker Jack. In less than three minutes it came up with a match: Isaac1.

Not a very strong password, Dr. B.

Now that he had the password, Victor entered it and scanned through the files. It didn't take long before he found what he was looking for: the complete case file on Detective Sergeant Gabriel McRay. Victor downloaded the entire file onto a separate flash drive.

Later, Victor drove back to the restaurant to return the keys to the valet's rack. He glanced through the restaurant's window to see the doctor seated next to his wife and talking animatedly to another couple. Victor smiled under his disguise. Still on his main course, Dr. B had no idea that his private world had just been infiltrated.

CHAPTER NINETEEN

Gabriel walked a good distance behind Victor Archwood as the younger man perused the various furniture showrooms at the Pacific Design Center. Apparently, Archwood was at the decorating stage of his remodeling. The thought of that fueled Gabriel's ire.

He knew what he was doing was risky. He knew Ramirez would ream him for it, but Gabriel could not resist. He was baffled by Archwood's ability to maintain his composure and was sure the killer would soon crack.

A young, attractive African American woman accompanied Archwood as he strolled around. At times, she'd walk alongside him. Other times she would bounce ahead like a cheerleader and enter one of the showrooms to eagerly point out some interesting adornment. Gabriel recognized her from the magazine photo with Archwood. He wondered who she was and why she would keep company with a murderer.

They were walking down a particularly boring stretch of stalls when Archwood glanced backward. Gabriel, feeling inept, ducked into a showroom selling lamps. He bided his time and then peered around the corner. Archwood was gone. Gabriel slowly reemerged and made his way down the hall. He peeked into every showroom but did not see the other man.

"May I help you?" a saleswoman called from the showroom across the way. She stood hopeful amid displays of Turkish glassware.

Gabriel shook his head.

Knowing he could get into trouble for following Archwood, Gabriel sighed and figured this was all for the best. As his eyes searched for an exit, he felt a tap on his left shoulder. He turned around to see Victor Archwood standing behind him.

"What a coincidence," the blond man said. "Running into you here."

Caught, Gabriel could only stare at the other man.

Archwood's lips curled into a grin. "You wouldn't be following me, would you?"

Heat reddened Gabriel's face, but he answered boldly, "I guess it's a free country. This is a public place."

"No, not really open to the public. You must have used your shiny sheriff's star to get in. I used a friend's resale number." Archwood leaned in close to Gabriel and asked in a low voice, "You won't arrest me for that, will you?"

Gabriel took an involuntary step backward. "Not under my jurisdiction."

The pretty girl walked up then, and Archwood slipped

an arm around her waist. "This is my girlfriend, Andrea Leighton." He smiled down at her. "This is Detective Sergeant McRay. You remember him from the trial, don't you, Dre?"

Andrea gave Gabriel a little low-slung wave, her arm tight against her body while her hand manically fanned the air in front of her. "Hi!"

"I think he's following us," Archwood confided to her.

Gabriel frowned at the other man, refusing to be intimidated.

Archwood continued, "Yep, I'm pretty sure we've been followed since we left the hotel. Gosh, Sergeant, next time don't be so obvious."

Unable to come up with an adequate retort, Gabriel shook his head and then brushed past the couple toward the elevator.

"I think maybe you're obsessed with me," Archwood called after him.

Andrea giggled. "That's understandable." She gave her boyfriend a peck on the cheek. "I'm obsessed with you too."

Archwood bent down and put his lips on Andrea's in a more intense kiss, only he kept his light eyes glued on Gabriel's retreating form.

BACK AT HIS desk in Commerce, Gabriel sat, his eyes closed. He pinched the bridge of his nose between thumb and forefinger and applied pressure. He was getting one helluva headache. He'd stupidly blown his cover, and now Archwood knew Gabriel was pursuing him.

Ramirez was right. Archwood could claim harassment.

I'd better let this go. Lord knows I don't want to, but I can't risk my job or anything else over Victor Archwood.

With a sigh, Gabriel reached out to a stack of papers waiting for him. What a fiasco. As he penned his signature on more documents from various state regulatory agencies, a call came through on his extension.

He eyed the phone warily. Had Archwood already filed his complaint?

"Detective McRay," Gabriel said as he picked up. He tried to keep the anxiety out of his voice.

"Detective, this is Mrs. Funston, Patrick's mother."

Gabriel swallowed in relief. Patrick Funston had been one of Archwood's victims. Gabriel knew Patrick's mother fairly well. Every homicide detective forged a tragic bond with the family of murder victims.

"How are you, Mrs. Funston?"

"Can we retry him?"

She was speaking of Victor Archwood, and Gabriel could hear tears behind her words.

"My husband says we can't," she continued. "But I wanted to hear it from you."

Gabriel said as gently as he could, "You can still try him in civil court for wrongful death."

"But we'd have to pay for the lawyers, right?"

"I believe so."

He knew the Funstons were struggling. They had scraped together enough money to send Patrick to college in hopes of giving him a better life. A wonderful student, he had repaid them by making them continually proud. He had been their only child too.

Gabriel listened as Patrick's mother grieved to him, knowing he was powerless to help her any further. When the call ended, Gabriel felt so twisted up inside that he realized he'd crunched up a Department of Justice paper in his hand.

He spread it out and tried in vain to press out the wrinkles. The damaged paper somehow brought Wendy Pennington's timeworn face to mind.

Suddenly, Gabriel stopped what he was doing, got up, and went to find the closed file on April Pennington.

When he returned to his desk, he opened the file before he could change his mind and reread Ming's autopsy report.

The epidemiologic findings are most consistent with the hypothesis that malignant arrhythmias occurred during maximal cocaine concentrations that increased concentrations of circulating catecholamines.

Jesus, Gabriel muttered to himself. He turned to his laptop and looked up the definition of catecholamines. Hormones—like adrenaline, he read. Gabriel then flipped through more of Ming's report.

Additionally, tachycardia alone may be sufficient to trigger a reentrant rhythm in a susceptible host. Cocaine may have also caused ischemia and infarction. Ischemia and infarction may have resulted in the dispersion of repolarization, which then created a substrate for arrhythmia.

Gabriel blew out a deep breath and looked up the

meaning of ischemia... Restriction of blood supply causing a lack of oxygen.

A trace amount of ouabain has been identified in the vitreous gel of the eye, signaling hyperkalemia.

Okay, what is hyperkalemia? Gabriel researched the word and saw it meant a seriously abnormal increase in potassium, which can increase the chance of irregular heartbeats or arrhythmia.

In the past, ouabain was used to assist in cardiac medical procedures, but it can also occur naturally in patients with cardiac issues. It is also the principal chemical in a compound called Acokanthera.

Turning once again to the Internet, Gabriel looked up Acokanthera and learned it was a compound found in plants. He also learned that it was poisonous. Somali tribesmen used doses of ouabain as poison for their arrows. The poison could stop a hippopotamus in its tracks, causing it to die from cardiac arrest. Analysis of some of the poison arrows yielded as much as five grams of ouabain on one small arrow tip.

Only 0.002 grams of ouabain were needed to kill a human being.

"I picked those up in Somalia."

Remembering Mr. King's words, Gabriel felt his own heartbeat quicken. He reviewed Ming's report again. Nothing more was found in the dead girl's body except for traces of antihistamines.

"Very sly," Gabriel said aloud.

One side effect of antihistamines is that they can suppress nausea. Gabriel knew that clever murderers gave their victims antihistamines because...

Poisons cause vomiting.

GABRIEL BUNDLED ALL the papers together haphazardly. He took the now-bulging file to Ramirez's office and knocked on the door.

"Hey, McRay," Ramirez called from his desk. "You and your partner ready for a case now?"

"I've got one," Gabriel replied and placed April Pennington's file on his lieutenant's desk.

CHAPTER TWENTY

E than Post sat in a chair and waited in the lobby of the coroner's office outside L.A. County General. His longish, light brown hair was tied back in a ponytail, and he wore a neatly trimmed beard and mustache.

Dr. Ming Li entered the lobby and extended her hand to the young man.

"Ethan?"

He stood up and shook her hand with a smile. "Dr. Li. Nice to meet you."

"You are my Cal State intern, correct?"

"The one and only."

Ethan had a gentle Bostonian accent. With his John Lennon round wire rims and a corduroy jacket, he reminded Ming of the quintessential bookworm graduate student.

"Great," Ming said. "So you aspire to be a forensic anthropologist, huh? Well, we get our fair share of bones around here. Come on, let's get you suited up."

A little later, Ming took Ethan into a large space affectionately known as the decomp room and introduced the intern to her deputy coroner, Geoffrey.

"Ethan is going to be with us while he works on his thesis," Ming explained.

After looking Ethan up and down, Geoffrey seemed legitimately pleased. "I went to Cal State LA myself," he told Ethan. "Good program. One of the top in the country."

"That's why I chose it."

Geoffrey led Ethan to a table on which lay a partially fleshed corpse.

"Who is it?" Ethan asked him.

Geoffrey shrugged. "Unidentified."

Ethan's eyes traveled the length of the corpse. "Is it a man? Woman?"

Ming chimed in. "Hard to tell with all that fat and flesh still adhering to the bones, isn't it? How are we supposed to know how protruding a cheekbone is or how large the supraorbital torus is until you take off the skin?"

Ming winked at Geoffrey as she handed Ethan a scalpel. "So have at it!"

～

AT FOUR O'CLOCK, Geoffrey peered into Ming's office. "Uh, how long do you want to let your guy work over that body?"

Ming's eyes widened in surprise. "Oh my God. I forgot he was here!"

Ming rushed into the decomp room and saw Ethan still slicing tissue away from the body. She felt bad, hearing his stomach growl.

"I'm a terrible taskmaster," she told him apologetically. "You didn't have lunch, did you?"

He shook his head and looked down at the shredded corpse. "It's okay. I'm not too hungry."

Ming laughed. "I'm so sorry. Please go home."

"Could I take you out to dinner instead?" Ethan smiled.

"I'll take you. It's the least I can do." Ming turned toward Geoffrey. "Would you mind cleaning up?"

Geoffrey surveyed the mess Ethan had made and then reluctantly nodded his head.

ETHAN INSISTED on buying the wine at dinner, and Ming relaxed for the first time since the trial. Like her, Ming's intern had a strong stomach and could eat heartily while discussing the effects of weather on the decomposition of a human body.

Ming found Ethan to be charming, sharp, and intuitive. His respect for her work was a flattering escape from somber Gabriel, who lately wanted to focus more on Victor Archwood than on Ming.

"I'M a little surprised to see you here again, Detective."

Mr. Todd King stood with Gabriel and Jonelle in what

he called his great room, which Gabriel would have called a living room. Once again, Gabriel observed the African art, the tidy and orderly decor.

"We have a few more questions relating to the deceased," Jonelle told the younger man.

Gabriel eyed his new partner carefully. Jonelle was not about to play good cop, and that threw him off balance. Dash would have made light, innocuous conversation to put Mr. King at ease, to ready his underbelly for Gabriel's verbal dissection. Now it appeared that Gabriel would have to find new footing after all these years. He had a game plan that he'd shared with Jonelle, one Gabriel hoped she would follow, but now he had his doubts.

"May we sit down?" He asked Mr. King.

The man looked around impatiently. "Is this going to take long, I have a lot of—"

"We have a few questions," Jonelle insisted.

Mr. King reluctantly gestured to a couple of chairs. The two detectives took their seats. Gabriel made a formal introduction of his partner Jonelle and then said, "I wanted to ask you about the products you bring into Somalia."

"I don't 'bring them in,'" Mr. King countered. "They are shipped by the organization I work for."

"Medical supplies, correct?" Gabriel asked.

"Who is your contact in Somalia?" Jonelle blurted as she pulled out her notepad and a pen.

Again, Gabriel regarded Jonelle. Dash would have allowed Gabriel to keep on the medical supplies track.

"I really don't understand what this has to do with April's death," Mr. King said.

"Your contact's name, please?" Jonelle pressed.

Mr. King crossed his legs; crossed his arms. "Mr. Abdi Ismail Samatar of Mogadishu. I'd have to look up his contact information."

Determined to get back on the medical supplies track, Gabriel said, "I'd imagine, Mr. King, that you must know something about these medicines you're supplying."

"Of course." The younger man brightened. Apparently, the subject excited him. "We're trained to answer questions regarding the items we bring. It's all aboveboard, you know."

"Of course," Gabriel used his words. "You must exchange interesting anecdotes with your English-speaking friends. I'll bet you compare your modern medicines to their homemade treatments."

"Actually, we do."

Gabriel nodded at the other man and remained silent. Jonelle observed this interchange and, after glancing at Gabriel, she said, "In return for some of these supplies, what do you get?"

Good, Gabriel thought appreciatively.

"Things like that." Mr. King pointed to what appeared to be a small, ornately carved wooden stool.

"Doesn't look very sturdy to sit on," Jonelle commented.

"It's actually a headrest," Mr. King explained. "And you are right. It isn't sturdy. It's not meant to offer a good rest. Would you like to see it, Detective?"

He picked up the headrest and handed it to Jonelle.

She hefted it in her hands and they heard the works

rattle inside. Worried she'd broken it, Jonelle handed it carefully back to Mr. King.

"It's very delicate," she told him.

Mr. King nodded. "They say the man who possesses it is known to have the ability to wake to action. With something so unstable, one is always alert."

He gave Gabriel a small, smug smile.

He's hiding something, Gabriel knew. It was all over that conceited face of his.

"Do they trade you anything besides art?" Jonelle pressed.

"Jewelry, little homemade things. Can I ask what this has to do with police business?"

Gabriel stood up and addressed Mr. King, "May I trouble you for a glass of water?"

Mr. King looked at his watch again and then nodded toward the kitchen. "Help yourself. There's Evian in the fridge."

"Would you like some Evian water, Detective Williams?" Gabriel asked her.

Jonelle shook her head and gave Gabriel a curious look, wondering what he was up to.

Gabriel walked into the kitchen and tried to compare the current topography to that of the coroner's photos. No dark granules were anywhere to be seen, and Gabriel took his time to view everything as he got his water bottle. The kitchen looked practically unused. Even the crockery hanging from the rack over the kitchen island looked brand new and was spaced evenly.

On his way out, Gabriel paused before a desk stacked with notes and mail. He looked around and, making sure he was alone, let his fingers separate the envelopes. He spied three letters from the same life insurance company. He made a mental note of the company name and then returned to the living room.

Gabriel held up the water to Mr. King as a gesture of thanks.

Jonelle was speaking. "So Mr. King, when was your last trip to Somalia?"

The dapper young man's mouth hinged open in exasperation. "Right before April died. You know that. I had just come home, remember?"

Gabriel took a sip of water. "How long did you and April do drugs together?"

The sudden change of subject caught Mr. King off guard. His mouth twitched. A subtle gesture, but Gabriel caught it.

"I believe I told you that we went to rehab. I don't do—"

"You both were in rehab?" Jonelle chimed in.

"Yes, we—"

Jonelle continued, "And when was that? What month, year?"

Mr. King looked up at the ceiling. "Uhh… I think it was—"

"Where did you go?" Gabriel leaned forward. "What facility?"

"Cliffside in Malibu," Mr. King answered, distracted. Apparently, he was still trying to muster up the dates of the rehab stay.

"How long did you two go for?" Jonelle asked.

"We went for sixty days. I think it was in September of—"

"Then how long have you both been clean?" Gabriel asked.

"Two years," Mr. King blurted out with annoyance.

Gabriel nodded. Jonelle's full lips pursed together.

LATER AS THEY were getting into their unmarked car, Jonelle asked Gabriel, "If Mr. King was clean, how come he would put up with a girlfriend that went back on drugs?"

"She didn't go back on drugs," Gabriel reminded her. "According to him, they've been clean for two years, remember?"

"That's what the man said, didn't he?" Jonelle smiled. "And if she wasn't on drugs, then she couldn't have died from an overdose."

"Right." Gabriel started up the car. "She had coke in her system, but it wasn't enough to kill her. I'd lay bets he injected April with cocaine after she was dead. He did it to cover for something he didn't think would be found."

"The ouabain."

Gabriel agreed, and as they pulled away from the house, he told Jonelle about the life insurance letters.

His partner raised her penciled eyebrows. "Pretty gutsy of you to search his place without a warrant."

"I wasn't searching. I was getting water and keeping my eyes open."

'So what's next?"

"What's next is to get a warrant to search the premises," Gabriel told her. "He's arrogant. Maybe arrogant enough to think he doesn't have to cover his tracks. That's what I'm betting on."

"How'd he do it though?" Jonelle asked. "Her prints were on the syringe."

In his mind's eye, Gabriel saw Wendy Pennington.

It's your job to find out how.

CHAPTER TWENTY-ONE

On the day Janet was to arrive, Gabriel was held up downtown, petitioning the court for a warrant to search Mr. King's home. Janet planned on renting a car, so he sent a text message with directions to his home from the airport.

Before leaving for downtown, he hid a key for his sister, made up the beds, and put a couple of new toys out for the kids. He left instructions on how to use his ridiculously complicated television that Ming had insisted on buying him.

On the way home from the courthouse, Gabriel stopped at the market. He planned on cooking dinner, and he picked up a few items including some kid-friendly food. Finally Gabriel pulled into his garage and jumped out of the car.

"Hey!" he called, opening the door leading into his home.

The place was surprisingly quiet. Gabriel put the

grocery bags down in the kitchen and looked around. He had been expecting an avalanche of attention with the kids jumping on him. He poked around, but the house was empty. Gabriel checked his cell phone and saw he had a message. He accessed his voice mail. Maybe they had missed their plane.

Listening to the message, he learned that Janet was staying at Shutters, a hotel near the beach. Gabriel quickly called the hotel and was transferred to her room.

"Hi," Janet answered on the first ring. In the background, Gabriel could hear the children talking and behind that, the television cartoon sounds he'd expected to hear in his own home.

"What are you doing?" Gabriel asked, perplexed.

"I decided to come here. I didn't want to put you out."

Gabriel scratched his head in confusion. "You're not staying here? I kind of planned on it."

"You're busy with your work and everything. It's no problem, Gabe. We're fine here."

Gabriel didn't reply. Disappointment stifled his speech.

"Do you want to meet for dinner?" Janet asked.

Gabriel glanced back into the kitchen at the grocery bags. "Why, Janet?"

"Why what?"

"Why didn't you come here like we planned?"

"I thought we'd be less of a burden at a hotel. I have a rental car. Why don't we meet—"

"I was planning to make you guys dinner. A barbeque. I mean I have the whole place set up for you."

"We'll come over for dinner," she assured him. "Give me half an hour."

OUTSIDE, the kids tore up the grass with their shoes. The backyard had undergone quite a change from its previous neglect, and the smell of a new wood fence, fresh grass, and jasmine filled the evening air.

Gabriel turned steaks on his new barbeque. Janet sat on one of the new patio chairs sipping a glass of wine.

Gabriel eyed his sister. His confusion had turned into hurt, and from there it had evolved into annoyance. He tried, however, to keep his tone amicable.

"You don't have to pay for a hotel. I made the place ready for you and the kids."

The children, keeping one ear on the adult conversation, immediately reacted to their uncle's invitation.

"I wanna stay here!" Liam shouted.

Amber raced over to her mother's side. "Please, Mommy, can we stay?"

"I think it's easier on Uncle Gabe if we—"

"It's fine," Gabriel interrupted as he stabbed the sizzling steaks with a fork.

Janet surveyed her brother. "We'll see you every day, Gabe, but we're already settled at the hotel."

Amber started crying.

"Cut that out, Amber," Janet commanded.

"You're mean!" Liam yelled at his mother.

"Okay, we're leaving now." She grabbed Amber by the arm as Gabriel stared dumbfounded at her.

"What's your problem, Janet?"

"I'm tired, okay? It's been a long day. Someday when you have kids you'll know what I'm talking about."

Amber's crying escalated.

Gabriel left the steaks, picked Amber up, and said gently, "Don't cry."

The little girl buried her face in his neck and held on to him.

Janet plucked Amber from Gabriel. "I knew they'd be overtired."

As Amber shrieked, Janet grabbed Liam's hand and moved into the house. "We'll see you tomorrow after a good night's sleep."

"I don't wanna go!' Liam cried, and his mother yanked his arm.

"I wanna stay here!" Amber sobbed and reached out her arm over her mother's shoulder toward Gabriel, who wasn't sure what he should do.

Janet wore a steely expression. "We'll talk in the morning."

Gabriel watched as they drove away. When he was alone again, he could do nothing else but save the steaks from burning. He had, however, lost his appetite.

IN HIS HOTEL SUITE, Victor Archwood reclined on his bed, holding his laptop and perusing a file on Gabriel McRay. This one was a good read, the transcript of a taped therapy session in which Gabriel had been hypnotized. Gabriel was reciting that his neighbor Andrew

Pierce had just molested him for the first time, and Pierce was threatening Gabriel not to tell anyone.

"*And if you do tell,*" *Andrew Pierce had told the little boy,* "*I'll drown your ma and pa and sister in my pool. Then you'll go into a foster home and nobody will talk to you. They'll know you told a secret that caused your family to die. And I, your only friend, will never speak to you again. So you'd better keep our secret, Little Buddy.*"

Victor lifted his eyes from the monitor. *Little Buddy...*

Victor had no conscious recollection of Gabriel ever touching him inappropriately, but then again, maybe he'd suppressed that memory just as Gabriel had suppressed the memory of Andrew Pierce.

It didn't matter, Victor thought with a grin. It was going to be a lot of fun to bring it all back for Detective McRay. This performance might just be Vic's masterpiece.

He lowered his eyes to the laptop once more and read that Andrew Pierce often chewed black licorice. Gabriel had developed a nervous phobia to the candy.

This is just too good...

The suite's doorbell rang, and Victor groaned. With his fingers, he swiped the page up to make it disappear from his monitor. He then shut his laptop and went to the door. Andrea bounded inside.

"Hi, baby," she called to him and gave him her perky little wave. "What are you doing?"

"Looking over some plans."

Andrea was content with his answer. She was always content with him.

· · ·

211

VIC TOOK her out to a café on Sunset where he listened to her recite what she did during the day. To be truthful, he only half listened because she bored him to tears. He was very adept at looking her straight in the eye and nodding as if he were interested. What he really did while she blathered on and on was take the opportunity to think and plan. The time served him well.

After they ate, Vic and Andrea returned to his suite to order a pay-per-view movie. As they lay on his bed, Andrea snuggled against his body. All Vic wanted to do, however, was return to his computer and read more of Gabriel's psychiatric file.

He felt Andrea's body curling close to his. She picked up his hand and played with his fingers. Vic had pale, tapering fingers—a musician's hands, Andrea liked to say. Hands that could make a classical guitar weep. She wanted those hands to play her like an instrument and often complained to Vic that he never gave her one hundred percent of himself. Even now, he heard her sighing with disappointment.

"What?" Vic asked, annoyed with her.

"I don't know..." Andrea pouted. "You're always so distracted."

Victor looked longingly toward his laptop, which waited for him across the room. *Delay, delay...*

"I want you to be yourself around me," Andrea told him.

Victor looked at her balefully. *Delete, delete...*

"I want to be close to you," she said in a childlike voice. "Let me in, Vic."

Victor watched his fingers as Andrea ran them softly along her full lips.

"Somebody wants attention," he stated.

Andrea rolled her eyes. "Not attention, exactly. It's more—"

Victor leaned over and closed her mouth with a kiss.

She wants to be let in.

Victor unbuttoned Andrea's blouse to reveal her full bust bulging out of the neon-pink bra she wore. He let his fingers move gracefully along her ample cleavage.

"Is this what you want?" he asked softly.

She murmured a response. He wasn't sure what she said. He didn't care, actually. He could operate like this, in the everyday world, but he had to keep a tight lid on his dark fantasies. There was another world to which he often retreated, the World of his Creation. In that world, Vic often reveled in what he would really like to do to Andrea Leighton.

Victor deftly unsnapped her bra, pulled it off her body, and tossed it aside. He knew that in time the temptation to fuse the two worlds together would become too much for him to bear. He would have no choice but to give in to the ultimate release.

Then I'll let you in, Andrea, he thought as he cupped one breast and ran his tongue in circles around her dark nipple.

Then I'll show you how to truly get close to me.

CHAPTER TWENTY-TWO

G abriel introduced Ming to his family while they visited Pacific Park on the Santa Monica Pier.

"You two should have a lot to talk about," Gabriel confided to Ming as they trailed Janet and the children through the aquarium.

"Why's that?"

"Janet was going to pursue a career in medicine," Gabriel told her and gave a nod toward his sister.

"What stopped her?" Ming asked.

"She chose to be a wife and mother instead."

Ming observed Janet walking ahead. "There are plenty of doctors who are also mothers."

"Yeah, but how can you really dedicate yourself to both? Besides, she didn't want some nanny raising her kids."

Ming paused and stared after Gabriel as he rejoined his sister and the two children. Was he insinuating that someone like Ming would have a stranger raise her children? What did he mean by bringing that up? And his remark about women being unable to dedicate themselves to two careers… What an old-fashioned, misogynistic statement! And yet her boyfriend seemed quite impressed with Janet's decision to forgo medical school.

In Ming's family, that decision would have been scandalous. Successful people pursued careers and excelled at them. She watched Gabriel laugh with his family and felt something go hollow inside her.

After the aquarium, they ate ice cream at the old-fashioned soda fountain and then did enough back-and-forths on Inkie's Pirate ship to make them regret eating.

They went up on the Pacific Ferris Wheel. As the ocean ebbed and flowed beneath them and the summer sun warmed them from above, Ming tried to engage Janet on the subject of medicine.

"If you like," Ming suggested, "I'm happy to show you what I do at the hospital."

Janet grimaced. "What makes you think I'd want to see dead people?"

"Well, I wouldn't show you that part of it," Ming assured her. "There's the forensic part of—"

"No thanks," Janet interrupted her and turned away to view the coastline.

Ming raised her delicate eyebrows in indignation and decided that she didn't care much for Gabriel's sister.

When they got off the ride, Amber tugged at her mother's shirt. "I have to go potty."

"I have to go too," Liam told Gabriel.

Gabriel gestured for Liam to follow him, but Janet took her son by the hand.

"It's okay, I'll take them both."

"I don't wanna go in the girl's bathroom," Liam said, pulling away. Janet grabbed his hand again and forced him along.

"It's just for a minute," she told her son.

Ming glanced at Gabriel, who watched them tread the wooden boardwalk to the restrooms.

To spare his feelings, Ming covered for Janet's behavior. "What an overprotective helicopter mom," she stated.

Gabriel did not respond, but he looked bewildered. Ming, fiercely protective over her lover, made a great effort throughout the day to avoid telling Janet off.

AT THE SAME TIME, in his suite at the Chateau Marmont, Victor was once again giving Andrea the attention she needed when the phone rang. Eager for a break, Victor picked it up from the bedside table.

He listened and then said, "Uh-huh. And it's fully soundproofed, right? Okay, wait." Victor grabbed a pen and a pad of paper with Chateau Marmont printed on it. He scribbled on the pad and caught Andrea looking at him. Victor rolled off the bed with the phone in hand.

"Okay, give it to me," he said as he moved into the bathroom.

Back on the bed, Andrea pouted, feeling neglected again. Hearing Vic speaking quietly, she rose and went to the bathroom door. She opened it wide and saw her boyfriend standing naked, hunched over the sink and studying the piece of paper.

His ass is so fine…

Andrea crept up behind him and peered over his shoulder. The paper was bare except for the number 8520. Victor, suddenly seeing her reflection in the mirror, crumbled the paper in his fist. He grabbed a lighter from where it lay on the bathtub near two candles and promptly lit the note on fire. He let it burn in the sink and immediately steered Andrea back into the bedroom.

"What's wrong?" she asked, giggling nervously. "What are you soundproofing?"

"I'm thinking of putting in a recording studio."

Andrea made a disbelieving face as she crawled back into bed. "Do you play?"

Victor seemed annoyed. "I plan on taking up the guitar. Or maybe I'll make a gym. Actually, it's too expensive; I'll probably toss the whole plan."

Andrea let it go, unwilling to risk making her boyfriend angry. Although Victor never hit her, never even yelled at her, Andrea could sense a storm brewing behind his eyes at times. The threat of thunder resided there, and something deep inside Andrea warned her to never allow that storm to unleash itself.

ARMED WITH A SEARCH WARRANT, Jonelle and Gabriel went through Mr. King's home.

"I don't really understand what you are looking for," Mr. King said in a tight voice.

"Well," Gabriel explained, "April's case involved illegal substances. This is more of a formality than anything else." He gave Mr. King a reassuring grin.

Something Dash would have done.

"We can tie this up, and we won't have to bother you any further," Gabriel added.

Mr. King made no response. He probably knew Gabriel's explanation was bull, but he wisely said nothing. He might have made their jobs easier by babbling nervously or running about hiding items, but instead, the man watched the detectives with a quiet reserve.

The investigators didn't know what the instrument of murder was, but Mr. King did. Given his controlled demeanor, Gabriel hoped he'd grow arrogant enough to reveal his secrets.

WHILE JONELLE HANDLED THE HOUSE, Gabriel inspected the garage. Like the house, the garage was orderly. White melamine closets lined both walls. The closets held the usual assortment of tools, brooms, fertilizers, cleaning supplies and a couple of gallons of paint.

Atop the closets sat labeled plastic containers: "Tax Returns 2009 to 2013," "Christmas," and "Halloween." An Audi, this year's model, sat gleaming in the middle of a clean, epoxy-coated floor.

This guy's garage is neater than my new house.

Gabriel stood wearing latex gloves on his hands and wondered what all the tight-assed structure was masking. He continued to open and inspect the closets, and while he did, he thought about his sister. He couldn't help it.

She doesn't trust me to take care of her children. She thinks I'll fumble it somehow.

Just because I'm in therapy, he told himself, doesn't mean I'm incapable of watching over two little kids.

Gabriel closed the last closet door and then stood near the Audi. A trickle of perspiration meandered down his face, and he wiped it away with his coat sleeve. It was warm in the garage and Gabriel would be happy to quit it. He weighed whether or not he should start rummaging through the plastic containers when his eyes fell upon a suitcase sandwiched between "Christmas" and "Halloween."

Gabriel pulled it down. A baggage tag still attached read MGQ LAX.

Mogadishu to Los Angeles?

Gabriel opened the case. It was empty. He ran his gloved finger around the inside, checking for any unusual lumps or bumps. He felt something crinkle when he pressed one of the sides. Tucked deep within a zippered interior pocket was a small plastic cosmetic case. Gabriel unzipped the bag, sniffed it briefly, and smelled something earthy. He shook it slightly. The inside held a crumbly residue that appeared to be some sort of plant material.

Gabriel grinned.

WITH HIS NEW evidence now safely deposited in the lab to be processed, Gabriel spent time with his family.

He hammered out plans with Janet regarding their father and got to know Liam and Amber.

He wasn't sure why he got such pleasure from their company, but he did. Gabriel had always lived behind a defense mechanism that had made him emotionless. He once confided to Dr. B that he didn't think he could ever love anyone. He wasn't sure what love felt like.

Now, Gabriel found it strange to realize that he did care for his niece and nephew. Like a rusted tap that had finally turned on, emotions were spilling into him—among them, fear that he might become alienated from his family again.

HE SHARED his love of nature with Janet and the kids by taking them hiking in the Santa Monica Mountains. The parkland was one of the reasons Gabriel had chosen the Sheriff's Department over LAPD. Having the mountains as part of his jurisdiction made working in the big city a much more pleasurable experience.

Amber and Liam played hide-and-seek through the oak trees and followed the creek along boulder-lined paths. Gabriel pointed out holes in the flatter rocks that were formed years earlier by Chumash Indian women who ground their pestles against the plentiful acorns. The children hunted for pestles and arrowheads and squealed at the cottontail rabbits that raced across their path.

Around lunchtime, Ming met them at Paramount Ranch with a picnic basket. The Old West movie set was open to the general public and was a local favorite for those with fertile imaginations. Gabriel handed the children toy pistols, much to Janet's chagrin.

"Oh, we don't play with guns!"

But it was too late.

"I'm gonna getcha, bad boy!" Liam yelled as he ran behind the saloon. "I'm the sheriff, not you!" He popped out and pretended to shoot his uncle.

Gabriel stood in his spot, grinning until Amber tugged at his shirt. "Play with us!"

Gabriel looked at her, looked at Liam, and then dramatically clutched his chest. "You got me. I'm no match for you."

He staggered against the doorway of the general store while Amber stood protectively in front of her uncle and fired off her toy gun at Liam.

Janet watched the game in resignation. Finally, she turned to Ming. "So how come you two aren't married yet?

Startled by the question, Ming was unable to respond. A full minute passed, and Ming replied with the only explanation she could think of.

"My work is very demanding."

"Oh." Janet sniffed and watched as Liam pretended to drag Gabriel to the jailhouse while Amber pulled at her uncle's waist, prodding him to escape.

Ming pursed her lips together, resenting the fact that Janet had successfully pushed her buttons. This wasn't fair. Ming had never given a thought to marriage until that strange moment when Gabriel presented her with a key to his house. Even then, her hormones had taken her by surprise.

Ming's father had always encouraged his daughter to study, then work, and do both without failure. Ming's mother was so unhappy with her father that Ming never considered marriage too bright an idea. But watching Gabriel romp with his niece and nephew... Was Ming missing something in her life? Was she not a complete woman?

"I guess you're waiting on Gabriel," Janet commented.

Ming's almond-shaped orbs settled on Janet then, and she was about to tell the other woman to stay out of her business when Gabriel came up to them, smiling and brushing dirt from his jeans.

"Hey, ladies," he said as he hefted the picnic basket. "Ready to eat?"

THEY CHOSE a table not far from the creek. While the children stayed at the water's edge trying to catch tadpoles, Ming pushed the uncomfortable subject of marriage to the far corners of her mind and talked to Gabriel about the Pennington case.

"What's the boyfriend's story?"

Gabriel sat down next to Ming and watched the kids as they played. "He's not saying much, but I think the girl became a drag on him. He seems to have reinvented himself somewhere along the way, and now he's this holier-than-thou type. My bet is that he tired of April and wanted her gone."

"Breaking up is so hard to do," Ming said sarcastically.

"Especially when there's life insurance money involved."

"Especially then," Ming nodded and grinned at Gabriel.

He met her smile. "Not to mention the plant material I found in his suitcase."

"No!"

Janet watched their discourse and, feeling ignored, yelled to her children. "Be careful over there!"

Gabriel immediately got up from the bench. "You kids all right?"

"Yes!" they called out merrily, content to be independent for the moment.

Ming poked Gabriel's leg. "You dog. You didn't tell me you found any plant."

"I hope it contains that poison you discovered. If it doesn't, we're sunk. I don't want to call the sister until we're sure."

Ming beamed at him, more than happy to be assisting her favorite detective. She turned to Janet. "The best part of my job is working with your brother."

Ming expected the other woman to ask them about their work together; the subject interested most lay people, but instead Janet dug into the picnic basket and pulled out a bag of pretzels. Ming observed Janet with irritation.

Guess this one could not care less about her brother's interesting career.

Gabriel wandered over to Liam and Amber and knelt

alongside them at the water's edge. Ming took the opportunity and said to Janet, "Were you and Gabriel close as children?"

"We got along." Janet munched on a pretzel.

That's not close.

Ming quietly warned herself to leave it alone, but she could not resist. "Did you two have sibling rivalry? I'm always curious about that, being an only child."

"He did his own thing, and I did mine."

You can be vague, sis, but I'm still going to dig.

"Were you closer to your parents?"

"I don't know," Janet answered and then called out to her kids, "Don't pick dirty things up from the water!"

Gabriel gave her a thumbs-up from the creek.

"I'll bet your parents were concerned about Gabriel," Ming dared to continue. "You know, during his difficult times."

"That's an understatement." Janet picked through the bag for another pretzel. "Even when their own grandchildren were born, they couldn't stop worrying over him." Janet, catching herself, quickly popped a pretzel into her mouth to keep from talking.

"Hmm," Ming murmured thoughtfully as she studied Gabriel's sister.

Janet tried to cover. "We were all concerned about Gabriel."

Ming wasn't so sure. She pulled a pretzel from the bag and leaned across the table toward Janet as if they were old friends.

"Do you want to have a girl's afternoon?" she asked

Janet brightly. "I could take you downtown to the clothing mart and we could go shopping."

"With the kids?"

"No. Gabriel will watch them."

"I'd better not." Janet stood up, brushed the crumbs from her shorts, and headed to the creek to join her children.

MING SPENT the night at Gabriel's, and they were in the process of christening his new bed for the umpteenth time. He kissed her neck as his hand gently worked its way around her firm breasts.

"Did your parents favor you over Janet?"

"I don't know," he whispered huskily.

Ming rolled her eyes. *Men... Did they have brains?*

"Think! Did they?"

"I don't know. Maybe." His tongue ran along her ear, causing goose bumps to rise. Normally, Ming basked in Gabriel's sensual attention, but thoughts of Janet were throwing ice water on her passion.

"Well, I think they did, and your sister is using her children to get at you."

Now Gabriel stopped what he was doing and looked Ming in the eye. "What are you talking about?"

"She knows how much you love them, and she's using them to have something over on you."

"That's her trip. I don't care." He went back to kissing Ming's neck, but she pushed him away. He stared at her, momentarily vexed.

"Then what's her problem?" Ming asked. "Because she definitely has one."

Gabriel regarded his girlfriend for a minute. Realizing that she was resolute about discussing something he had no desire to talk about, he let out a long breath.

"Leave it alone, Ming." He rolled onto his side and fluffed the pillow under him in frustration. "I just want to be a part of my family again."

Surprised at the pang of jealousy she felt at that, Ming turned on her side as well, facing away from him. She tried to sleep, but her eyes wouldn't shut. She wondered how long she'd be able to keep her mouth shut.

CHAPTER TWENTY-THREE

"Good morning, Dr. Li."

Ming looked up from her desk and saw Ethan, already outfitted in his scrubs. She smiled. "Look at you, ready and willing."

This time, Ming had Ethan stand alongside her during one of her examinations. She worked on the corpse of a female that was found in an abandoned warehouse in Vernon. The remains were all but skeletal. Ming found Ethan to be an attentive apprentice. He reminded Ming of herself as a student, dedicated and eager to learn.

After the examination, Ethan offered to buy Ming lunch.

"I can't keep going out with you," Ming told him.

"But you can't work all the time, Dr. Li," he replied. "Besides, I have an exam coming up that I definitely need your help with."

Ming acquiesced and they went into Chinatown.

THE WAITER SET down a teapot and two glasses and then took their order. Ethan poured tea into the small cups and handed one to Ming.

"There's something I've wanted to ask you," Ethan began.

Ming gingerly sipped her tea. She hoped the graduate student was not going to get personal. First of all, he would be overstepping his bounds. Secondly, Ming had no desire to discuss her private life after Janet had so successfully attacked it.

"Do you feel," Ethan said, "That the Suchey-Brooks method is a reliable way to determine the age of a person at death?"

Ming nodded in relief, only too pleased to remain within her comfort zone. The Suchey-Brooks method determined someone's age by analyzing the surface of the pubic symphysis, which is robust and has ridges in a young person but flat or hollowed-out in someone older. The longer a person lives and walks around, the longer the two symphyses at the front of his body rub against the connecting cartilage. This continual use or rubbing eventually wears down the ridges, and thus provides a forensic anthropologist the means by which to determine a corpse's age.

"I go by that standard," Ming told her intern. "It's a respected aging method."

Ethan sipped his tea thoughtfully. "I have to tell you, I'm a big fan of yours."

"Of me?"

"Yes." Ethan grinned at her perplexed look. "You're Ming Li. You have this premiere job and a great reputation. I admire that."

Ming felt herself glow. Sometimes, after being with Gabriel, she forgot her own worth. It was refreshing to be reminded that she was a woman of achievement. She watched as Ethan refilled her teacup.

"I feel extremely grateful to have this internship. I want you to know that." He raised his own teacup in a toast. "To you."

Ming blushed prettily and raised her glass.

IN THE AFTERNOON, and because it was their last day, Janet permitted the kids to visit Ming's offices along with an LASD substation. Although she was invited to tour the lab, Janet opted to wait in the lobby with Gabriel and Amber.

Liam, however, jumped at the opportunity to inspect Ming's macabre domain. She obliged the little boy by showing him a clean examination room. She let him hold the various instruments and explained what she did with them.

"You mean you cut someone in the middle, all the way down?"

Ming nodded.

"And you pull back their skin?"

Ming nodded again and smiled to herself. She had a way with children.

"Cool!" He looked at Ming in a new and interesting light. "You're gross."

"I've been called worse."

"Can I watch you do it?"

"No." She began steering the boy out the door.

"Please?"

"I think your mother is missing you."

On the way out, they passed Geoffrey chatting with Ethan. Ming introduced Liam as her boyfriend's nephew and then caught herself.

"I mean, he's Detective McRay's nephew."

Geoffrey gave Ming a conspiratorial wink.

The two men shook hands with Liam, who felt very adult at that moment.

"Is your boyfriend here?" Ethan asked Ming.

"Detective McRay is, yes, right outside. Would you like to meet him? He just submitted some evidence that's being screened at the Trace Analysis Unit at your alma mater."

Geoffrey looked impatient. "We were just heading out for a coffee, if that's okay."

"Of course," Ming said, a little surprised. Introspective Geoffrey had never struck her as the social butterfly type.

"I would be interested in meeting a detective," Ethan interjected.

Ming exchanged glances with Geoffrey. "Okay," she said, and let Liam lead the way to the lobby.

~

WHEN THEY JOINED JANET, Gabriel, and Amber, Liam ran up to his sister and pointed at Ming.

"She's weird!" He broke out giggling and teased his sister. "She cuts people open and takes out their guts!"

Amber dropped her jaw and eyed Ming in horror, which caused Liam to laugh even more.

Gabriel smiled and looked over at Ming, who was not amused in the least.

"I take it you had fun," Gabriel asked the little boy.

"Yep."

"If you had fun in a morgue," Gabriel said, "Then *you're* weird."

Liam playfully punched his uncle in the leg. Liking the game, he continued trying to wrestle Gabriel.

"Detective McRay," Ming began, "This is one of our interns, Ethan Post."

Gabriel, holding Liam at bay with one hand, held out his other hand to Ethan who shook it. "Nice to meet you," Gabriel said and grinned as he maneuvered a squirming Liam under one arm, securing him.

"Liam," Janet warned as she watched them roughhouse.

"Very nice to meet you," Ethan echoed to Gabriel.

"I see you've met Liam." Gabriel laughed as he held the boy.

Liam grunted fiercely and struggled to escape his uncle's hold, but he was clearly having fun.

"That's enough, Liam," Janet said tensely.

Gabriel, eyeing Janet, released his nephew.

"This is my sister, Janet, and my niece, Amber," Gabriel said.

Janet shook Ethan's hand, and Amber did not shake hands but offered up a shy smile.

"Janet, this is Deputy Geoffrey Wallace," Ming said. "He's been indispensable to me."

Janet exchanged pleasantries with Geoffrey.

Gabriel nodded to the redheaded deputy. "She's not working you too hard, is she?"

"Always!" He pulled at Ethan's sleeve. "Let's bounce."

"Uh, yeah, sure." Ethan smiled at the assembly and then dutifully followed Geoffrey to his car.

AT THE SUBSTATION, Gabriel's fellow officers made much of the children. Two uniformed policemen allowed Liam and Amber to ride around the block with them in a squad car and run the siren and the emergency lights. Seeing her children happily occupied, Janet took the opportunity to bow out to the nearest Starbucks for coffee.

Gabriel watched her depart as he and Ming waited outside in the parking lot for the children to return.

"Do you see that?" he asked Ming. "Janet will let them ride around with two complete strangers, but she won't leave them alone with me for a minute."

This time, Ming didn't bother to cover. "I told you, she's got a jealous power trip over you."

No, that's not what it is, thought Gabriel, and the realization spread over him in a thick black cloud.

Ming, who could read him well, put a hand on his arm.

"What is it?"

Gabriel swallowed, wondering if he could verbalize the terrible revelation he'd had.

"She doesn't want me alone with the kids because she's afraid I'll hurt them." He looked at Ming. "She thinks I'm a sick person who can't be trusted around children. A pedophile."

"No…" Ming protested.

Gabriel squeezed her hand and then moved off to lean against the wall of the building.

CHAPTER TWENTY-FOUR

After Janet and the kids departed for the airport, Ming asked Gabriel if he wanted to see a movie. He told her he would rather head to the gym for a workout.

Ming didn't argue. During Gabriel's forgotten hours, those times he would have a memory lapse, he had gone to the gym—a subconsciously safe choice where he could escape his marauding emotions and seek shelter in his physical body. She knew he was depressed.

As Gabriel's old Celica backfired out of the driveway, Ming picked up the phone.

She had Janet's cell phone number; the overprotective mother wouldn't leave Liam alone in the lab with Ming without a contact exchange.

Ming angrily punched in Janet's number. The other woman picked up on the first ring.

"Janet, it's Ming."

"Ming, we're about to board the plane..."

"This won't take long. I want you to know it is an extremely low person who holds her kids for ransom. I know Gabriel better than anyone, and I can tell you that no one would treat your children better. And here's something else for you to think about, you judgmental bitch, when Gabriel was a boy, younger than your own son, he loved you so much, he protected your ass by getting raped by a monster!"

Ming slammed the phone down. Her heart banged against her breastbone. Suddenly she felt ashamed. What did she just do? Gabriel was going to be furious with her!

ALTHOUGH HE PUT up an indifferent front to Ming, the idea that Janet truly thought of him as a child abuser made Gabriel feel terrible. When he arrived at the gym, he looked forward to working out his frustrations in peace.

He did forty-five minutes on the treadmill and then worked out at the weight pile. As he bench-pressed, the tension began to ease off his body. He closed his eyes, and his arms shook with effort as he hefted the barbell for one final press.

Someone above him asked, "Would you like a spot?"

Gabriel opened his eyes and saw Victor Archwood standing over him. The sight of the killer made Gabriel nearly drop the barbell, which Archwood deftly caught before the weights crashed onto Gabriel.

"Whoa," the blond man cried, "What are you trying to do, kill yourself?"

Gabriel sat up on the bench and glared at Archwood. "What are you doing here?"

"Working out."

Gabriel's eyes roamed the room, unwilling to believe that the Malibu Canyon Murderer stood a foot in front of him. At last, he focused on the younger man. "Get the hell out."

Archwood shrugged and used Gabriel's own words. "I guess it's a free country. I can work out where I please."

"Not here, you can't."

"I think I can."

"I guess you think you can do anything since you got away with killing seven people."

Archwood leaned down and whispered, "Eight."

Gabriel flew off the bench and stood, buff and menacing, before Archwood. The veins in Gabriel's arms bulged, pumped with blood from his workout. A vein in his forehead stood out from the sheer rage pumping through him at Archwood's intrusion.

How dare he show up here?

Gabriel curled his hand into a fist and took a step toward Archwood.

The killer remained perfectly calm. "What are you going to do, Detective Sergeant McRay? Are you going to hit me? Go ahead and do it. Then you can join your Detective Sergeant partner in jail."

Gabriel halted in his tracks, now acutely aware of the roomful of onlookers watching and waiting for something to go down.

"Can I call you Sergeant for short?" Archwood asked.

Giving the younger man a savage parting look, Gabriel stormed past him and left the gym.

WHEN HE ARRIVED HOME, Gabriel saw Ming and had to remind himself as to why she was still in his house. She had a key, of course, and could come and go as she pleased. A flare of annoyance lit through Gabriel. He wanted to be by himself tonight. Seeing Archwood had stressed him out, making him tense all over again. Knowing his old, moody demons were trying to roost within him, Gabriel nodded to Ming and quickly headed for the bathroom before she could sense his irritation.

"What's wrong?" she called, sensing it anyway.

"Nothing," he muttered.

He stepped into the bathroom and locked the door behind him. He turned on the shower and hoped the water would rinse away his foul mood.

Closing his eyes, he let the spray hit his face and went through all the possible reasons as to why Archwood would show up at the gym. Being an investigator, Gabriel put no stock in coincidences. Archwood had learned where Gabriel exercised, and he had joined the gym. But why? What could he hope to gain by bothering Gabriel?

I wish I could have smashed him in the face. I wish I could have done that.

That would be an effective measure of keeping Victor Archwood away.

Gabriel turned around and let the water pound his back. Maybe that was the other man's goal, to cause

Gabriel to lose his job or land in jail. Sure, why not? That way, Archwood would remain the wronged man and Gabriel would forever remain the bad cop.

It's okay, Gabriel told himself and took a calming breath. *I get it now.*

Archwood was trolling, throwing out lures, but Gabriel was not going to take the bait.

Wrapping a towel around his waist, Gabriel exited the bathroom, only to find Ming waiting right outside the door.

"What are you doing?" He was irked to find her hovering in the hallway like a phantom.

"I did a bad thing," Ming blurted out. "I called Janet."

Gabriel stared at her and wondered if the day could possibly get any worse. He then bypassed Ming and headed for his bedroom, where he began to dress.

Ming trailed Gabriel and wrung her hands as she confessed, "I told her she was a bitch and that as a boy you showed more bravery than she would ever have in her whole life."

Gabriel stepped into a pair of sweats and pulled on a T-shirt. Ming stood in his doorway with pleading eyes.

"I know I shouldn't have butted in, but you protected her when you were young and she should acknowledge that. You've always been protective of other people, Gabriel. You're a wonderful uncle, and you'll make a wonderful father!"

At that last remark, Ming sniffed back tears. "I'm sorry. I'm so sorry. I have no filter."

Gabriel sat on the bed and looked pensively at his

girlfriend. Finally, he waved her over. Ming came forward and slipped into his arms.

Strangely enough, Gabriel felt his annoyance pass the moment he felt Ming's body touch his. It was so like Ming to do what she did, and so like Gabriel to stuff it all inside. Another strange phenomenon—Gabriel had never thought of himself as a father, and Ming had just said he'd make a wonderful one. The idea had never occurred to him before.

Gabriel felt Ming hiccup against him.

"What am I going to do with you, huh?" He smoothed her lovely hair. "What should I do with a woman who speaks her mind... *all* the time?"

Ming looked up at him with a tear-stained face. "How mad are you?"

"I'm not mad."

"You sure?"

He nodded.

Ming sniffed and wiped her eyes. "You seemed upset before. What's wrong?"

Gabriel tightened his arms around her and shrugged. "Nothing."

His encounters with Victor Archwood were better left unmentioned.

CHAPTER TWENTY-FIVE

D r. Raymond Berkowitz removed his glasses and rubbed his eyes. Gabriel had told him that Janet suspected her brother might abuse her children.

"Did she say such a thing?" he asked his patient.

"She didn't have to. Her actions said it all."

Dr. B surveyed Gabriel. He sat in his usual chair, calm and composed, but there was a slight hitch to his voice. He didn't ask Gabriel how Janet's assertion of him made him feel. The answer was obvious.

An abuse victim, especially a male victim, can often feel like a failure for being incapable of protecting himself from the abuse. The message society sends is if a male is abused, he can't really be a man. If he really is a man, then he couldn't have been abused.

Even though Gabriel knew intellectually that as a child he had no way of protecting himself, it didn't matter. Self-blame played a big role.

Acknowledging the fear, acknowledging the helplessness and the pain, that was the key to any therapy. Having those feelings validated by those around helped alleviate the shame and the self-blame.

Gabriel valued his sister's opinion. He had told Dr. B that. Now Janet not only invalidated Gabriel's internal struggle, she made matters worse by letting him know that she considered him a perpetrator.

Dr. B replaced his glasses and leaned toward Gabriel.

"Who do you think is responsible for Janet's fears?"

"Apparently, I am." Gabriel shrugged. "It doesn't matter, does it?"

"It matters," answered Dr. B. "Who is responsible?"

"If it never had happened—"

"It happened. And it's part of your reality. Who is responsible for the fears Janet is having?"

Gabriel said nothing, so Dr. B said it for him.

"Janet is responsible for her fears. Do you agree?"

Gabriel remained silent, but his blue eyes were focused on his therapist.

Dr. B continued. "You cannot control her thoughts, Gabriel. They are hers to process as she will. You haven't threatened anyone; you haven't given her any cause to worry about her children. These are manufactured fears that she has. Knowing that you have no control over what Janet thinks or feels, what do you do?"

"I don't know," Gabriel replied. "Try to explain things to her."

"But you cannot control her thoughts or feelings. So what can you possibly do about it?"

Gabriel sighed. "Let it go, I guess."

Dr. B paused to study the dark-haired man struggling

next to him. "The key to any situation out of your control is to not let it own you." He gave his patient a gentle smile. "That's a lot harder to do than to say, isn't it?"

"Extremely."

As Mrs. McRay squirmed in front of her computer's camera, she appeared and then disappeared from Gabriel's view.

"Can you see me okay?" she asked her son.

"No. Ma, you have to sit right in front of it."

"But I look like terrible from that angle!"

Following his appointment with Dr. B, Gabriel had returned to the bureau and now sat at his desk, becoming rather dizzy watching his mother come in and out of focus. He had convinced Mrs. McRay that frequent video chats with his father might keep Gabriel at the forefront of Pete's mind.

His mother sat to the side, looked over her shoulder at the camera, and smoothed her hair. "How do I look now?"

He smiled in amusement. "Like a movie star."

She seemed pleased. "How's work? Getting the bad guys?"

He thought briefly of Victor Archwood. "Trying. How's Dad?"

"I'll get him right now." She grimaced at the camera. "Anything to get away from that."

Gabriel watched his mother walk out of sight. He heard her cajoling her husband, but the words weren't clear. Pete McRay walked into view, looked once at the monitor, and then tried to walk away, but his wife urged him to sit down.

"Hey, Dad," Gabriel called tentatively.

His father gave the computer a suspicious look and then turned to his wife.

"It's Gabriel," she explained. "Can't you see him? Say hello."

Pete McRay looked back again at the monitor and then pushed himself out of the chair, obviously done with the matter. Mrs. McRay tried to grab his hand, but he shook her off and then wandered away.

Gabriel's mother reclaimed her seat, and the camera caught the weariness in her features even though she put up a carefree front. "Don't worry, Gabe. He's going to have a good time today. That care facility you and Janet picked out has a wonderful day program." She looked at her watch. "They should be here any minute to pick him up."

The smile had long left Gabriel's face, but he tried to be reassuring. "As soon as I can, I'll come up to see you both. I want to help."

"We don't need any help."

Something crashed in the background, and his mother, slightly panicked, looked to the left. "I've got to go, Son. I'll call you on a real phone later."

The call ended, and Gabriel gazed at the paused image of his mother. Meshing with his family was not going as well as planned. He'd hoped that the video chats would keep him engaged with his father, only now it looked like Pete McRay refused to oblige the computer's camera.

With regards to his sister, Gabriel could barely communicate with her. For one thing, he felt like a pariah around Janet. Although Dr. B's advice was well intentioned, it didn't help much. And Janet, apparently unable to forgive Ming's verbal bashing, didn't seem inclined to keep the lines of communication open with her brother.

Gabriel slowly closed his laptop. He caught Jonelle looking at him from Dash's old desk, and she instantly dropped her eyes to her own computer, embarrassed to have been caught snooping.

He cut her a break and said, "I think the lab should have that residue from Mr. King's suitcase identified sometime this week."

"Oh, good!" She nodded with too much enthusiasm. "I'd like to nail his stuck-up ass."

A clerk approached Gabriel and handed him an envelope.

"This just came for you," the clerk stated and then walked off to make more deliveries.

Gabriel turned the fine linen envelope over in his hands and saw it monogrammed with a red wax seal. The seal looked like a small blood blotch with the letter "A" stamped into the center.

"Whatcha got?" Jonelle leaned in from her cubicle. She seemed eager for a chance to make more conversation.

"I don't know yet." Gabriel opened the envelope, and a pile of purple and gold Mylar confetti spilled onto his lap. He pulled out what appeared to be an invitation. Two theatrical masks, comedy and tragedy, were embossed at the top of an ivory-colored card which read:

.   .   .

A MASQUERADE BALL
  (and housewarming!)
  For Victor Archwood
  5155 Willow Lane
  Corral Canyon, Malibu
  Costumes are mandatory.
  Revelers unmask at midnight!

"SON OF A BITCH," Gabriel muttered.

"What?" Jonelle asked.

"Archwood."

He tossed the invite to Jonelle, who read it.

"He's got nerve." She shook her head. "I'll give him that."

Gabriel cursed under his breath, and Jonelle regarded her partner.

"You want to join me for lunch today?" she asked.

A LITTLE LATER, the two of them made their way across the parking lot opposite Steven's Steakhouse, one of Gabriel's favorite eateries in Commerce.

"You gotta ignore that invitation," Jonelle said as they headed toward the restaurant. "If Archwood starts harassing you, then get a restraining order on him."

"The only way to restrain that guy is to kill him."

Jonelle pulled her partner to a stop. "That kind of

talk," she said soberly, "will only get you into trouble. Why don't—"

Jonelle's speech halted and Gabriel saw her narrow her brown eyes in consternation at something behind him. He turned around to see Victor Archwood loitering in front of the restaurant. Gabriel's jaw dropped. The killer must have followed him here from the bureau, which meant that Archwood had Gabriel under surveillance.

The asshole has been watching me!

"That's it. That's *it*..." Gabriel growled and moved forward, wanting nothing more than to put his fist through Archwood's face.

Jonelle's arm blocked his path. "He wants this reaction from you. You can see that, can't you?"

Gabriel glanced at Jonelle and restrained himself. He reminded himself this was Archwood's plan. Jonelle, however, surveyed her new partner with doubt, apparently unwilling to trust Gabriel's resolve.

She pointed a finger in his face. "Stay here."

Jonelle turned her ample form and started walking swiftly toward Archwood. Gabriel watched her cross the street and reach the restaurant, where she immediately started drilling into Archwood. Gabriel couldn't hear what she said due to the cars whizzing past, but the blond man put his hands up in innocent protest and backed away from her. Jonelle gestured to Gabriel to come forward.

As soon as he crossed the street, Archwood popped out from behind a parked truck and joined Gabriel.

"Do you need her to fight your fights?"

"Back off."

"I'm only wondering why you stopped following me."

Jonelle called from the restaurant door, "Come on, Gabe!" She shook her head at Archwood.

"Isn't it weird how our lives are running a parallel course?" Archwood taunted. "I mean you have a new house. I have a new house. You have a black partner, I have a black girlfriend."

"Happy for you, Vic." Gabriel took a controlled breath as he neared the entrance.

"Are you going to follow me again or —?"

Gabriel whirled on the younger man. "Get the fuck away from me! I don't want to see you. Our business is done, remember? You're a free man."

Archwood sidled next to him. "Yeah, but we're family friends from the old neighborhood. You and I have a relationship."

Gabriel felt the rage course through him and consciously forced his fists to stay at his sides. "We don't have a relationship," he said tightly. "If you know what's good for you, you'll stay far away from me."

With that, Gabriel strode through the door that Jonelle held open for him. She waggled her head once more at Archwood and then turned to follow her partner.

WHEN THE TWO cops had disappeared inside the restaurant, Victor looked down and viewed the digital recorder he'd hidden in his hand. He pressed the "back" button and listened.

"I don't want to see you," Gabriel's recorded voice said.

Vic then fast-forwarded to, "We don't have a relationship," and finally, "If you know what's good for you, you'll stay far away from me."

Satisfied, Vic got into his BMW to return home. There, he planned to use the new sound-editing software that his friend Sergio had so graciously provided him.

IN THE RESTAURANT, Jonelle slid into the seat across from Gabriel and looked him in the eye. "What's going on here, Gabe?"

Tense, feeling it in his shoulders, Gabriel replied, "He's messing with me, that's all."

"Why'd he ask if you were going to follow him again?"

Gabriel eyed Jonelle guiltily. "I tailed him one day. He saw."

Jonelle frowned. "He's crazy. You know that. Why would you get up in his business?"

"Because he shouldn't be out free to kill again."

Jonelle's brown eyes softly sympathized for a moment in agreement, and then her features hardened. "Messing with Victor Archwood can only get you into trouble. And now how are you gonna shake that crazy bastard?"

CHAPTER TWENTY-SIX

High up in the Santa Monica Mountains, in a place called Corral Canyon, Victor Archwood's home stood sentinel on a craggy hilltop. The canyon, a popular destination point for hikers, promised not only the spectacular view but a collection of oddities as well.

A large circular rock formation, a prayer circle, was an easy hike from the Archwood manse. A smattering of caves surrounding the prayer circle made good hiding places from which to spy on those walking the concentric pathways. An old convertible, perhaps abandoned in the 1970s, lay partially buried in the dirt with a bush overgrowing the half-submerged hood. The entire front end of the car poked out of the ground as if it were caught exiting hell. Its front lights were gone, but the round, empty spaces still stared like eyeless sockets in a fleshless skull.

Rabbits jumped, and deer roamed, and vultures flew

overhead in their own prayer circles, waiting for something to die.

The Archwood home, built partly against a boulder-studded hill, was accessible by a long, steep driveway.

Inside, Vic worked on his computer. Near him, Andrea Leighton watched a TV show and chatted on her cell phone with a friend.

When Andrea finally ended her call, she looked over at her boyfriend, who was still intent on his work. The two sat in the room that bordered the kitchen, a room large enough to hold two sets of sofas.

Bored, Andrea rolled off one of Vic's large wrap-around couches, turned off the flat screen television, and picked up her tablet.

She hit a button, and her favorite playlist began streaming through the stereo speakers. Subtly dancing, nodding her head and gyrating her hips, she made her way toward an open cardboard box filled with compact discs and record albums. Andrea plopped down next to it and began poking through the contents. She pulled out a remastered CD set called *Teen Dreams* and some old vinyl records from the 1960s. She figured these belonged to Natalie, Vic's ugly-ass mother.

Wondering why Vic would keep anything of his mother's, Andrea perused the yellowed album covers one by one. She pulled out a Platters album, and read the list of songs. Her eyes snagged on one title: "The Great Pretender."

Andrea sat back and regarded Vic. He was too engrossed to pay her any mind.

The song's title reminded her of something her journalistic mind had filed away. She crept back to the couch and opened her laptop. As Vic worked soundlessly a few feet away, Andrea accessed his trial transcript online. In minutes, she honed in on the notes the Malibu Canyon Murderer wrote to Detective Gabriel McRay.

One had read, "You are a Great Pretender."

Andrea ran her tongue across her glossed lips and lifted her eyes once again to her boyfriend. His lithe fingers tapped the keyboard, and his handsome face was set in the utmost of concentration.

She watched him carefully. So she had found a familiar song title in an old pile of music. So what? It probably had nothing to do with a killer's notes. Still, "The Great Pretender" remained stuck in her head throughout the night and refused to leave.

THE FOLLOWING DAY, Andrea Leighton found herself waiting outside the homicide bureau in Commerce. She watched Gabriel McRay exit the building and head toward a beat-up old car. She appeared at his side as he unlocked the drivers-side door.

"Detective McRay?"

"Miss Leighton." Gabriel immediately scanned his surroundings, searching for Archwood.

"I'm alone," she assured him. "I wanted to ask you something."

Gabriel continued to survey the area, apparently convinced that Archwood lingered nearby. Finally, he settled his eyes on the girl. "Yes?"

"Did you receive a note calling you a great pretender?"

"One of the suspect's notes to me said 'you are a great pretender.' Why do you ask?"

"No reason."

Gabriel appeared doubtful. "Talk to me, Miss Leighton."

"I was just curious about the note, that's all."

"Would you like to grab a cup of coffee?"

She shook her head.

Gabriel cocked a thumb toward the bureau's door. "We could go inside. You're perfectly safe in there."

"I'm not in any danger," she told him.

Gabriel leveled a serious gaze at the young woman. "Miss Leighton, your boyfriend is extremely dangerous."

"I wouldn't go around saying that, Detective McRay," Andrea warned. "Innocent until proven guilty, remember? I guess you don't. Vic told me you don't follow any rules."

"I don't follow any rules." Gabriel gave small laugh and shook his head. "He of all people made that observation, huh?"

Andrea shrugged and then grew self-conscious. Vic would be so angry with her if he knew she had spoken with Gabriel McRay.

"Well, thanks so much, Detective!" Andrea waved her teeny little wave and then practically sprinted away from Gabriel.

"Miss Leighton," he called after her.

Andrea ignored him and headed to her own car. Filled

with many questions, Andrea Leighton made the decision to live without the answers.

"DID YOU HAVE FUN?"

Gabriel was on the phone with his niece, and Amber was telling him about a birthday party she went to where the kids painted clay figurines and then ate pizza. Gabriel sipped a Dos Equis and listened to her enthusiastic chatter, content to learn how she spent her days. Of his sister Janet, he learned very little for his dialogue with her was brief. Even if Janet had a mind to talk, Gabriel could barely converse with her, knowing of what she thought him capable.

Despite that, Gabriel felt good.

It was Friday and his weekend had started the minute the lab confirmed that the plant material found in Mr. King's possession was Strophanthus gratus, a woody liana that hung from trees in Africa, boasted fragrant flowers, and whose seeds contained ouabain used for poisoned arrows.

Jonelle had wanted to bring Mr. King in for questioning immediately, but Gabriel convinced her that they didn't have enough evidence to assure his guilt. After all, Mr. King could claim that April found the plant material and somehow ingested it herself. Ming had provided them the mechanism of death. What Gabriel needed to know was the manner of death. How did Mr. King do it?

Rest assured, Your Highness, I will find out.

Gabriel took another swig of beer. Bringing these

clowns to justice was what it was all about for him, and for the first time since the trial, Gabriel felt positive about life.

He heard the doorbell ring and angled his head curiously toward the house. Ming wasn't expected to get off work for another hour. Besides, she had her key.

"Can we talk tomorrow?" he asked the little girl, who reluctantly gave her permission. Gabriel ended the call and walked into his house. He moved to the front door and opened it. Victor Archwood stood on his front stoop.

"Hello, Sergeant."

"Get off my property," Gabriel told him squarely.

"You never RSVP'd to my housewarming. Are you coming?"

"No."

"Why not? It's going to rock. It's the hot ticket in town from what everyone says."

"Because I don't want to see your face," Gabriel said. "Now get lost."

He moved to shut the door, but Archwood blocked it with his foot. Gabriel stared at the younger man in astonishment. Did he want Gabriel to shoot him?

"Oh, come on Sergeant McRay. You of all people should want to see the hidden lair of Victor Archwood. I know you do."

Gabriel took a step closer to the blond man. "I told you to leave."

"What's the matter?" Archwood rested his hands on his hips. "Aren't you man enough to face me on my own turf?"

Gabriel eyed the younger man steadily.

The abuse rendered you powerless…

"I'm not afraid of you, Vic. I'm just not allowed to give you the kind of punishment I think you deserve. So stop tempting me."

Archwood smiled, white teeth under his black sunglasses. "I think you're afraid. What a poser you are, Mr. Badass Cop. All nightstick and no balls."

Gabriel seriously considered kicking the younger man to the tree-stippled sidewalk, but he held his anger in check. The killer looked pretty dandy these days: designer sunglasses, designer house. Right up there with movie stars and famous sports figures.

Gabriel itched to catch Archwood off his game, and the younger man was begging for a confrontation. Perhaps Gabriel should give him one. He could put himself out as a lure. Archwood would try something, of that Gabriel was sure. And when Archwood made his move, Gabriel would bring the bastard to justice once and for all.

Before he could change his mind, Gabriel said, "Okay, Vic. I'll be there."

Archwood appeared overjoyed. "I knew you couldn't resist. You can bring a guest. Why don't you bring Dr. Li?"

The blond man began walking toward a shiny, silver BMW parked in Gabriel's driveway. "Oh, and don't forget it's a costume party. Revelers unmask at midnight."

The late afternoon sun lost its warmth as Gabriel watched Archwood enter his luxury car. *And I'll be ready when you take off your mask, Vic.*

CHAPTER TWENTY-SEVEN

"Was there anything at all unusual about the body? Anything at all?" Gabriel spoke on his office phone to Ming. "Absolutely no defensive wounds?"

"No," Ming responded emphatically. "If he tried to force her to inject herself, she put up no struggle. At least none that is indicated on her body."

Gabriel scratched his head in frustration. "He couldn't have just willed April to poison herself."

"Maybe he talked her into doing drugs again. Maybe he pretended to get high with her, but slipped her the poison."

"Then where is the syringe containing the ouabain?"

"Probably in the trash," Ming said. "Are you gonna search the city dump for one syringe? Talk about a needle in a haystack!"

Sullen, Gabriel flipped through the report. "The trash was searched. Nothing was found."

He looked at the photos of April's body.

"There are a lot of track marks on her," he said, unwilling to give up. "On her arms and legs, but one on her neck. What's that all about?"

"She went for her jugular," Ming replied. "Some of her peripheral veins had sclerosed, so she had to inject the large central veins. It's risky, but users do it."

"She didn't inject herself," Gabriel curtly reminded Ming. "Not for two years. I find it amazing that people will continue to hold someone's past against them."

He stopped himself from saying more. He was projecting, of course. Thinking of his sister and what she thought of him.

"You're right," Ming spoke gently. "Somehow Mr. King administered the drug without her fighting. Maybe while she was asleep, huh?"

"Maybe." Gabriel calmed down. "We've got poison on the premises, brought in by the suspect. We've got a girl with the poison in her system, but what we don't have is the proof that he gave it to her." Gabriel closed the file and rested a reflective hand on it. "I won't take the chance of another killer getting acquitted."

"What are you doing tonight?" Ming asked, wisely changing the subject.

"Going to a costume party."

"Really?" Surprise raised her voice. "Whose? And how come I'm not invited?"

"You won't like the host."

"Whose party is it?"

"Victor Archwood's."

Ming gasped, paused for a moment, and then said, "You're kidding, right? That's not funny, Gabriel."

"You're right. It's not funny."

"Don't you dare go. I'm coming over."

"Ming, I'm still at work."

"Then I'll meet you at your house."

"DO YOU WANT TO GET FIRED?" Ming exclaimed as she entered Gabriel's bedroom. "You can't go near that man!"

Gabriel fastened his shoulder holster. "He's not going to let this go, Babe."

"You'll have to ignore him then." Ming watched as Gabriel tucked his Redhawk revolver into the holster. "What are you doing with that?"

"Archwood blows it, I blow his head off."

"Gabriel, if anything bad happens to him, your life is ruined. This—" Ming threw her purse onto the bed. "This is a terrible idea!"

Gabriel moved to a mirrored closet door and fitted his jacket over the holster. "Remember what happened the last time he wanted to confront me? He tried killing me. I say let him try again."

Ming sighed, crossed her arms, and then looked resolutely at Gabriel. "Then I'm going with you."

A laugh, sarcastic and short, escaped his lips.

Ming held her ground. "I am. Someone has to make sure you don't do something rash to mess up your life."

Gabriel took a last look in the mirror where he eyed Ming's reflection. A moment passed, and he walked over to her and lifted a gentle hand to stroke her cheek.

"I won't do anything to mess up my life," he promised. "But if I have an opportunity to find one crack in his armor, I'm gonna take it." Gabriel pulled away and picked up his car keys. "You can stay here."

"I'm going," Ming argued.

"No, you're not."

Gabriel thought a moment and then went to his closet. He pulled his police special from a secret hideaway deep within. After double-checking the striker block safety, he handed the gun to Ming. She stared at the Smith and Wesson M&P, fascinated by its slate gray solidity.

"That's in case things get weird tonight," Gabriel told her. "Who knows what that douche bag has planned? Keep the doors locked and the gun handy."

His phone beeped, causing the both of them to jump slightly. Gabriel checked his cell display. There was a forwarded call from his office voice mail. He gestured to the weapon in Ming's hand.

"Be careful with that," he said as he accessed his voice mail. "It's loaded. Keep the safety on."

Gabriel retrieved the message and listened. After ending the call, he held the phone in his hand and stood motionless, thinking.

"What is it?" Ming asked, still marveling at the gun in her hand.

"I got a call from Andrea Leighton, Vic's girlfriend. She wants to meet me before the party, alone."

"Why?"

"She didn't say." Gabriel picked up his car keys. "But

it could be important. She tried talking to me a couple of days ago."

He gave Ming a kiss on the lips and a squeeze on the shoulder. Neither reassured her.

And then he walked out the door.

As soon as Gabriel left the house, Ming moved to the kitchen counter and the little basket where her boyfriend kept his mail.

She rifled through the various bills and advertisements and came upon a printed card—Archwood's invitation.

A Masquerade Ball

Ming's fingers began to tremble as she read, and the paper shook in her hand.

5155 Willow Lane

Oh, he can't go there alone, Ming thought anxiously.

Costumes are mandatory.

Ming lifted her eyes from the card and wondered what kind of mask she could wear to fully hide her fear.

As evening fell, Gabriel leaned against his idling Celica, parked down the road from Archwood's home. One limousine after another drove by, and Gabriel surmised they were heading for the "hot ticket in town."

He'd always liked the Santa Monica Mountains, but tonight the hills and chaparral were shadowy and black around him and Gabriel felt spooked. The fact that he was about to enter Victor Archwood's "lair" didn't help to liven his spirits.

A few minutes passed, and then a black Jetta pulled up beside him. Andrea Leighton was behind the wheel.

She hopped out and gave Gabriel her trademark wave. "Hi, Sergeant McRay!"

He nodded his hello.

"Did you bring a costume?"

"No." Gabriel observed Andrea's look of disappointment.

"Vic knew you wouldn't wear a costume," she said and returned to her car.

She reached through the open window and pulled out a large paper bag, which she promptly thrust into Gabriel's hands. "So he bought you one."

Gabriel glanced down at the bag and then squinted at Andrea. "Is this what you wanted to talk to me about?"

"Yes."

"I'm not going to wear a costume, Miss Leighton."

"But you have to. The bouncers won't let you inside the house without one. Don't you want to come inside?"

Gabriel viewed the fancy cars humming past them. "Are you sure you don't want to tell me anything else?"

Andrea smiled as she bounced back to her car. "What's there to tell?"

Gabriel watched her enter the Jetta and then drive up the winding street. He reached into the bag and pulled out the latex mask of a killer clown. The mask boasted a wicked, sharp-toothed smile, but it was a clown just the same. The irony wasn't lost on Gabriel.

"Nice," he muttered derisively.

It was going to be one hell of an evening.

CHAPTER TWENTY-EIGHT

G abriel parked amid all the cars that lined the narrow canyon road leading up to the Archwood house. As he walked along, he pulled on pieces of the clown costume and felt like an idiot. But he had to wear it. He did not come all this way to be rejected at the door.

Holding the mask in his hand, he paused at the bottom of a long, steep driveway.

"Gabriel."

Surprised to hear his name, he turned around.

Ming stood near the mailbox, wearing a Venetian-style Mardi Gras mask replete with long feathers and sequins. Her long hair and sensuous figure gave her away.

Gabriel strode over to her. "Ming, what are you doing here? I told you to stay—"

"I'm sorry." She lifted nervous fingers to his cheek. "I was afraid to be alone. I want to be with you."

"Ming..." Gabriel began and then read the anxiety in

her eyes. He wondered why she cared so much about him.

"Please go home," he begged.

"No."

Gabriel exhaled, gave her one last weary look, and then positioned the evil clown mask over his head.

"A clown?" Ming asked him.

"Archwood picked it for me." Gabriel took Ming's hand, and the two of them trekked up the driveway. Slowly, a modern one-story house came into view.

"Good gracious," Ming said. "Where'd he get the money for this?"

Gabriel swallowed in amazement. He could barely afford his fixer-upper, and Archwood had built an architecturally stunning home. Rows of glass windows shined behind rich wood trim and elegant stonework. Looking around, Gabriel could already make out an ocean view, and they were only halfway up the drive.

'Didn't you know," he replied, staring contemptuously at the house. "Archwood is the shit nowadays. On everyone's A-list." He turned to his girlfriend. "Makes you sick, doesn't it?"

Ming squeezed his hand. "Come on. Let's see what he's hiding."

THERE WERE two bouncers standing guard at a solid-steel front door, which was open. Gabriel queued up behind a row of people waiting to be admitted. As he neared the entrance, he craned to see inside the house.

The stacked stonework reached beyond the exterior walls and wound itself into the interior, smartly bringing the outside in. Issuing from inside the house was the loud thump of bass and techno music. The place was overrun with people.

"Name?" a burly Polynesian man who was built like a sumo wrestler asked.

"Gabriel McRay." He brought Ming forward. "And guest."

Ming was reluctant to go inside, and Gabriel pressed on the small of her back as the bouncer nodded and let them pass.

The couple stood awkwardly in the midst of what apparently was a rollicking party. The music thumped against their ears, competing for dominance over the sound of happy voices and clinking glasses.

A row of glass doors, now wide open, lined the walls across from them and beckoned the visitor to walk across a nicely appointed living room. Beyond the doors lay a sleek lighted pool and a spectacular view. The city lights spread out to the left like a blanket of sparkling gems. The ocean spanned in front of them, bathed in a softly forming fog. Near the pool, a bartender manned a well stocked bar, handing out drinks to those waiting in line.

Gabriel looked around, amazed. Didn't they know who was buying their booze? Didn't they care?

All the guests were masked. Many of the women wore elegant Venetian masks similar to Ming's. Others had chosen costumes of the standard Halloween variety, frightening or grotesque. One guest was dressed like the

Phantom of the Opera. Another wore the Scream mask with his mouth open in a frozen howl.

A woman rushed by them, calling to someone named Jim. She was dressed as a belly dancer and her diaphanous face veil trailed behind her. A man wearing a ragged beanie stared meanly at the newcomers from across the room. His face was replete with fake cuts bound by primitive black "stitches" that twisted his features. Although the man thought he was freakishly cool, his fake wounds reminded Gabriel of the autopsy images of Archwood's victims. Stab wounds had marred their bodies as well; only their wounds had been tragically real.

Ming shivered against Gabriel.

"Are you cold?" he asked her.

"Nervous."

He put his arm around her.

"Where do you think he is?" Ming asked.

"Hard to tell." Gabriel continued to observe the man with the stitched wounds.

"Canapé?"

Gabriel and Ming turned to see a waiter wearing a tux under the Jigsaw mask from the movie *Saw*. His pasty white face, red glowing eyes, and protruding red-spiraled cheeks made him a monstrously intimidating kitchen staffer.

"No, thanks," Gabriel answered flatly and watched the waiter move off.

He and Ming made their way through the living room, feeling out of place and vulnerable as two mice in a snake pit.

They peeked into an empty study. Here too, a row of glass doors lined one wall, which led to the backyard. The rest of the room was covered in panels of padded wine-colored leatherette. A large single painting hung opposite Archwood's expansive desk. It was of a fey, big-eyed child with blood spilling from her eyes. The painting was eerily beautiful and looked expensive.

Ming couldn't tear her gaze from it, so Gabriel gently pulled at her sleeve. "Come on."

They returned to the living room and stood in the thick of the revelers. People sloshed drinks on them, and the bass of the music mimicked their own rabid heartbeats.

Gabriel observed a group of people catering to a tall, black-shrouded figure whose back was to them. Gabriel nudged Ming and nodded toward the figure. At that moment, the dark one turned, and Gabriel saw Death.

The man inside the Grim Reaper costume apparently noticed Gabriel at the same time, and confidently strode over. Ming gasped, and Gabriel took her hand. Archwood wore a hood over a grinning skull mask. In his hands, he held a plastic scythe.

"I should have known," Gabriel told him when he joined the couple. "Death incarnate."

"I'm Poe's Masque of the Red Death," Archwood said from behind the skeletal grin.

Gabriel remembered the story from his college English. "About the plague, right? That fits you, Vic."

Archwood chuckled. "I won't say anything about the clown costume. Welcome to my home, Sergeant McRay."

He held out his black-gloved hand to Ming, "A pleasure, Dr. Li."

Unwilling to shake hands with the man who had tried to murder her, Ming took a subconscious step closer to Gabriel.

Archwood let his hand drop. "Would you two like a drink?"

Gabriel glanced at Ming who was frozen, the eyes behind her mask riveted on Archwood's grinning skull.

"No, thanks," Gabriel responded for her.

A sexy Cat Woman came up then and entwined her arm through Archwood's.

"You remember Andrea, don't you?"

"Shhh! You weren't supposed to tell!" she said as she snuggled close to him.

"Sorry, Dre."

The Cat Woman nodded to Gabriel. "Hello, Detective McRay."

"Miss Leighton."

Andrea the Cat curiously cocked her whiskered mask toward Ming.

"Nice to meet you," Ming said mechanically and without introducing herself.

"Well," the Grim Reaper said, "Look at the four of us. We should go out sometime."

Gabriel suddenly felt claustrophobic. Was it due to the hot latex mask he wore or Archwood's suggestion of a double date? Ming must have felt it too, for she turned her head this way and that, looking for something.

"Excuse me, I need to use the bathroom."

Andrea took the cue and pointed left. "That way. First door down the hall."

Ming looked anxiously back at Gabriel. "How will I find you?"

He scanned the crowd with disdain. "I guess I'm the only clown around here. You'll find me."

Archwood snickered at that but stopped when Gabriel swiveled his sharp-toothed clown face toward him.

Ming meandered off, looking furtively around, spooked at any little thing. Observing her, Gabriel regretted he had let her come inside. He knew he should take her home.

Archwood unraveled Andrea's arm from his. "Dre, go check on the food and make sure they've started serving the lamb."

"Okay." Andrea gave her hyper little wave to Gabriel. "Nice seeing you again, Detective McRay."

Archwood's death mask watched her bounce off, and then it focused on Gabriel. Behind the mask, Gabriel sensed Archwood bristling with energy, as though he could barely contain his excitement. And yet the younger man was attempting to act very casually.

"Would you like a tour?" Archwood asked.

"Sure."

As they began walking, Gabriel reached under his clown vest and settled a waiting hand on the Redhawk. He quietly unlatched the safety—just in case.

Archwood led him down a long hallway and paused at a set of closed double doors. "Here's a room that would interest you." He swung the door wide to reveal a large master bedroom with a king size bed, a grand fireplace, and more astounding views. Archwood cocked his head and held the door open in invitation.

Discomfited, Gabriel continued down the hallway, feeling exposed, as perforated as Swiss cheese, even behind his disguise. He heard rustling, and in an instant, Archwood was by his side again.

"Pull something," Gabriel told the Grim Reaper. "Give me any reason, because you don't know how badly I want to take you down."

"Oh, I get that, Sergeant. But if I pull something on you..." Archwood wheeled in front of Gabriel and halted him in his tracks. "You'll never see me coming."

The younger man then turned and walked ahead. "So give the gun a rest, okay?"

OUT IN THE crowded living room, Ming wandered around uneasily, searching for Gabriel. A man wearing a mask that displayed only the bloodied upper half of a mouth tipsily approached Ming.

"Hey, babe, can I get you a drink?" he slurred.

The forensic pathologist in Ming stared gravely at his mask, noting that a person who had truly lost half his face would have already expired from exsanguinations.

Ming shook her head, still studying the man's mask, and the jawless would-be admirer moved off to greener pastures.

GABRIEL STOOD and watched Archwood's flowing black robes disappear around a corner. What an arrogant bastard. Jonelle was right. Gabriel needed to avoid having anything to do with Victor Archwood. Being around the killer was toxic, and Gabriel would only poison himself by being near the man.

He turned and headed back toward the main hall. Dr. B was right. By focusing solely on Archwood, Gabriel had not dealt with his anger toward Dash. He'd had enough therapy to know that ignoring his issues would not make them go away. Gabriel needed to get Ming, get out of here, and get on with his life.

He entered the thick of the party, fed up with the brazen masks and the thumping music. The partiers disgusted him. Archwood was a serial killer, and these people were drinking his liquor and eating his food. They might as well have dressed like dogs, or pigs, or worms.

Gabriel searched the room and spied a woman with long dark hair and a feathered mask. He weaved his way through the partiers until he reached her.

"Let's go," he announced.

The lady turned to face him. She wasn't Ming. Gabriel mumbled an apology.

He began to circuit the crowded room, turning one Venetian mask around after the other; only none of the masked ladies were Ming. He thought he heard her call his name, and he moved in the direction of the kitchen.

"Coming through!" a waiter dressed as Winnie the Pooh cried as he exited the kitchen, carrying a tray loaded with food.

Gabriel stepped back to let the waiter pass and then swore he heard his name again.

"Ming?" he called toward a darkened hall beyond the kitchen.

Gabriel entered a luxuriously long butler's pantry where glass-covered cabinets held china plates and twinkling crystal. At the end of the pantry was a closed door.

He walked over and opened the door. Gabriel felt for a light switch and flipped it on to reveal a large laundry room. It was empty, save for a lone Mardi Gras mask lying on the silent washing machine. Curious, Gabriel picked up the mask, which sparkled in his hands. It didn't belong to Ming.

Suddenly, someone grabbed him from behind and he felt a sting in his bicep. Gabriel's arms immediately went up, clutching the person behind him.

"I said you wouldn't see me coming," Archwood whispered and retracted the hypodermic he'd plunged into Gabriel's arm.

Instantly, the room turned in a circle and Gabriel opened his mouth to yell, only nothing came out, and he dropped to his knees.

ARCHWOOD CAUGHT Gabriel before he did a face-plant to the stone floor, then quickly removed the clown mask and produced a strip of duct tape that he plastered over Gabriel's mouth.

He then pulled off Gabriel's clown costume, and quickly removed the Redhawk revolver, his keys, his wallet, and his cell phone, and dumped them into a nearby drawer. Rolling up the clown suit, Archwood threw it into the dryer. He then fit a costume of ragged clothing onto Gabriel's inert body and pulled a latex zombie mask over Gabriel's head. Archwood worked quickly and quietly. Under the mask, Gabriel's eyes were closed. He was out.

Archwood reached into another cabinet and grabbed a bottle of gin he'd stowed there earlier. Twisting the cap off, he poured the alcohol liberally over Gabriel's zombie mask and chest area. Archwood quickly surveyed the scene. Satisfied, he opened the door and strode to the front entrance.

He spoke to the burly bouncer. "There's this dude who's had too much to drink. Can you drag him over to a chair so he can sleep it off?"

The bouncer accompanied Archwood to the laundry room and hefted Gabriel over his shoulder. He carried him over to a chair in the living room and sat him down, surrounded by all the guests. For all intents and purposes, Gabriel looked and smelled like a passed-out partier. If any of the other revelers noticed the zombie at all, they were soon ignoring him.

Archwood returned to the laundry room and put on Gabriel's costume. He pulled the killer clown mask over his head and tucked his own Grim Reaper costume away.

~

MING WAS WALKING in fretful circles. She couldn't find Gabriel anywhere. She went from room to room, searching; scared she might end up alone with Victor Archwood. Where was Gabriel?

The blossoming panic was about to make her short of breath when she felt a tug on her shawl. She turned to see Gabriel.

"There you are," she said in relief. "I didn't know what happened to you."

"I'm leaving," Archwood the Clown told her in his best impression of Gabriel's voice. "I can't take this anymore."

The noise of the crowd and the music made his harsh whispering acceptable to Ming.

"Okay," she said loudly. "I'll follow you back to—"

Archwood the Clown shook his head. "Vic's gotten away with everything. It's too much!"

He abruptly turned on his heel and scurried to the front door, leaving Ming gaping after him.

"WAIT!" Ming chased him. She tripped over the extended legs of a zombie passed out in a chair. Righting herself, she pushed her way through the crowd.

When she made it to the front door she saw the clown dashing down the driveway.

"Gabriel!" she cried anxiously and took off after him.

Her high heels made it difficult to negotiate the steep drive and Ming's heart pounded as she watched Gabriel run down the street, jump into his car, and take off without a word to her. She shot a terrified look back at the house.

Was he leaving her behind?

Taking off her shoes, Ming skittered down the driveway. She jumped into her own car, locked the doors, and immediately dialed Gabriel's cell phone.

VICTOR ARCHWOOD, driving Gabriel's car, heard the phone ring and ignored it. Once out of the canyon, he pulled off the clown mask and wiped the sweat from his brow. He drove straight to Sergio's house in the Miracle Mile.

Vic drove down the cracked narrow driveway to a detached garage out back, where Sergio was waiting for him.

"Can you make this car disappear?" Vic asked his friend.

Sergio eyed the old Celica disdainfully. "Why don't you sell it for scrap?"

"It needs to disappear."

Sergio nodded. "Sure. Can I come to your party now?"

"Yeah," Vic replied. "In fact, you can drive me back home."

MING KNOCKED on the front door of Gabriel's beach house, feeling the ocean mist creep under her pashmina.

"Gabriel!" she yelled and pounded on the door again.

Finally, she used her key to enter and could see he hadn't come home yet. She quickly called his cell phone, only to get his voicemail again. Bewildered, Ming sat on the couch and wondered what to do.

She decided she would wait for him and give him a piece of her mind when he returned. Gabriel should not have abandoned her like that, no matter how upset he was. Feeling odd and out of sorts, Ming sat back to wait.

THE MORNING SUN streaming through the windows woke her up. Ming looked around, mildly surprised that she had fallen asleep. She could see that nothing had changed overnight. Gabriel had not returned home.

Rubbing her tired eyes, Ming reached for her phone and called Gabriel's cell. Again, he did not answer. Distraught, Ming had no choice but to return to her own home in Los Feliz.

Once there, she forced herself to wait a couple of hours. She did some laundry. She paid some bills. When she could no longer stand waiting, Ming called Gabriel's cell phone. This time, to her surprise, he picked up the call.

"Gabriel? Where are you?"

"I don't want to see you," he growled.

Ming was stunned. "What? Why?"

"If you know what's good for you, you'll stay far away from me."

"What?"

"We don't have a relationship."

"Gabriel!" Ming cried breathlessly. "What's going on?"

The phone disconnected. Ming immediately tried him back, but he wouldn't answer.

Ming called his cell phone several times over the next few hours. She drove back to his house in the evening and taped a note on his refrigerator. She e-mailed him dozens of times. Unable to do or say anything more, she realized she was late for a dinner appointment with Ethan.

AT THE RESTAURANT, Ming was dismayed and kept checking her cell phone for messages. She called her office exchange twice to see if Gabriel had tried to contact her.

"I'm sorry," she finally said to Ethan. "I'm not much company tonight."

"What's wrong?"

"My boyfriend." Ming paused and felt the tears press against her eyes. "He's gone. He's disappeared and…"

Ethan put a concerned hand on hers.

Ming continued in a perplexed voice. "I don't know where to look for him. He's not at home."

"Did you call the police?"

"He is the police." Ming sighed. "He's not exactly missing. I spoke to him a couple of hours ago."

Looking at her, Ethan called over the waiter and ordered a bottle of Heitz cabernet. "I think you need a drink."

"I need to know what's going on."

Again, Ethan clasped her hand. "People like to get away sometimes. I'm sure he'll be back."

Ming pulled her hand away to wipe her eyes. "I'm sorry. We came here to discuss your class notes."

"The notes can wait," Ethan told her. "Consider me a friend, Dr. Li. Tell me what's going on."

"I'm so worried. He's been driving himself crazy. A case he worked on came to trial, and his partner was accused of planting evidence. Because of that, the killer walked away free, and since then, Gabriel has been a wreck."

"The detective I met, right?"

Ming nodded desperately and watched the waiter uncork their bottle of wine. As he filled their glasses, Ming said, "I just need to know if he's okay."

CHAPTER TWENTY-NINE

G abriel awoke to discomfort in his upper arms. As the cloud of sleep broke away, he realized he felt more than discomfort; his shoulders ached badly, and pain pulsed through his limbs. Something sharp was digging into his wrists, and he had the ugly sensation that he was about to be ripped apart.

He opened his eyes to blurred vision. He couldn't focus on any one thing, and a wave of nausea started at his stomach and ended in his mouth where he swallowed back bile. He felt stretched, as if he were on a medieval torture rack. Strange though, because he imagined he should be lying down, only he wasn't. Fighting for lucidity, Gabriel moved his head and looked up. His arms were above him, and as his vision cleared, he could see his wrists were manacled. The manacles were hoisted upon a long hook from the ceiling. He was hanging by his arms.

His legs... His legs were being pulled away from his torso. Gabriel looked down his suspended body and could see that his ankles were tied to some sort of heavy weight that prevented him from swaying. He could see also that he was naked.

"Sleeping Beauty awakes!"

Gabriel looked up miserably. Victor Archwood was sitting in one of two wingback chairs across from him. Between the chairs stood a smart-looking table with a bowl of ice and a washcloth rolled on top. Gabriel's eyes roamed what appeared to be a large, windowless room. A sleek wood stairway with a modern utilitarian railing ascended to the left. Rich wood molding detailed the ceiling and floor, which was smooth, glossy cement.

Archwood rose lightly and approached Gabriel. In his hand he carried the washcloth. Gabriel tried to speak, but nothing came out. The movement of his lips was hampered, which led him to another bleak revelation: his mouth was taped shut.

Archwood gently dabbed Gabriel's forehead. The washcloth was cool and damp.

"You're sweating, Sergeant. Is it too hot in here? I made it a little warm for you, I mean, under the circumstances." Archwood's eyes scanned Gabriel's body. The washcloth dabbed at Gabriel's neck. "You keep yourself very cut. Kudos to you."

Gabriel felt the damp fabric lightly dust over his chest hairs, sweep a bit under his arms, and then glide down to his hips. Archwood met his eyes. Gabriel heard the washcloth drop to the floor and he felt his heart drop at the same time.

Don't you dare. Don't you freaking dare...

Gabriel felt his groin caressed and he jumped as if electrocuted. The manacles clinked as his arms jerked.

"Now, Sergeant," Archwood began as he massaged Gabriel with a little more intensity. "This is nothing to be ashamed of."

Again, Gabriel tried to speak, tried to protest, but the tape frustrated his effort.

The blond man watched the ministrations of his hand for a couple of minutes and then looked at Gabriel with a grin. "You say no, but your body says yes. Oh, yes..."

Archwood bent down and went to work on Gabriel with his mouth. Gabriel shook his head. A startling vision of Andrew Pierce appeared in his mind—Andrew with a seven-year-old Gabriel, touching the boy in places he shouldn't, taking Gabriel's childhood away from him. Gabriel groaned behind the duct tape. This wasn't happening again. It couldn't happen to a grown man. He was a cop, for God's sake! He had a life...

He shook his bound wrists, trying to unhook himself. He tried kicking, but his legs could only twitch, stretched as they were. Archwood continued uninterrupted. And then there was only the sensation at Gabriel's crotch, something too primal and magnetic to fight. Gabriel tried to control himself, but he couldn't help it. He came in waves, with his body shuddering, vaguely aware that Archwood's hands were still on him, but that the younger man had pulled his face away to view his captive.

Shutting his eyes, Gabriel refused to acknowledge him.

"Somebody's happy," he heard Archwood say with amusement.

An eternity seemed to pass in the space of seconds, and then Archwood spoke again. "Oh, come on now, Sergeant. Don't be bashful. It's not like it hasn't happened to you before. Didn't your molester ever give you a blow job?"

At that, Gabriel opened his eyes to see the other man wiping his hands on the washcloth and grinning at him. Archwood tossed the washcloth onto the table and then moved close to Gabriel.

"I like this. I like having you here and... having you. I would think you'd like that as well. In case you're wondering, you're still in my home. *Mi casa es su casa*, as the saying goes. I'm going to tear that tape off, but I don't want to hear any bullshit." He grabbed an edge of the duct tape. "Understand?"

Gabriel nodded. He could barely breathe and needed the tape removed. Archwood stripped off the tape, and Gabriel gasped in a breath. For a moment, he could only gulp air into his mouth. Fresh thoughts of Andrew were making his insides petrify. The idea of what just went down with Victor Archwood threatened Gabriel's sanity.

"Well?" Archwood asked.

"My arms." It was all Gabriel could muster. Archwood quickly surveyed Gabriel's arms.

"Oh. I guess they would hurt, wouldn't they? All right, Sergeant, hang in there." Archwood winked at his joke then walked out of Gabriel's sight. He returned a moment later with a stepladder and a stun gun.

"I'm going to let you down and you are going to walk straight to that bed behind you. If you do anything else,

I'll give you this." He waved the stun gun in front of Gabriel's face.

Archwood pulled over a stepladder and climbed up. "It was a bitch getting you up here. I almost hate to let you down." He pushed up at Gabriel's cuffed wrists, which sent twin jolts of burning pain through Gabriel's arms. "That's okay, Sergeant. Moan if you like. I enjoy hearing the sounds you make."

Gabriel fell and Archwood caught him under the arms, slowly bringing them both down. Being hugged in this way by his nemesis caused the nausea to return, and Gabriel was afraid he would vomit. He could smell the skin of Archwood's face and neck, so close to his own—a faraway wisp of expensive cologne and, more apparent, the scent of Gabriel's own musk. He was going to vomit.

Archwood gently released Gabriel to the cold floor and unlocked the cuffs on his ankles.

I could try it now. I could bash his head in.

But when Gabriel tried to lift his arms, they wouldn't work. Archwood hoisted Gabriel to his feet and helped him hobble to a hospital bed. His legs felt spongy. He couldn't figure out why. His ankles and wrists stung. Gabriel could see a flat-screen television on the wall opposite the bed and a long bureau that held all manner of medical items which he wanted to focus on but couldn't. Other than the TV, the walls were bare and stark white. To his immense relief, Archwood laid him out on the bed.

"That's better. Now relax." Archwood proceeded to pull thick leather straps from somewhere under the bed and through the mattress. He tightened them around

Gabriel's calves and thighs and then around his upper and lower arms. "Gotta give those wrists a break. Your ankles are looking bad too. I'll put something on them." He went to the bureau, humming a little tune, something familiar to Gabriel—a song from the musical *Anything Goes*.

In a moment, Archwood was back with a tube of antiseptic cream. He squeezed a bit on his finger then carefully applied the white cream to the abrasions around Gabriel's ankles.

"Vic," Gabriel began.

Archwood glanced at him but made no reply. He continued humming. Gabriel now recognized the song: Cole Porter's "Easy to Love."

The salve soothed Gabriel's burning ankles; the pillow behind his head was soft—lulling temptations in a hellhole. Gabriel had to be careful. He needed to keep his wits sharp, but the fog in his head and the gentle humming... *Good God!*

"What are you doing?" The words creaked out of him.

The humming stopped. "I'm tending your wounds. What do you think I'm doing?"

"No... What do you want from me?"

Archwood moved to Gabriel's wrists and gently rubbed cream on the red scraped flesh. "I think I made it pretty clear what I want from you."

"The crown chakra," Gabriel said weakly.

Archwood paused, perplexed, and then he smiled. "No, I don't want your skills, Sergeant. I don't need help from anyone anymore."

"Then what the hell do you want?"

"Ask me another question, and I'll get out the duct tape. Do you want the duct tape?" Archwood halted his actions, looked at his captive, and waited.

Gabriel stared at him and then shook his head. Archwood nodded satisfactorily and continued humming as he applied the cream. When he was done, he unfolded a sheet and laid it upon Gabriel, neatly tucking it in all around. Then he stepped back to survey his work.

"Okay. It's been over a day since you've had anything to eat, so I'm going to fix you something special. Now, I know you are somewhat of a gourmet chef, so don't hold my cooking against me. I hope you like polenta."

Gabriel continued to stare at him. Archwood seemed to blur in and out of focus. Gabriel's mind was having trouble catching up with each moment.

Archwood chuckled, reached down and cupped Gabriel's chin. "Don't look so mystified, Sergeant. Chill out. Think of this as a vacation of sorts." Archwood released Gabriel's chin and then hopped up the stairs.

Gabriel's head swung forward and he tried to get his bearings. He was bound; he could see that. He tested the straps. The ones on his legs would not budge, but the strap on his lower right arm gave a bit. He pulled and pulled on that one, feeling it loosen. He had to stop every couple of minutes as the exertion made him dizzy and he thought he might puke.

Archwood must have hit him with one powerful drug. But where and when? Gabriel could not focus. Any one thought he captured seemed to slip away the next moment.

He put his hands on me, Gabriel suddenly remembered with revulsion.

Hell, did he put his mouth on me?

Gabriel let his eyes trail down the length of his body, but then he jerked his gaze away, feeling his heart pound, refusing to believe such a thing had happened. It couldn't have happened. Did it happen? This was all part of a nightmare that started at the trial and seemingly would not end.

But it is real, Gabriel thought.

He had become Archwood's prisoner.

Gabriel strained mightily against the loose strap again. Exhaustion forced him to stop, and a strong thumping threatened to crack open his head. Archwood had said a day had gone by, but Gabriel could not remember yesterday. What did he do? Gabriel pushed against the strap, bent his elbow outward and tried to slide his forearm from underneath the leather bond. How did Archwood get at him? Wait, he was at a party—a party at Archwood's house!

Ming! Where was Ming?

The barrel of a gun pressed Gabriel's hand flat against the sheets. Archwood was standing over him, obviously displeased.

"Look up, Sergeant. Do you see that camera mounted on the ceiling?"

Gabriel looked up. He'd missed it. A small camera was mounted on the ceiling. Another camera hung at a different part of the room above a door he hadn't noticed before either.

"What did I say about bullshit? Do you want me to shoot the tendons in your hand?"

"You're fucking crazy," Gabriel muttered and noted that the gun was his very own Redhawk.

"I'll ask again. Do you want me to shoot the tendons in your hand? Yes or no."

"No."

Archwood slammed the gun butt down on Gabriel's hand, which forced an abrupt yell out of his captive. He then tightened the forearm strap as Gabriel's hand swelled and the breath shook in and out of his lungs. Without another word, Archwood jogged back up the stairs.

CHAPTER THIRTY

"I don't know where he's gone." Ming held the phone to her ear and paced around the study in her Los Feliz home. "Are you sure he didn't call you?"

"He didn't call," Jonelle told her.

"And he hasn't shown up for work at all?"

"No. He's still not here."

"I can't figure it out..." Ming said, bewildered.

"Look," Jonelle offered over the phone. "Give him some space, and you'll see. Gabe will be in the office tomorrow, bright and early."

Ming hung up the phone, knowing she had to get to work too. But where was Gabriel? And why had he left her like that?

GABRIEL DIDN'T MOVE. Even though he was thirsty and he had to take a piss, he didn't move. He didn't want to give Archwood the satisfaction of seeing him squirm. Every so often, Gabriel would glance up at the camera. Curiosity eventually got the better of him, and he craned his neck to see the bureau. Some vials and syringes were placed on clean paper towels. A few prescription pill bottles were grouped together, but Gabriel couldn't make out the names. He figured that Archwood had used some sort of knockout drug on him—benzodiazepine perhaps. The loss of consciousness, nausea, amnesia, and lack of willpower, all were symptoms of hypnotics, popular with fraternities, apparently popular with serial killers as well.

Think! You have to get out of here!

Gabriel continued scanning the items on the bureau, when his gaze halted on a tube of lubricant standing in plain sight. Dread formed in his gut.

That was left for me to see, Gabriel knew.

Somehow Archwood knows. He knows what happened. He knows it can break me. He wants me broken.

Gabriel had grossly underestimated his foe. All this time, he thought Archwood desired nothing more than to taunt Gabriel into publicly losing his temper. How wrong he had been...

The room became insufferably quiet. Gabriel heard only the breath whistling in and out of his nose. His eyes moved across the room. He could see now that the wing-back chairs were outfitted with restraints on both the arms and the chair legs. A manacle was attached to a heavy iron staple that protruded from the bureau. The bureau itself was built into the wall. Gabriel swallowed dryly, craving a drink of water.

He heard a distant click, very audible in the quiet of

this room, and then the tap-tap of footsteps. Archwood descended the stairs with a tray of food held aloft and Gabriel's gun tucked into his pants.

"Hungry?"

Archwood put the tray and the gun on the bureau then bent over the side of the hospital bed. With an electric hum, the back of the bed rose until Gabriel was in a seated position. Archwood reached to adjust the bed table.

"I have to use the restroom," Gabriel said.

"Now?"

Gabriel nodded once.

"Can you wait?"

Gabriel shook his head.

Archwood sighed as he looked over the steaming tray of food. "Great."

Holding the gun with one hand, he loosened the straps with the other. "What a stupid frigging hassle." Archwood waved the gun at Gabriel. "Okay, stand up."

Gabriel slowly got out of the bed. Archwood nudged him along with the gun toward the closed door across the room. Gabriel was aware of how much his muscles ached. He felt awful. The younger man opened the door for him.

"Go on."

The bathroom was modern, industrial, and consisted of a large, deep tiled shower with no shower door and a toilet and sink. A roll of bath tissue sat on the toilet lid. Archwood leaned against the doorjamb, watching him.

Gabriel hated this. He hated being under a spotlight. He was being exposed, and he assumed the violations had only just begun. He had to give Archwood a lot of credit. The predator knew his prey. Gabriel went to the toilet, lifted the seat, and let his urine flow. He wouldn't look at Archwood. When he was done he went to the sink and turned on the faucet. There was a mirror above the sink where Gabriel caught sight of his desperate reflection.

"Soap?" he asked.

Archwood opened the cabinet underneath the sink and pulled out a towel and a bar of French-milled soap. The wrapping was already off, but the bar of soap was new and smelled of sage. Gabriel washed his hands and as an afterthought bent down and washed his face.

Gabriel placed the soap on the sink where it swam to the left slightly. He ran his swollen hand under the cold water and then took a long drink from the faucet. Afterward, he picked up the towel.

"Wait," Archwood said.

Gabriel stopped, wet black hair framing his face. Archwood watched the water drip down Gabriel's neck.

"You're really here..." the younger man whispered, more to himself.

Gabriel dried his face and hands, wondering if he had the strength to throttle Victor Archwood with the towel.

Archwood put the gun to Gabriel's head. "Now, come on and eat your dinner."

~

THE BOWL CONTAINED what looked like Cream of Wheat.

"It's polenta with mushrooms and chorizo. The chorizo gives it a little kick." Archwood sat beside Gabriel and dug the spoon into the polenta. Another humiliation—Archwood intended to feed him. He told Gabriel he didn't trust his hands being free.

"Where's Ming?" Gabriel demanded.

The other man ignored the question and tried putting the spoon into Gabriel's mouth.

Gabriel took it, and then spat the polenta onto the floor. "Where's Ming?"

The corners of Archwood's mouth dragged down as he spooned up more meal. He grabbed Gabriel by the hair and brought both the spoon and his blue eyes close to Gabriel's.

"I could always put my dick in your mouth, Sergeant," Archwood said. "Which would you rather swallow?"

The words were a sucker punch to Gabriel. He'd been threatened like this once before, long ago. His insides felt twisted. He couldn't answer.

The abuse rendered you powerless

Archwood grinned and pulled his face away. "She left, okay? Dr. Li isn't here. Are you happy now?"

He merrily slipped the spoon into Gabriel's mouth.

Archwood broke off break off a small piece of a baguette, which he dipped in olive oil. "Would you like some bread?"

Gabriel wondered if Archwood was lying about Ming being safe. He also wondered how Archwood knew of his Achilles heel. If anything could weaken Gabriel it was his experience with Andrew Pierce.

Archwood stuffed the bread into Gabriel's mouth.

"Tasty, isn't it? It's from a bakery on Melrose. How 'bout some wine?"

Archwood didn't wait for a reply and moved to the bureau. Gabriel forced the bread down. It wanted to stick in his throat.

Gabriel eyed Archwood's back. "How long before the poison kicks in, Vic?"

The other man laughed without turning around and said, "Oh, my cooking isn't as bad as all that, is it?"

Archwood returned to Gabriel with a brimming wine glass. "Have you ever heard of Heitz?"

He lifted the glass to Gabriel's lips, which remained closed.

"Come on, Sergeant. It's just wine. This is their Martha's Vineyard Cabernet. It goes well with this type of meal."

"You're quite cultured now, aren't you?" Gabriel said with the rim of the glass glued against his lower lip.

"Prison is a great place to catch up with one's reading. I used the time to educate myself." Archwood tilted the glass and watched Gabriel drink. "You like?"

His prisoner didn't answer.

"Take another sip," Archwood prodded. "Go ahead." He watched Gabriel carefully and then smiled as he set the glass down.

"I ordered a bottle last night at dinner. Dr. Li thought it had a very fine palate, but I don't—"

Gabriel jerked against his bonds. "What?"

"—think she realized how expensive it was."

Archwood retrieved the spoon.

"You leave Ming alone," Gabriel said as the spoon hit

his teeth. "You stay away from her. She's nothing to you!"

Archwood succeeded in plunging the spoon into Gabriel's mouth.

"Stop it!" Gabriel spat out the polenta once again.

The metal spoon chinked loudly against the dish as Archwood scooped up more of the white meal. He forced another spoonful into Gabriel's mouth as Gabriel struggled to turn his face away and strained at the bonds holding down his arms and legs. Polenta ran down his chin as he yelled out, "You motherfucking asshole!"

Archwood quickly jabbed another spoonful at him, and another, the spoon mostly hitting Gabriel's face. Then Archwood abruptly stood up and pinched Gabriel's nostrils. When Gabriel automatically opened his mouth for air, Archwood put the rim of the bowl against his lips and shook polenta down Gabriel's throat. Gabriel choked and sputtered. Archwood then slammed the bowl down on the bed table and backhanded Gabriel across the face, sending bits of polenta flying.

"She's nothing to me?" he said. "She's nothing to you! Not anymore. She was a momentary blip on your radar."

Gabriel could only wheeze and fight for air. Archwood tersely picked up the bowl and tossed it on the tray along with the bread and the olive oil. He turned his back on Gabriel, and his hands clenched the edge of the bureau, hard enough to turn the knuckles white. A moment later, Archwood grasped the wine and took a deep swallow straight from the bottle. Gabriel's convulsing had reduced itself to a mere hacking. Archwood turned around and roughly wiped a cloth napkin across Gabriel's face, chin, and neck.

"Look what you've done," he muttered and released Gabriel, who went limp save for a few coughs. Archwood disappeared into the bathroom, and the water ran as he washed his hands. "It's not that I dislike Dr. Li. We both know she's smoking hot. She just shouldn't be in your life, that's all. You're damaged, Gabriel. We're both damaged. We share that history."

Gabriel stared into his lap, trying to catch his breath. When he looked up again, the room skewed.

Oh, no...

His wary eyes traveled to the bureau where the wine glass stood near an open vial. The haze was creeping back in. *No, no, not now. Not now. I...*

Archwood had returned and was cleaning up; wiping dried polenta off the floor, off the bed sheet, from the leather straps encircling Gabriel's arms. He ignored his captive. Soon, he picked up the tray and climbed the stairs, while the objects in the room danced for Gabriel.

GABRIEL FELT a tugging of the straps, and he opened his eyes to see Vic.

"Liquid Ecstasy. Get you in the mood."

"Don't do it," Gabriel uttered, not sure if he was intelligible.

"Huh?" Vic asked. "Didn't catch that."

Gabriel surmised that he was unintelligible. He felt himself being flipped over onto his stomach. He tried to form words but nothing came out. *Please don't.* The straps went tight again.

He felt something warm and wet drop onto his lower back and his mind began to close down.

Words were whispered very close to Gabriel. They crawled into his ear like insects. "You and I are going to take a trip back to San Francisco."

But Gabriel's mind was already in San Francisco where Andrew Pierce was holding him down.

"Little Buddy."

Little Buddy. That's what Andrew had called me. The Skipper.... Andrew!

Gabriel felt the weight of the other man as he climbed on top of him.

Andrew pushed his hand against my mouth. It hurt but I couldn't scream.

The other man took a rough hold of Gabriel.

"Well, you can scream all you want, Sergeant. I'd like to hear it."

How could you? I looked up to you, Andrew. We were friends.

All movement on the bed came to halt.

VICTOR LET GO of Gabriel and climbed off the bed. He stood looking down at his captive for a moment. He then knelt beside Gabriel and studied his face, half-planted in the down pillow.

"We were friends," Vic murmured. "Good friends."

Gabriel did not seem to see or hear him. Vic sighed and leaned against the side of the bed, thinking. Finally, he whispered, "I can't take from you what I want you to give."

The blond man reached for his pants and put them on. He pointed at his captive. "By the time I'm through with you, you'll want to give me everything you have to give. Do you hear that, Sergeant?"

Vic walked over and shook Gabriel's arm. "Hey. Have you gone catatonic? Do you want a shower?" He spoke loudly in Gabriel's ear. "Do you want to take a shower?"

No response. Vic shrugged and then left Gabriel to go into the bathroom.

He returned a few moments later and addressed his prisoner. "I've started the shower for you. I have soap, shampoo, but no razors. I'll shave you when you need it." Vic rolled his eyes and loosened the leather straps. "Dammit, Gabriel, come on!" He pulled Gabriel to his feet, where Gabriel wobbled unsteadily.

GABRIEL ONLY BECAME aware of his surroundings when he stepped into the water, which was hot, but comfortable. The water ran over him. He couldn't think. He was numb. Gabriel looked toward the door, figuring Archwood would be standing there, but the doorway was empty. It didn't matter. He was dizzy. He wanted to throw up. Nothing mattered. Gabriel only wanted to melt under the hot water. He reached for the soap.

CHAPTER THIRTY-ONE

Ming sat at her desk and gazed at the silent phone. No word from Gabriel, no calls. Perhaps he had run up north to take refuge with his family. Ming had been hesitant to contact Janet. Ever since she'd verbally reamed Gabriel's sister, Ming figured that she'd never talk to the woman again. Ming hesitated, and then picked up the phone.

After a few rings, Janet's voice mail picked up.

"Hi, Janet. It's Ming. Please listen to this message. Gabriel is missing, and I want to know if he's with you or your folks." She paused and then said, "I know I was very rude the last time we spoke, but your brother has left his house and refuses to talk to me. Please call me and let me know if he's with you. I only want to know that he's safe."

~

IN HER LARGE house in Seattle, Janet listened as Ming left her message. When the phone rang and Janet saw "Dr. Ming Li" on the caller ID, she rolled her eyes and refused to answer the call. Ming Li may be some hotshot doctor, but she had no class. That horrible phone call Janet had received at the airport with Ming swearing at her and calling her names. No one had ever spoken to Janet like that before.

So Gabriel had run off. No doubt he was avoiding his loudmouth girlfriend. Janet didn't blame him for that whatsoever.

DOWN IN SANTA MONICA, Victor Archwood was dressed in cut-offs and a tank top. He parked his BMW near the beach. He pulled a skateboard from the trunk, hopped on, and skated down a couple of alleys, making his way toward Gabriel's bungalow. The summer sun shone on his light hair. Anyone noticing him would do so only because he resembled a good-looking surfer and not an ex-killer with a prisoner tied up in a secret room.

Vic arrived at Gabriel's house and opened the front door with the key. Once inside, he grabbed the duffle bag and stuffed shorts, pants, shirts, anything he thought the other man might pack up. Finally, he picked up Gabriel's laptop and shoved that into the duffle bag as well.

Pausing, Victor observed the small home. He knew Gabriel was fastidious and wouldn't leave food to rot, so Victor tossed any perishables into a trash bag and dumped the bag into the outside garbage pail. He dragged the trash to the street and wiped his hands on his shorts. Operation Deconstruct Gabriel was moving along nicely.

He then returned to the house and searched the drawers for any bills the detective might have incurred. He found them stacked in a small basket in the kitchen. Everything Vic had read in Gabriel's case file pointed to an intensely private man who, despite suffering from post-traumatic stress disorder, was very responsible. No matter how messed up Gabriel had been he'd always managed to keep on top of his debts. Vic rather admired that.

He felt euphoric as he dug through Gabriel's things. Everything Gabriel owned now belonged to Vic. He was amazed at how good it felt to know he commanded power over the detective. He'd always been so intimidated by Gabriel. Well, not anymore. He knew how to control Gabriel now.

He rummaged through a couple of drawers and saw some keys, pens, an old paycheck stub, and a television channel lineup from a cable company. As Vic pushed the drawer closed, something oval rolled into his view.

An involuntary shiver ran down Vic's spine and he winced as the oval object sparked a memory. An instant flicker of flame shed weak light on a mental room engulfed in black.

Victor reached into the drawer and pulled out the Easter egg his grandfather had made for him long ago. His eyes blinked in rapid sequence, and he heard his grandfather's voice, thick with a Russian accent. The flame grew brighter in Vic's head, illuminating the black room. So many trinkets filled that room. A blue plastic cowboy hat. A toy robot frozen with one arm up and one arm down—

I had no idea how to put in the batteries.

Quiet words, whispered words, a Russian accent.

Dedushka…

Vic flipped his fingernail against the clasp of the egg and it instantly opened like a box. He used his thumb to snap the lid closed. Mechanically, he opened the box and closed it again.

One arm up and one arm down…

Cobwebs hung over a gray-sheeted bed.

Run from this room!

Victor forced his mind to fast-forward to a different time, to a night bloated with fog, where he stood on a balcony overlooking a furious ocean.

Gabriel McRay had been there with him. Gabriel had thrown Grandfather's gifts over the railing. There had been three delicately fashioned boxes in total: the Easter egg, a Christmas tree, and two entwined hearts. Once upon a time, there had been candy inside them.

The candy was Dedushka's secret.

We had other secrets between us too. Didn't we?

Vic threw the egg back into the drawer, and it rolled like a sneaking demon into the black depths. He slammed the drawer shut as anger thundered through him. Gabriel McRay had kept this box to trick him!

ALONE IN THE BASEMENT ROOM, Gabriel stared at a

television program that he was not watching. Nothing on TV could supersede the real-life drama Gabriel was reliving in his own mind. He couldn't remember all that happened last night, and he was racking his brain. He remembered Vic crawling on top of him, and then things went blank. His memory was blocked, just like before.

Gabriel felt a groan wanting to escape, and he suppressed it down deep into his belly, where it hung there, weighing him down. Whatever happened last night, Archwood had reawakened terrible memories, and now Gabriel's head was once again filled with the most disturbing recollections of Andrew Pierce.

Tied down, he couldn't escape his mind.

He heard the door upstairs open, and he steeled himself for whatever might come his way.

Victor Archwood appeared, and in his hand, he held Gabriel's duffle bag. Archwood did not look at him, and Gabriel said nothing. The noise from the TV was a welcomed distraction. Archwood laid the duffle bag on the small table between the two chairs. He took Gabriel's laptop from the bag and set it down. He then began pulling Gabriel's clothing from the bag and folding the items neatly into the bureau drawers.

Archwood has been in my home, Gabriel thought as he watched the other man. *He's gone through my things*.

"Do you pay your bills online or should I use your checkbook?" Archwood finally spoke.

He had his bills? Gabriel stared at the other man unbelievingly.

"Do you pay your bills online," Archwood repeated angrily, "or should I write a check?"

"I pay online. Why are you doing this, Vic?"

Archwood swiveled his face toward Gabriel's. "That was very cagey of you, Sergeant, to keep something of mine without asking me."

Tickertape of possibilities quickly ran through Gabriel's head as he tried to figure out what Archwood was referring to. Then he remembered.

The Easter egg... He must have found the egg.

Archwood walked to the bed and hovered over Gabriel like a blond ghost. He studied his captive for a long while and then put his index finger in the center of Gabriel's forehead. He pressed hard, pushing Gabriel's head back against the pillow. Gabriel could feel a fingernail gouging his skin. After a moment or two, Archwood retracted his hand.

"I have to know," Gabriel said as the other man gazed at him.

"What do you need to know, Sergeant?"

"You drugged me."

"I did," Archwood confirmed.

After a moment, Gabriel whispered, "What else?"

"Can't you remember?" The other man's lips curved into a grin, which slowly evaporated in the heat of a blossoming rage. "Maybe nothing happened at all. Maybe you're having the sick and twisted fantasies of a perverted pedophile."

Gabriel squinted up at him. "Is that what all this is about?"

Archwood ignored the question. "It's the not-knowing that really eats at you, doesn't it, Sergeant? Makes you think you might be losing your mind." Archwood turned away. "Well, better to lose your mind than your heart, I always say. Since last night was obviously not too memorable for you, we won't discuss it anymore."

"I'll kill you, Vic," Gabriel told him.

"Nice talk coming from an officer of the law." Archwood walked over to the wingback chair, picked up Gabriel's laptop, and plopped into the chair. "Should we check your e-mail?"

He logged into Gabriel's e-mail and read silently as his prisoner watched him.

"Ming Li is a pain in the ass." Archwood grimaced. "She's sent you a million e-mails. How obnoxious."

Archwood typed rapidly and then read his reply out loud for Gabriel. "Ming, stop bugging me. I will get in touch with you when I work things out." He looked over at Gabriel. "Does that sound like you?"

The mention of Ming caused a wave of panic to roll through Gabriel. How could Archwood possibly get to her? Ming herself wouldn't get within a hundred miles of the killer, but Archwood claimed to have had dinner with her. Was it a lie made up for Gabriel's benefit? It had to be a lie...

Suddenly, Archwood perked up in his chair.

"What do we have here?" he said in a singsong voice. "Pictures!"

Gabriel felt his pulse rise.

"I almost forgot about your niece and nephew." The Malibu Canyon Murderer held the laptop up so Gabriel could see the pictures of Liam and Amber. "So cute. The little one takes after you. Oh, and here's Mom and Dad.

The caption says Mom and Dad, Seattle. That's touching."

Archwood accessed Gabriel's address book. "I'm assuming McRay means relative. Yep, here we are. 12247 Bodega Drive. Mom and Dad."

"Don't even think about it," Gabriel warned.

"Or what?" Archwood teased. "You met my family. It's only fair I get to know yours. Think I ought to introduce myself to your family?"

"Leave them alone."

"That's up to you, Sergeant. The ball is in your court, as they say."

This is what Andrew did, Gabriel thought.

He threatened to kill Janet if I didn't answer when he came calling...

"Tell you what," Archwood said from behind the computer. "You act nice to me and they won't ever have to see my face."

Gabriel felt his insides crumble at the memory of Andrew Pierce uttering the same sentiments. Powerless to do anything else, he watched Archwood delve through all his computer files, picking apart his private life like a vulture on road kill.

CHAPTER THIRTY-TWO

Ming read the e-mail from Gabriel and shook her head. *Stop bugging me?* He disappears from her life and that's all he has to say? She crossed her arms and stared dumbfounded at the e-mail message.

Ethan entered her office in a rush. "Sorry, I'm late. I lost track of time."

Ming wasn't angry. In fact, she had forgotten all about Ethan. Her long dark hair fell in an unbrushed mass about her face. Under her lab coat, her clothes were wrinkled.

Not really wanting to think about work, Ming gave her intern some random filing. After a few minutes, she announced he could go home, but Ethan chose to stay and do the busywork. Despite her current anxious state, Ming found herself respecting the graduate student's sense of responsibility and the fact that he seemed genuinely concerned for her welfare.

Around lunchtime, Ramirez and Jonelle entered her

office. Ming felt her heart drop upon seeing their serious faces. Had they come to deliver bad news?

"Where is he?" The anguish in Ming's voice caused Ethan to pause at the file cabinet.

"That's what we hoped you would tell us," Jonelle replied.

Ramirez stepped forward. "When you last spoke to Gabriel, what did he say?"

"Why?" Ming asked, her eyes darting between both visitors. "What are you doing here? What do you know?"

Ramirez noticed Ethan then and refused to speak further. He looked to Ming for an explanation.

"Oh, this is my intern, Ethan Post." Ming turned to the student. "Ethan, this is Lieutenant Miguel Ramirez and Detective Jonelle Williams."

Ethan extended his hand to both officers. They politely shook hands with him and then turned their attention back to Ming. Ethan took the cue and excused himself.

When the door closed behind the intern, Ming turned to Ramirez.

"When I last spoke to Gabriel he was so angry," she said. "He told me he didn't want to see me anymore."

Ramirez exchanged a surprised glance with Jonelle, and then he held out a letter to Ming. "I got his resignation in the mail this morning."

"What?" Ming's eyes widened in disbelief and she took the note. Reading it, she shook her head wildly. "No. There is no way Gabriel would quit his job."

Ramirez shrugged. "We were hoping you could explain this."

Ming continued shaking her head. "He would not leave me and he would not quit the bureau. No way."

"When was the last time you saw him?" Ramirez asked.

"At Victor Archwood's."

The lieutenant grimaced—a mixed look of disbelief and revulsion. "What the hell were you doing there?"

"Archwood wouldn't stop harassing Gabriel," Ming explained quickly. "He was having this party, and Gabriel saw it as an opportunity..."

Her voice trailed off as she saw Ramirez's expression darken. He then pursed his lips into a tight line and shook his head. After a moment, he asked, "And then what happened?"

"Gabriel left. He said he couldn't take it anymore and ran out of there."

Jonelle asked, "And you haven't seen him since?"

"He told me we don't have a relationship anymore." Ming grabbed a tissue from a box on her desk, but her eyes remained dry.

Ramirez looked steadily at Ming. "It says in his resignation letter that he needs time to deal with what Dash did. McRay has never been the most stable person. Maybe he needs time alone somewhere."

Ming crushed the tissue in her hand. "No, that doesn't make sense. He just moved into a new house, he's rebuilding relations with his family..."

Ming trailed off, remembering how hurt Gabriel had been over Janet's suspicions of him. But he had been handling it. He'd been dealing with it.

With a more determined voice, she said, "He wouldn't leave."

"Then what should we do?" Jonelle asked her.

"Send someone to question Victor Archwood," Ming said as she trashed the tissue bits. "That's the last place Gabriel was seen. Maybe Archwood knows something."

"But you saw Gabriel leave the premises," Ramirez stated. "On what grounds do I have to bother Archwood?"

"On the grounds he's a psycho killer!" Ming yelled. A moment passed and she composed herself. "One of your team members has gone missing, Miguel. Are you sure you don't want to trust your gut on this one?"

Ramirez didn't answer.

"With all that Gabriel has been through," Ming pressed, "have you ever known him to run away?"

The short lieutenant sighed and fished for the pack of Winstons in his pocket.

"Fine," Ramirez muttered. "I'll think of some excuse to go harass Archwood. Next they'll be asking for my badge."

ANDREA STOOD at Victor's front door, giggling with excitement. She reached out and rang the bell. Tonight she wore a designer coat over a red lace bustier, red lace panties, a red garter belt, and silky red stockings. She stood in black stiletto heels and waited for her boyfriend to answer.

When Victor opened the door, she traipsed inside like a fashion model and said, "I have a big surprise for you!"

She let the coat drop to the floor.

"Happy anniversary, baby."

Victor gave her an approving smile. "What a nice present. But I didn't realize it was our anniversary."

Andrea threw her arms around her handsome boyfriend. "It's only a couple of months, but why not celebrate every minute?"

Victor looked wistfully toward his study, and Andrea tugged at his shirt collar.

"Uh-uh," she told him. "You're not paying attention to anything else but me tonight. Got that?" She turned her eyes toward the study. "What's in there anyhow? What are you working on?"

"Business," he answered, and then he added ominously, "And it's private business. That's one room that is off limits to you, okay?"

She rolled her eyes and lifted her face up to kiss him. He gripped her shoulders hard.

"Look at me," he demanded.

Feeling a little pain from his tight grip, Andrea met her boyfriend's eyes.

"Say you understand," Vic said.

"Ouch." She wriggled under his hands. "I understand. You can have your dumb room."

Vic loosened his grip and then kissed her lips. Andrea, relieved to have her lover back, playfully took his hand and began to skip toward the master bedroom.

Vic reluctantly followed her.

. . .

She tossed herself onto the big bed and then stretched out seductively, making sure she showed off her new lingerie. Observing her, an idea occurred to Victor, and he suddenly became more animated. He dimmed the lights and lay down next to her with a smile.

"What a pretty outfit," he said, playing with the hooks on her bustier.

She giggled and reached her hand into his slacks. Pleased with what she found, she unzipped him. She nibbled his neck while she kept her hand in his pants. He took hold of her hair and pushed her head down toward his groin. Andrea acquiesced, and soon Victor was closing his eyes and his breathing got heavier.

A minute or so passed, and he opened his eyes to watch the up and down motions of his girlfriend's head. While she was otherwise engaged, Vic very carefully reached out his hand and picked up a large, heavy book on his nightstand. He glanced down at Andrea who was busy with her eyes closed. Victor carefully raised the book.

He leaned it against one of five unmarked call buttons on an intercom affixed beside the bed.

Then he took hold of Andrea and bade her stop.

"Turn over," he commanded.

Wiping her mouth, Andrea leaned back against the pillows. Vic spread her knees apart and tucked his hands under her derriere. He licked the sweet flesh of her thigh, trailed his tongue toward the center between her legs and then bit her cinnamon skin.

~

DOWN IN THE BASEMENT, with only the bathroom light illuminating the secret room, Gabriel heard a woman cry out. He quickly looked toward the television, but the set was dark. He then realized the sound was coming from the intercom speaker. Breathy, intense gasps filled the room—over and over again, punctured by a cry.

Vic's killing Miss Leighton, Gabriel decided, knowing he could do nothing but bear witness to her death. Unless his finger was pressing the intercom button, no one would be able to hear his protests.

Then a long, luxurious moan hit his ears. The poorly lit basement room echoed with female giggles.

With some shame, Gabriel realized that the sounds he had heard were not yelps and cries of pain, but of sexual pleasure. Hating Archwood all the more for showing him what he was missing, Gabriel pressed uselessly against his bonds and then hung his head at this new indignity.

Minutes passed. Gabriel had no clue as to how many. He felt himself on the verge of sleep, when he heard the door click above the stairs. He watched Archwood enter, wearing only a robe and carrying with him the memory of a woman's perfume.

Archwood sat next to Gabriel on the bed.

"How did you like the evening's entertainment?"

Gabriel made no reply.

"She sure can howl, can't she?"

Angry, Gabriel turned his face toward the wall. Archwood grabbed Gabriel's chin and forced him to look at him. In response, Gabriel yanked his head away.

"If it's any consolation," Archwood said, "I'd much rather be with you than her."

Now Gabriel did turn to face his nemesis. He stared at the other man in disbelief. Did Archwood think Gabriel was jealous?

The younger man leaned over and gently kissed Gabriel on the lips. He drew back to tenderly regard his captive.

"Do that again," Gabriel told him evenly, "and I'll tear your mouth off with my teeth."

Archwood's pale cheeks reddened, and he began to shake with anger. "Why?" he asked furiously. "Why do you have to fight me?"

He promptly stood up and moved to his array of pills and vials, where his fingers rifled through the collection. He plucked a small bottle from the bureau and shoved the drug in Gabriel's face.

"Permax," he announced. "A dopamine-enhancer used by victims of Parkinson's." Archwood wasted no time in filling a syringe.

"You can drug me all you want, Vic. To me, you're still a murdering bastard."

In response, Archwood rammed the needle into Gabriel's vein and watched the syringe empty.

Too soon, Gabriel imagined he saw masks—comedy and tragedy, only all the comedic smiles morphed into frowns. He saw Andrea Leighton in her kitty-cat mask, meowing and pawing at Archwood, who wore a mask of normalcy. He saw Jonelle dressed as the Canadian Mountie Dudley Do-Right, and that made Gabriel smile.

From afar, he heard Archwood cursing and telling Gabriel that he needed to be broken like a wild horse. Gabriel felt maneuvered around. He felt the straps loosen and he knew he should try breaking free. But he was having an out-of-body experience, and by the time the decision to free himself surfaced to Gabriel's conscious mind, the straps were tight around his limbs once more and Archwood's breath was in his ear.

He thought it strange that the gym shorts he wore stayed put. And then there was the unexpected sting of another needle. He was sure he felt that in his shoulder. For a moment Gabriel felt nothing, he was floating, feeling the objects in the room undulate gently about him like ripples on a lake. And then he could swear Archwood held an object against his nose. Did he want Gabriel to smell something? Gabriel wanted to laugh, thinking the idea ludicrous. But then he inhaled the scent of black licorice—a scent that instantly pulled the trigger of a mental gun that fired a bullet so explosive into Gabriel, it tore the breath from his body.

CHAPTER THIRTY-THREE

J anet's phone rang. She looked at the Caller ID and saw that it was Ming again.

Rolling her eyes, she picked up the phone.

"Yes?"

"Don't hang up."

"What do you want?" Janet asked curtly.

"I just want to know if you've seen Gabriel lately."

Janet could sense unshed tears in Ming's voice. Still, who did she think she was, expecting things to be all right between them?

"Is he still missing?" Janet asked, frustrated with herself that she cared to know.

Ming seemed anxious to vent because her words came out in a flood. "Yes, and he gave his resignation. You know how much he enjoys his work. You know he wouldn't quit. I was hoping he had come up to see you."

"Why would you think that?"

Ming went silent as if shocked by the question. Then she said in a strained voice, "Because he loves you. He gets so much comfort from you, your parents... Your children."

Now, it was Janet's turn to be silent.

"If he's up there," Ming begged, "please tell me."

Janet bristled, refusing to pity the other woman. And wasn't this just like Gabriel? Always drawing attention to himself. Obviously, her brother had drawn in a little pet dog named Ming Li who followed him around and pandered to his ills.

"He's not here," Janet replied. "If you do see him, could you tell him to quit being selfish and call his mother?"

"There's something wrong, Janet. Gabriel would not disappear like this."

"He disappeared from our lives for many years, Ming. No words, no contact, no returned phone calls. This is what Gabriel does."

"You're wrong," Ming told her. "You are absolutely wrong."

Janet chewed at her lower lip and asked herself, do I really have to be on the phone with this person?

No, I do not.

So Janet hung up.

ARCHWOOD RAN the razor blade down Gabriel's neck. In the quiet of the bathroom, the sound of the blade moving wetly along his flesh seemed amplified. Archwood worked methodically, wiping the razor against a towel or running it under water.

When he first came at Gabriel with the razor, Gabriel was sure that the killer had some sort of torture in mind. Maybe he wanted to peel at Gabriel's flesh with the small blade. Instead, Archwood moved Gabriel to a chair in the bathroom, cuffed his wrists, and then rubbed shaving foam on his cheeks, chin, and throat.

Humming "Easy to Love," Archwood shaved Gabriel.

At times, their eyes met in the mirror, and Gabriel thought he saw longing in Archwood's gaze. Not sexual desire, but some sort of longing. Gabriel wondered what the other man wanted that he hadn't already taken.

Now finished, Archwood wiped Gabriel's face with the towel and, while holding the Taser, untied him.

"Okay, let's go back."

He prodded Gabriel toward the bed and lightly pushed him with the Taser to lie down. Archwood strapped Gabriel's right arm first and then his right leg. As he made his way to the left side of the bed, the intercom buzzed, cracking the silent shell of the room. Both men gaped at the intercom.

Archwood quickly crossed the room and pressed the call button. "Yes?"

"It's the police."

Archwood paused, eyed the floor in quick thought, and then said, "I'll be right there."

Gabriel watched him jog up the stairs. He heard the now familiar click of the door shutting. His eyes dropped to the bed. Archwood had left two of the leather straps unclasped.

ON HIS SECURITY MONITOR, Victor could see two uniformed cops standing at his front door. Taking a deep breath, he walked to the door and opened it wide. He gave the cops a genial smile.

"What can I do for you?"

"We're sorry to bother you, Mr. Archwood. We've had a complaint about excessive dog barking."

Vic arched an eyebrow. "That's odd, seeing that I don't own a dog."

The cops appeared embarrassed. Vic sighed inwardly. He could make them get a warrant. He could give them a hard time. Instead, he showed his straight, white teeth in a renewed smile and said, "Would you like to come in and see for yourself?"

They were more than eager. Vic struggled to keep the fake smile on his face. He would have to do something about the annoying Dr. Ming Li. The cops stepped into the foyer.

"You've got a beautiful home, sir."

"I like it."

They walked around, their duty belts squeaking as they moved. One cop came perilously close to the wall panel that hid the secret basement door as he paused to view the painting of the bleeding, ethereal child.

"Interesting picture," the cop said.

"It's a Ryden. From his Blood series."

The cop made a murmuring sound as if he knew of the painter. He didn't, Vic was sure. The cop moved away from the secret door, and Vic felt a pang of relief.

DOWNSTAIRS, Gabriel yelled out toward the ceiling, "Hey! I'm down here!"

He struggled with the two bonds that claimed him, but they wouldn't budge. He reached as far as he could to touch the locking mechanism on the side of the bed, but his fingers fell short.

THE TWO UNIFORMED policemen made a cursory inspection of each room, commenting to Vic when something impressive about the decor struck them. It was all bullshit, Vic knew. They were looking for Gabriel McRay. They weren't going to find him.

"Thank you for being cooperative, Mr. Archwood."

"I certainly wouldn't want my imaginary dog to be a nuisance to the neighbors," Vic said as he accompanied them into the backyard.

GABRIEL USED all his might to push against the leather strap with his arm muscles while pulling at it with his free hand to loosen it. He kept hunching his right shoulder upward, trying to get his arm to slip through. It was excruciatingly hard work, but soon his efforts paid off. He was able to slip his arm out of the bond. He grabbed the straps holding his right leg and began to shake and pull violently at them.

VICTOR WALKED the two policemen to the front door.

"We're sorry to have bothered you," one of the cops apologized.

"No trouble at all, officers." Vic watched them walk the down the driveway to their squad car.

IN THE SECRET ROOM, Gabriel broke free. He ran across the smooth floor, raced up the stairs, and grabbed the door handle.

At that same moment, the door swung open and Gabriel received a face full of pepper spray. Snarling like a rabid animal, Archwood nearly emptied the can on him. Gasping, Gabriel clutched at his face and hobbled backward. Archwood then zapped him with the stun gun. Gabriel didn't even feel the stairs as he toppled down them.

CHAPTER THIRTY-FOUR

Jonelle Williams tapped on Lieutenant Ramirez's office door.

"May I come in?" she asked.

He gestured for her to enter. She closed the door behind her and took a seat in the chair opposite his desk. Ramirez wore a glum look as he twirled a plastic stirrer in a mug of coffee. A couple of case files sat untouched upon his desk, and Jonelle pointed to them.

"Something new?"

"Uh, yeah. I was going to brief you on one of them."

Jonelle waited, but her superior did nothing except stir his coffee, which appeared to be cold.

"Are you waitin' on Gabriel?" Jonelle ventured to ask.

The question came unexpectedly and Ramirez raised his intense brown eyes to hers.

"I guess I am. Stupid, huh? We've got work to do here."

Jonelle sighed. "It's not stupid. I keep looking at his

chair, thinking I'll see him there. You'd think he'd want to clear his desk."

Ramirez pushed the coffee away and thoughtfully rested his chin on his hands. "Everything's still there?"

"Everything's still there."

"Archwood is clean, Jonelle. Two of our guys searched his place thoroughly and saw no sign of McRay."

Jonelle leaned forward in the chair. "This is so freaky. It's like he just up and disappeared."

Ramirez changed the subject. "Where are you on the Pennington case?"

"The lab confirmed that the plant-like substance Gabriel found contains the poison that Dr. Li identified as ouabain."

Ramirez chuckled and shook his head. "McRay... He drives me loco, but damn if he doesn't have good instincts."

"What should we do?" Jonelle asked. "Before he left, Gabriel told me we needed proof that Mr. King used the poison before we can go forward. I would agree."

The Mexican lieutenant didn't reply. He was too preoccupied, wondering where one of his best detectives had run off to and fighting the temptation to open up a missing person's case in Gabriel's name.

A STEEL-BLUE SKY hung above Janet as she sat on a deck chair next to her mother. Seattle was blessed with a clear day, and Janet and Mrs. McRay sat on chaise lounges outside. They watched the kids run circles around their grandfather at the water's edge. Although the sun was bright, the two women wore light sweaters. Mrs. McRay's salt-and-pepper hair ruffled in the breeze that moved in from the locks. Janet noticed that her mother's gaze was well out upon the water and not on the children.

"What are you thinking about, Ma?"

Mrs. McRay pulled her sweater tight with hands that were chapped and red.

"I'm thinking of last times," the older woman said.

Janet squinted in the cool sunshine and waited.

Mrs. McRay watched the water. "I breastfed two children."

Worried that her mother might be losing it from stress, Janet opened her mouth to question that remark, when Mrs. McRay continued.

"At some point, I nursed you and your brother for the last time, but I don't remember when. I've been trying to think back, but for the life of me, I can't remember."

Mrs. McRay turned her face up to the sun and closed her eyes. "Don't you think last times should be heralded somehow? Inscribed in stone or celebrated? I can't remember the last time your father and I had a normal conversation. I know it took place, but I can't recall it."

Janet reached out and held her mother's dry hand.

The children splashed water on each other while Pete McRay warned them to be careful.

"Why isn't he calling, Janet?"

Janet squeezed Mrs. McRay's hand, knowing that she missed her son. Janet had read that sorrow on her mother's face the moment she'd arrived.

"Now, that's a last time I do remember," Mrs. McRay said and opened her eyes to view the water again. "I made myself remember touching Gabriel's face, just in case it didn't happen again."

Janet felt her heart break. No matter how badly her brother acted, her parents remained faithful to him. Janet wanted to launch into her usual diatribe against Gabriel; to remind her mother how selfish and immature he was, how he tossed people out of his life like so much garbage. But something in Mrs. McRay's eyes stopped her. That, and the way her children lit up when they talked about their uncle. Most of all, Janet held her tongue because of something Ming said.

It's the lowest person that holds her kids for ransom.

I don't do that, Janet reminded herself. People couldn't blame her for being concerned about Gabriel's issues, could they?

Judgmental bitch…

Sometimes people who were scarred didn't function properly. Her first obligation was to protect her own children. Who could blame her?

Janet tried to veer her thoughts back to how much pain Gabriel caused his mother, but Ming's accusing voice would not be silenced.

When Gabriel was a boy younger than your own son he loved you so much he protected your ass by getting…

Janet bit at a hangnail, surprised to feel the pressure of tears building against her eyes. She glanced at her children and inwardly prayed that they would always look out for each other, be kind to each other.

He protected you.

Janet tore the hangnail off. Suddenly, a cold fear fell upon her. The minute the resentment vacated her heart she felt afraid for Gabriel. Ming had said he'd gone missing. What if something bad had happened to him? Should she tell her mother? She looked desperately at Mrs. McRay.

"What's wrong, honey?" her mother asked.

Janet didn't reply. She didn't want to worry the older woman.

"Excuse me, Ma." She hoisted herself up from the lounge. "I need to make a phone call."

CHAPTER THIRTY-FIVE

Ming received Janet's call on her cell phone as she sat in traffic on the freeway. She eagerly answered the call, thinking maybe Gabriel had shown up in Seattle.

"Yes, Janet?"

"Have you heard from him yet?" Janet asked.

Ming's shoulders fell. "No, I was hoping you had."

The two women fell silent on the phone, not quite knowing how to handle each other. Janet spoke first.

"Can't the police try locating him?"

"No," Ming told her. "Everyone thinks he's run off. I don't know, Janet. I don't know what to do! Even though he told me on the phone he didn't want to see me, I refuse to believe it. Am I crazy?"

"No," Janet replied. "You know him better than anyone."

"That's right. And this is not like him. He would not run off." Ming was quiet for a moment and then said, "I know he ignored you and your parents. He feels bad about that, Janet. He really does. That's why you all are so important to him now. Gabriel would not run away!"

"Do you want me to fly down?"

The offer surprised Ming. At first, she wanted to jump at the chance to have a compatriot around who believed her. Someone who had a stake in finding Gabriel, just like she did. But then Ming remembered how much Janet disliked her. Things would be awkward between them.

"You don't have to come down. At this point, there's nothing to be done." Ming paused. "Look, I'm sorry. I know I said horrible things to you. It's a fault of mine."

JANET'S first inclination was to agree but found herself mute as she tried to cut a clear path through her emotions. There didn't seem to be a clear path.

"Well, if you don't need me," she said, "I won't come. But please call if you hear anything, anything at all. I'll do the same."

MING ENDED the call with Janet and kept her eyes on the line of cars ahead on the highway. With some sadness, she realized that she didn't have any friends. There was no one she could call and commiserate with. Her parents lived across the country, and she didn't have the kind of relationship with them in which she could cry on their shoulders. Ming never had to cry on anyone's shoulder—not before she met Gabriel. She'd been safe, ensconced in the hard exterior of her busy career. The consummate over-achiever.

Gabriel's issues had brought out the nurturer in Ming. His humor encouraged her wit. He brought out a passion in her that toppled her to-do list. Above all, Gabriel knew how to make Ming feel feminine. As cliché as it might sound, he made her feel like a woman.

Ming wouldn't have minded if Janet came down. The two of them might not become friends, but they could certainly join forces in hunting down Gabriel. They did have him in common.

MILES away from where Ming was stuck in traffic, Victor Archwood was cuffing Gabriel to the treadmill and asking at what level he would like to work out.

Relieved to be away from the bed, Gabriel undertook an advanced workout. As soon as he started jogging though, he realized how out of shape he was.

Gabriel swiveled his head to survey Archwood as he changed the bedding.

"I suppose it's useless to ask how long you intend to keep me chained up," he called out.

"If you would stop fighting me," the other man responded, "I wouldn't chain you up."

Gabriel didn't believe that. Archwood enjoyed keeping him subdued, but there was a reason the other man hadn't killed him. What exactly did Archwood want? Gabriel watched his feet as they ran on the belt. *I could pretend to be his friend. Maybe I could gain the advantage that way.*

Finished with the bed, Archwood retrieved Gabriel's gun and moved over to the treadmill. He observed Gabriel's labored breathing, slowed the speed, and then rested his arms on the machine.

"I know you think I'm crazy," he commented as he watched Gabriel jog. "But you've got to understand, I'm different than most people."

That's an understatement.

Feigning civility, Gabriel asked, "How so?"

"What comprises most people's lives, Sergeant? What do most people do every day?"

Gabriel kept his eyes on the moving belt below him. He didn't relish trading philosophies with a murderer, but he figured he ought to keep Archwood relaxed, maybe get him vulnerable. It was an interrogation technique, although Gabriel didn't employ it much. Dash was the one who was good at earning people's trust.

Dash!

Gabriel shrugged. "I don't know, Vic."

"I'll tell you," Archwood said. "Eat, play, work, screw and sleep. That's it. And while they're doing one, they're most likely thinking about the other."

"But not you." Gabriel tried to keep the sneer out of his tone.

"I didn't say that. I think about those things a lot, only I want more." Archwood gazed at the gun in his hand. "I don't get upset if someone is rude or cuts me off on the road. You know why? Because I know I can make that person die. He doesn't know that, but I do. It's a pretty liberating feeling."

Gabriel gave him a sidelong glance. "Being a murderer is liberating?"

Archwood's blue eyes found his. "Don't tell me you've never experienced that power behind your badge, Sergeant. If I'm not mistaken, this lethal weapon belongs to you. And you've used it, haven't you? You used it well, as I recall. If your career allows you that kind of freedom, what's to stop me?"

"It's called a conscience, Vic."

"Yeah, but what is it good for?"

Gabriel grimaced. *Fuck pretending to be his friend.* Just the sight of Archwood turned Gabriel's stomach. And he had to bring up Gabriel's checkered past. This was the same man who viciously dug holes into innocent people.

I can't let him turn the tables on me, Gabriel thought. *Even if he's good at it.*

"Then it's all about feeling powerful, right, Vic?"

"I don't have to feel it. It doesn't come and go. It's always there. It's who I am."

Gabriel nodded. *And I don't have a clue as to what you're talking about, you psycho-prick.*

Aloud he said, "And how'd you get that way?"

Archwood's baby-blues blinked with sincerity. "Glinda the Good Witch told me she'd share the secrets of the universe with me if I sucked off her wand. Are you trying to psychoanalyze me, Sergeant?" His shoulders shook with laughter. "You can't outthink me. Don't even try."

Still laughing, Vic freed Gabriel's hands—and Gabriel

immediately lurched forward and wrapped them around the younger man's neck.

Just as fast, Gabriel felt the hard nose of the Redhawk press into his abdomen.

"Go ahead and regret it," the blond man hissed in Gabriel's grip.

Gabriel loosened his hold and Archwood shook him off and pointed the gun in his face. Gabriel stood, weighing his options. He could tackle Archwood and take his chances with being shot.

Archwood cocked the gun and aimed for Gabriel's upper arm.

"I won't kill you, Sergeant. I'll just make you bleed. And then I'll go after everyone you care about. It will be my pleasure. Did you forget we had a deal?"

Gabriel wavered.

"Who will be first?" Archwood pressed. "Dr. Li? Mom or Dad? What about the little girl? She might be nice company for me."

At the thought of Amber, of any of them, being confronted with Victor Archwood, Gabriel's shoulders fell. With the keen sense of a wild being, Archwood saw Gabriel's resignation and quickly took the opportunity to use the gun to prod Gabriel back toward the bed.

"I do like bringing out the beast in you. But don't piss me off too much, Sergeant, or your loved ones will lose their lives."

He shoved his captive down on the mattress.

"You enjoy taking lives," Gabriel countered. "Don't you, Vic?"

"And I remember every life I took." Archwood pulled

the leather straps across Gabriel's arms and legs. "They made me what I am today."

"A murderer," Gabriel grunted as the straps went tight.

The blond man, less tense now with Gabriel incapacitated, sat on the bed. "You still don't get me, do you?"

"What don't I get, Vic? How special you are?"

Archwood quickly cuffed Gabriel's cheek with the gun. "Watch it, Sergeant."

Gabriel's face stung but he continued to glare at the other man.

Archwood didn't appear fazed. "Now that you bring it up, I will say that I am special. I've found a way to tap into certain forces."

"Is that right?" Gabriel's voice oozed with sarcasm.

It was dangerous to taunt Archwood. The man claimed to have access to Ming and knew how to find Gabriel's family. But Gabriel refused to succumb to his enemy's need for control. The thought of being dominated by Victor Archwood, in both body and mind, was something he had to fight.

Helplessness and powerlessness are nearly intolerable to males.

Dr. B had driven that point home. Gabriel had been a mere child when Andrew molested him, unable to protect himself. He had lived with the self-blame and the resulting emasculation for his entire life and refused to go through it again. But Gabriel didn't want to bet on whether or not Archwood would go after his family and Ming. The man had killed before and he would kill again.

Archwood, oblivious to Gabriel's inner dialogue, prattled on. "I've used these forces to improve my powers. I admit I am the ultimate hedonist."

Gabriel regarded the younger man with contempt. "Yeah, well, everyone pays for their fun in the sun."

"I see." Archwood smiled. "Are you gonna make me pay, Sergeant?"

"That would be *my* pleasure."

The blond man laughed. "It's funny how I can be myself around you. Only you know the real me. That makes you very special yourself."

He lifted his hand and softly traced Gabriel's face; gently touching the mark the gun had left on Gabriel's cheek.

"I need you... too much, I think." His hand moved to Gabriel's hair, and he fingered the dark curls. As a child, Vic had loved playing with Gabriel's hair, which had been much longer then.

"Do you get it now?" Archwood asked softly.

Gabriel looked his nemesis in the eye. "I don't get it, Vic. I guess I'm too dumb. And I can't figure out why you haven't killed me yet. Why don't you tell me the reason?"

Archwood gazed at him for a moment and then looked away in disappointment. "I'm going out. We need some things." He hesitated and then quickly kissed the top of Gabriel's head. "I won't be long."

CHAPTER THIRTY-SIX

Andrea Leighton walked up Victor's driveway, struggling with a large canvas tote bag. She had ordered two dinners to go from a trendy new cafe in Beverly Hills and wanted to create a romantic date night with her lover. Wanting this date to be a surprise, she parked down below on the street. Out of breath but excited, Andrea snuck around the side of the house to the pool patio which offered the best view. She quietly set the bag down and pulled out a white linen cloth that she fluffed over the patio table. Then she produced from the bag a thick hurricane candle and a bottle of good red wine, which she opened to aerate.

Andrea peered through the glass doors leading into the study and was pleased to find the room vacant. She'd sneak into the house through here, find her boyfriend, and yell, "Surprise!"

Turning around, she surveyed the view with satisfaction. Perfect, she congratulated herself. A spectacular sunset was forming over the ocean.

She put her hand on the knob and was about to enter the study when Vic suddenly emerged out of nowhere. Andrea quickly ducked out of sight, not wanting to spoil her surprise just yet. Crouching low, she peeked through the glass doors. Strange how Vic materialized like that. One moment the room was empty; the next moment he stood in front of that weird painting.

Vic walked out of the study and disappeared from view. Andrea waited, biting her lower lip, when she heard the sound of the garage door opening. She rose and placed a fretful hand upon the glass.

What if he's leaving for the night?

No, she had asked Vic earlier if he planned on going out, and he said no. Maybe he needed to run a quick errand. Determined, Andrea opened the study door and entered the house with the canvas bag. She went directly into the kitchen, laid the food out on two plates, and placed them in the oven to warm.

She marched to the butler's pantry and plucked two crystal wine glasses from the cupboard, which she then placed on the table outside. The colors of the sky had now blended into a vivid watercolor of yellows and oranges.

Andrea gave a little "humph" of frustration and trudged back into Vic's house. She looked out the front window, hoping to see her lover's car coming up the drive. No sign of him yet.

Restless with anticipation, worried that Vic might be out for the night, Andrea wandered back into the study.

She leaned against Vic's desk and tapped her long, sparkly fingernails on the surface. Her eyes fell on the painting of the creepy child.

Vic had warned her more than once to keep out of this room, although she could plainly see that there was nothing of interest in it. He didn't even keep his computer here.

Andrea had a vague memory of Vic mentioning a recording studio or a gym that he wanted to be sound-proofed. He told her he'd scrapped the plan, but she wondered if that was a lie. Her boyfriend enjoyed scheming and keeping secrets. It heightened Andrea's interest in him but also drove her crazy.

She moved over to the padded, wine-colored wall and softly kicked out a curious toe. Her foot met with a hard thud. She continued along the wall, giving soft little kicks to the paneling. When her eyes stared directly into those of the bleeding child, Andrea's foot hit a hollow panel. She pushed on the leatherette and the panel popped forward, bringing the bloody teardrops two inches closer to her face.

Amazed, Andrea tugged at the panel's edge and discovered it slid easily to one side. Revealed behind the panel was a heavy-looking steel door with a combination lock.

She looked around guiltily, alert to any noises. She glanced toward the glass patio doors. Outside, the sky was shedding shimmering purple light over the city. The fragrance of the dinner warming in the oven crept into Andrea's nostrils.

She pulled at the steel door, which of course, being

locked, would not budge. The curious journalist in her, however, refused to be satisfied. She spun the numbered dials of the combo lock uselessly for a good minute. Frustrated, Andrea reached to slide the panel back into place when...

8520

He burned it with a lighter.

Her heart began thumping and she lifted her manicured fingers.

Eight... five... two... zero...

The lock mechanism engaged with a click. Andrea pressed her hand against the heavy door and slowly pushed it open. A single stairway of glossy wood steps descended toward a source of light she couldn't identify. Andrea took a tentative step down.

VICTOR DROVE his BMW through the winding streets. Although he'd been let down by Gabriel, his disappointment was dissipating. What did it matter if Gabriel wasn't on the same page as him? They were together, weren't they? Gabriel was safely ensconced in Vic's wonderful house. The thought of it gave Vic no end of pleasure.

Stopped at a traffic light, he brought out his iPhone, and to lighten his mood, accessed the surveillance camera application. As the site loaded, Victor pondered over what he would feed them both tonight. He also wondered if he would need to drug Gabriel again. He hoped not. Perhaps they could have dinner in peace without struggles and harsh words.

The site loaded and Victor smiled. Gabriel appeared on the small screen. There he was, tied up and calm, waiting for Vic to return. Gabriel had nothing else in his life now except to wait for Vic. His world could not turn without Vic. Victor kept the phone in his hand as he drove, enjoying the ability to observe his captive remotely.

Got to hand it to technology. It certainly has made my life easier.

ANDREA CREPT down the steps and found herself in a large room. She first saw a treadmill planted in front of a flat-screen TV bolted to the wall.

Why is his gym behind a locked d—

Her eyes froze upon seeing a man with wild black hair lying under a sheet on what looked like a hospital bed. She then registered that wide leather bands strapped both his arms down.

He saw her too.

My God, it's Detective McRay!

"Miss Leighton?" he asked in a disbelieving voice.

VIC GLANCED AGAIN at the phone and nearly swerved into oncoming traffic. Gabriel was looking desperately at something and talking.

~

"ANDREA," Gabriel began in a quaking voice.

She stared at him, stupefied.

"Call 911," he told her.

Her mouth worked, but she made no sound. She didn't move.

Gabriel pushed against the leather straps. "Help me. Please!"

Andrea put her fist to her mouth and shook her head.

Gabriel licked his dry lips and tried to stay rational. "Go call the police. Tell them what you've seen down here."

"Wh-what are you doing here?" she asked in a tremulous voice.

He looked down at his bonds and strained against them. "Please get me out of these."

Andrea jerked her eyes around the room, taking in the bureau with its bizarre collection of syringes, pills, and bottles.

"Hurry," Gabriel pleaded.

She rushed over to him and pulled at the leather strap binding his right arm.

"What is all this?" She searched for a clasp. "Why are you down here?"

"Ask your boyfriend." Gabriel watched her struggle. "I think there's some sort of locking mechanism on the other side."

She began to cry. "I don't get what's going on!"

Gabriel, suddenly remembering, looked up at the camera.

"Get out of here," he told her and then added wildly, "For God's sake, go now!"

ANDREA, in shock, nodded and began backing up. She couldn't take her eyes off the man in the bed. He was talking to her, pleading with her, but she couldn't process what he was saying.

Detective McRay—tied up! He looked pale and haggard. How long had he been here? What was he doing here? Could Vic have...?

The man needs help!

Andrea backed up toward the stairs, all the while staring at Gabriel. As her hip hit the railing, she abruptly turned to run up the stairs.

Archwood stood a few steps above her. The door behind him was shut tight. A squeak of fear escaped Andrea's lips and she froze. Gazing at her, Archwood began descending the stairs, taking one casual step at a time. Andrea backed away from him.

THEY CAME into Gabriel's view and he groaned in despair. Archwood glanced at Gabriel then looked back at Andrea who was stock-still with fright.

Gabriel spied the Redhawk tucked into Archwood's jeans.

"Don't," he said from the bed and quickly tried to recall everything he'd learned about talking down an armed and angry man. "Think about it, Vic. You like Andrea. You wouldn't like it she was gone for good, would you? She cares for you. Think about if she was truly gone…"

Victor moved to the bureau and balled up a clean washcloth. He stuffed it deep into Gabriel's mouth. Gabriel choked for a moment and his eyes watered, but when he once again focused on Archwood, he shook his head vehemently and strained against the leather bonds.

Archwood watched Gabriel struggle. "Now look what you've done," he said to the terrified girl. "You've upset him."

Somehow Andrea found her voice. "I w-wanted to surprise you."

Archwood pulled the Redhawk free. "I am surprised."

He walked toward Andrea, backing her up toward the bathroom until she was standing in the shower stall.

GABRIEL, suffering behind the gag, could no longer see the couple when they disappeared into the bathroom, but he heard Andrea say, "I won't tell anyone."

"I know," Archwood assured her gently.

Then the gun discharged three times. The room fell into silence.

Gabriel's head fell back dispiritedly against the pillow and he ceased struggling. He heard water running in the shower. Archwood exited the bathroom, holding Gabriel's gun. He moved toward the bed. Gabriel turned his face to the wall as Archwood stretched out next to him. For a couple of minutes, nothing was said; no movement was made. Only the sound of water running and the metallic smell of blood permeated the room. Archwood prodded Gabriel's chin with the still-warm muzzle of the revolver.

"Hey," he said, "look at me."

Gabriel wrenched his head toward the other man.

"She blew it, okay? I liked Andrea. I did. But what's done is done." Archwood tucked the gun back into his pants. "She's a popular girl though. We can't just bury her. People will ask questions."

For a minute, Archwood seemed to sink into himself. Gabriel watched in morbid fascination as the younger man's lips moved, talking silently as he stared at the bathroom door, reflecting on what lay beyond.

After a minute or so Archwood gathered himself together. He sat up and ruffled Gabriel's hair. "No worries. I'll take care of it."

He pulled the cloth from Gabriel's mouth. "She brought dinner. I'll get it ready for you."

Gabriel knew it was useless to speak, so he didn't bother. He could only watch Archwood as he walked to the stairway.

Archwood spoke as he climbed the steps. "After she drains I'm gonna have to make a little noise in here with the saw. I'll turn the volume up on the TV so you can enjoy your food."

CHAPTER THIRTY-SEVEN

The sound of a power saw cut through Gabriel's ears, and he winced. Before him on a bed tray was a fancy-looking chicken dinner. Archwood had freed Gabriel's forearms so he could maneuver a plastic fork around, but Gabriel felt anything but hunger.

The whine of the saw sliced the air again and the growling of metal on bone made his insides clench. Someone was talking on the television, and the room filled with laughter. Gabriel looked up at the screen. A show about funny home videos was on. A live audience was being entertained.

Gabriel had his own entertainment. The saw screeched against Andrea Leighton's body once more. The audience on TV laughed.

If I don't get out of here, I'm going to start laughing too. The high-pitched giggle of the terminally insane.

At last, the sawing stopped. Archwood exited the bathroom, sweating, the surgical scrubs he wore dripping in blood spray. He trudged past Gabriel and went up the stairs.

Gabriel had to breathe through his mouth. If he smelled the blood he would barf all over the chicken dinner and then what would Vic say? As he watched the other man depart, something prodded Gabriel's memory. Something about the clothes Vic wore. His rattled mind tried to pin it down.

A minute or so later, Archwood hustled down the steps with a pack of heavy-duty garbage bags. He paused to survey his captive.

"Don't wait for me." The blond man waved genially at the untouched meal. "Go ahead and eat before it gets cold."

He disappeared into the bathroom, and Gabriel closed his eyes.

HE DIDN'T FEEL his eyes open in wakefulness. They simply focused again on his surroundings. He heard the television and looked up. A new show was on. The chicken dinner had magically disappeared, but Gabriel's forearms were still free. Amazingly, he could lean his head forward enough to touch his own face. This was a sheer triumph.

God, I'm becoming that desperate.

Archwood sat cross-legged on the floor laying down sheets of newspaper. Next to him was a cardboard box. He glanced over at Gabriel and grinned.

"You checked out," he said. "Sort of fell asleep with

your eyes open. Scared the hell out of me for a minute." Archwood turned back to the box and shook his head. "Really freaky, Sergeant."

He then asked Gabriel if he wanted to watch a movie or watch the news. Gabriel couldn't bring himself to fake normalcy, so he did not answer. Archwood chose a comedy on a movie channel.

It didn't matter what played on television because Gabriel couldn't take his eyes off what Archwood was doing on the floor. Gabriel watched as Archwood pulled out Andrea's Dodgers cap and set it down on the newsprint. Then Archwood pulled locks of Andrea's streaked hair from the box. He used a hot glue gun to stick the hair to the interior back and sides of the hat. He worked carefully, but off and on he'd watch the show, and if something struck him as funny, he'd laugh, nod at Gabriel, and then return to his task. Eventually, Archwood set the hat down to dry and then pulled Andrea's two severed hands from the box.

For a while, Archwood caressed the hands, gently touching the polished fingernails. When the movie ended, Archwood switched to a news channel. As he concentrated on the nightly news, Archwood ran the fingernails lightly up and down his face.

Gabriel swallowed in disbelief. He was sure he had witnessed just about every depraved act under Archwood's watch, but seeing Vic caress himself with the dead girl's hands took the depravity to a whole new level.

Feeling his stomach churn, Gabriel forced his eyes toward the television. He wanted to shut out the image of Archwood touching his face with Andrea's hands, but he couldn't. Behind the gruesome scenes imprinted in Gabriel's mind, a newscaster was talking about tornado victims in the south.

Gabriel looked over at Archwood again. The young, handsome man was now wrapping Andrea's hands in plastic wrap. He wrapped them tightly and then sealed them in a freezer-proof bag. He then reached for the hat with the hair attached. After adjusting the strap for a better fit, Archwood placed it on his head.

On seeing the man wear his girlfriend's baseball cap, his face encircled by her streaked hair, Gabriel had to speak.

"That's so fucked up, Vic."

Archwood winked at him conspiratorially. "What do you think? I could darken my skin, wear her hat and sunglasses. It might be a nice challenge."

"You are one sick, *sick* motherfu—"

"Oh, I'm not getting close enough to anyone who knows her, but from a distance, sitting in her car, waving her little wave—" Archwood gave Gabriel Andrea's coquettish trademark wave. "That's all I need to do."

"And her hands? What are they for?"

"Fingerprints, Sergeant. Where Andrea's going, she's going to need a full set."

Gabriel couldn't help himself. He had to ask. "And where is she going?"

Archwood's lips contorted into a mischievous smile and he hopped to his feet. He walked over to his prisoner and leaned down until his nose practically touched Gabriel's. The smell of glue filled Gabriel's nostrils and Andrea's hair tickled the skin of his cheekbones.

"I can't tell you all my secrets, Sergeant. Then I wouldn't be any fun." Archwood's blue eyes twinkled, and he bounced happily to the center of the room where he collected the wrapped hands.

"Be right back. I wanna dump these in the freezer before they turn."

He left Gabriel to bask in the memory of the murdered girl's hair on his flesh. Gabriel willed his brain to think of something else, anything to keep him grounded in reality. That's when he realized where he'd seen scrubs similar to the bloodied ones Vic wore earlier. They came from the office of the county medical examiner—Ming's office.

MING PERUSED the body before her on the table. After a moment, she handed the scalpel to Geoffrey and walked out of the autopsy room. Geoffrey followed her.

"Are you okay?"

Ming peeled off her mask and scrubs and entered the hallway. She leaned against the wall, staring at nothing. Geoffrey's freckled face turned pink. He knew better than to butt into Ming's business, but he felt insecure seeing his boss like this. Besides, she didn't seem to mind Ethan the intern getting personal with her.

"You want me to finish up for you?"

"No, I'll be okay."

"Where's Ethan today?" Geoffrey asked.

Ming shrugged. She didn't know. Didn't care.

Geoffrey's face turned a shade rosier. "He's sure different from the other students we've had."

Ming closed her eyes. "How so?"

"He's got a strange technique and never gets grossed out."

"That's good, isn't it?"

"Oh, he's good."

Ming looked at Geoffrey. He met her gaze with a secretive smile. If Ming didn't know any better, she might mistake his rosy cheeks for a blush.

"Geoffrey?" She queried.

He *was* blushing. Ming raised an eyebrow.

They heard something down the hall and saw Ethan turn the corner. He waved and walked toward them. Ming observed Geoffrey who fell into instant elation upon seeing the intern.

"Sorry I'm late again," Ethan told them. "The traffic was a killer."

"Poor guy." Geoffrey patted Ethan on the shoulder. "Ready to get started?"

"Absolutely." Ethan then turned to Ming. "Want to go to dinner tonight? I'm free, and I'm buying."

Ming shook her head

"I can go," Geoffrey volunteered.

Ethan glanced at him with slight irritation and then masked it with a smile. "Cool."

Both men seemed buoyant, excited about life. Ming, on the other hand, felt deflated, as if the life had drained from her.

Her cell phone rang, and she answered it.

"Hi, Janet." Ming left the two men and headed into her office.

"Any news?" Gabriel's sister asked.

"No."

"Are you okay? You don't sound so good."

"I'm fine." Ming dropped into her desk chair.

"I'm coming down."

"No, don't," Ming told her. "You have your mom and your dad to take care of. You have your husband to tend to. You have a son and a daughter who need you. You have a life."

A few uncertain seconds passed before Janet spoke. "You have a life, Ming. Good gracious, you're famous in your field. I'm just one mom among millions."

"Gabriel thinks that being a mom is pretty impressive."

"He does?"

"I don't even know if I can have children."

"You haven't tried!" Janet paused. "Have you?"

"No."

"Well, there you go. Don't think you can't until you try. But becoming a renowned forensic pathologist, now that's something you don't see every day."

Ming sighed pensively. "You try hard enough at something, you get good at it. You breathe it, eat it, and live it —you get good at it."

"That's not true," Janet said. "I know I wouldn't be any good at it."

Ming reached out her hand and flicked away a stack of death certificates awaiting her signature.

"Are you still there?" Janet asked.

"Do you regret not pursuing medicine?" Ming asked, straight to the point as usual.

~

IN SEATTLE, Janet smiled. Gabriel had warned her that Ming never minced words, and the doctor had certainly lived up to her reputation. Did Janet have regrets? She sometimes felt that she did, although she knew she was blessed in many ways. Perhaps she'd been looking for something to feel bad about. She couldn't blame that on Gabriel.

Janet suddenly recalled the expression on Ming's face when the subject of marriage had come up. She remembered the melancholy behind Ming's voice when she said how much Gabriel loved being around Liam and Amber.

Could it be that Dr. Ming Li envied her? How ironic would that be? *And all I've ever done is throw a wet towel over my worth.*

For a moment, Janet thought about her wide circle of friends. Ming Li was totally obnoxious, but Janet had a feeling that Ming would never talk about her behind her back. She had a hunch that Ming would always be truthful; that she'd make a loyal friend. She certainly was loyal to Gabriel.

"You could volunteer in the medical field," Ming continued over the phone. "You could even go back to school if you wanted."

"I'm okay with it," Janet said. "I'll just live vicariously through you."

Amber entered the room and whined, "When are we gonna eat, Mommy? I'm hungry."

Janet held a finger up, motioning to her daughter to wait. "Uh, Ming, I've got to go—"

"Yeah, I hear her wanting you."

"Let me know if anything changes, okay? And Ming?"

"Yeah?"

"You're strong. Try to stay that way."

GABRIEL WAS on the treadmill again. He welcomed the relief from being tied down. He hoped the exercise would preserve his mind as well as his body because he was beginning to feel hopeless. He had felt hopeless once before, when, as a child, Andrew had told him that his parents approved of the abuse. Thinking they'd abandoned him to a miserable existence, Gabriel had felt plenty hopeless then.

Since Archwood had given him the option of watching television during the workout, Gabriel asked to see the news. No one, other than the police that first time around, had come enquiring about him. Nor was there any word of his disappearance on the news.

Where was Ming? Was she all right? It frightened Gabriel to consider how Archwood had acquired those scrubs. Had his lover met the same fate as Andrea Leighton? Or did Archwood keep Ming prisoner as well? Could she be locked away in another room in this hell house? No, Gabriel convinced himself. Ming had to be alive and safe because Archwood would tell Gabriel if he'd messed with her. The killer enjoyed taunting his captive too much to let that opportunity pass.

Gabriel thought about Ming constantly. He missed the way she made him smile. He missed her quirky humor and how it cut cleanly through the black fog of his moods. He missed the feel of her body against his own and the way her skin carried the scent of an exotic spice. With Ming nearby, he wasn't lonely. He missed her badly.

Gabriel tested the restraint on his wrist. The metal cuff held tight. He continued to jog and felt like a hamster in a cage, running on an exercise wheel and going nowhere.

The key in any situation out of your control is not to let it own you.

Who had said that? Oh, yes, Gabriel remembered. That was Dr. B. Or had it been Ming?

I'm not going down without a fight, he recited silently. I will not cave in and lose my mind.

He heard the click of the door—his ears were so attuned to it by now—and he looked with trepidation to the stairs. When he saw Archwood, Gabriel halted in mid-step and nearly fell over as the belt of the treadmill moved away from his feet. He quickly righted himself and continued his rapid walk, but he couldn't take his eyes off Victor Archwood.

The man was wearing Andrea's hat and hair. He had darkened his pale skin to a near brown color on his face and hands. Red, shiny, stick-on nails adorned his fingers. He wore Andrea's Fendi sunglasses and a long-sleeved baseball shirt mimicking Andrea's style. Of course, he was too tall, but from a distance, Archwood looked similar to his dead girlfriend. A scary, gerrymandered Andrea Leighton.

"Well?" Victor turned in a circle and then gave Gabriel Andrea's trademark mini-wave. "Pretty good, huh?"

Gabriel considered lying, but whatever was breaking inside him made him unable to care anymore if Vic killed him. He was fast plummeting to insanity himself, carrying on conversations like this with a lunatic.

"You'll never pass," Gabriel said bluntly.

"Like I said, I won't get that close to anyone who knows her."

Gabriel nodded toward Andrea's hat. "And where's the rest of her?"

Archwood wandered over and picked up a water bottle from the floor near the treadmill. "Under the cabana. I'm not much of a mason, but I can pour cement. I took a break to do these." He wiggled his fake, sparkling manicured fingernails under Gabriel's eyes and then held the water bottle to Gabriel's lips.

"What's the matter, Sergeant? You seem troubled."

Gabriel tried not to look at Archwood as he drank.

What's the matter? You're standing there impersonating your dead girlfriend, whom you shot to death with my gun and buried in your backyard. And did I mention that I'm currently handcuffed to a treadmill? And when I'm not here, I'm tied down to a bed, where I'm drugged and God knows what else. I'm not quite sure. Can't remember 'cause I'm back to experiencing memory lapses again. What could possibly be the matter?

Don't go crazy, Gabriel warned himself. Don't start

believing this is the real world. This is Vic's world, the world of a dangerous mental case.

I don't belong here.

But even as he said it, Gabriel felt his tenuous grasp on reality slipping.

MING USED her key to enter Gabriel's house and could instantly see he had packed up and left. His kitchen had been cleaned out, and his laptop was gone. She walked through his house, amazed he could have taken care of all his business and then abandon everything—his new house, his job, and her.

Ming sat on his couch and looked around, depressed. It was Saturday night, and the two of them would have most likely gone out to a movie. Or maybe Ming would have nudged Gabriel over to Disney Hall for a symphony. He would do as he always did, patiently weather whatever cultural event to which she dragged him, and then lean close to whisper in her ear, "This show can't top you."

It was a corny line, but she loved hearing it just the same. Ming glanced toward the window. The weather was fine tonight with a full moon rising. Maybe the two of them would spend a quiet night at home and dine outside. She would play sous-chef to Gabriel as they made dinner together. They had cooked plenty in his little railroad kitchen on Bay Street. It hadn't mattered that the kitchen was small. The only thing that mattered was that they were together. Gabriel had felt he had to improve himself by upping his lifestyle. Ming had been afraid Gabriel would toss her aside in his quest for self-improvement. What she had feared had come to pass.

Where *was* he? Why did he leave? Ming wandered into Gabriel's bedroom and opened his closet door. She pulled out the navy pea coat that was her boyfriend's favorite. The coat had belonged to his father and meant a lot to Gabriel. Strange that he left it behind too. She lay down on the bed, holding the coat, and rested her cheek against the rough fabric. She closed her eyes and fantasized that if she held on tight enough, Gabriel might materialize within his abandoned clothing.

CHAPTER THIRTY-EIGHT

Victor, toting his laptop case, used Andrea's key to enter her apartment to execute his plan. After searching through her messy bedroom, he found her passport and computer. He logged in and sent an e-mail from "Andrea" to himself:

"Vic, I'm going to Iran to do a film documentary. It's been a dream of mine to become a serious journalist."

Vic then logged into his own laptop, waited to receive her e-mail, and then replied, "Please don't do that. I think it's dangerous for a woman to go there alone. The embassies are advising against all travel for U.S. citizens."

He returned to her computer and typed, "I have to. This one will win me an award. I promise to be careful."

Vic then shuttled off e-mails from Andrea's computer to her mother and father, her general group of friends, and her boss at the production office. Vic then logged into her Facebook page and posted a notice about her upcoming documentary and travel plans.

He pulled her suitcase from the closet and tossed in some clothes, shoes, and makeup. Returning to her computer once more, he looked up information from the Iranian Visa Service. Andrea could procure a press visa within days rather than have to wait the usual month. Using the dead girl's credit card, Victor booked a flight to Frankfort International Airport that would then connect to Tehran. He made online arrangements with the post office to stop her mail.

Unlike Gabriel, Andrea would definitely forget about food rotting in her fridge, so Victor left all her perishables in there. He surveyed the apartment once more and left some Iranian travel brochures on her bedside table. After making sure nobody was outside, Victor exited the apartment, toting Andrea's suitcase.

He drove Andrea's car home and pulled it into his garage. He threw a tarpaulin over it, and in an exhausted daze, went straight into his bedroom. He felt so tired he even skipped saying goodnight to Gabriel.

DOWNSTAIRS, Gabriel wondered if it were day or night. The thick and endless silence of the sound-proofed room gave him no indication. He could only garner the time based on Archwood's comings and goings and on the rare occasions when they watched the news on television. While Gabriel assumed he slept during the night, he never knew how late or early he fell asleep or at what time he awoke. He assumed it was nighttime now because Archwood had brought him dinner earlier. Only Gabriel had fallen into a fitful nap, and now he wasn't sure if it was morning or the middle of the night.

I'm not going to be able to keep my mind intact much longer. How can I?

Gabriel glanced hopefully at the stairs and then mentally berated himself. This was another problem developing. Since Gabriel wholly depended on Archwood for food, drink, and entertainment, he found himself anticipating his captor's arrival on a daily basis. Although he didn't trust the other man not to kill him, Gabriel had to rely on Archwood for his very life. The paradox messed with his head.

Suddenly a low rumbling sound moved through the house. The bed began to shake and the floor shivered.

Gabriel was no stranger to earthquakes, having lived in Southern California most of his adult life. Still...

Gabriel pushed and pulled against his bonds, but as usual, they held tight. Behind him, he could hear vials and bottles knocking off the bureau. A crack appeared in the wall next to him and then ran like a mouse along the foundation, about a foot above the floor.

This frigging house is going to come down on my head, and I'm helpless as a baby!

The shaking then stopped as suddenly as it started. Gabriel took a relieved breath and heard the door click above him. Archwood descended the steps two at a time, calling Gabriel's name.

He came over and stood sentinel by the bed, waiting

for aftershocks. When none came, he sighed and sat down next to his captive.

"What a shaker, huh?" Archwood must have seen the anxiety on Gabriel's face for he lifted a hand and gently brushed Gabriel's hair with his fingers. "Don't worry, Sergeant. We're all good now."

OUTSIDE IN VICTOR'S BACKYARD, the cabana's crude foundation cracked and split. Part of the structure aborted and slid down the hill. The protesting earth pushed up Andrea's severed arm until the limb poked out between two pieces of broken cement. It remained upright like the stalk of a sorrowful gray flower that cut the full moon in half.

CHAPTER THIRTY-NINE

The following day, Vic darkened his skin, inserted brown contacts to cover his blue eyes, and did his best to piece together an outfit worthy of Andrea Leighton. Putting on Andrea's hat and hair as a final touch, he went to the Iranian Visa Service to apply for the visa.

If the woman wearing a jilbab over her hair had any suspicions about the overly made up "woman" standing across the counter before her, she didn't voice them.

Archwood-as-Andrea was asked to submit a full set of fingerprints. Nodding to the line behind him, he told the scarf-clad woman that he would move aside to allow her to help the others. He moved to the end of the counter and, after pulling his sleeve over his fist, he extracted Andrea's right hand from his right coat pocket and one by one dipped each of her fingers in the inkpad then pressed them onto the form. He did the same with the left hand.

Nobody saw. People babbled on their cell phones or got angry when the line didn't move fast enough for them. Vic felt completely at ease. He knew he could get away with anything he wanted. The I-world created the perfect climate for him. All the idiots were too engrossed in themselves to notice anything but their toys.

When Vic was done, he handed the forms to the lady, thanked her, and walked out with Andrea's two hands lolling around in his coat pockets.

GABRIEL'S abrupt departure bothered the investigator in Jonelle Williams. It struck her as odd that no one had seen her partner. It was one thing to leave, but to disappear entirely? To Jonelle, there was a big difference.

She asked Ming to meet with her at the bureau.

"Tell me everything that Gabriel told you the last time you saw him," Jonelle asked.

Ming took a seat in Gabriel's vacant chair and stared pensively at the items adorning his desk.

"We didn't talk much at the party. It was loud, and Gabriel was upset."

Jonelle absently tapped her gold bicuspid with her fingernail. It was a weird habit, she knew, but it helped her think. "Were you ever apart from Gabriel or were you with him the entire time?"

Ming reflected on that for a moment. "I went to the bathroom, but that was it."

"You saw him after you made the trip to the bathroom?"

"Yes." Ming slid open Gabriel's desk drawer. Amid the pens, paper clips, phone chargers, and other miscellaneous office supplies, she glimpsed a photo of the two of them, taken only a few months before at the beach. She took a shaky breath.

Jonelle crossed her arms over her buxom chest, thinking. "How about before the party? Anything you two talked about? Anything out of the ordinary happen?"

Ming closed the drawer, leaned back in the chair, and tried to remember. "He didn't want me to go. But after he left, I drove there to meet him."

Jonelle gave Ming a strange look. "You drove to Victor Archwood's separately?"

Ming nodded.

"Then how'd you meet up with him? You saw him at the party?"

"No, I met him on the street. I knew I'd get there first because he was meeting Victor Archwood's girlfriend beforehand."

"Andrea Leighton?" Jonelle cocked her head. "Why was he meeting with her?"

"She wanted to talk with Gabriel."

"About what? Did he say?"

Ming shrugged. "It was nothing. She wanted to make sure he had a costume and gave him one. Gabriel said Archwood handpicked it for him."

Jonelle's dark brown eyes gazed steadily at Ming.

"What, Jonelle?"

The detective shook her head. "Just thinking is all."

~

Vic received Andrea's travel visa within a couple of days. Revolving in his own world, caught up in his newest performance, Victor neglected his showcase home. The pool sat unused, and spiders spun webs in the corners of the outside bar. The cabana stood at the far edge of the property, broken and ignored.

The visa was stamped into Andrea's passport, and it was time for the final act.

Archwood-as-Andrea went to the airport, checked her suitcase into the baggage area and then showed Andrea's passport to TSA security. The security agent looked at the passport, squinted at Vic, and hesitated.

If the man had any qualms that the "woman" in front of him did not match the thumbnail picture in the passport, he did not show it. Perhaps he figured Andrea was having a bad hair day. The TSA agent stamped the boarding pass and ushered Vic forward.

Adrenaline pumping, high on the moment, Vic headed toward the departure gate.

In no time at all, he was boarding the plane with a rather industrial-looking carrying case.

The plane was semi-full with plenty of passengers but had enough empty seats to trade, if someone had a mind to. Archwood-as-Andrea took the assigned seat and waited until the female flight attendant came by to count the passengers.

"Andrea Leighton." He smiled and indicated the checklist in her hand. "But I may hop to another seat later."

"Okay." The flight attendant seemed too preoccupied to care.

He patiently waited until the aisle was crowded with passengers settling into their seats. He then stood up and made his way toward the bathroom. In the privacy of the small bathroom, Vic removed Andrea's hat/wig and opened the carrying case. He cleansed his face and hands of makeup and then wet his blond hair, carefully slicking it back. He heard the pilot make an announcement and felt the plane shake from the last of the baggage being loaded into the cargo compartment.

Victor doffed "Andrea's" traveling clothes and folded them into the case. He then pulled on a repairman's pants and shirt, and a neon yellow vest that had the word "Servisair" with two strips of reflective tape adorning the back. Next came work boots. Finally, Victor donned a short brown wig and topped it off with a repairman's cap. He stuck a tiny "v" of brown beard below his lower lip – something Sergio called a "pussy tickler." Vic knew it would draw attention away from his other features. Finally, he closed up the case and exited the bathroom.

"What is it?" the same flight attendant asked in concern and for a moment Victor wondered if he still resembled Andrea. He searched the attendant's face for any confusion or recognition.

"Wrong plane," he said with a slight Southern drawl. "I thought there was an issue with the water pressure, but y'all are good to go."

"Whew!" the flight attendant said in relief as Victor Archwood strode rapidly off the plane, bypassing the people still boarding the jetway.

CHAPTER FORTY

Jonelle sat in her gray cubicle in the bureau and glanced at Gabriel's empty desk. Despite the resignation letter they'd received, Ramirez still had not placed anyone in that cubicle. In fact, Gabriel's personal items still remained on his desk. Nobody had bothered to remove them. It was as if Gabriel's compatriots knew something was awry. Nobody truly believed he was gone. And yet...

Jonelle tapped her gold bicuspid reflectively and then picked up the phone. She called Ming Li.

"Why didn't Gabriel wait until the party to meet up with Andrea?" Jonelle asked. "He must have known she'd be there. Why did he meet her beforehand? Did he say?"

"I told you, she gave him a costume."

Jonelle was insistent. "She could have given it to him at the party."

Ming went silent and Jonelle waited, giving the other woman a chance to remember.

"He told me she tried to contact him once before," Ming told her. "Gabriel was concerned she might have something important to tell him. Something about Archwood."

"She'd contacted Gabriel before?" Jonelle asked.

Ming confirmed that she did.

Jonelle thanked Ming and ended the call.

Willing to follow up on Gabriel's lead, Jonelle did some research on Andrea and called her offices at Truth TV. Jonelle was surprised to hear that Andrea Leighton had left abruptly to film a documentary in Iran.

GABRIEL DECIDED that if he couldn't fight back with his body, then he would have to fight back with his mind. He had to throw Archwood a psychological curveball, but how? This was not Gabriel's forte, but he had no choice.

What are Vic's weaknesses?

Archwood had refused to pursue the effect the brass egg had on him. It was a handmade gift from his grandfather, the one who had abused him. Unlike Gabriel, who sought out the assistance of a therapist, Archwood refused to delve into the inner workings of his mind. Exploring that betrayal didn't interest him—or perhaps it frightened him.

What if Gabriel brought it up? Would he be capable of using it against Vic?

When his captor brought down two breakfast dishes, Gabriel decided to give it a go. After all, he had made some progress. His lower arms remained free now. That meant he had gained Archwood's trust.

His captor handed Gabriel his plate and dragged a wingback chair over to the bed so he could eat with him.

Talk to him normally. Take the trust to a new level.

Gabriel stabbed a plastic fork around in his scrambled eggs and wondered how to begin.

"Do you remember we used to talk, Vic?"

Archwood nodded as he ate.

"You were pretty young," Gabriel continued. "I wasn't sure if you'd remember."

"I remember more than you think."

Archwood appeared to be in good temper, willing to be engaged. Gabriel would have to tread carefully. Any odd thing might set his nemesis off. A flash of memory hit Gabriel then—the image of his brother-in-law, Michael, expressing concern over what might set Gabriel off. If only Michael could see him now...

"You used to confide in me," Gabriel offered.

"I have no secrets to confide, Sergeant. My life is an open book."

"You have a lot of secrets, Vic. I'm one of them."

Victor gave him a cryptic smile as he lifted his coffee cup. "Yes, you are, aren't you?"

What would Dr. B say?

Get him talking about his childhood, Gabriel thought silently.

Then throw his grandfather at him.

"I have very clear memories of you as a child."

"Do you?" Vic asked, the smile still prominent on his face. "Just how clear are those memories? I thought you had blocked them. Tell me, have I helped you break through, Little Buddy?"

Gabriel stared at Archwood, amazed at how effortlessly the killer had turned the tables on him. How could Vic possibly know...? How could he know the nickname Andrew Pierce had given Gabriel?

Archwood chuckled and bit into a piece of toast.

Gabriel observed the self-satisfied look on the other man's face and felt the rage begin to build. Archwood had a take-no-prisoners attitude when it came to dominating a situation. Well, two could play at that game.

"Why don't we talk about your grandfather, Vic?"

Archwood's grin crumbled from his face and he shot his prisoner a dark warning look. He stood up, removed Gabriel's plate, and set both their plates on the bureau.

"Are you ready to work out?" Archwood asked.

Gabriel felt the anger clawing at him, wanting to break free, wanting Archwood to shoot him dead—anything to get out of this hell.

"Let's talk about the fact that you're punishing me for the wrongs your granddad did to you."

Archwood reached over and tightly gripped a fistful of Gabriel's dark hair. He lowered his face close to his captive's. "Where are you going with this? What are you trying to prove?"

Unable to hold back, Gabriel's free hand darted out and grabbed hold of Archwood's head. He immediately smacked his forehead hard into the other man's nose.

Archwood's hand flew to his face as he stumbled backward. Gabriel saw blinding white for a millisecond, but it was worth the pain. Breathing heavily, Archwood looked into his hand, saw blood, and then stared severely at Gabriel.

A few moments passed, and Archwood's features relaxed. He sniffed once, wetly, and spit blood into his palm. He then swatted a paper towel from the roll on the bureau and pressed it against his nose. He regarded Gabriel once more.

"Is this your brilliant plan? To agitate me?" Archwood dropped the towel into a waste can. "You've got brawn, Sergeant, but you have a serious lack of brains."

Archwood returned to the bureau, picked up the breakfast plates, and walked toward the stairwell. He paused at the bottom and gave Gabriel a solemn look. "I did warn you what would happen if you pushed me too far."

Gabriel's anger instantly fled, chased by stone-cold anxiety. He'd blown it.

"Dr. Li is going to die today," Archwood stated. "And you have only yourself to blame."

He flipped off the light switch and walked up the stairs, leaving Gabriel to spend the rest of his morning in darkness.

JONELLE AND MING were at the coroner's offices sitting in front of Ming's computer and looking at Andrea's Facebook page. They viewed the post regarding the documentary. They read how Andrea had hired a cameraman. They saw a photo of the interior of a hotel room whose caption read: "Home Sweet Home in Shiraz."

The most recent post read, "Very scary here. They do not like journalists, and they hate Americans even more."

"Oh, come on," Ming said as she studied the page. "She's in Iran?"

"Apparently so."

Ming turned to Jonelle. "Gabriel leaves. Andrea leaves. You don't think it's a bit strange that everyone who comes into contact with Victor Archwood leaves town?"

"Her Facebook page says she arrived in Shiraz."

"Did you contact the embassy?"

"Where? In Iran?" Jonelle gave Ming a "don't-be-stupid" look and then said, "I spoke to the airline already. Andrea Leighton checked in and boarded her plane. A flight attendant even remembers speaking to her." Jonelle sighed. "Believe me, I checked it out."

Ming stood up and began to pace the floor of her office. She finally halted and looked squarely at Jonelle. "Tell me this doesn't strike you as weird! Andrea Leighton, of all people, suddenly transformed into a serious documentary filmmaker? Really?"

"I'll admit it sounds strange, but she was on that plane."

Ming shook her head. "It doesn't make sense. Just like with Gabriel. It makes no sense at all." Her eyes suddenly dropped to her wristwatch and she sighed in frustration.

Grabbing her purse, Ming headed to the door.

"Where are you going?" Jonelle asked.

"Home," Ming answered. "Ethan is coming from

school to meet me at my house, and I'm late. He needs help on his thesis. I don't know how the hell I'm going to help him. I can't think straight anymore."

With that, Ming walked out the door, which closed slowly behind her.

~

ETHAN STOOD in Ming's Los Feliz living room and poured wine into one of her rarely used fancy stemware pieces.

"Are you sure you want to drink wine before you work?" Ming called from the couch.

"I'll be all right."

He kept his back to her and surreptitiously added some Rohypnol into the wine. He mixed it with his finger then wiped his hand against his shirt.

"It will help me relax." He turned toward her with a smile. "Just as it will for you."

Today Ethan would make Ming fall for him. He would make love to her until her eyes filled with lazy satisfaction. Then he would bring out the large knife he'd brought with him, hidden in his student's satchel. He planned to take his own pleasure by betraying that love she felt for him. He would giddily watch her surprised face as the one she trusted now destroyed her. And afterward, he would bring her severed head back to Gabriel.

Look, Sergeant! I've brought you a present! A head in exchange for the headbutt.

Ming took the glass from Ethan, gazed absently into its scarlet depths, but set it down with a sigh. She crossed her arms and leaned forward in thought. Ethan lifted the glass and proffered it to her once again.

"Drink," he prodded. "You look like you need it."

Sadly, Ming tasted the wine and met Ethan's eyes. "Good choice again."

She took a deeper swallow and then ran her finger around the rim in contemplation. Soon, she became weepy and abandoned the glass once more.

"Boyfriend problems still?" Ethan sat next to her. "Gabriel, right?"

Ming nodded, wiping her eyes. Ethan put an arm around her and nodded sympathetically.

"COME HERE." He pulled her close to him in a friendly hug.

His arms, not muscular like Gabriel's, his chest, not solid and firm like Gabriel's, made Ming yearn for her detective even more. She felt empty inside as if everything meaningful had vacated her life. She felt Ethan's whiskers on her neck, and she pulled away. She didn't want this type of comfort. She wanted Gabriel.

Ethan brought the glass to her lips again. Not wanting to disappoint him, she took one more sip and then set it down.

"I wish I could cheer you up," he said.

"It's okay. Not your job."

"Who says?" He lightly ran his fingers back and forth along her bare arm.

Warmth slowly spread through her and Ming eyed her glass of wine. She had only taken a few sips. Maybe she was exhausted and didn't realize how much Gabriel's absence had taken a toll on her.

Ethan's hand went to her neck and gently massaged the tense muscles there. She let it stay, maybe because she wanted to relax. Ming couldn't pinpoint a reason because her thoughts were fuzzy. She sighed and let her shoulders drop.

"That's right," he said in a soft voice. "Let it go..."

Ethan was being so kind, Ming thought. So kind. She closed her eyes and surrendered to his massage. Now both hands were rolling along her shoulders, around her neck. She leaned back against him and swallowed. Funny, her mouth seemed dry all of a sudden.

"You want more wine?" Ethan asked, and his voice seemed far away even though he sat right beside her.

She shook her head and realized she didn't feel like talking. She felt her blouse rise up and Ethan's hands on her back. She felt her bra unclasp and her breasts tumbled free. They felt good to be free. Still...

Ethan's hands crept around to her chest. He was gentle, not at all grabbing or rushed. Ming moaned softly; she missed a man's touch. He turned her around and placed his lips on hers. His whiskers tickled slightly, but Ming didn't care. His tongue burrowed its way between her lips and, while she should have protested, somehow she couldn't bring herself to verbalize any words.

His body was touching hers now, his lips were on her earlobe, his breath in her ear, and he whispered, "Let go, Dr. Li. Let me make you feel good."

Ethan kissed her neck and bent his head at her breasts. He became a more ardent lover now, and Ming shook her head. Was she missing Gabriel so much that another man could stand in? She lifted her hand and pushed Ethan away.

"I really can't," she told him weakly and wondered if she'd spoken loud enough because now Ethan appeared quite aroused. His hands seemed to be moving too fast for her. She'd push one of his hands away, but then the other would be somewhere else on her body, cupping her breasts, tugging at the zipper of her pants. "Ethan..."

He stopped her mouth with a kiss—his tongue probed her, his lips crushed against hers. This was not Gabriel. This was not what she wanted. Ming pulled her face away and gave Ethan a stern look.

His eyes were wet, his breath was heavy, but what captured Ming's attention was his mustache. The left edge of it was peeling off his skin.

She opened her mouth to comment but instead found herself gaping at Ethan—maybe because her mind felt hazy and she wasn't her usual sharp self. She studied her intern's face for other irregularities and found them. His nose seemed swollen and he wore makeup to hide a slight bruising under the eyes. And speaking of eyes, Ethan was wearing green contact lenses. Odd that she never noticed that before. Ming reached out a perplexed hand and ran her fingers through his hair. Underneath her fingernails, she felt netting.

Ethan was wearing a wig. Why?

He wore a fake mustache and had changed the color of his eyes. Why?

Ming's heart began to pound, a rhythmic tattoo of realization. Her breath came out in a rush.

Ethan isn't Ethan... He's

His face hovered inches from hers. She could smell his breath.

Victor Archwood!

The taste of his mouth was on her tongue. His hand was holding her naked breast. His thumb gently rubbed the nipple.

Omigod, Omigod—

Ethan/Archwood closed his eyes as his head bent at her breast. She felt his mouth, his teeth against her flesh. He must have mistaken her hammering heart for a sign of sexual excitement, for now his fingers worked diligently at her pant's zipper and successfully tugged it downward. In an instant, his searching fingers had crept inside her thong like a tick searching for a fleshy part on which to latch.

There is no Ethan—it's been Archwood all along!

The realization bore into her brain. When Ming felt Archwood's fingers push inside her, and she heard the man who tried to kill her grunt pleasurably like a pirate discovering glistening treasure, she grabbed his hand. Steeling herself, Ming pulled it from her body.

He looked up at her curiously, and she instantly looked the other way, unable to meet his eyes.

"I can't," she forced herself to say.

"Yes, you can."

"No." Ming pushed herself away from him and quickly zipped up her pants, refusing to look at his flaking mustache; worried she'd give herself away. She pretended to be ashamed. "I shouldn't lead you on."

Ming struggled to clasp her bra, and panicking, she

simply pulled her shirt over her cockeyed bra and grabbed her purse.

Don't look him in the eye! He'll see right through you!

"Where are you going?" he asked, and Ming could hear a threat behind his calm tone.

Ming rifled through her purse for her car keys. "I—I have to get back to work."

He's in my house! Victor Archwood is in my house!

Archwood/Ethan stood up and began walking toward her. "Your boyfriend's gone. I'm here. Be with me."

Ming froze. *He's talking about Gabriel!*

Ming commanded her legs to move. She had to keep away from him. She backed toward the front door. Her head was beginning to ache, and a scream threatened to escape her throat.

"Sit down," he commanded and pointed to the couch.

Ming shook her head wildly. "No, I-uh-gotta go."

Where is Gabriel, you bastard? What have you done with him?

Ming's shaking fingers found the doorknob and twisted it. The blessed sky opened up behind her and, feeling the scream about to tear through, Ming ran for her car.

When she was safely away, safely driving, safely down the block, the scream nearly broke her in half as it filled her car.

CHAPTER FORTY-ONE

"Calm down, Ming," Ramirez told her.

"You calm down, you asshole! It's Archwood!"

"That kid you introduced me to?"

"Yes! He's Archwood!"

A black and white uniform entered Ramirez's office. Ming, Jonelle, and Lt. Ramirez stood, waiting for his report. "We just checked your house, Dr. Li. There's no one there."

"My God..." Ming shuddered violently. "Victor Archwood was in my house."

Ramirez reached for a cigarette, but Ming swiped the pack from him. "What are you going to do about it?"

"How do you know this guy is Archwood?"

"Fuck you, Miguel! I saw him!"

"Would you give me my pack?"

Ming threw it across the room.

Ramirez stood his ground. "This department cannot

tolerate another run-in with Victor Archwood. Did he threaten you?"

"No, but—"

"Did he hurt you? Rob you? Did he break into your house?"

Ming shook her head desperately.

"Then what offense did he commit?"

Ming could only gape at Ramirez, unwilling to believe what she needed to say. "He was trying to have sex with me."

Ramirez grimaced at her in disgust and promptly retrieved his pack. "Okay, so he attempted rape—"

Ming shook her head and sat helplessly in a chair. "No, he didn't."

"Then what did he do?" Ramirez asked emphatically. "Why was he there?"

"He was pretending to be Ethan, saying he needed help with his studies."

"I can't arrest Archwood for dressing up like some student, Ming!"

"But he's killed Gabriel."

That gave Ramirez pause. He exchanged glances with Jonelle. "How do you know?"

"He said Gabriel is gone." Ming hung her head.

"Unless this Ethan or Archwood, if they are one and the same, does something to you, I can't do anything to him."

Ming, desperate, looked over to Jonelle for help.

Gabriel's partner stood in the corner and stared back at Ming like a deer caught in headlights. Jonelle then pursed her full lips together and dropped her gaze to the floor. Too new to the bureau, unwilling to jeopardize her job, Jonelle shrugged apologetically.

Ming glared at them both and stood up. Striding to the exit, she said, "Fine. I'll handle it myself."

"What does that mean?" Ramirez followed right on her heels.

"It means I'll handle it myself!" Ming slammed the door on her way out.

JANET CALLED AGAIN, only Ming didn't answer her cell phone. She was too busy browsing through a theatrical prop shop in Studio City. Outside, the summer sidewalks burned, but Ming walked around with a perpetual chill. Victor Archwood had gone to great lengths to get close to her... Why? Why didn't he simply kill her when he had the chance? And he'd had numerous chances, Ming thought with a shiver. Sitting across from her at dinner, sitting on her couch—God, she'd wined and dined with that freak, thinking him a graduate student in need of mentoring.

Feeling violated and angry, Ming strode purposefully up and down the aisles of props, unsure of what she was looking for but determined to find something that could be used to fool a maniac.

Maybe Archwood had wanted to watch her pine for Gabriel. Maybe that had given his sick mind some sadistic pleasure. But something nagged at the outer edges of Ming's consciousness. She could still feel Gabriel everywhere she went and refused to believe he was "gone" as Archwood had stated. She had to find out if Gabriel was still alive. There was a reason Archwood had kept a close watch on Ming, and she intended to find out why.

Ming still had Gabriel's Military and Police special. She had no idea how to use the gun, but that was one secret she intended on keeping.

She walked down paths of fake appliances, fake books, hollowed-out computers, and plastic fireplaces. She felt unreal herself, so nightmarish were these last few weeks. If only she had kept her cool after she had realized Ethan was Archwood. She could have followed him or held the gun to his head and made him tell her where to find Gabriel.

How am I going to pull this off?

Ming could not believe what she was about to do. She wasn't a detective. In her safe world, she didn't go looking for risks, and yet she was about to confront a murderer. What other choice did she have? No one else would help her.

Just then Ming chanced upon an entire medical section. Canes, wheelchairs, and crutches lined the walls. One display shelf featured fake plaster casts and plastic orthopedic boots. Ming inspected one of the casts and saw that it opened like a book on well-disguised hinges. Inside was a hard foam padding.

An idea struck her. She could cut out the padding and insert the gun inside the cast. She would then confront Victor Archwood, and he, thinking Ming was unarmed and at a disadvantage, would have his guard down. Then she would pop open the cast at the right moment and shove the gun in his face.

Let's see how well he can act then, Ming thought and took the fake cast to the cashier for purchase.

IN MONTEREY PARK, Jonelle knocked on Dr. B's office door. He invited the detective to take a seat, but she shook her head.

"I want to ask you a question about Gabriel."

Knowing that Jonelle's relationship with Gabriel had its roots in rocky terrain, Dr. B clasped his hands together defensively. "That's all privileged infor—"

"It's just one damn question, Doctor."

Dr. B fell silent.

"You know Gabriel as a patient and a friend. I need you to tell me honestly, would he run?"

"No," Dr. B answered without hesitation. "As long as I've known Gabriel, I have never known him to quit on himself or quit on anyone else. I've seen him frightened, and I've seen him angry. But he's always met his challenges head-on. I'm quite perplexed by his departure. It's not like him."

Jonelle nodded, conflicted, and now faced with her own challenge. Archwood was a sensitive subject. The LASD wanted to put as much distance as possible between itself and him. A search of Archwood's place had turned up nothing. Gabriel truly might have left Los Angeles. After all, they had letters, they had e-mails—

they even had Ming's admission that she had spoken to Gabriel about his leaving town.

"What's on your mind, Detective Williams?"

Jonelle stood clumsily in front of the psychiatrist and then slumped into Gabriel's usual chair. "I want to do the right thing but I cannot break protocol."

"Okay." Dr. B nodded patiently. "What is tempting you to break protocol?"

"A bad feeling," Jonelle admitted. "I don't want to cause trouble for the bureau, but things don't feel right in here." She put a hand over her solar plexus.

"You mention protocol." Dr. B crossed his arms and rested them on his desk. "Do you honestly think all the answers can be found in a government-issued pamphlet or a textbook?"

Jonelle shook her head.

"I'm not a detective," Dr. B said as he pushed up his ever-slipping glasses. "But if I've learned anything from Gabriel, the best investigators always follow their gut feelings."

THE CITY LIGHTS of Los Angeles glittered in the distance, offering endless possibilities of fun, food, and people. But the area directly surrounding Victor Archwood's darkened home held the covert silence of the mountains.

Ming Li limped on her fake cast, throwing shadows on a moonlit trail and feeling the cool steel of the M&P pressing against her calf.

If Victor Archwood caught her snooping, Ming intended to tell him that she had left something at his house the night of the party and had returned for it. It was a lame excuse, but maybe it would buy her time to get the gun out of the cast before he attacked her.

Ming circled the perimeter of the house to find a way inside. With some difficulty, she hoisted herself over the block wall that separated the front yard from the back. She kept to the edge of the yard, trying to work up the courage to approach the house. She could see the pool and the wet bar. No lights shone from the house, which seemed to be untenanted.

A Santa Ana breeze kicked up and the pool water began to ripple. On the edge of the breeze, Ming caught a malodorous, yet familiar scent.

She swallowed and looked upwind. The silhouette of a small, unfinished hut hung against the black line of the distant ocean. Warm air caressed Ming's face and she grimaced. With some reluctance, she limped toward the structure.

As she drew nearer, Ming could see some sort of gazebo, still in the framing stage. Half of it had slid down the hill. She leaned over, daring to peek over the edge of the cliff. Yes, bits of splintered wood and cement pieces reflected the moonlight on the earth below.

The odor assailed her nostrils once again, pungent and strong. Ming no longer needed the breeze to tell her where to look for the source. It hung right here next to her. And she didn't have to try to figure out what the smell was. Ming knew it well enough. It was the stench of a decomposing body.

She felt something break inside her, and a moan escaped her lips despite her efforts to stay quiet.

In despair, Ming hobbled over to what was left of the gazebo and forced herself to climb over chunks of foundation to inspect it.

"Please, Gabriel, don't let it be you," she whispered to no one.

She saw a human arm poking out between two pieces of broken foundation. The arm was black, past the bloat stage. Ming looked around helplessly and then found a piece of roof tile. She pushed the cement pieces apart and began to dig around the arm, which soon fell over, unattached to a body and missing its hand.

Ming cringed and then began digging more intensely, scooping up earth and tossing it away. Bits of a dark plastic bag came up, torn apart by wildlife. Soon she uncovered a face.

Animal activity had eaten the flesh away from the lips, exposing the teeth and giving the corpse a permanent sneer. The eyes were gone, along with the nose. The rest of the flesh was blackened, like the arm, making it impossible to readily identify the corpse. Ming prodded the face with the tile, dislodging it from the earth, and was alarmed to see the head without a scalp, without any hair.

Her breath came out in a desperate rush.

Reaching into her pocket, Ming pulled out a small tissue pack. She removed the tissue and wound the plastic casing around two of her fingers. She studied the corpse's face through her clinical eyes and then pressed her wrapped fingers against the eyebrow ridges and along the mandible and chin.

A minute passed. Ming sat back and felt warm tears course down her cheeks. She let the plastic fall from her fingers and covered her face with her hands. She began to sob.

This was the body of a woman. It shamed Ming to feel such relief. Archwood had killed someone and buried her here.

But the body was not Gabriel's.

Sniffing back her tears, Ming hoisted herself upward to face the silent, shadowed house. Dragging her sleeve across her wet face, she hobbled toward the glass doors of the master bedroom. Maybe Archwood slept. Ming emboldened herself by visualizing "Ethan" waking up to a gun pressed against his temple.

She peered through the glass doors. A cold shiver ran down Ming's spine upon seeing the bed perfectly made at this late hour. She swallowed, opened the door, and entered the room. Standing solo in the middle of Archwood's bedroom, Ming felt sickness creep into her stomach and wanted nothing more than to turn and run back the way she came.

She toyed with the idea of removing the gun hidden in her cast to hold for protection. But what if Archwood should overtake her? She would lose her only chance of survival. Besides, if she panicked and killed Archwood right off the bat, she might never know what had become of Gabriel.

Thinking of her lost love made her petrifying feet move, and Ming crossed the threshold into the hallway.

She began limping toward the living room. The house was preternaturally quiet, and her fake cast made tapping sounds against the stone floor no matter how carefully she set her foot down.

Along the hallway, Ming passed a couple of doors. One door hung open like a broken jaw. She paused at the threshold and dared to peek inside. As her eyes adjusted to the dark, she made out what appeared to be a guest bedroom. The bed here was also made with military precision. Ming held her breath and listened, alert for any sounds, but nothing issued forth. She backed away and continued down the hall.

A tiny green light, flashing near the ceiling, caught her eye as she rounded a corner, but Ming ignored it. If she had observed its source further, she would have discovered the flashing green pinpoint belonged to a security camera.

She walked by a vestibule where she saw a phone resting on a small table. She didn't see Victor Archwood posed like a statue deep within the darkened recess. Only the white of his teeth showed behind an impish grin.

As Ming passed, he leaped out and shouted, "Boo!"

Ming uttered a shocked yell and Archwood grabbed her. He quickly twisted her arms behind her back and held her tightly.

"You're an amateur, Dr. Li," he said lightheartedly and then dragged Ming toward his secret room.

CHAPTER FORTY-TWO

Although it was the middle of the night, Jonelle sat at her home computer, searching the names of students on the Cal State registrar's list.

Her young son, Trevor, came into the den of her small Torrance home. The den served as both TV room and her office.

"You still up, Mama?"

"Hi, Baby." She reached her hand out to him. "Couldn't sleep?"

Trevor rubbed his eyes and went to his mother. He laid his head against her abundant chest.

Jonelle held him as she studied the information on the monitor.

Minutes later she called Ramirez at his home and, with no apology for waking him up, said, "In case you're interested, there is no Ethan Post at Cal State LA, and as soon as I can get a babysitter, I'm goin' on over to Victor Archwood's."

～

INSIDE HIS SECRET ROOM, Archwood released Ming once they were down the stairs. She immediately scampered backward, keeping her frightened eyes trained on him, fully expecting an attack. Archwood, however, leaned casually against the stair rail and gave her a rogue's smile.

Ming's trembling hand slowly lowered toward her cast. Archwood observed her and then shrugged amicably to something behind her. Ming dared to turn her head and then her breath caught in her throat.

Gabriel stood not ten feet away, watching Ming with a stunned expression.

"Gabriel!" Ming cried and stumbled over to him. She threw her arms around his neck. "Oh, Gabriel!"

His eyes traveled over Ming in disbelief, as if she were an apparition. At last, he spoke. "Let her go, Vic."

Still leaning against the railing, Archwood pulled a strand of Ming's hair from his shirt. "You know I can't do that."

"Gabriel!" Ming clutched at her boyfriend—at his face, his hair, his broad shoulders. "Thank God!"

One of his wrists was cuffed to a long, built-in bureau, but Gabriel pulled her close with his free hand. He gazed over her head at Archwood.

Ming squeezed Gabriel in her arms. "I knew you were here! I knew you didn't leave. I knew it!"

Archwood rolled his eyes and strode over to the couple. "Okay, okay, Dorothy understands she's not in Kansas anymore." He pulled Ming away from Gabriel and turned her around to face him. "What happened to your leg, Dr. Li?"

Ming shook Archwood's hands off her. "It broke."

"When?" His brows furrowed in suspicion.

"Whenever. What do you care?"

Archwood smiled wickedly. "I'm only concerned."

"Let her *go*," Gabriel said, more intensely this time.

Archwood's eyes slid over to Gabriel like a snake. "Keep quiet."

Ming also regarded Gabriel. His face was pasty white, which made the dark circles under his haunted, hunted blue eyes stand out like two bruises. She felt her heart break, wondering what tortures her boyfriend had endured.

Archwood returned his attention to her. "I'm glad you joined the party, Dr. Li. Sorry about your leg, but I'll make accommodations for it."

"Leave her alone!" Gabriel yelled and strained at the manacle holding his wrist.

Archwood, resenting the protectiveness he heard in his captive's voice, left Ming and strode over to Gabriel. "What? Do you want to make another deal, Sergeant?"

Unobserved, Ming reached down toward the cast on her leg.

"What exactly will you do for me if I let her go?" Archwood smirked. "Will you be my bitch for all time?"

"Fuck you, Psycho!" Ming cried out dramatically and flicked the clasps on her cast.

Only, they didn't open. The hinges stuck.

Horrified, Ming tugged at the clasps, instantly broke two fingernails, and then pounded the clasps with her fists. She gasped at Archwood, who gave her a strange look.

"What are you doing, Dr. Li?"

Ming continued to pound and pull on the cast.

Archwood shook his head. "Talk about psycho..." He moved over to Ming and grabbed her. "You're not very polite, you know. Telling me to fuck off in my own home."

He jerked Ming around to face Gabriel. "What say you and I put on a show for the sergeant here? He's been crazy bored. I think he'll be entertained watching me fuck *you* in every hole you have."

Gabriel lunged forward, and half the bureau splintered off from the wall.

Archwood, astonished at this show of strength, immediately threw Ming to the floor, grabbed the Redhawk from the bureau, and slammed the gun butt across Gabriel's face.

As he whipped the gun against Gabriel, Ming screamed for Archwood to stop. With his one free hand, Gabriel alternately defended his face against the blows while trying to grab the gun from Archwood. The younger man, however, kept ducking away. Gabriel gave one giant heave, and the bureau detached completely from the wall. He lurched toward his assailant, but Archwood immediately turned and dragged Ming upward. He shoved the gun in her side.

"I'll put your bullet in her," the younger man gasped, out of breath. "You know I will."

Gabriel wiped his hand across his face. Blood dripped from a gash on his cheek, and his swollen lower lip bled freely. His breath came in and out in deep, slow waves. He glared steadily at Archwood and lowered his hand.

Glancing at the damage to the bureau and the wall, Archwood pushed Ming aside and quickly unlocked the cuff on Gabriel's wrist. Holding the gun under Gabriel's chin, Archwood prodded him into one of the wingback chairs. He wasted no time in cuffing Gabriel's wrists to the armrests and his ankles to the chair legs. Archwood then stood up and smoothed his hair. He turned to Ming and waved the gun at the bed.

"Go."

Ming dropped into the chair opposite Gabriel. Archwood came over and pulled her to her feet.

"I can't lie down!" She dropped again into the chair. "It puts too much pressure on my leg."

"Lying down puts pressure on your leg?"

"Yes. It's the way the leg was broken."

Archwood gave her a dubious look. "So you stand all day on your broken leg?"

Ming stubbornly remained in the chair. "If you were a real forensic anthropologist, *Ethan*, you'd know the different ways bones break."

Archwood suppressed a grin and his eyes wandered the room, finally coming to rest on the pharmacy he kept on the bureau. "Then sit if you like, Dr. Li." He bound Ming's wrists to the armrests. He then tried to get the leg restraint around the cast.

"Don't!" Ming cried out. "I mean it's too painful."

Archwood tugged harder, but couldn't make the strap longer. "All right, this thing won't fit around it anyhow."

He moved to the bureau. "I think someone as tightly wound as you, Dr. Li, needs to loosen up a bit."

Gabriel lifted his battered face. "Vic..."

Archwood perused his medicinal stash and then picked up a vial. He proudly displayed it for Ming.

"Have you ever heard of ketamine hydrochloride?"

"Yes," Ming answered bravely. "It's an animal tranquilizer used by vets."

"Very good. The intelligent Dr. Li knows her pharmaceuticals. Do you know what else it's used for?"

"For God's sake, Vic—" Gabriel began.

"Keep quiet, Sergeant. You're the audience today. But you, Dr. Li, are going to be my star performer."

Archwood filled a syringe with the liquid. "Ketamine has a street name called Special K. It's usually sold as a powder, but I got my hands on liquid ketamine. I'm not great on dosages, but I do know a little too much can cause delirium, make you kind of wobbly on your feet."

"Vic," Gabriel said. "Listen to me. You said we had a relationship."

The younger man paused.

Gabriel looked desperately at Ming, then wiped his bloodied mouth against his shoulder and continued talking. "You doing this to her can only cause problems between us, right? I'm here. I'm with you now."

Archwood gave Gabriel a somber look. "If only I could believe you, Sergeant. But I know you'll say or do anything to protect the ones you love."

"You let her go," Gabriel insisted, "and I'll stay with you. You know a lot about me. You know I'll remain true to what I say." He looked earnestly at Ming. "I'm staying

391

here. Vic is my friend and he needs someone who understands him. Our lives have always run a parallel course. This was meant to be. I know that now."

Both Archwood and Ming seemed struck speechless. A tender look spread over Archwood's features.

"It's okay, Vic." Gabriel nodded gently toward Ming's chair. "She can go. If she calls someone, I'll tell them I'm living here of my own accord. There's no proof I've been abducted. You have the gun. Should anyone come here and I say something different, you can shoot me dead."

The younger man stared hard at Gabriel, trying to gauge if he was lying. Slowly, Archwood pivoted and walked over to Ming. He knelt down in front of her. He freed one of her wrists and then looked back at Gabriel.

Gabriel felt relief flood his body but made an effort not to show it.

Then suddenly, Ming kicked her leg up and the cast hit Archwood squarely in the groin. He made an "oof" sound and doubled forward. Ming kicked him hard again, causing Archwood to fall sideways. The syringe fell on the plunger, depressed, and lost its liquid. Ming struggled to free her other hand.

Archwood groaned on the ground, curling himself into a ball.

"Gabriel!" Ming wrenched her wrist free. She frantically tugged at the strap binding her ankle.

Gabriel jerked his chair forward as Archwood lurched to his feet. The younger man swayed for a moment, and then a growl escaped him. He lunged over to Ming, grabbed her long hair, and violently shook her head back and forth.

"What the hell, bitch?" Archwood then bolted for the stairs.

"Ming!" Gabriel said. "Are you okay?"

Rattled, Ming took a moment to get her bearings.

Gabriel pushed and pulled against his bonds. "Can you get loose? Baby, try!"

Ming struggled to release herself.

But then Archwood was back with a baseball bat. He strode right at her, swung hard and clubbed her cast. Ming cried out and Gabriel heaved his chair once more toward her. Archwood whirled on Gabriel.

"I will fucking brain her if you make a move!" Archwood raised the bat again, aiming for Ming's head. Then with one fast swipe, he hit her cast again. Ming yelled and the fake cast simply broke in half. With the bat raised for another go, Archwood stared at the two pieces in amazement. Nestled within the foam of one of the broken halves shone Gabriel's M&P.

Archwood dropped the bat and guffawed. Shaking his head, he picked up the two cast pieces and examined them.

"Beautiful," he said in admiration. He plucked the gun out of its hiding place and tossed it onto the bureau. He then approached Ming, who sat rigid in her chair. Archwood brought his face close to hers.

"Now, *that* was a worthy performance, Dr. Li. Brava." Archwood's eyes searched the floor near Ming's chair. "Where the hell did the ketamine go?"

"It's right here," Ming announced and raised the syringe with her free hand. She rammed the needle directly into Archwood's carotid artery. A squirt of blood flew from his neck at least two feet.

Archwood made a high-pitched squeal as he backed away and pulled the syringe from his throat. He stared at it, astounded.

Gabriel worked against his restraints, watching as Archwood stumbled to the bureau. The younger man clutched at his swelling neck and grappled for the gun.

Ming got her ankle loose and threw herself toward Gabriel's chair. She worked frantically to unclasp his bonds. Archwood wobbled on his feet and pointed the gun directly at her. He pulled the trigger and the shot went off.

Ming cried out as the bullet ripped through the wing of Gabriel's chair and lodged itself in the opposite wall.

Finally loose, Gabriel immediately whipped around the back of the chair. He covered Ming's body with his own and at the same time edged them both out of Archwood's line of sight.

"Fucking ingrates," Archwood whispered as he squeezed off another round. This time, the shot went wild and the bullet found purchase in the bathroom door. Gabriel looked behind him to see the blond man wavering, the gun unsteady. Archwood fired again, but this one hit the ceiling. Then came a crashing sound as Archwood fell to the floor, the fingers of one hand hooked on a bureau drawer handle and the other hand holding his neck. The gun fell to his side. A sprinkling of pills and broken glass vials surrounded him. He struggled to breathe and stared at Gabriel, but his eyes seemed unfocused. Gabriel slowly pulled himself to his feet and began walking toward him.

"Careful!" Ming blurted as she crawled on the floor after her boyfriend.

"Go get help," he told her.

Ming noticed that Gabriel moved warily, with the stealth of prey avoiding capture.

"Don't worry." She pulled herself to her feet. "I hit the carotid so if there was any drug left, it will go straight to his brain."

Ming headed for the stairs and Gabriel lifted the younger man onto the bed. Archwood mumbled something unintelligible and his head lolled to one side.

Gabriel pulled on the straps and tied his nemesis down.

MING LIMPED up the steps to the study where she found a landline phone. The fake cast had provided little protection from Archwood's attack with the bat, and her leg was screaming now. She dialed 911.

DOWNSTAIRS, Gabriel watched Archwood as he fought for lucidity. The blond man's breathing had evened out, although his neck had swelled under an expanding purple bruise. Gabriel rubbed his hurt jaw reflectively. He could not stop staring at Archwood.

A drop of blood oozed from the needle mark on his neck.

If there was any drug left it will go straight to his brain.

A random thought suddenly occurred to Gabriel. The mark on April's neck...

She went for her jugular, Ming had said.

But she didn't do it. Mr. King had stabbed April's neck, going for a central vein. The ouabain went straight to her heart and killed her.

"What did you do, Sergeant?"

Archwood had recovered, and his head rolled from side to side, viewing the binds on his arms. He looked back at Gabriel with venomous eyes.

"Get over here and undo this," he said. "Get over here quickly, or you know what I'll do? I won't just kill Dr. Li. I'll cut her up while she's alive. I'll rub her dead parts all over you. You'll be responsible for her suffering. For her screams."

Gabriel dragged his eyes away from Victor Archwood.

IN ARCHWOOD'S STUDY, Ming held the phone to her ear and tried to ignore the painful throbbing in her leg. "And please patch me through to Lieutenant Ramirez of the LASD."

"That's a different division, Ma'am—"

"I'm Dr. Ming Li of the county ME-Coroner's office, goddammit, and I'm in the home of a serial killer! You fucking connect me right now!"

"One moment, please."

Ming waited. "God-damned bitch," she whispered and the tears began to fall. She didn't know why she picked this time to go hysterical, but now the crying wouldn't stop. When Ramirez got on the line, her words were barely perceptible.

"Miguel, Oh my God, Miguel!"

"LAPD has two units en route, and Jonelle's already on her way. I'm heading over right now. Where is Archwood?"

"We tied him up. He's on th-the bed."

"Okay. Okay..."

"He-he's got possible carotid thrombosis." Ming's breath hitched in her throat.

"All right... You're going to be all right."

Ming heard some background talking, and then Ramirez returned to the line. "Ming, I've got Dr. Berkowitz on a three-way call. He wants to talk to you. Stay on the phone with him until Jonelle arrives. I'm on my way."

∽

"WHERE'S DR. LI, SERGEANT?"

Gabriel did not answer.

"Come here." Archwood stretched his neck as if he were trying to appease a pulled muscle. "Get me out of this. You don't think you're going to get away, do you? Do you really think you can go out in the world and be one of them?"

Gabriel gazed at his nemesis.

"That's right." Archwood nodded to him. "You think

you're gonna leave this house and be free? I'm the only one that understands you. I know you inside and out. Now get over here or I swear I'll cut her up. I'll cut her up, and you'll sleep at night with her head on your pillow."

Gabriel rose to his feet. After a moment's hesitation, he approached the bed and began unclasping the straps.

Ming wiped at her eyes and her nose as she spoke into the phone. "He's been torturing Gabriel. I can't even tell you—it's like mental torture."

"We'll deal with it, don't you worry."

Ming heard the sounds of approaching sirens and felt her limbs go soft with relief. "I hear them. I hear them coming."

"It's almost over. You'll be all right. Just stay calm." Dr. B's voice, soft as velvet, began to soothe her ragged nerves.

"I'm trying." Ming sniffed back tears.

"Where's Gabriel now?"

"Downstairs. He's guarding Victor."

"You left him alone with Archwood?"

A paralyzing streak of fear jolted Ming.

"I don't think that's a good idea. I'm sure you've heard of the Stockholm syndrome, and Gabriel has been under Archwood's control for a while. Ming?"

But Ming had already dropped the phone and was running toward the secret door. She nearly tumbled down the stairs, and when she reached the bottom, she skidded to a stop on the smooth cement floor and froze.

GABRIEL HAD Archwood in his grip and was punching him hard. With every hit, Gabriel's mouth set tighter while the blond man groaned and twisted like putty in his hands.

"You wanted to break me?" Gabriel allowed Archwood to fall to the floor and then he hoisted him up again by his hair. "This is what I do when I break."

He roundhoused the younger man in the face, caught him, and then threw Archwood against the wall. Before the other man hit the ground, Gabriel was on top of him again, punching him in the torso, in the face.

"Don't!" Ming cried tearfully from where she stood.

Gabriel looked up at her with startled blue eyes, his bloodied fist poised for another hit. Ming rushed over to him.

"No more." She pushed her body against Gabriel's, which caused him to let go of Archwood who slid to the floor in a crumpled heap of bruised flesh and blood spatter.

Ming held Gabriel fervently, burying her face against his chest as if she wanted to crawl inside him. Gabriel swallowed and looked down at the other man. Then slowly, he drew his arms around Ming. He hugged her tightly, closed his eyes, and breathed in the scent of her hair.

CHAPTER FORTY-THREE

They insisted he spend one night in the hospital so they could run tests. Gabriel told them he would submit to tests, but would not spend the night. He refused to go anywhere near a hospital bed.

Ming and Jonelle stood outside his room and waited for the doctor to finish up the examination.

Ming dropped her gaze to her leg, which now had a very real splint on it thanks to Victor Archwood. "He's being pretty closemouthed," she confided to Jonelle.

"I asked him for a statement," the other woman said.

"You did? Did he give you one?"

"No, not yet. But he asked me to get a warrant to search Mr. King's home again."

"What?" Ming's brows furrowed in concern. "That's all he had to say?"

She sighed and anxiously chewed at a fingernail. After the ambulance had taken Archwood away, Gabriel had stood outside with his fists colored in Archwood's blood to watch the dawn paint the sky yellow and pink. He wouldn't talk to anyone. He simply stood and studied the sky.

Janet had called a number of times, and Ming gave her a brief rundown of what had befallen Gabriel. Janet went dead silent on the phone. When she finally spoke, she assured Ming she would handle explanations with her mother. Janet asked if she could come to Los Angeles and help out, but Ming told her that taking care of Gabriel's parents would be help enough.

The doctor exited the room and Ming moved over to him. They spoke quietly for a couple of minutes, and then she returned to Jonelle's side.

"He got a good pistol-whipping, but nothing broke." Ming rubbed the exhaustion from her eyes. "At least nothing physical is wrong with him. But the physical problems aren't what worries me."

MAKING use of her good leg, she drove Gabriel back to Santa Monica. She had to, seeing that her boyfriend's car had disappeared into thin air.

When he walked into his home, Gabriel seemed momentarily displaced.

"What's the matter?" Ming asked anxiously.

"Nothing," he answered. "I just thought we were going back to my apartment."

Gabriel stood in the middle of his living room like an awkward visitor. He swallowed. "I need to walk to the beach." He moved to the front door, rested his hand on the knob, and paused. He eyed the splint on her leg. "Do you think you can come?"

THE TWO OF them walked in silence. They walked slowly, impeded by her use of crutches and Gabriel's apparent bewilderment at the zooming cars, the rollerblading beachgoers, the tourists, and the general hubbub of Santa Monica. Ming noted that he seemed to relax when they finally settled down on the warm sand. She felt joy and relief to have her boyfriend back but worried that Archwood might have succeeded in his goal of damaging Gabriel. As she pondered what kind of conversation to make, Gabriel spoke first.

"You kept a secret." He gazed at the rippling ocean.

She eyed him, puzzled.

"The gun," he reminded her. "In the cast."

"Oh." Ming tucked a lock of hair behind her ear and forced a smile at the horizon. "Cheap thing wouldn't open. And you were a good actor. You promised him you'd stay."

She snuck a look at his face. She wanted to make sure that Gabriel's promise to Archwood had indeed been a ruse and nothing more.

"How'd you know to come to the house?" he asked.

Ming felt a rush of emotion that caused unwelcome tears to well in her eyes. "Even though you told me to go away and leave you alone, I refused to believe it."

Gabriel turned to her. The sea breeze ruffled his dark hair. "I never said that."

Ming looked heavenward and hoped the tears would

fall back inside her head. She wanted to be strong. This was no time to fall apart. "The worse thing for me was thinking that you didn't want me in your life anymore. I mean you do so well alone. I know sometimes you prefer it that way."

Ming felt him studying her closely and, self-conscious, she pretended to concentrate on the breaking waves.

"He was right about one thing," Gabriel said as he regarded her. "He said I would do or say anything to protect those I love. That's when I knew I was capable of it."

"Of what?" Ming's voice cracked as she tried not to cry. "Of protecting someone?"

Gabriel lifted a hand to her face and gently wiped away the falling tears. "Of loving someone."

THAT EVENING, Gabriel answered a knock to find Dr. B standing on the front step.

"I hope you don't mind." He held up a bag of food. "The meal is from my favorite restaurant, the Meatery. I thought you could use some dinner."

"You didn't have to do this, Raymond," Gabriel said, surprised to see the psychologist at his door.

"I thought maybe you'd want to talk."

Ming appeared beside Gabriel and motioned Dr. B inside. "Would you like to stay and join us?"

Dr. B replied that he would.

. . .

NOTHING MUCH WAS SAID during dinner, but afterward, Ming made a great show of needing to clean up the dishes, even though they'd only used three plates. That left the two men to talk in private.

"Are you going to be okay with all this going public?" Dr. B asked.

Gabriel studied his wrists, which were still abraded from the ties he'd twisted against. "Man, I don't want to go there again. Not like this. I know I have to, but...Vic knew things, Raymond. He knew all about Andrew Pierce. He knew what Andrew did to me. How the hell could he know that?"

"It's very strange." Dr. B paused a moment to think and then said, "You were drugged. Could you have let it slip?"

Gabriel released the breath he'd been holding. "Maybe. I can't be sure. I only know the whole thing brought it back. You know what I mean?"

"I understand you were tied down."

Gabriel nodded warily, knowing his therapist would bring everything to light. Sometimes, it felt safer in the dark.

"Do you feel ashamed of that?" Dr. B asked. "Ashamed that as a man, especially as a cop, you couldn't break free?"

"It got to me," Gabriel admitted, "being tied down like a dog."

"I bring it up because I don't want to see you punishing yourself over it. It was a very clever move on Archwood's part to tie you down. Bondage makes one submissive. The goal, of course, is to get the victim mentally submissive as well as physically. You have to realize that was Archwood's plan. He wanted you to see yourself as powerless, as ashamed, as helpless." Dr. B chewed his lower lip. "Damn, the guy's fucking good."

Gabriel had never heard Dr. B cuss before and it made him smile. How long had it been since he smiled? And the doctor's words did make him feel a little better. However, the next subject Dr. B brought up wiped the smile from Gabriel's face.

"And whether or not he faked the sexual assaults, they were still a terrible trigger for you, bringing you back to the place you fear the most."

Oddly enough, Gabriel did not feel the usual stab that came along with the mention of the molestation. He had to face it so many times with Archwood, it seemed to have been burned right through him.

"He wanted to torment me with it, I'm sure. But I had a lot of hours to come to grips with it."

"And did you?"

Gabriel shrugged. "I had no choice. I had to find some way to deal with it or go insane."

"So how did you deal with it?"

Gabriel tried to catalog his many whirling thoughts. "I kept telling myself he wasn't going to beat me with it. That I was going to fight him any way I could."

"Do you think you succeeded?"

Gabriel sat back and gazed at Dr. B. "Why did you come over tonight, Raymond?"

"I came over tonight not as your therapist but as your co-worker and friend. Friends help us get through hard times, Gabe. That's the joy of being part of a community. You do realize you are part of a community, don't you?"

"I never really considered it."

Dr. B leaned toward his patient and the glasses slid down the bridge of his nose. "I know your pattern when things get tough is to isolate yourself. I want you to understand that isolation is one part of self-loathing. Self-loathing is part of self-blame. I don't want to see you isolate yourself over this. It's not the right move, but you'll be tempted to do it."

Gabriel eyed his therapist. Didn't reply.

"That's why community is more important to you now than ever." Dr. B pushed his glasses into place. "A person can never quite get past self-hatred unless he realizes he belongs. When you are nourished by a sense of family and community, you learn that you belong. It's through others that we learn love and awareness of ourselves. Try not to isolate yourself, even if that path feels comfortable to you. I would advise you to walk the more unfamiliar path."

THE FOLLOWING DAY, Ramirez asked Gabriel to return to Archwood's house and help them piece together the details behind Andrea's murder. Archwood himself was now in police custody, remanded to the Twin Towers Correctional Facility's medical ward downtown.

Police personnel crawled through every inch of Archwood's home. Crime Scene Unit officers combed the debris that once was the gazebo and Andrea's tomb. In

Archwood's enormous walk-in closet, officers pulled out various costumes and uniforms, elaborate theatrical makeup that included latex and foam appliances, a collection of colored contact lenses, fake teeth, F/X makeup, trauma kits, bald caps, and a variety of wigs. In the study, the wine-colored paneling was stripped from the walls. The investigators wanted to know if Archwood was hiding any additional secret rooms.

The door to Gabriel's prison hung open, beckoning the visitor to enter if he dared.

As they walked toward it, Ramirez risked a glance at Gabriel.

"Hey, *ese*," he began, "because of you, we got another chance at Archwood. You nailed him."

Gabriel made no comment.

Ramirez licked dry lips and stared at the yawning door. "Hey, remember when I said I was your friend?"

Gabriel shot him a look but said nothing.

The short, dark man swallowed noticeably, apparently finding it hard to verbalize what he wanted to say. Finally, he gave up trying to come up with anything original. "Well, I am."

With that, Ramirez descended the steps first.

DOWN IN THE BASEMENT, two mobile crime scene unit technicians dusted the treadmill for fingerprints. Jonelle crouched near the broken bureau and made notes on the contents of Archwood's pharmacy still littering the floor. They didn't hear the others come in.

"This is what I need," a CSI tech with a paunchy

stomach said. "Cuffs on a treadmill. Maybe I'd actually lose weight if I were chained to it."

The other one sniggered, looked up, and caught sight of Gabriel. The tech nudged his partner, and they both fell silent and went back to their work.

Ramirez told them to shut up although the techs no longer spoke. He looked at Gabriel, who stood by stoically.

Jonelle got to her feet to greet her partner. As she approached, her large brown eyes moved from the meat hook in the ceiling to Gabriel.

Ramirez waved his hand casually in the air, perhaps to minimize the unease. "Just point out where you were when he shot Miss Leighton."

Gabriel pointed to the bed and felt a wave of sickness hit his gut. The mattress, bedding, everything had been torn apart by the evidence crew.

They'll find bits of me on that bed. My hair, my skin…

"Oh my Lord," Jonelle muttered. She moved to the bed and the locking mechanism that Archwood had constructed. Taking hold of one of the thick leather straps, she regarded her partner. "He planned this for a long time, didn't he, Gabe?"

Gabriel didn't answer, just stared at the strap in her hand. It was dirty, stained with his sweat.

Ramirez gently tapped Gabriel's elbow. "Has anything been moved or is it just as you remember?"

"It's as I remember."

Gabriel watched Jonelle return to Archwood's pharmacy, his collection of pills and vials. He watched her hand pause above some used syringes.

Gabriel crossed his arms. Ramirez headed toward the bathroom.

"So Archwood stood about here, and Miss Leighton was already in the bathroom?"

Gabriel nodded and then glanced back at Jonelle. Her mouth hung open as she looked from the syringes to the bed and back again.

Ramirez, evidently sensing Gabriel's discomfort, barked at Jonelle. "Leave that shit for now. We don't know if they've photographed it yet."

"I would have died," Jonelle announced. "I would have died screaming. You're a survivor, Gabe. You survived him."

Ramirez cleared his throat in an attempt to keep things professional. "So, McRay, you witnessed Archwood pull the gun out here—"

"He took the gun out earlier," Gabriel told him. "He backed Miss Leighton into the bathroom and then stood where you are when he shot her."

Gabriel's eyes found a stray bullet hole in the bathroom door, a reminder of his last struggle with Victor Archwood.

You think that somehow you're gonna leave this house and be free, Sergeant?

Gabriel put a hand to his forehead.

"Did you see her after she was shot?" Ramirez asked.

I know you inside and out.

"Yeah," Gabriel answered plainly. "In pieces."

CHAPTER FORTY-FOUR

Back at home, Gabriel experienced odd, momentary flashes of what he could only imagine was post-traumatic stress disorder. Laying on his couch or bed, watching television or reading a book, an unexpected jolt of panic would rip through him. Thinking the straps bound him again; he'd jump up and shake out his arms and legs to prove nothing fettered him. Gabriel found this embarrassing when it happened around Ming.

But she was good to him. She didn't judge or advise him, and Gabriel felt grateful for that. Her presence comforted him. After a couple of days, the constricted feeling passed, and Gabriel began to feel more like himself.

His mother wanted to come down, but Gabriel wouldn't hear of it. He promised that he would head north as soon as he could. He needed to see his father again.

Fellow officers from the bureau called, even workplace associates he barely knew gave him attention. Gabriel understood what Dr. B meant about healing through community and felt grateful for everyone's concern, but he did not want to be perceived as a victim.

This was because he no longer felt victimized. He drew strength from the fact that he had made it through. It reminded him of something Dr. B had said long ago.

A survivor confronts the trauma, incorporates it into his or her life history, and then uses the trauma as a source of strength.

Archwood had certainly provided a forum in which Gabriel confronted his trauma.

Things weren't perfect, of course. All those changes he had manifested in his life: a new house, a new partner, the public knowledge of a previously private wound, he found them difficult to navigate. Gabriel needed to find his footing on this new path.

Only Ming remained the one constant in his life.

Around his sister, who called him nearly every day, Gabriel still faltered. He spoke to Janet but kept an emotional distance. Although she encouraged Gabriel to talk to Liam and Amber, he made excuses. He couldn't help but think Janet's kindness stemmed from a sense of sibling obligation.

During one of their brief phone conversations, Janet let her exasperation show. "The kids are dying to see you, Gabe," she pleaded. "Won't you please come up again? How about if I bring them to you?"

"Don't," he countered. "I'm too busy right now. Got a lot to catch up on. I've got to wrap up the case I was working on."

She asked him what she should tell Liam and Amber. "They'll want to know why you won't see them."

Gabriel didn't reply. He didn't want to reject his sister like in the bad old days, but couldn't live with the feeling that she thought of him as a monster. He figured now he was even more "damaged" in her eyes and therefore more dangerous.

"I guess I can tell them you are feeling sick," Janet mused aloud. "It wouldn't be far from the truth, would it?"

~

"JANET'S TELLING the kids I'm sick," he told Ming later. "That's a great way to sum it up."

They lay in each other's arms on his bed, listening to Billie Holiday sing about someone who was easy to remember and hard to forget.

"She's trying to make it easier for them to understand," Ming replied, surprised to find herself defending Janet.

Gabriel's fingers trailed softly along Ming's bare arm and that reminded her of something she would sooner forget.

"He kissed me," she confessed.

Gabriel didn't respond but his touch seemed to get more protective.

"I didn't know it was Archwood," she added miserably. "I don't know why I let another man get close to me. We were drinking wine... I was messed up because I thought you had run away. He—he got close enough to—"

"You were drugged."

She paused and looked at her boyfriend.

Gabriel didn't meet her eyes, but his tone stayed reassuring. "If he gave you wine, it was tampered with. Trust me on that one."

Ming scowled and felt both relief and anger. Archwood had drugged her. That's why she had kissed him. The bastard.

"I wish that syringe had stopped his breathing. I wish I'd killed him."

Gabriel's fingers continued to drift along the smooth skin of her arm. "No, you don't. Don't wish to be on the same level as Archwood." He sighed. "Not that I practice what I preach. I sent him to the hospital."

"Oh, you're not punishing yourself for that, are you? Look what he did to you."

"It wasn't about what he did to me that made me want to tear him apart." Gabriel regarded Ming. "It was what he was going to do to you. At least this time it was less a reaction on my part and more of a conscious decision."

Billie Holiday sang softly, and Ming shivered, remembering Archwood's threats all too clearly. After a moment, she shook off the memory and put a delicate hand upon Gabriel's face.

"I want you to know," she told him, "you're not alone in this. Whatever you need—"

Gabriel grasped her hand, kissed her palm, and then

began to make love to Ming because that is what both of them needed the most.

A PERSISTENT KNOCKING drove Gabriel from the bedroom. He struggled into shorts as he stomped through his house. Swinging open his front door, he saw Miguel Ramirez standing outside, holding a large foil covered tray.

"Seriously?" he asked his lieutenant.

"Let me in, *Vato*. This shit's burning my hands."

Gabriel stepped aside as Ramirez made his way into the kitchen.

"My wife made chicken with chocolate *mole* for you," he said.

Gabriel followed him inside and watched in amazement as his testy boss dumped the tray on the counter.

Ramirez shook out his heated hands and appraised Gabriel. "Oh, hey. Did I interrupt something?"

Ignoring the question, Gabriel lifted one corner of the foil. "This smells delicious."

"There's rice too." Ramirez rubbed his palms against his slacks. "And those *frijoles* are homemade, McRay. None of that canned crap. I don't know why my wife insisted on making everything from scratch."

Gabriel leaned against his kitchen counter and surveyed his superior. He had a feeling that Pilar Ramirez wasn't the one who had done the insisting. "This was very kind of you, Lieutenant."

Ramirez nodded impatiently and then paused to regard Gabriel. "How are you?"

"I'm good."

"When are you coming back to work? I've got a nasty unsolved from the eighties that could use your expertise."

"A cold case?" Gabriel asked.

"That's right. Not high profile at all."

"I'll take it."

Just then, Ming exited the bedroom and walked into the kitchen wearing nothing but Gabriel's flannel shirt and a pair of his socks. Ramirez caught sight of her and rolled his eyes.

She self-consciously lowered the hem of the shirt over her shapely legs.

"I see your leg is healed," Ramirez said.

"Getting there. Would you like to stay for dinner, Miguel?"

"No, I would not," he replied. "I wouldn't dream of it."

He headed to the front door. As he let himself out, he turned back to Gabriel with a wink. "*¡Buen provecho!*"

CHAPTER FORTY-FIVE

"The Tell-Tale Heart" by Edgar Allen Poe came to Gabriel's mind. The famed story featured a murderer speaking boldly to the police with his victim buried right below the floorboards on which he stood. But that murderer suffered a case of guilty paranoia. Mr. King didn't act guilt-ridden at all. He simply seemed annoyed at another visit by the police. Still, Gabriel likened the scene to the "The Tell-Tale Heart" because, like that murderer, Mr. King had been arrogant enough to hide the key to his undoing in plain sight.

Jonelle detained Mr. King in the entry hall as Gabriel made his way into the "great room" with its collection of African art.

Mr. King hustled to the doorway, apparently trying to determine the object of Gabriel's search, but Jonelle steered him back to the entry.

"I'd appreciate you staying where I can see you, Mr. King."

"What exactly is he looking for?" He tried to move past Jonelle again. "Didn't you already search the entire place?"

"Mr. King, please remain standing where you are."

And then Gabriel appeared at the doorway. In his gloved hands, he held the small, wooden headrest. He regarded his suspect. "Anything more you want to tell me about this, Mr. King?"

The other man's eyes widened. Gabriel smiled genially. No tough tactics, he thought. Just get him talking.

Without warning, Mr. King grabbed a nearby vase and swung it hard at Jonelle.

Her instincts were good. She ducked her head away, but he got her shoulder. The policewoman yelled and went down to the tiled floor as Mr. King bolted outside.

Gabriel quickly moved to his partner. "Are you okay?"

"Fine! Get him!" Jonelle's hand went to her hurt shoulder. Proper police procedures circled in her head like cartoon stars. *Demonstrate alertness. Be emotionally in control. Force must be controlled and used wisely with a purpose...*

Gabriel sprinted out the front door after Mr. King.

He shouted out a warning, but the other man refused to stop. Running down the residential street, Mr. King looked around frantically then grabbed a neighborhood boy riding past on a bicycle.

Gabriel skidded to stop, wondering if Mr. King planned on using the kid as a human shield. Instead, Mr. King flung the protesting child aside, picked up the bike, and hurled it at his pursuer.

That only made Gabriel angry. Mr. King fled but Gabriel pounced and tackled him on a lawn. He pinned Mr. King's arms behind his back and used his knee to keep the man facedown on the grass.

"How low class can you get?" Gabriel reached inside his jacket to the nylon handcuff holder attached to his belt. He cuffed Mr. King's hands behind his back and pulled him to his feet. "What will the neighbors think?"

BACK INSIDE THE HOUSE, Gabriel ran his gloved fingers along the seams of the headrest and then finally turned one of the legs. It detached from the body. The inside of the headrest was hollow. Gabriel shook it slightly, and a syringe fell out. He retrieved it and held it up to Mr. King, who sat on the couch, shoulders drooped, hands cuffed behind his back.

"Not a bad idea," Gabriel commented, "hiding it in the artwork. Chances are it would never be found."

Mr. King met his gaze. "Then how did you know it was there?"

"You told me." Gabriel deposited the syringe in a puncture-proof tube. "You held the headrest and said, 'with something so unstable, one should always be alert.' I can't think of anything more unstable than a murder weapon."

MUCH LATER, after they had booked Mr. King at the

Twin Towers downtown, the two detectives drove back to Commerce.

"Don't say it," Jonelle warned.

"Don't say what?" Gabriel asked.

"Don't say I spent too much time deciding what textbook move to make instead of fighting back."

"I wasn't going to say any such thing." Gabriel maneuvered through the downtown traffic.

Jonelle noticed a hole in her nylons. She felt a pulsing pain in her shoulder and a tender spot on the back of her head. "It's strange, you know. No school prepares you for shit when it really goes down."

"It prepares you. Don't beat yourself up about it."

Jonelle rubbed her shoulder. "Did you ever get in touch with the sister, Wendy Pennington? She ought to know about Mr. King's arrest."

"I tried contacting her," Gabriel said. "But her phone number is disconnected, and I have no clue where to find her."

Jonelle clucked in pity. "What a shame. After all that…"

It's more than a shame, Gabriel thought. Wendy was robbed of the chance to feel vindicated. The woman had most likely fled town in an attempt to escape one more injustice. While Gabriel could sympathize, he knew that nobody escaped the trials of life. They caught up to you wherever you went.

～

ONCE HE WAS BACK at his house, Gabriel opened the

windows of his study to let in the ocean air. He then relaxed in one of the armchairs he'd bought for Liam and Amber and picked through the file on the cold case to which he'd been assigned.

The victim of the case was a young girl named Nancy Lewicki—only fifteen years old. She had gone missing after school one spring day in 1988, and no one had ever heard from her again. Although they'd never found her body, Nancy had been presumed dead.

As the wheels in Gabriel's mind began to turn over the possible scenarios, he barely heard the phone ring. Picking up the receiver, he put it to his ear without taking his eyes from the aging case notes.

"Hello?" he murmured.

"Sergeant?"

Gabriel tensed up, and the file slid from his lap. *What...?* How did Archwood know his home phone number?

He knows everything about you, remember?

"What the fuck, Vic?" Gabriel forced himself to say.

"I miss you."

Gabriel closed his eyes, wondering if he should hang up, wondering if Archwood had escaped incarceration. Wondering if, by some bizarre twist, he would open his eyes and find himself caged in the secret room once more.

Then Gabriel heard a commotion in the background with a female voice pleading, "I don't know how he got it!"

A male voice, stern and demanding, got on the line. "Who is this?"

"This is Detective Gabriel McRay with the LASD. Who the hell is this?"

"Doctor Levine. My apologies, Detective. Seems even with his entire face covered in bandages, our prisoner here can charm the cell phones off our nurses. Won't happen again."

In the background, Gabriel heard the female apologizing to the doctor and one other voice—a male guard, perhaps, berating Vic. Behind all that, Gabriel distinctly heard Vic call out, "It's not over, Sergeant. Not for us. Not ever."

More commotion and raised voices, and then the call abruptly cut off. Gabriel stared at the phone for a long moment and then hung it up. He glanced at the case file on the floor and wondered briefly if he should get himself a new line of work.

THE FOLLOWING MORNING, as Gabriel mowed his backyard lawn, Ming appeared on the patio holding a suitcase. He halted, wiped the sweat from his brow, and surveyed her.

"What are you doing with that?" He gestured to the suitcase.

"I've got to get home. I wanted to say goodbye."

Puzzled, Gabriel shut down the motor. He could tell from her wistful expression that she wanted to stay. Ming looked at her watch, pouted slightly, and then moved back into the house.

"What's going on?" he called as he followed her. He found her at the front door.

"I need to exchange some of my clothes."

"So?" He shrugged. "We'll go over to your place later and do it."

"I have bills to pay, Gabriel," she said dispiritedly and opened the door. "I have potted plants that need watering."

He reached across her and closed the door. "Don't go."

"I have to get home sometime. Besides, your—"

"I want you to stay," Gabriel interrupted.

A car horn sounded outside, two friendly beeps. Ming looked toward the honking with some resignation.

The beeping continued and Gabriel grimaced. "That's mighty annoying."

He reopened the door and saw Liam and Amber standing on his stoop.

In unison, they screamed, "Surprise!"

Amber threw her arms around her uncle, and Liam danced around him. Gabriel, astounded, saw Janet exit the car, carrying two suitcases.

Liam hopped up and down. "Mom says we're staying here for a whole week! My dad is coming down, and they're going to stay in a hotel, but we get to stay with you! Hey, can you show me how to shoot a gun?"

Gabriel could only stare at them, unsure whether or not he was hallucinating. He looked at Ming, who smiled pensively at him. Janet set down the cases on the front step, stood behind her children, and regarded her brother.

Liam continued, "Maybe we could go to Disneyland or Six Flags or—"

"Liam…" Janet mildly scolded her son.

Liam caved in. "Or we could just hang out on the beach." He looked back at his mother to see if she approved of his revised tactic. She did so with a nod.

Amber, who had been hugging Gabriel tightly, pulled back and surveyed his bewildered face. "Are you still sick?"

Gabriel swallowed, unable to believe his family stood in his entryway.

"Mommy says a kiss cures all boo-boos." She waved him down to her and promptly planted a kiss on his cheek. She pulled away to observe him. "All better now?"

Gabriel regarded his sister, who gave him a warm smile.

"Much better," he said.

Janet acknowledged Ming with a grateful nod. Ming, in turn, made a subtle hello to Janet and the children. As the kids scrambled into Gabriel's house and Janet went to hug her brother, Ming walked down the path to her car. She pulled away unobtrusively to let Gabriel catch up with his family.

CHAPTER FORTY-SIX

M ing paused in front of the Matterhorn at Disneyland to pull at the cotton candy stuck in her hair. Liam and Amber walked ahead with their parents, eating the sweet sticky stuff that had, in the crowd, somehow left their hands and ended up on Ming's head.

She confided to Gabriel who stood nearby, "If you ever want kids with me—*don't*."

Gabriel reached out and pulled threads of blue candy from her hair. Rubbing it off on his fingers, he said casually, "I think I'd have to marry you first."

Ming chortled. "Oh my God, Detective, that means we'd have to actually live together."

"Wow. I forgot about that. Never mind."

Ming gave her boyfriend a crooked smile. "Was that a proposal?"

"Was what a proposal?"

"You mentioned marriage just now."

Gabriel tapped his chin in contemplation and his expression turned serious. He then got down on one knee and took hold of Ming's hands. She looked at him in disbelief.

"Dr. Li, would you do me the honor..." He let her dangle and then he grinned. "Of riding on Small World with me?"

"You jerk."

Still grinning, Gabriel hopped to his feet.

"I may have something to say about the subject, you know," Ming warned him.

Gabriel put his arm around her and steered his lover toward Fantasyland.

The theme park had been Liam's idea, but Gabriel agreed to immerse himself in the "happiest place on earth." He felt he deserved some fun. He realized more than ever that happiness was a daily choice and he would choose it today. Besides, Fantasyland seemed as good a place as any in which to make life-changing decisions.

The couple met up with Janet and her family at It's a Small World. The clockwork tower sparkled and played tinny-sounding music as people boarded the boats that would take them into the ride. The kids immediately swarmed Gabriel as they boarded, but Michael nudged Liam, and the little boy whispered something to his sister.

"Oh!" Amber squealed, "I forgot!" The little girl obediently climbed over to sit between her parents.

Ming watched the goings-on with a suspicious eye.

The party watched the mechanized children in their beautiful costumes sing about one moon and one sun and how a smile needs no translation. The boat glided through each colorful, glittering part of the world.

Gabriel took Ming's hand in his and held it. She rested her head against his shoulder and closed her eyes, content to hear the music and be right where she was most comfortable, at Gabriel's side.

She felt something slip onto her finger and she opened her eyes. Glistening under the colored lights was a solitaire diamond ring. Ming stared at the ring and then looked up to see Janet, Liam, Amber, and Michael twisted around in their seats, watching Ming with excited smiles.

Ming finally lifted her face to Gabriel who nonchalantly gazed at the performing dolls. As the boat swept into the last turn, she saw a poster hanging near the signs for good-bye that said in five different languages, "Ming, will you marry me?"

Only then did Gabriel turn to his girlfriend.

"Well?" he asked her. "Got anything to say?"

Resting her head once more upon the shoulder of the pea coat, elated to feel the man radiating from inside, Ming murmured, "I'm going to say yes."

"THERE'S someone here to see you, Sgt. McRay."

Gabriel was knee deep in the cold case. As he studied the old suspect profiles, he grew as frustrated as the detectives who had preceded him years before. He nodded his acknowledgment of the clerk and then finally pulled himself away from his desk.

Wendy Pennington stood in the lobby of the homicide bureau.

She held her big purse protectively against her bony chest as if it would somehow shield her from the misfortunes of a predatory world. Despite her shield and her defiant posture, water filled Wendy Pennington's eyes. The woman looked as though a strong wind could break her to pieces.

"You did good," Gabriel said as he approached her. "April's killer is in jail because you didn't give up on her. She was worth it to you. To have someone to fight for you is a blessing."

Gabriel couldn't help but think of Ming.

Wendy Pennington spoke in a voice choked with tears, "You didn't give up on me either."

Gabriel regarded the woman kindly. *When you are nourished by a sense of family and community, you learn you belong.*

"That's because you were worth it too, Miss Pennington."

Behind the hardened street demeanor, a beautiful, youthful smile bloomed on her face.

In that smile, Gabriel found his footing once again.

– THE END –

And now, an excerpt from the
fourth Gabriel McRay book,
In Twilight's Hush.

IN TWILIGHT'S HUSH

"Please sit down, Detective McRay."

Gabriel took off his jacket and hung it over the back of the chair. With some reluctance, he took a seat at the cloth-covered table.

The psychic held out her hand to him. "Take it. I need everyone to join hands."

Gabriel took the hand of Carmen Jennette. He felt an instant cat-like sensuality emanate from her touch and made a quick survey of her in the dim light. He'd heard she was of Creole blood from Louisiana. Her dark brown hair fell in curls over her shoulders and her skin boasted hints of smooth cocoa, which made Gabriel wonder if she didn't have some African genealogy behind her. He could swear he caught flirtation in Carmen's glittering green eyes, but he ignored it. Wouldn't a real psychic sense his heart belonged to another woman? He noticed that Nancy's jacket lay across Carmen's lap. Stiff, faded, the jean jacket served as a supposed bridge to the nether-world. What a bunch of nonsense.

Gabriel grasped hands with Nancy's mother. Pauline Lewicki regarded him with eyes that brimmed with hope.

Controlled and in her element, Carmen said, "I need everyone to clear his or her mind of any straying thoughts. Just concentrate on your breath. Everyone take a deep breath and let it out slowly."

A white pillar candle threw dancing shadows on the wall and gave off a heady aroma. Next to him, Gabriel heard Pauline take a shaky inhalation as if her body could not hold air. On the opposite side of the table, Len Lewicki seemed to be barely breathing. Paul, Nancy's brother, kept his bloodshot eyes on the candle, his lips pinned to a horizontal line.

"Visualize bright, white light," Carmen murmured in a voice that stroked like a velvet glove. "It is surrounding you. Let it clear your mind. Breathe."

The words struck a familiar chord with Gabriel. He tried to remember where he'd heard similar phrases.

"Take deep breaths and let them out slowly. Visualize the light."

Then Gabriel remembered. A couple of years before, he had sat with Dr. B and received the same directive.

Watch the light. Listen to my voice. Take deep, slow breaths…

Did Carmen aim to hypnotize the present party? Is that how psychics pulled off their stunts? Gabriel focused on the candle, which sent a thin plume of smoke into the air. Above the dancing flame, Gabriel watched Paul Lewicki shake like a volcano about to erupt until his father threw him a fierce glare, which quelled the trembling.

Carmen furrowed her brows in concentration. "I'm seeing mountains."

"Nancy loved the mountains," Pauline whispered to no one in particular.

Paul muttered incoherently under his breath. Gabriel reckoned that a man with a fragile mental state probably should not be exposed to a ghost gathering.

"I'm not getting a clear picture," Carmen said and gave a small shake of her shoulders. She sat up straighter in the chair. "We are seeking the help of our spiritual guides to lead us to Nancy. We want to focus only on those who can enlighten us about Nancy. Come forth."

A silence fell upon the room. Gabriel's eyes shifted toward Paul Lewicki again. Nancy's brother screwed up his face as if he were about to cry out.

Carmen's grasp of Gabriel's hand suddenly tightened and she sucked in a sharp intake of breath. She captured the breath for what seemed an extraordinarily long time and then slowly released it.

"I see an ocean." She gripped Gabriel's hand firmly. "Gray water—not blue. Cold."

Pauline Lewicki gave a little gasp, and Gabriel felt her hand tremble in his. He knew what she was thinking. She anguished that her daughter lay in some cold, disconsolate ocean.

Grief is a taxing burden to bear. Unrequited hope is tortuous. Gabriel witnessed each of the Lewickis display the strain tonight as they had for thirty years.

He fired a disparaging look toward Carmen, but the

psychic did not notice. Her eyes were shut and words floated from her mouth in a hushed monotone.

"I smell pine trees and damp air. I feel concrete underneath me—no, granite. I can see the variations in the stone. Gray, black and white. Smooth to the touch. There's a rumbling on the street where I sit. A trolley car."

Pauline Lewicki opened her eyes and looked beyond Gabriel to her husband. Len's eyes were open wide, and the couple shared an anxious glance. Between them, Paul Lewicki sat still as a stone, except for that tic agitating the corner of his mouth. The poor wretch seemed distracted by the candle, whose capering flame mocked his misery.

"The granite steps lead to the front door of a house," Carmen whispered. "There is loneliness here and the fear of being alone."

Paul's eyes shifted to Carmen. Pauline's hand squeezed Gabriel's as if holding on for dear life. And there was something else, something that dragged Gabriel's heart down to the pit of his stomach.

Carmen whispered, "A terrible danger is close and hidden within the guise of a friend."

Len Lewicki blurted out, "Where are you, Carmen? Can you see? Can you see any street signs—anything?"

The medium, with eyes still closed, shook her head fervently, not in response to Len, but against some unseen terror.

"A smiling, brutal friend," Carmen said. "Callous. Selfish with an insatiable need."

Gabriel watched a tear make a track down Pauline's cheek.

"Nancy," Pauline pleaded, and her nose began to run. "Where are you, Sweetheart?"

For a terrible moment, Nancy's mother reminded Gabriel of the watery corpse of his nightmare, filled with a flood of sorrowful emotion. A deluge so powerful, that when it broke, it would leave nothing behind except a bloodless shell that would desiccate into brittle and forgotten bone. Frightened, Gabriel broke his handhold with Pauline and Carmen.

The psychic kept her eyes shut, but Nancy's mother looked at Gabriel in concern. He took a deep breath. He would stay no longer. The only valid means of returning Nancy to her family, dead or alive, was gumshoe detective work. Not psychic phenomena. Not hocus-pocus. And certainly not this debasing tribute to Carmen's ego.

"We're done." Gabriel addressed the closed-eyed psychic. "Don't you think this family has gone through enough torture? What exactly are you trying to get out of this, Carmen? You see mountains. You see oceans. What's next? The fucking rings of Saturn?" He tossed an apologetic glance toward Pauline and Len. "Pardon me."

Facing Carmen again, Gabriel shook his head. "Getting visions from the great beyond about Nancy... What are you really after?"

The shades of Carmen's eyes rolled up, revealing two emeralds, which glittered at Gabriel. "The messages I'm receiving today are not about Nancy, Detective. They are about you."

Gabriel shivered involuntarily but held his defiant posture.

"The granite stairs. The duplex. Your childhood home, correct?"

He held his tongue.

"And the false friend was real, wasn't he? He was a monstrosity that burned a brand onto your psyche. I saw what that man did to you, and now I understand."

Gabriel felt his face go ashen. The room seemed a dead weight around him, a crush of heavy stones upon his chest. Len and Pauline regarded him with a mix of compassion and curiosity. Nancy's brother gaped at Gabriel with an expression that he didn't quite decipher, for humiliation blotted out Gabriel's senses.

Carmen continued in a gentle voice. "Your suffering gives you great empathy for the victims of the cases you work. Perhaps this is the reason Nancy sought you out."

"You'd better stop while you're ahead," Gabriel told her in a voice prickling with menace. He rose from his seat and put on his coat. He then addressed the Lewickis. "Give me time. That's all I ask. I promise to bring Nancy back to you, but please, do not ask me to participate in any more of this lunacy."

In Twilight's Hush
will be released Summer 2019
For updates:
www.facebook.com/lauriestevensbooks
or *www.lauriestevensbooks.com*

ABOUT THE AUTHOR

Laurie Stevens is the author of *The Dark Before Dawn* and *Deep into Dusk*. The novels have won over a dozen awards. Her short stories and articles have been published in numerous magazines and anthologies. Laurie lives in the mountains outside of Los Angeles, California with her husband, three snakes, and a cat.

To learn more about the author, please visit her website at www.lauriestevensbooks.com.